The Fire in the Stone

▼

▼

▼

The WESLEYAN EARLY CLASSICS OF SCIENCE FICTION SERIES

General Editor
ARTHUR B. EVANS

The Centenarian
Honoré de Balzac

*Cosmos Latinos: An Anthology of Science Fiction
from Latin America and Spain*
Andrea L. Bell and Yolanda Molina-Gavilán, eds.

Caesar's Column: A Story of the Twentieth Century
Ignatius Donnelly

Subterranean Worlds: A Critical Anthology
Peter Fitting, ed.

Lumen
Camille Flammarion

The Last Man
Jean-Baptiste Cousin de Grainville

The Battle of the Sexes in Science Fiction
Justine Larbalestier

*The Yellow Wave: A Romance of the Asiatic
Invasion of Australia*
Kenneth Mackay

The Moon Pool
A. Merritt

*The Black Mirror and Other Stories:
An Anthology of Science Fiction from
Germany and Austria*
Mike Mitchell, tr., and Franz Rottensteiner, ed.

Colonialism and the Emergence of Science Fiction
John Rieder

The Twentieth Century
Albert Robida

*The Fire in the Stone: Prehistoric Fiction
from Charles Darwin to Jean M. Auel*
Nicholas Ruddick

The World as It Shall Be
Emile Souvestre

Star Maker
Olaf Stapledon

The Begum's Millions
Jules Verne

Invasion of the Sea
Jules Verne

The Kip Brothers
Jules Verne

The Mighty Orinoco
Jules Verne

The Mysterious Island
Jules Verne

H. G. Wells: Traversing Time
W. Warren Wagar

Star Begotten
H. G. Wells

Deluge
Sydney Fowler Wright

ALSO BY NICHOLAS RUDDICK

Christopher Priest (1989)

British Science Fiction: A Chronology, 1478–1990 (1992)

(Editor) *State of the Fantastic* (1992)

Ultimate Island: On the Nature of British Science Fiction (1993)

(Editor) *The Time Machine* by H. G. Wells (2001)

(Editor) *Caesar's Column* by Ignatius Donnelly (2003)

(Editor) *The Woman Who Did* by Grant Allen (2004)

(Editor) *The Call of the Wild* by Jack London (2009)

The Fire in the Stone

*Prehistoric Fiction from
Charles Darwin to Jean M. Auel*

NICHOLAS RUDDICK

▼

▼

▼

Wesleyan University Press

Middletown, Connecticut

Published by WESLEYAN UNIVERSITY PRESS, Middletown, CT 06459
www.wesleyan.edu/wespress

Printed in the United States of America

54321

LIBRARY OF CONGRESS CATALOGING-IN-PUBLICATION DATA

Ruddick, Nicholas, 1952–
    The fire in the stone : prehistoric fiction from Charles Darwin to Jean M. Auel
/ Nicholas Ruddick.
        p. cm. — (The Wesleyan early classics of science fiction series)
    Includes bibliographical references and index.
    ISBN 978-0-8195-6900-4 (cloth : alk. paper)
        1. Science fiction—History and criticism. 2. Evolution (Biology) in literature.
3. Prehistoric peoples in literature. I. Title.

PN3433.6.R83 2009
809.3'8762—dc22   2008049861

*Wesleyan University Press is a member of the GreenPress Initiative. The paper used in
this book meets their minimum requirement for recycled paper.*

Psychology will be based on a new foundation, that of the necessary acquirement of each mental power and capacity by gradation. Light will be thrown on the origin of man and his history.

—Charles Darwin, *On the Origin of Species* (1859)

We can realise now, as no one in the past was ever able to realise it, that man is a creature changing very rapidly from the life of a rare and solitary great ape to the life of a social and economic animal. He has traversed most of this tremendous change of phase in something in the nature of a million years. His whole being, mind and body alike, betrays the transition.

—H. G. Wells, *Mr. Belloc Objects to "The Outline of History"* (1926)

[B]ipedal, tool wielding, meat eating, xenophobic, hierarchical, combative, competitive. . . . Full of the possibilities of the future, laden with the relics of the past.

—Stephen Baxter, *Evolution* (2002)

Contents

▼

Preface

▼

At the beginning of H. G. Wells's story "The Grisly Folk" (1921) the narrator, contemplating the scanty remains of prehistoric human beings in a museum case, borrows the words of the prophet Ezekiel to ask, "Can these bones live?" (607). By the end of the story, the long dead relics do seem to have come back to life. The narrator, acting as Wells's mouthpiece and referring to scientific research into human prehistory, concludes, "This restoration of the past is one of the most astonishing adventures of the human mind" (620). I could not agree more. My own expertise being literary not anthropological, I focus here on those "restorations" of human prehistory that are worth reading as fiction, regardless of their scientific accuracy. Yet in so doing I suggest that these prehistoric narratives, by opening up a new realm to the popular imagination, also played a role in the astonishing adventure.

Anyone interested in human prehistory quickly discovers that the mind is rarely more changeable than in the contemplation of its own evolution. I recur frequently in this study to the radical revision of ideas about human origins brought about by the Darwinian revolution. A century and a half of hindsight helps us understand why the new light shed on human nature and culture by the evolutionary sciences simultaneously enlightened, dazzled, and blinded those who first experienced this illumination. Existing terminology could not easily accommodate conceptual novelty, and outdated words pressed into new meanings frequently constrained their users in unexpected ways.

Recent history has revealed to us how sexism and racism, especially of the quasi-scientific kind, can lead to injustice and atrocity. In acknowledgment of this danger, we today try to employ an inclusive language that does not discriminate on the grounds of gender or ethnicity. The consciousness of the late nineteenth and early twentieth century was rarely raised so high in this respect. Yet silently to "translate" the sexist and racist diction of this period into today's more sensitive terminology may produce misleading results.

To take an example: a century ago, European and North American writers about human prehistory constantly used the phrase "our ancestors" to refer to the close kinship that they felt with certain favored prehistoric peoples—most notably, the Cro-Magnons. They did so partly as a means of dissociating themselves from disfavored peoples, such as the Neanderthals, whom they had erroneously "dehumanized." Today, we know much more about the great antiquity and tangled lineage of our species, and we may often be tempted to chastize early prehistorians for their naïveté or presumption.

Yet it is probably more useful to demonstrate as frankly as possible what these pioneers felt or believed about human prehistory and to explain why they did so. As Stephen Jay Gould eloquently put it, "If intelligent people invested intense energy in issues that now seem foolish to us, then the failure lies in our understanding of their world, not in their distorted perceptions" (*Panda's Thumb*, 149). Our disagreements with the past should not prevent us from trying to understand it in its own terms. For if we can do so, we are likely to see more clearly how almost all scientific truths about human evolution, including those we currently hold dearest, are really provisional hypotheses, based on the data available, colored by many kinds of unscientific desire, and often with the gaps filled in by preconception and prejudice.

To take another example: in the oft-quoted line from Tennyson's poem *In Memoriam* (1850), "And let the ape and tiger die" (cxviii, 28), the phrase "the ape" might be glossed today as follows: "the mythical common ancestor of human beings and living nonhuman primates that, thanks to one of the more egregious errors of nineteenth-century recapitulationism, was thought to inhabit the bodies and minds of civilized human beings and cause their continuing propensity for savagery and unrestrained sexual desire." But it is awkward, to say the least, constantly to be either paraphrasing obsolete ideas in this way or signifying one's disapproval of them by the use of scare quotes. Once "the ape" has been properly framed in its historical context, there is no reason why the phrase, deriving from an exploded fallacy though it might be, cannot be used today without further qualification to summarize the Victorian viewpoint.

In this study I shall use certain words and phrases, for example, "modern savages," "missing link," "primal horde," "fossil man," "Aryan race," as they were used in early prehistoric science and fiction, even though such usages are no longer standard in scientific discourse. On the first appearance of each of these terms I shall explain in the main text or in a note what they once signified and why they are now obsolete. I shall thereafter allow "Primitive Man," "Eternal Woman," and the rest of their quaint crew to stand as naked as they were created, without the fig leaves of quotation marks.

Acknowledgments

▼

I originally planned this book to show how the enlarged temporality opened up by the Darwinian revolution acted upon the imagination of the later nineteenth century and in the process brought the genre of science fiction into being. The first half was to have been on the fiction of our prehuman origins, the second on the fiction of our posthuman destiny. Fairly early in my reading, it became to clear to me that the post-Darwinian fiction of human origins deserved a book to itself and that "science fiction" didn't describe its subject properly.

My first debt is to those bibliographers—especially Marc Angenot, Nadia Khouri, Gordon B. Chamberlain, and Steve Trussel—who have identified the works constituting the neglected genre of prehistoric fiction. I'm also deeply grateful to the University of Regina, which has supported my research unwaveringly over the past twenty-five years, and which named me President's Scholar for 2002–04 on the basis of my original research plan.

My President's Scholar award enabled me to visit the Science Fiction Foundation Collection at the Sydney Jones Library, University of Liverpool, to read hard-to-obtain texts; Andy Sawyer made me warmly welcome there. I also visited Paleolithic sites in the Vézère and Lot valleys, as well as the Musée National de Préhistoire at Les-Eyzies-de-Tayac-Sireuil, the Musée de l'Homme in Paris, and the Musée des Antiquités Nationales at Saint-Germain-en-Laye. Julie and Brian Coote were hospitable and helpful hosts at La Boissière near Mouzens; Britt and I have fond memories of the magnificent view from the terrace of La Boulangerie over the Dordogne valley.

I'm indebted to Susan Robertson-Krezel and her staff at Interlibrary Loan at the Dr. John Archer Library, University of Regina, for their ability to track down my abstruse requests. Thanks also to Michelle Windisch for her assistance with micromaterials. I'm grateful to my honors and graduate students in my courses "Wells, Darwin, and Scientific Romance," "Prehistoric Romance: Intersections of Science and Desire," and "Science and Sex in Nineteenth-Century Fiction" for their enthusiastic response to course material that was sometimes at a primordial stage of formulation when I presented it to them. My colleague Carlos Londono Sulkin of the Department of Anthropology, University of Regina, was kind enough to read parts of the manuscript from an anthropologist's perspective and make many useful comments. Thanks to Judy Peace, Printing Services, University of Regina, for her assistance with the illustrations.

Many thanks to Suzanna Tamminen, director of Wesleyan University Press, and Eric J. Levy, former acquisitions editor, for their rapid and enthusiastic response to my proposal for this book. I'm very grateful to Gary K. Wolfe for his many useful suggestions in his report on the manuscript. Thanks also to Parker Smathers of Wesleyan University Press for his guidance during the later stages of the project. I owe a special debt to Arthur B. Evans for his unstinting encouragement and assistance.

Finally, I'd like to thank my father: my interest in human prehistory began in about 1956 when he adorned the playroom in Waterpark Road with parietal paintings of hunters and animals in the Spanish Levantine style of Valltorta.

Small parts of this book have appeared, usually in a different form, in the following articles: "Sexual Paradise Regained? C. J. Cutcliffe Hyne's *New Eden* Project," in *Foundation: The International Review of Science Fiction*; "Jules Verne and the Fossil Man Controversy," in *Science Fiction Studies*; and "Courtship with a Club: Wife-Capture in Prehistoric Fiction, 1865–1914" in the "Science Fiction" special issue of the *Yearbook of English Studies*, edited by David Seed. Please see the Works Cited section for full references.

Notes on References

▼

In the main text and endnotes, the abbreviation "q.v." following a name refers to the entry headed by that name in the Works Cited section. It is used chiefly to refer to whole works or to identify unpaginated sources such as Websites.

If unfamiliar foreign words or phrases are used in the text, a translation immediately follows in parentheses. Unless otherwise credited, translations are my own.

As is conventional, the locations of French archaeological sites are identified by the name of the *département* (administrative division) following in parentheses.

Endnotes are used chiefly to direct the reader to further relevant readings in literature or paleoanthropology.

For the sake of concision, the Prehistoric Chronology contains only the events and works mentioned in the main text.

The Works Cited section contains entries for all works of prehistoric fiction referred to in the text and notes, but does not include works of other kinds that are only briefly mentioned.

The Fire in the Stone

▼

▼

▼

Introduction

The Fiction of Hominization

> There are four simple themes in the paleoanthropological debates. . . . Who was our ancestor? Where did it first arise? When did we break away from the rest of the animal world? And, Why did it happen?
>
> —Roger Lewin, *Bones of Contention* (1987)

What Is Prehistoric Fiction?

Prehistoric fiction will here be taken to consist of novels and stories about prehistoric human beings.[1] For reasons soon to be made clear, none of these works is more than 150 years old. Most are set, however, a very long time ago during human prehistory; that is, during the period between the emergence of the first hominids and the invention of writing. The fundamental human characteristic, the one that first set us apart from our closest ape relatives, is bipedalism: we are vertical primates.

Human prehistory began, then, when a still imprecisely identified ancestral hominid first assumed a fully upright posture, probably more than five million years ago. Prehistory ended—and history began—when humans attained the ability to record events for posterity in a written language. Writing is a very recent invention, so human prehistory was hundreds of times longer than recorded history. The Paleolithic period (the Old Stone Age) alone lasted about 2.5 million years and ended circa 10,000 B.P. (that is, 10,000 years "before the present").[2] Writing, or at least record-keeping in decipherable symbols, probably began no earlier than 6,000 B.P.

The scientific study of prehistoric human beings is called *paleoanthropology*. To try to determine what human life was like during prehistory, paleoanthropologists examine the material evidence. Until very recent advances in genetics, this evidence chiefly took the form of (exceedingly rare) fossilized hominid bones, and (more common) stones and other durable materials purposefully modified by human hands. Clothing and wooden artifacts are too perishable to survive for millennia, so we cannot know for sure if Stone Age "cavemen"[3] ever wore animal skins or carried oak clubs.

Moreover, we know very little for certain about the culture of prehistoric human beings. Those intangible aspects of life that we consider essential features of our humanity, such as languages, customs, and beliefs, leave very few traces in the archaeological record if there is no writing to record them. Nevertheless, because we are human and believe that "Man himself is the most fascinating animal that ever existed on the face of the earth" (Oliver, viii), we are eager to fill in the great gaps in our knowledge about our ancestry. At least in theory, paleoanthropologists do this with "deductions and informed speculation" tempered by scientific caution (Leakey, *Origins Reconsidered*, 181), while writers of prehistoric fiction require "facts, speculation based on facts, and imagination" (Kurtén, *Singletusk*, 203). But the scientists, the novelists, and their readers are all animated by a similar curiosity about human origins. As the paleoanthropologist Alan Walker puts it, "I need to know where we all came from; I need to know, in a much bigger sense, what all of us are doing here" (4).

Prehistoric Fiction and Science Fiction

Prehistoric fiction, hereafter abbreviated "pf," is a speculative literary genre dependent on extrapolations from scientific or quasi-scientific discourse. In the densely branching genealogical tree of popular literary genres, pf is very closely allied to science fiction (hereafter "sf"). Indeed, some authorities consider pf a branch of sf. *The Encyclopedia of Science Fiction* (1993), for example, contains a theme entry entitled "Origin of Man" (Clute and Nicholls, 894-895) as well as shorter entries on writers particularly associated with pf from Stanley Waterloo to Jean M. Auel.

However, in the *Encyclopedia*'s entry on "Anthropology," Brian Stableford notes that stories dealing with past human evolution "are often seen as 'borderline' sf at best" because they "participate hardly at all in the characteristic vocabulary of ideas and imaginative apparatus of sf" (41). What this "apparatus" would seem chiefly to consist of is a series of motifs associated with the *future*, and in particular with space and time travel in or into futurity. Indeed, most sf readers, myself included, would probably agree that sf is preeminently the fiction of the human or posthuman future.

Both sf and pf are speculative genres, though in slightly different ways. The logic of temporality—time's one-way arrow—debars all witnesses to the future. In contrast, there *were* human witnesses to prehistory or we would not be here today. Yet there are no eyewitness *accounts* of prehistory: by definition, a surviving eyewitness account of an event signifies that history has begun. The prehistoric past and the future are both ultimately unknowable from the position of the present. The *historic* past, on the other hand, defined by its bequest of written documentation to the present, may be undecidable but it is not unknowable.

Good sf typically projects current (that is, historical) trends into the future. By suggesting where we might end up tomorrow, good sf reminds us about the possibilities implicit in our present circumstances. Good pf also tells us about ourselves today, but does so by reminding us of the great journey in time that we have traveled to get here. It provides speculative scenarios of *hominization*, namely, the evolutionary process that made us the kind of species that we are. Good sf engages the question, What does it mean to be a member of the human species? by speculating plausibly about our destiny; good pf engages exactly the same question by speculating plausibly about our origin. As an aesthetic criterion, plausibility is far more important in both genres than fidelity to science.

If pf and sf seem at odds in their temporal orientation, they are generically very close. As we shall see, they can interbreed fruitfully, so they are not of different generic "species." But perhaps their most fruitful recent joint outcome (see the Coda below) has come about through collaboration rather than mating. I see pf and sf, not as sibling rivals, nor as identical twins, but as something between those conditions: as fraternal twins, born from the marriage of science and the speculative imagination.

Fiction about prehistoric human beings is not a monolithic or even a unitary phenomenon. "Pure pf"—to adapt a phrase used by Steve Trussel (q.v.)—which is set exclusively in prehistory, is the kind that overlaps least with sf. Pure pf most often has a modern third-person narrator who recounts prehistoric events without explaining how he or she acquired knowledge about them: Jean M. Auel's Earth's Children series is a well-known example. But pure pf can also have a prehistoric first-person narrator who recounts events without any explanation of how s/he is transmitting them to the present, as in Elizabeth Marshall Thomas's *Reindeer Moon* (1987).[4] Whether the transmission of the narrative is rationalized or not, pure pf works conceal the time machine that makes them possible. Pf, like sf, is inconceivable without fantastic vehicles in which to make imaginary voyages outside the bounds of history.

But not all pf is pure. Writers, especially those associated with genre sf, have often ventured into prehistory with the help of explicit time machines. In Michael Bishop's *No Enemy but Time* (1982), for example, the protagonist undertakes a time travel experiment to visit the habilines of early Pleistocene Africa. In *Child of Time* (1991) by Isaac Asimov and Robert Silverberg, scientists use a time machine to snatch a Neanderthal child from the Middle Paleolithic and bring him into the narrative present. I shall henceforward refer to these generically hybrid works—most of them sf with a strong prehistoric element—as "prehistoric sf."

But prehistoric sf need not contain an explicit time machine. Works in which prehistoric humans survive into modernity involve figurative time travel that is sometimes, but not always, naturalized scientifically. In Arthur Conan Doyle's *The Lost World* (1912), Professor Challenger and his team "virtually" travel back in time when they mount the remote South American plateau where dinosaurs and apemen have avoided extinction. In Philip José Farmer's "The Alley Man" (1959), a Neanderthal man has been plucked forward in time by the author so he can be used to represent by analogy dispossessed ethnic minorities on the margins of modern American urban society. In Fred Schepisi's movie *Iceman* (1984), a caveman accidentally frozen in a glacier "travels" forward into the present via cryogenic suspended animation.

Fictional descriptions of prehistoric people and events are the result of a fantastic (that is, not realistic) narrative strategy. It is fantastic because time travel, literal or otherwise, is impossible in the physical universe as currently understood. Time machines, however they may be rationalized, are devices operating on magical principles. Yet pf, sf, and their hybrids are all characteristic cultural products of a post-Darwinian scientific age. Before such genres could exist, the concept of "deep time," the sine qua non of evolutionary theory, had to have been formulated. (The metaphor of "depth" is a nod to geology, the science that first discovered via excavation the new, unexpectedly vast temporality associated with planet Earth.) In pf, prehistoric humans occupy those few upper strata of deep time that immediately underlie the vanishingly thin layer that we inhabit and refer to as history. By contrast, sf, though aware of the deep temporal context, concerns itself with the future destiny of us who occupy that thin surface layer of historical time.

In both pf and sf, past and future time are conceived of as visitable, observable, reportable. In both genres, temporality is implicitly reconfigured spatially, typically as a river whose upstream and downstream are equally accessible to explorers from the present. Sf writers veer downstream, often allowing time's current to carry them ecstatically into a transcendent realm. Pf writers go against the flow: they may believe, or want to believe, in human progress, but at bottom they cannot forget that we are a species bound by terrestrial gravity. They recall Darwin's preferred trope: man has *descended*. Geology, not ballistics, is the keynote of the fiction of hominization. Pf writers dig in the hope of more fully disclosing the human brain and heart.

The Idea of Prehistory

For millennia human beings have eagerly or anxiously speculated about what the future might hold. Such speculations, fantastic or otherwise, have been preserved in literary form since at least classical times. Though "science fiction" is a very recent appellation, some of sf's most characteristic futuristic motifs have an ancient provenance, making it difficult to pin down a precise origin for the genre. For example, the literary lunar voyage dates back as far as Lucian of Samosata (2nd century A.D.), while the notion of artificial human beings was familiar to the medieval alchemists.

The origin of pf, on the other hand, can be located quite precisely in time and space. There can be no pf without a generally accepted concept of human prehistory, and such a concept did not exist until the second half of the nineteenth century. Indeed, Glyn Daniel in *The Idea of Prehistory* (1962) identifies a specific year, 1859, as the annus mirabilis that saw the acceptance by educated people in Britain and France of human antiquity beyond the 6,000 years or so traditionally allowed by the biblical chronology (69).

In April 1859 the English geologists Joseph Prestwich and John Evans visited the pioneering French archaeologist Jacques Boucher de Perthes in Abbeville on the banks of the Somme River in northern

France. Boucher de Perthes had long argued, without much success in his homeland, that because flint tools and the bones of long-extinct animals were often found in association (that is, close together in the same geological stratum) in the Somme gravels, the tool-makers and the animals must have been contemporaries. At Abbeville the two Englishmen were shown the material evidence by Boucher de Perthes in situ. What they saw was supported by similar evidence that had recently been gathered at Brixham Cave and other English sites, and the pair were entirely convinced.

Prestwich presented his conclusions to the Royal Society on 26 May 1859 and Evans presented his to the Society of Antiquaries one week later (Prestwich, 121–128). From Prestwich's paper, states Robert F. Heizer, "we may date the birth of modern prehistory" (94). As November of that same year saw the publication of Darwin's *Origin of Species*, the work that more than any other successfully challenged traditional ideas about the origin and development of living organisms, 1859 was an annus mirabilis for prehistory indeed.

In the early nineteenth century, the great French naturalist Georges Cuvier had hypothesized that successive "revolutions" accounted for the stratified fossil record of extinct species. According to Cuvier, immutable species were successively created by God, then destroyed by him in cataclysms, of which the biblical Deluge was probably the latest. To many, Cuvier's oft-quoted statement of 1812, "There are no human fossil bones,"[5] strongly suggested that human beings, like other living species, had been created very recently. "Human recency" was both an affirmation to the faithful that God had created the world specifically for mankind, and an encouragement to scientists "to seek evidence of Him in the details of natural history" (Van Riper, 5).

Cuvier's "catastrophism" enjoyed considerable authority among scientists eager to reconcile the Mosaic account of creation with new geological and paleontological data. Yet after 1859 nothing less than a "great and sudden revolution in modern opinion"[6] brought prehistoric humanity irreversibly into being. Charles Lyell's uniformitarian geology—gradualist, requiring no supernatural interventions—had undermined catastrophism, and provided the necessary millions of years of prehistory as the temporal foundation for both Darwinism and paleoanthropology. Evolutionary transmutation had been revealed to be interminably slow, yet the intellectual revolution that succeeded this revelation was very rapid.

In 1863, Lyell began the first chapter of his *Geological Evidences of the Antiquity of Man*, the work that epitomized the spirit of the "great and sudden revolution" in Britain, with the sentence, "No subject has lately excited more curiosity and general interest among geologists and the public than the question of the Antiquity of the Human Race" (1). Two years later, *Pre-Historic Times* by John Lubbock (later Lord Avebury) was a British best seller, popularizing both the word "prehistory" and the emerging idea that the world of our prehistoric ancestors could be reconstructed by reference to "modern savages" (the standard nineteenth-century term for peoples deemed still to be living in a primeval fashion).

It was in France where the first attempts were made to dramatize the lives of prehistoric human beings in fiction. There are at least two major reasons for this. First, the French quickly developed a proprietary interest in human prehistory because so many of the significant early archaeological finds were made by French savants on French territory. French readers were naturally curious about the lives of these earlier "Frenchmen" who once dwelt on the banks of the Somme, Seine, or Vézère,[7] and their curiosity was better satisfied with imaginative fictions than with dry factual reports.

Second, ideological conflicts specific to France about human evolution and its relation to national progress stimulated fictional expression. France felt itself to be falling behind other leading Western nations technologically. Some blamed the conservatism of the Catholic church, others diagnosed a more general cultural *dégénérescence* (degeneration). Most agreed, though, that there was an urgent need to educate French youth in modern scientific possibilities. From 1863 on, Jules Verne developed a palatable, popular, and lucrative method of doing this in his great series of "scientific fictions," the *Voyages extraordinaires* (Extraordinary journeys). Thanks to Boucher de Perthes and his successors, France led the way in the emerging science of paleoanthropology. "From the start," the archaeologist priest Abbé Henri Breuil would later declare, "the study of Prehistory was essentially French" (18). It was therefore almost a patriotic duty[8] to claim the new literary territory opened up by this discipline: "le roman préhistorique"[9] (the prehistoric novel) was born.

There is a continuous and rich tradition of French pf from 1861 to the present. This study, however, will focus primarily on the equally rich, if not quite so lengthy, tradition of pf in the English language that begins in 1880 and includes novels and stories published mainly in Britain and the United States. This Anglophone pf tradition is very little known: some readers probably believe that it begins with Jean M. Auel's best-selling *The Clan of the Cave Bear* (1980). As I shall show, however, Auel's first novel, the founding text of a subgenre of contemporary romance fiction, represents only a recent stage—albeit a major one—in the evolution of the pf tradition in English.

Because pf began in France, because there was much early Anglo-French paleoanthropological interchange, and because early English pf had existing French models to work from, I shall begin my survey of the historical development of pf with the founding works in French, most of which are almost unknown in the English-speaking world. In later chapters I shall also discuss major works of French pf that are available in English translation, such as J.-H. Rosny *aîné's La Guerre du feu* (1911, translated as *Quest for Fire* in 1967), and a small number that are not, such as Edmond Haraucourt's *Daâh* (1914). I shall deal, too, with a few major pf novels that have been translated into English from other languages, such as Johannes V. Jensen's *Bræen* (1908) and *Det tabte Land* (1919) (translated from Danish as *Ice* and *Fire*, the first two books of *The Long Journey* in 1923),[10] and Stella Carr Ribeiro's *O Homem do Sambaqui* (1975, translated from Brazilian Portuguese as *Sambaqui* in 1987).

The first three chapters of this study survey the historical development of pf from its post-Darwinian origin through the emergence of prehistoric romance with Auel's *The Clan of the Cave Bear*. My concern here will be to highlight those works worth reading (and occasionally to warn against those that are not) and site them in the evolving literary-historical and scientific context. In so doing I identify distinct (though closely related) British and American pf traditions that descend from a common French ancestor. This ancestor gave birth to a vigorous French pf tradition that has been for most of the recent past too little known in the Anglosphere.

The remaining four chapters each focuses on a central theme of the fiction of hominization: "Nature and Human Nature" (on the evolutionary divergence of human nature from Mother Nature); "Sex and Gender" (on aboriginal differences between men and women and their consequences); "Race or the Human Race" (on whether human beings have descended as one species or as several subspecies); and "A Cultural Triad: Language, Religion, Art" (on the origin and evolution of three of the most important elements of human culture).

Even as the fiction of hominization seeks to understand how we became human, it raises questions about our destiny. The Coda focuses on a recent major pf novel, *Evolution* (2002) by Stephen Baxter, which in the course of its action time travels from the very distant past to the even more distant future. I offer this work as a concluding paradigm of good pf, one that provides the kind of insights into our evolved human nature characteristic of the genre at its best, while incidentally illuminating the generic relationship between pf and sf. Finally, a tabular Prehistoric Chronology relates major pf works to significant developments in paleoanthropology.

The Poetics of Prehistoric Fiction

Pf contains a significant number of little-known works that are well worth reading for pleasure and studying as literary texts. But does this body of works, relatively neglected by critics,[11] require a special approach when one is undertaking its aesthetic evaluation? Is there, in short, a poetics specific to pf as a genre? There have recently been two attempts to answer the question, What makes *good* pf? The critics whose views I summarize raise between them most of the main issues associated with the aesthetic evaluation of pf. Yet their conclusions are so widely different that I find it impossible to imagine how both can be equally correct. Having evaluated their claims, I outline a third, less extreme approach to the poetics of pf that I myself shall take.

Charles De Paolo's views on pf were first expressed in his article "Wells, Golding, and Auel: Representing the Neanderthal" (2000), then more fully in his book *Human Prehistory in Fiction* (2003). The latter begins with a statement of intent: "An efficient approach to the study of prehistoric fiction would position a work in its intellectual context, compare it to other works of its kind, and determine whether a writer employed available scientific resources effectively" (1). By this De Paolo means that pf writers achieve critical credibility by ensuring that their characterization, plot, thematics, and so on, accord with "normal" paleoanthropology at the time of composition. "Normal" here alludes to Thomas S. Kuhn's definition of "normal science" in *The Structure of Scientific Revolutions* (1962): "research firmly based upon one or more past scientific achievements, achievements that some particular scientific community acknowledges for a time as supplying the foundation for its further practice" (10). In De Paolo's view, good pf writers will test prevailing research-based scientific theory and produce from their informed positions "adumbrative and inventive" texts (126); bad pf writers simply ignore the theory.

By way of example, De Paolo evaluates various pf writers' use of Neanderthal characters. In "The Grisly Folk," H. G. Wells "indiscriminately embraces conservative ideology and incorrect interpretations" of Neanderthals (4); in "The Day Is Done" (1939), Lester del Rey "missed a dramatic opportunity" offered by the Mount Carmel discoveries in the 1930s[12] to develop the idea of "the indivisible unity of the human family" (4); William Golding's "benign imbecile[s]" in *The Inheritors* (1955) are based on the "misconstruction" of Marcellin Boule (see chapter 2) and on the discredited pseudoscience of phrenology (5). By contrast, the plausibility of Neanderthal culture as depicted in *The Clan of the Cave Bear* is due to the "paleoanthropological authenticity" (113) of Auel's text. De Paolo concludes that pf's function is to supplement the science: "Imaginative literature that is insightful or anticipatory can augment anthropological discourse and make scientific theory more accessible to the general reader" (145).

Joseph Carroll in his essay "Adaptationist Criteria of Literary Value: Assessing Kurtén's *Dance of the Tiger*, Auel's *The Clan of the Cave Bear*, and Golding's *The Inheritors*" (2004) does not mention De Paolo, but offers precise counterarguments to him nonetheless. Carroll's essay is an application of a larger Darwinian project, namely, to understand literary works as an aspect of humanity's "adaptive need to make sense of the world . . . to produce cognitive order" (164). "Adaptive" in an evolutionary context means "conducing to survival." Literary works that evoke in the reader empathy and compassion for characters are adaptive in that these emotions are likely to improve the reader's social integration; for a member of a highly social species, such an improvement conduces to survival. Narrative strategies that allow a coherent functional integration of elements are adaptive in that they conduce to the reader's cognitive advantage; such an advantage improves the odds of survival for a member of a highly intelligent species. Moreover, both literary qualities conduce to the likely "survival" of a text by increasing its adaptive value to its readership.

For Carroll, Björn Kurtén's *Dance of the Tiger* (1978) is a "bad work of art" because it is "not true to human nature" (167): its integrity of conception is sacrificed to the attempt to preach an implausible hypothesis about Neanderthal replacement. As for *The Clan of the Cave Bear*, it is a "soap opera" (173) transposing the author's narcissism into the Paleolithic. Suffering from a "failure of historical imagination"

(176) and characterized by "stylistic and tonal vulgarity," Auel imposes a contemporary woman's consciousness on prehistory, resulting in "absurd perspectival misconstructions" (177). By contrast, William Golding's manipulations of point of view in *The Inheritors* are "an integral part of the total artistic order" (178). Golding realizes that understanding Neanderthals "requires not just arranging the furniture in the cave, as Auel does" (179): it involves, for example, getting inside a mind that is incapable of planning ahead. *The Inheritors* is a "tour de force of technique" and "an instance of a large and generous moral nature" (182).

My own position on what makes good pf lies between De Paolo's and Carroll's, though rather closer to the latter. While I respect De Paolo's clarity of purpose and willingness to reconstruct how a pf work might have emerged from paleoanthropological theory, I have three main objections to his approach. First, I believe that the value of any literary work—be it sf, pf, or prehistoric sf—that extrapolates from scientific ideas has very little to do with its author's adherence to normal science, even when the work thematically foregrounds scientific theory. For example, a time machine is no more scientifically credible than a magic carpet. It is, as Wells himself frankly confessed, a conventionalized item of quasi-scientific "jiggery-pokery" (Preface, viii) that grants a minimally sufficient plausibility to a fantastic idea: that evolution might be advanced or reversed rapidly enough to be perceived and evaluated as a moral process. Time machines have never been part of normal science and probably never will be, but it is impossible to describe the course of human evolution in a work of fiction without the overt or implied use of such a device.

Second, paleoanthropology in its short history has never been a body of knowledge stable enough to be theoretically "normalized" in the manner of, say, physics or chemistry. The study of human origins is a highly speculative hybrid discipline (Leakey, *Origins*, 12) based on a very small body of physical evidence. The accidental discovery of one or two fossil bone fragments has the potential to bring about a revolution in the field. As I write, for example, a major readjustment to the human lineage is being contemplated thanks to the discovery of a jawbone and skull in Kenya. This new fossil evidence indicates that *Homo erectus* did not derive from *Homo habilis*, as previously thought, but that the two hominid species coexisted for half a million years.

Paleoanthropology is ideologically very highly charged because of what it promises to reveal about our origins *and* it is extremely vulnerable to subjective distortion because the objects of its scrutiny are very closely related to the scrutineers themselves. Its history indicates that paleoanthropology is also more vulnerable than most other sciences to serious, long-lasting distortions caused by deliberate fraud. Pf world-building is likely to be more successful if it is motivated by the writer's desire to understand human nature rather than by rigorous adherence to unstable paleoanthropological hypotheses.

Third, I think that the value of any artistic work chiefly resides not in its ability to supplement or augment other discourses, but in its aesthetic success. The key to any literary work's aesthetic success lies in its literariness, namely, in its capacity as an artfully arranged verbal structure to generate a rich plurality of meanings. Didactic, dogmatic, or propagandistic literary works, in which authors attempt to impose a single interpretation upon the reader, usually achieve little aesthetic success. Such works demonstrate insufficient respect for the complexity of potential interactions between the inherent suggestiveness of human language and the reader's imagination. I believe, for example, that one of the reasons that *The Inheritors* is a great novel (here I am entirely in accord with Carroll) is because to read it is to inhabit the consciousness of "benign imbeciles" yet to feel no contempt for them. On the contrary, our sympathies are enlarged even as we are brought harshly up against the constraints of our human nature.

But I am reluctant to dismiss, as Carroll does, the lesser achievements of Kurtén and Auel. The main problem with *Dance of the Tiger* is not so much with dishonesty of ideological conception—Kurtén is, I think, entirely sincere—but with two-dimensional characterization and weak plotting; his sequel, *Singletusk* (1984), is a considerable improvement on both counts.

As for Auel, though she is not an elegant stylist, the interplay of character and plot in *The Clan of the Cave Bear* is compelling—if one accepts her premise that a Cro-Magnon woman could have a fully modern consciousness. True, this premise challenges plausibility not only because Auel's feminism might not seem easily transposable to prehistory but also because she deviates from generic expectations when portraying prehistoric female characters. A historical survey of pf reveals that before Auel, authors, though often treating female characters with sympathy, rarely allowed them to develop over the course of the plot; most fall into a limited range of feminine stereotypes. For readers prepared to accept that women might always have been capable of becoming fully human, even if men or circumstances rarely allowed them so to be, Auel's novel is extremely engaging: it broadens our vision of human possibility, even of human nature. (In Auel's later novels, Ayla, having become a paragon of all the virtues, fails to develop further, and these works are accordingly weaker.) Read thus, *The Clan of the Cave Bear*, an innovative and sociologically important fiction, expresses adaptive value as Joseph Carroll defines it.

I

Generic Evolution

From Boitard's *Paris before Man* to London's *Before Adam*

From a status like that of the Crees,
Our society's fabric arose,—
Develop'd, evolved, if you please,
But deluded chronologists chose,
In a fancied accordance with Mos
es, 4000 B.C. for the span
When he rushed on the world and its woes,—
'Twas the manner of Primitive Man!

　　　—Andrew Lang [and E. B. Tylor],
　　　　"Double Ballade of Primitive Man" (1880)

The French Origin of Prehistoric Fiction, 1861–1875

The central issue of the first French pf was the existence of the "fossil man" so categorically denied by Cuvier.[1] *Paris avant les hommes* (Paris before man) (1861) by Pierre Boitard (1789–1859) was a posthumously published work by a writer who died in the annus mirabilis. Though no literary masterpiece, "the first Darwinian narrative" (Angenot, "Science Fiction," 62) and the originating work of pf is a frontal attack on the "preconceived opinions of the late Master Georges [Cuvier]" (Boitard, 252). It is an overt time travel story: the narrator, having fallen asleep reading Cuvier, dreams that he is taken back 12,000 years in time by a demon who warns him to leave his preconceptions about human prehistory at home. He observes the future site of Paris three hundred meters under water, and after being introduced to extinct monsters of earlier geological periods, he is taken by the demon to an actual cave, the Grotte de Souvignargues in southern France.[2]

There the narrator is confronted by a revolting creature resembling an orangutan, in the company of his equally disgusting family, all covered with stinking filth. Boitard then summarizes the material evidence from many French sites to prove that Cuvier was wrong; fossil men (and women) certainly existed. Moreover, our ancestors were not Adam and Eve but demi-apes whose lives were anything but Edenic. Boitard's scatological portrait of our foreparents is correctively satirical: it is no accident that his cave dwellers are strongly reminiscent of Swift's Yahoos in part 4 of *Gulliver's Travels* (1726).

Boitard's aim is to promote the new scientific account of human origin, one shockingly different from, yet truer than, the biblical and Cuverian accounts. A full decade before Darwin's *Descent of Man* (1871), Boitard was arguing that we do better to celebrate the distance that we have ascended on our own initiative from our lowly origin, than to lament how far we have fallen from the scriptural Eden. The frontispiece of *Paris avant les hommes* shows "fossil man" caped in an animal skin brandishing a stone ax as he stands protectively in front of his mate and infant (fig. 1.1). This awkwardly drawn, unsigned image[3] may be the earliest incarnation of the popular-culture icon of the caveman.

The next significant work of French pf was published only four years after Boitard's, but in the intervening time there had been an explosion of knowledge and speculation about human prehistory. In 1863 alone, Thomas Henry Huxley's *Evidence as to Man's Place in Nature* had provided a powerful anatomical argument for the close cousinship of humans and apes; Charles Lyell's *Geological Evidences of the Antiquity of Man* had concluded that there were unshakable geological proofs of humanity's lengthy descent; and Louis Figuier had produced in *La Terre avant le Déluge* (translated as *The World before the Deluge* in 1865) the first best-selling chronicle of deep time from the Precambrian to the Quaternary appearance of man, illustrated with striking scenic engravings by Edouard Riou.

Moreover, by 1865 excavations had begun at many subsequently notable and productive archaeological sites including Les Eyzies, La Madeleine, and Laugerie Basse in Périgord; Edouard Lartet and his English collaborator Henry Christy had shown that people of the Reindeer Age (the Upper Paleolithic) had made accomplished mobiliary (portable) artworks;[4] and Neanderthal man had been recognized as an extinct hominid type and given a binomial designation, *Homo neanderthalensis*, that suggested he was of a lower order than our sapi-

Figure 1.1   Boitard's fossil man protects his family.

ent selves. Already a process had begun without which there can be no effective pf: prehistoric human beings had begun to be differentiated, with certain individuals promoted to the rank of worthy ancestors and others demoted to savagery or animality. Already lineages were being sketched and allegiances mapped out. In short, the question of *whether* there had been prehistoric men had been settled; now it was a question of *which* prehistoric man was our forefather.[5]

L'Homme depuis cinq mille ans (Five thousand years of man) (1865) by Samuel-Henry Berthoud (1804–91) employs a narrative strategy still current in pf that strives, as Stephen Baxter recently put it, "to dramatize the grand story of human evolution" (567), namely, an episodic rather than a temporally unified narrative.[6] It takes the form of a sequence of chapter-length episodes in chronological order, each offering a glimpse of human life at a particular evolutionary stage. In *Evolution* (2002), his major contribution to this pf subgenre, Baxter starts at 145 million B.P. and ends circa 500 million years in the future. Berthoud, living at a time when absolute dating was impossible and human prehistory was still a novel concept, begins 4000 B.P. and ends in A.D. 2865. His narrator notes that while the ancient Egyptians were enjoying an advanced civilization, ancestral Frenchmen were huddling in caves while floods ceaselessly inundated the terrain. After discussing prehistoric tools and weapons found in the Paris area, he informs us that he will now offer "a sort of little novel" dramatizing primeval customs (25). This episode, "The First Inhabitants of Paris," constituting chapter 4 of Berthoud's book, is the first pure pf narrative.

A tribe, ruled by an old man, appears on the uninhabited banks of the Seine after having fled north from the Vézère to escape their enemies. They are delighted by the prospect of the easily fortifiable Ile de la Cité and by the butte of Montmartre with its accommodating caves. The men are small and robust with long reddish hair; the women are blonde and wear necklaces of animal teeth. Energetic as a result of their ceaseless war with necessity, they expel the bear (fig. 1.2) occupying the best cave and make fire to fend off nocturnal carnivores. Then they settle down diligently to their industries: hunting, tool manufacture, and artwork for the men; cooking, tailoring, and jewelry-making for the women. The old chief having invoked the protection of the sun god, social development proceeds apace.

After the cave becomes too crowded, the tribe construct a lake village on stilts. While the men fish, the women wash their hair in the river: these first Parisians had a passion for hygiene, filth being a product of modern civilization! Soon the young settlement is besieged by jealous foes, but the attackers are defeated; the captured warriors are sacrificed to the sun god, and their women enslaved. The enemy chief's captured daughter is found to have a remarkable ability to domesticate animals and heal with herbs. (Here Berthoud anticipates Auel's Ayla by more than a century.) Consequently she is fully adopted by her captors, who are wise enough to exploit talent in whomever it is found. In this way Berthoud celebrates the foresight of the founders of Paris, and reminds his own "tribe" of modern Parisians to adhere to their ancestral virtues, be they martial or compassionate. His utopian, Rousseauesque fantasy could hardly be more tonally different from Boitard's excremental vision, even though both writers identify troglodytic savages as the ancestors of the modern French.

Jules Verne (1828–1905), whose literary career was just beginning in the early 1860s, took a conservative position on the fossil man controversy, probably because he was reluctant to accept those aspects of the new scientific "materialism"[7] that conflicted with his Catholic faith. Verne's third novel *Voyage au centre de la Terre* (1864, revised

Figure 1.2   The cave bear expelled by Berthoud's founders of Paris.

1867, translated as *A Journey to the Centre of the Earth* in 1871–72), is a geological fantasia fictionalizing and humanizing the same journey through deep time that Figuier undertook in *La Terre avant le Déluge*.[8] But how to deal with the culminating appearance of man? In the 1864 first edition, Verne's answer was to avoid the issue entirely. Yet so imperatively did fossil man demand attention that his exclusion from a work with a strong geological theme was soon no longer possible. The Paris International Exhibition of 1867 contained public displays of prehistoric artifacts, including Edouard Lartet's epoch-making discovery at La Madeleine (Dordogne);[9] the guidebook to the exhibits was written by the fiercely anticlerical prehistorian Gabriel de Mortillet; the possibility of man's Tertiary origin was seriously discussed at the International Congress for Prehistoric Anthropology and Archaeology held during the Paris Exhibition.[10]

The 1867 reissue of *Voyage*, illustrated by Edouard Riou, contains two more chapters than the first edition. Now, toward the end of their subterranean odyssey, Professor Lidenbrock and his nephew Axel (the narrator) find a human skull associated with the bones of prehistoric animals. The Professor eagerly discourses on the possible major significance of this find in light of the recent discovery of a human jawbone unearthed by workmen at Moulin-Quignon (Somme) under the direction of Boucher de Perthes. Verne probably refers to this "discovery" because its authenticity was seriously in doubt. Indeed, by 1867 the Moulin-Quignon jaw was generally dismissed as a hoax,[11] and it remains one of the most notorious frauds in the field of paleoanthropology, if not quite on the level of "Piltdown Man."

Lidenbrock, unaware of the unfolding scandal of Moulin-Quignon back in Europe, enthusiastically supports the authenticity of the jaw and the existence of fossil man. But then the travelers come across a well-preserved corpse of "Quaternary man" (211) and shortly thereafter they glimpse a herd of living mastodons shepherded by a man over twelve feet tall (fig. 1.3). In retrospect, the narrator doubts his own eyes: "No human being could exist in that subterranean world. . . . The very idea is insane" (219).

Verne, however, would like his readers to believe in the living reality of the mastodons and their herdsman, because such phenomena, together with the evident recency of the Quaternary man's death, undermine Lidenbrock's naïve materialist confidence in fossil man. Couldn't the discoveries of stone tools in association with extinct animals be accounted for by the *continuing coexistence* of the "prehistoric" toolmakers and the "extinct" animals in the subterranean world? Might not Cuverian catastrophes in the form of landslips and earthquakes explain why archaeologists keep unearthing these tools and bones in association? For Verne, then, if fossil man is a living species, he cannot be an extinct human ancestor, and the Mosaic account of creation, as elaborated by Cuvier, remains (just about) intact. Verne's vignette of the giant herdsman is a product of the author's reluctance to abandon the biblical account of human origin. Verne's readers would have to wait thirty-four years until he was prepared to revisit the question of prehistoric man in fiction.

Boitard, Berthoud, and Verne were nonspecialists who introduced prehistoric sections into their fiction, buttressed with references to experts, in order to engage in the fierce ideological debate that was directly about fossil man and indirectly about man's place in nature.

Figure 1.3 Verne's subterranean explorers glimpse a gigantic mammoth herdsman.

The author of the first pf novel proper was himself an experienced archaeologist with a bold imagination. Adrien Arcelin (1838–1904) was
one of the discoverers of Solutré (Saône-et-Loire) in east-central
France, Europe's richest Paleolithic "kill site." Here the men of
the Reindeer Age, close to the limit of human habitation during the
Würm glaciation about 20,000 B.P., probably ambushed migrating
herds of reindeer and wild horses, dismembering the corpses with ex-
quisitely fashioned stone knives shaped like laurel leaves.

   In 1870, Louis Figuier had published *L'Homme primitif* (translated
as *Primitive Man* in 1870), a popular synopsis of new paleoanthropo-

logical discoveries in a format similar to his *La Terre avant le Déluge*. It included thirty-nine full-page plates by Emile Bayard depicting reconstructed scenes from prehistoric human life. Twelve of the most striking of these plates had been engraved from preliminary sketches by Adrien Arcelin that had been inspired by his excavations at Solutré. Perhaps the most famous of these plates (137) shows wild horses, stampeded by hunters, plunging over the edge of the steep escarpment known as La Roche de Solutré (fig. 1.4).

We now know that such events almost certainly never happened. The animal bones lie far from the bottom of the Roche and none show multiple fracture patterns typical of such a fall. It seems that Arcelin, carried away by accounts and images of North American Indian buffalo jumps that had filtered into European popular culture via Lewis and Clark's diaries, George Catlin's paintings, and James Fenimore Cooper's novels, had figuratively clad his prehistoric Solutreans in the garb of the Plains Indians. Thanks to the success of *L'Homme primitif*, the icon of the horse jump embedded itself in popular culture even before Arcelin's novel was published, reappearing in several later works of pf.[12] Here, then, early pf reveals its generic proximity to the emerging body of fiction about the untamed American West[13]—and, as is sometimes the case in Western fiction, the aboriginals are viewed more sympathetically than the invading settlers.

Arcelin's novel, *Solutré, ou les chasseurs de rennes de la France centrale. Histoire préhistorique* (Solutré; or, the reindeer hunters of central France. A prehistoric story), was published under the anagrammatic pseudonym "Adrien Cranile" in 1872.[14] The narrative, framed as a time-traveling dream vision, has a melodramatic plot turning on a clash of races, but it is competently written and commendable for its resistance to the more simplistic scientific racism of the time.

The narrator, Alexandre, hypnotized by a glittering stone as he lies sleepily below the Roche de Solutré, is transported with his friend Dr. Ogier, a local savant, back to prehistoric times. There they meet the aboriginal Solutreans, a short, dark-haired people who are a common ancestor of the Lapps, Finns, Estonians, Tartars, and Eskimos.[15] The Solutreans, however, are led by an Aryan[16] outsider, the beautiful I-ka-eh, daughter of the late chief: "She had the mixture of strength and refinement that one rarely finds except among the purest Indo-Europeans . . . and her foot . . . wouldn't have dishonored a Parisienne" (46). I-ka-eh is reluctantly betrothed to a native warrior whose Neanderthal features suggest that he is a throwback to the ape. Spurned by

Figure 1.4 Arcelin's Solutrean hunters stampede horses over a cliff.

I-ka-eh (who now favors Alexandre), the brute betrays his people to blond Aryans who are about to invade the area for its flint mines.

Yet though the invaders are ancestral Frenchmen, Arcelin's sympathies are with the peaceable reindeer hunters. (The novel's publication in the aftermath of France's military humiliation by Prussia may well account for Arcelin's preference for the aboriginals over the blond invaders.) The Solutreans have no knowledge of war; their meat supply being plentiful, they have never had any reason to fight anyone. Taking his lead from I-ka-eh, who loves her adopted tribe more than the race of her birth, Alexandre chooses the humanist path; ironically, this requires that he lead his hosts into battle. But he is too late: his outnumbered Solutreans on the Roche are soon encircled by the ruthless Aryans with their superior weaponry. Meanwhile, Dr. Ogier, who has joined the Aryans, spouts a crude racial determinism: the Solutreans are vermin destined to be exterminated by their betters. Inevitably the Aryans triumph, and I-ka-eh in despair throws herself off the Roche. Alexandre wakes from his dream, but when he later disinters the skeleton of a disfigured woman at the foot of the cliff, the authenticity of his adventure is proven.

Arcelin's modern editor feels that in 1872 *Solutré* was too poorly understood to be successful (10); certainly it has never received the recognition it deserves as the first pf novel. Instead, that honor has usually been given to Elie Berthet's *Romans préhistoriques: le monde inconnu* (1876). This, the first French pf novel to be translated into English (as *The Pre-Historic World* in 1879), is the most recent common ancestor of both the French and English pf traditions. Berthet (1815–91) was no archaeologist like Arcelin; though science had been his passion since childhood, he had made his living as a prolific *feuilletoniste* (writer of fiction for serialization in magazines) until, with the new popularity of human prehistory, he found a subject that harnessed both his literary talent and his scientific imagination. *The Pre-Historic World* is not strictly a novel but a trilogy of novellas, each set in Paris at a different epoch. By the 1870s prehistory was no longer one nebulous stretch of time but an increasingly well established sequence of demarcated periods.

As early as 1836, even before "prehistory" had been conceptualized, the Danish archaeologist Christian Jürgensen Thomsen had successfully proposed a tripartite progressive chronological sequence—a Stone Age, followed by a Bronze and an Iron Age—corresponding to what the relics were made of. In 1865 John Lubbock had coined the terms

"Paleolithic" and "Neolithic" to distinguish between the Old Stone Age of the hunter-gatherers and the succeeding Age of Polished Stone, during which pastoralism and agriculture were invented. From 1866, Edouard Lartet had named the cultural phases of the Paleolithic after animals whose fossilized remains were typically found at French sites: in ascending order, the Hippopotamus Age, the Age of Cave Bear and Mammoth, and the Reindeer Age. And between 1867 and 1873, Mortillet had subdivided Paleolithic industries chronologically and named them for French "type stations": Chellean, Mousterian, Solutrean, and Magdalenian.[17]

Speculative portraits of human evolution in the 1870s were everywhere strongly colored by a set of assumptions, philosophical rather than scientific in nature, that can be conveniently labelled "progressionism." This doctrine, whose spiritual father was Cuvier, assumed "that life has risen from simple to more complex forms throughout the successive eras of the geological past. [It] does not imply actual phylogenetic descent from one form to another, but rather a succession of more and more advanced creations until finally man appears as the crowning achievement" (Eiseley, 353). Such a doctrine accorded well with the popular nineteenth-century faith in progress. And in the view of many of his contemporaries, Herbert Spencer's universal "law" of evolution (from 1862), which stated that all organisms progressively developed from simple undifferentiated homogeneity to complex coherent heterogeneity, satisfactorily reconciled progressionism with Darwinism.[18]

From a progressionist viewpoint, human evolution was a linear evolutionary process in which peoples universally progressed through predetermined phases, though at different rates. Progressionists took it for granted that modern savages had failed to progress as far as Europeans. A writer of pf who in 1876 aimed to dramatize hominization could do no better than to revisit one familiar geographical site— Paris, for example—and reveal its prehistory as a series of progressive stages. Hence the three sections of Berthet's *The Pre-Historic World*: "The Parisians of the Stone Age"; "The Lacustrian City (Age of Polished Stone)," and "The Foundation of Paris (Age of Metals)."

Berthet places his characters, vividly drawn stereotypes adapted from existing romance genres, in a defamiliarized Parisian setting. He invites his reader to marvel as much at unchanging human nature as at the fact that hippos once haunted the Seine. In part 1, a maiden, Deer, is coveted by an atavistic brute named Red, though her heart belongs to Fair Hair, a blond, artistic proto-Celt. Eventually, the hero dispatches the hairy throwback with an arrow and restores the distressed damsel to her family. The ascendant trajectory of the Parisian bloodline is secured by the union of hero and maiden.

Part 2, set in a lake dwelling by the Seine, has a more elaborate plot reflecting the increased complexity of proto-Parisian society in transition from the Neolithic to the Bronze Age. The Aryan hero, Light-Foot, seeks to purchase the lacustrian chief's daughter with a dowry of precious bronze artifacts that he has acquired in the east. Berthet suggests that there is a correlation between the elevated status of women in this early agricultural community, the elevated feelings that "were beginning to be evolved from the ruder instincts of the primitive race" (157), and an elevated body count as amorous and political rivalries led to tribal warfare.

Part 3, set in pre-Roman Gaul, centers on the intrigues of a rich widow and the consequent endangerment of her beautiful daughter. Once again, the future destiny of Paris is at stake, and the tiny island fortress in the Seine is only saved from destruction because the joviality already typical of the Gallic character allows a looming vendetta to be resolved in laughter rather than blood. This episode, which contains a Druid, a Bard, and a heroic Gaulish warrior named Dumorix (who wears a winged helmet), is a direct ancestor of the famous *Astérix* comic strip in subject, theme, and occasionally even in tone.

One later pf work by Elie Berthet is also of interest: a short visionary text, "Un Rêve: L'Homme tertiaire.—L'Anthropopithèque" (A dream: Tertiary man.—anthropopithecus) (1883). It was written to serve as the prologue to the 1885 reissue of *Romans préhistoriques*—retitled *Paris avant l'histoire* (Paris before history)—acknowledging the even greater antiquity of man as suggested by recent scientific findings. In a scene anticipating *The Time Machine*, Berthet's dreamer, with the goddess of Science as his guide, travels vertiginously backward in time to the age of Tertiary man.[19] He finds himself in what looks like Egypt but is actually Thenay (Loir-et-Cher) in central France, scene of the first discovery of Tertiary stone artifacts by Abbé Bourgeois in the 1860s.

There the dreamer encounters our small, hairy "precursors" (5), who are bipedal but have opposable big toes that suggest an arboreal origin. He feels a mixture of anger and fear, protesting to his companion, "these aren't men, but monkeys!" (6–7). But Science calmly replies that no species of monkey anatomically resembles these anthropopitheci (man-apes). He then watches our remote ancestors split flint nodules using controlled heat from a fire and then knap (that is, shape) the fragments into tools. While amphycions (extinct bear-dogs) devour an unburied corpse by night, our precursors sleep soundly in their aerial dwellings.

The vision having ended, the dreamer proves unwilling to accept what he has seen. He tells Science that as no bones of Tertiary man-apes have yet been found, they remain only theoretical entities. But Science informs him that the findings at Thenay have been confirmed by others in Auvergne and Portugal. The dreamer protests that God *must* have created modern man all in one piece, but receiving no response, wakes up, at which point the story abruptly ends. Berthet strongly implies that Science does not deign to reply to the dreamer's final assertion because her counterevidence has spoken for itself: we *do* descend from these precursors.

Berthet's assertively materialistic "Dream" would shape Jules Verne's response to Science's disconcerting claims about human origins, and usher in a new subgenre: lost-race prehistoric sf. Verne felt that if it could be shown that semi-arboreal anthropopitheci were actually still alive on Earth, then the evolutionist position would be undermined. Inconveniently, however, before Verne could reply to Berthet, a precursor's fossilized bones were found.

Missing Links in the Fin de Siècle

Before turning to pf in English that followed the 1879 translation of Berthet's *Romans préhistoriques*, I shall sketch the course of human evolution as it was popularly perceived during the Victorian fin de siècle. It should be remembered that absolute dating of paleoanthropological remains—that is, calculating their actual age in years—was impossible until the development after 1945 of chronometric techniques such as radiocarbon and potassium/argon dating. Before then, only the relative age of remains could be known with any certainty, and this was by means of stratigraphy, namely, by comparing the depth and thickness of the geological strata in and near which the remains were found.

Human beings were thought to have descended from arboreal apelike creatures who may have lived as long ago as the Miocene epoch in the Tertiary period. These tree dwellers, perhaps motivated by a self-perfecting creative force—progress, if no longer directly under divine supervision, seemed as natural as breathing even to agnostic

Victorians—sought the dignity of an upright posture. They timidly descended to the ground, thereby losing their tails and prehensile feet (rudiments of which remained to disprove omniscient design) and gradually raised themselves from an apish, knuckle-walking posture.

Now vulnerable to terrestrial predators, they took to living in caves, invented weaponry for self-protection, and learned to make fire and clothing to keep themselves warm; the climate cooled as the Quaternary period began. In the succeeding ice ages, their expanding brains helped them to become cunning and ruthless hunters of animals far more powerful than themselves, such as the woolly mammoth and the cave bear. As their posture, confidence, and morals improved, they started to produce art and pottery and entertain religious beliefs. It was commonly believed that a series of invasions from the east by more advanced peoples had at different times replaced aboriginal populations in western Europe. Such invasions had been responsible for the extinction of the Neanderthals, for the disappearance of the Cro-Magnons, and for major innovations associated with the Neolithic period, such as permanent artificial shelters (for example, the Swiss lake dwellings first discovered in 1853), the domestication of animals, pastoralism, and agriculture.

Today, new fossil discoveries, more sophisticated dating techniques, and advances in human genetics have produced a complex, ever proliferating hominid genealogical tree. By contrast, in the nineteenth century, a paucity of material evidence and a progressionist mentality together gave rise to a simple unilinear ascending sequence of human development, often visualized as rungs on a ladder:

Such a schema owed little in its conceptual origin to the "bushy" tree of life as sketched out by Darwin, much more to the ancient figure of the *scala naturae* (scale, or ladder, of nature), more commonly known as the great chain of being. Hence Victorian prehistorians sought confirmations of the sequence of human evolution in the shape of fossilized "missing links" in the chain, links that clearly revealed the transition between simian and human form. The general public, finding the Darwinian concept of common ancestry hard to grasp, instead anticipated the discovery of fossils of creatures that were half ape, half modern man.

The most familiar prehistoric humans, the Neanderthals, whose existence had first been recognized in 1857, were held to occupy the "man-ape" rung on the ladder. Huxley had correctly argued in 1863 that Neanderthals were much more like human beings than apes. It was he who first popularized the phrase "missing link" the following year ("Further Remarks," 587), and a drawing of his is perhaps the first British depiction of the icon of the caveman (fig. 1.5). Nevertheless, for reasons later to be discussed, for most of the next hundred years Neanderthals would find themselves harshly "dehumanized."

But what of the "ape-man"? In 1868 Ernst Haeckel, the German evolutionist, had published his brilliant, though dangerously over-assertive, popular exposition of man's place in the new Darwinian cosmos, *Natürliche Schöpfungsgeschichte* (translated as *The History of Creation* in 1876). In it, he stated that the remains of an *Affenmensch* (ape-man) would one day be found. He even named this putative creature *Pithecanthropus alalus* (speechless ape-man) and located its probable home in the former continent of Lemuria, now mostly sunk beneath the Indian Ocean (2:300, 326).

Darwin, more tentative than his German disciple, had in *The Descent of Man* posited the likely existence of "connecting-links" (1:185) between apes and men and located them in Africa (1:199). On the question of the location of the cradle of humanity Darwin would eventually be proved more correct than Haeckel, but in one of the stranger stories connected with the quest for human origins, the Dutch surgeon Eugène Dubois, inspired by Haeckel to search what was left of Lemuria, did indeed discover remains of an ape-man missing link at Trinil, Java, in 1891.[20] "Java man" was named *Pithecanthropus erectus* by Dubois; it was later reclassified as one of the widely dispersed species of early hominids known as *Homo erectus*.

Meanwhile, the inhabitants of the upper rungs of the ladder were starting to come into focus. The first significant discovery of fossilized remains of anatomically modern humans was made by Louis Lartet at Crô-Magnon (Dordogne) in 1868. These specimens, physically more imposing than the average nineteenth-century European,

Figure 1.5　Huxley's sketch of a caveman.

were quickly embraced as ancestral Frenchmen. From this moment the Cro-Magnons (as they would thenceforth be known) would be viewed in popular culture as favored ancestors, especially by those who feared that modern white Europeans had become racially degenerate. By contrast, discoveries in 1901 of two modern *Homo sapiens* skeletons in one of the Grimaldi Caves near Monaco were more coolly welcomed, as these ancient inhabitants of the Côte d'Azur were reckoned to have been "negroid" in appearance.[21]

British Prehistoric Fiction, 1880–1914

In pf, the "unearthing" of a Paleolithic stratum under the familiar terrain of modernity is a common metaphorical strategy, though its rhetorical function varies. When Berthet tells us that mammoths laid down the trail now known as the Boulevard Montmartre, he chiefly means us to marvel at how much the urban amenities of Paris have improved since the Stone Age. But what struck Andrew Lang (1844–1912), Scottish polymath and author of the first pf story in English, was how little his contemporaries had transcended their prehistoric heritage. As he noted to his friend H. Rider Haggard in 1886, "we are all savages under our white skins" ("Dedication," v). Lang's jaundiced observation was not untypical of the cynical, interrogative spirit of the Victorian fin de siècle. His fellow-Scotsman Robert Louis Stevenson gave paradigmatic expression to the idea of civilized man's inner ape in *The Strange Case of Dr Jekyll and Mr Hyde* (1886), while Haggard himself in *She* (1887) suggested that even the possessor of the greatest female beauty would eventually have to yield to the hideous monkey within.

Lang's "The Romance of the First Radical: A Prehistoric Apologue" was first published in *Fraser's Magazine* in 1880.[22] It is set on the prehistoric French Riviera; perhaps Lang had been inspired by earlier discoveries at the Grimaldi Caves (from 1872). Its protagonist is Why-Why, a rebel from birth against the "despotism of unintelligible customs" (289) imposed by tradition and the medicine man: the blind worship of totems, misogynistic sexual taboos, cruel and disfiguring initiation rituals. Though Why-Why and his mate go into exile like their radical descendants Percy and Mary Shelley, they are tracked down and murdered by their own tribe for having dared to disobey the injunction against endogamy.

But Lang wrote his "apologue" (a short allegorical narrative conveying a moral) not so much to celebrate the belated flowering of Why-Why's progressive initiatives in the nineteenth century, as to suggest that his fellow Victorians' confidence in their superiority to those they deemed of lower race was hardly warranted. Did not so-called civilized people stubbornly retain such utterly irrational taboos as, for example, the law against a widower marrying his deceased wife's sister, or the Lord's Day observance regulations banning Sunday entertainments? Lang here uses pf to dramatize the anthropologist E. B. Tylor's theory of survivals in *Primitive Culture* (1871),[23] while his social critique anticipates that of J. G. Frazer, whose *The Golden Bough* (1890) includes an inventory of "savage" beliefs that Christianity retains with only minor modification.[24]

Despite Lang's promising start, there were few other significant British pf works published before World War I. One was *Zit and*

Xoe: Their Early Experiences (1886)[25] by Henry Curwen (1845–92), a "whimsical romance" (Henkin, 174) in which millions of years of hominization are compressed into the escapades of one primal human couple. Curwen's satiric targets are not easy to distinguish, though they probably include utilitarianism and Victorian gender stereotypes. Today it is tempting to read the novel as a comic pastiche of the pf genre, but this is misleading, in that *Zit and Xoe* actually precedes the crystallization of generic clichés. Nevertheless, *Zit and Xoe* certainly foreshadows Roy Lewis's droll masterpiece *What We Did to Father* (1960), for example, in the attribution of middle-class vernacular to prehistoric characters for comic effect.

A more important pf work is the five-part novella "A Story of the Stone Age" (1897) by H(erbert) G(eorge) Wells (1866–1946), who as a former pupil of T. H. Huxley was well qualified to explore the theme of human origins in fiction. By temperament, however, Wells was much more attracted to the question of human destiny, and probably conceived his Paleolithic romance as a prelude or junior partner to his similarly structured, but longer novella "A Story of the Days to Come" published in the same year as "Stone Age."[26] Wells's major work of pf would come to be considered outdated by its author and has never received much attention from critics.

Set 50,000 B.P. in the Thames valley, "A Story of the Stone Age" centers on a love affair between the advanced young hero Ugh-Lomi and the fleet-footed maiden Eudena. Their tribe's atavistic leader, Uya, covets Eudena, so the pair must leave the tribe to save her from his brutal attentions (fig. 1.6). Thanks to Ugh-Lomi's invention of the stone ax and equestrianism, the couple (unlike Lang's doomed visionaries) survive the hardships of exile, return to their natal hearth, and defeat the tribe's retrogressive elements, to the benefit of their descendants: ourselves. Like Berthet, then, Wells dramatizes a watershed moment in prehistory when two men, one progressive and one atavistic, compete for a woman near the future site of a great city, the fate of civilization hanging on the outcome.

The only other significant British work of pure pf of the pre-1914 period is not so much neglected as forgotten—except by Thomas D. Clareson, who correctly calls it the "most original" of early prehistoric novels in English (187). This is *The Master-Girl: A Romance* (1910) by "Ashton Hilliers," the pseudonym of the Quaker writer and zoologist Henry Marriage Wallis (1854–1941). This work is worthy of renewed attention in that its feisty female protagonist Dêh-Yān

Figure 1.6 Wells's Uya woos Eudena as Ugh-Lomi watches helplessly.

strongly anticipates Auel's Ayla. Hilliers's sixteen-year-old Magdalenian protagonist is over six feet tall and the strongest unmarried girl of
her totem clan. She falls in love with a man from an enemy clan who
has broken his leg, and invents the splint to save his leg (and later the
bow and arrow to defend him from a cave bear).

Hilliers's narrative clearly has a feminist aim: Dêh-Yān is an exceptional woman, mentally superior to the "routine-ridden, unimaginative
men" (74) who dominate her society. Her eventual rise to the effective
leadership of her tribe is a sign that female worth was recognized by
prehistoric people. Consequently, her tale is meant as a reproach to
modern people who share the views of the professor of ethnology with
his "mid-Victorian conceptions of the functions of womanhood"
(10)—and who, at the opening of the external narrative frame, has discovered a fossilized engraving celebrating Dêh-Yān's prowess.

Of other Edwardian pf, the episodic *In the Morning of Time* (partly
serialized in 1912)[27] by the Canadian poet and novelist Charles
G(eorge) D(ouglas) Roberts (1860–1943) is one of the very few anglophone works to show the influence of French pf. For example, the
chapter called "The Finding of Fire," in which the advanced protagonist Grôm successfully learns fire-making and gains the love of the
maiden A-ya, is clearly patterned on J.-H. Rosny's *La Guerre du feu*
(see below, chapter 2). Moreover, Roberts's frequent, graphic, and
slightly stilted depictions of violent conflict between animals and
men, or among hominid races at different stages of development, are
stylistically reminiscent of Rosny.[28] Roberts averred in his "Author's
Note" to the 1924 reprint of the novel that "the imagination must be
held under curb by a vigilant regard for the results of the painstaking
investigations of the scientists" (5). But that did not keep him from
capitalizing on the public fascination with dinosaurs and missing
links by pitting them anachronistically against one another in the
chapter entitled "The King of the Triple Horn" (fig. 1.7).

Also capitalizing on this fascination was Arthur Conan Doyle's
prehistoric sf novel *The Lost World* (1912). Doyle had fewer scientific
scruples than Roberts: the remote South American plateau where
ape-men and dinosaurs attack Professor Challenger and his team is
simply a faraway place where the laws of evolutionary plausibility can
be conveniently suspended. Yet *The Lost World*, one of the most exciting adventure tales ever written, is not totally shallow. Doyle is alert
to the ironic thematic possibilities opened up when civilized men return to the jungle, amusingly noting the survival of primeval traits in

Figure 1.7 Roberts's dinosaurs threaten an ape-woman and her baby.

the civilized Edwardians. For example, Challenger himself is both emotionally and physically atavistic: his brilliance is easily eclipsed by his violent irascibility, while the ape-men burst into laughter at his close resemblance to their chief (153).

Moreover, Doyle slyly pokes fun at those dubious offspring of evolutionism, eugenics and racial memory, made fashionable in earlier American pf by Stanley Waterloo and Jack London respectively. For example, Doyle's protagonist, Ned Malone, goes on the Challenger expedition to impress the lovely but reluctant Gladys, having been informed by his "race-memory" (4) that as a male he must win his mate by undertaking a daring feat. On his return he discovers that his instinct had been a little deficient: Gladys had simply been eager to get rid of him so she could marry a wimpish solicitor's clerk.

American Prehistoric Fiction, 1894–1914

There are three main reasons why pf took firmer root in the United States than in Britain before the First World War. First, in the Darwinian aftermath there was a greater reluctance in the United States to adopt a purely materialistic or monistic view of human origins, and consequently a greater urgency to use pf to rewrite Genesis in a manner that reconciled science and theology. This reluctance may have been a legacy of the New England Transcendentalist tradition, reinforced by the influence of the dominant American prehistorian of the nineteenth century, the fiercely anti-Darwinian Louis Agassiz of Harvard. Second, during this period of tremendous expansion of American economic power, it seemed both self-evident and patriotic to offer progressionist hominization scenarios dramatizing the providential apotheosis of American values: in short, to reveal that in the United States, "The pattern of history was upward" (Russett, 2).

Finally, as R. W. B. Lewis (q.v.) effectively demonstrated, American culture had already developed a complex relationship with the figure of Adam. By the orthodox interpretation of a national myth of origin, the first man, ruined in the corrupt Old World, had gone to remake himself in the unfallen Eden of the New. More cynical readings of this myth in the light of the closing of the Western frontier and the excesses of the Gilded Age suggested that the New Adam might have had as many flaws as the Old. Had he not violently occupied his New Eden at the expense of its aboriginal inhabitants? Whatever the case, pf offered itself as a genre that could both celebrate and interrogate America's buoyant sense of its own exceptionality.

The first important American pf novel was *From Monkey to Man; or, Society in the Tertiary Age: A Story of the Missing Link* (1894) by the Chicago lawyer and classical scholar Austin Bierbower (1844–1913). This awkwardly written but inventive novel attempts a tentative reconciliation between scriptural and evolutionary narratives of origin. It suggests that motifs found in Hebrew and classical mythology can be read allegorically as memory traces of the clash between two divergent kinds of Tertiary ape-man, only one of which was progressive enough to give rise to modern humans. For example, the serpent of Genesis as a symbol for theological evil derives from the actual threat that snakes posed to our arboreal ancestors; the Fall of Man comes from a racial memory of the glaciation beginning the Quaternary period, when one species of ape-man stayed in the north and froze to death (fig. 1.8).

Figure 1.8 Eve recast by Bierbower as an ape-woman.

The more progressive Ammi (whose name evokes both "American" and "Adam") emigrated south from the "Eden" of their primal jungle home and survived. Eventually, Bierbower implies, their descendants would regain the lost paradise (the United States) thanks to their spirit of enterprise and self-reliance. Though its analogies are unsophisticated and sometimes forced, *From Monkey to Man* represents an important early recognition that pf can profit as much from exploiting as from rejecting the traditional scriptural myth of origin.

Stanley Waterloo (1846–1913), a nationally known Chicago journalist, was the first English-speaking writer to specialize in pf. *The Story of Ab: A Tale of the Time of the Cave Man* (1897) was more successful and influential than Bierbower's novel, partly because it has better-drawn, more sympathetic characters. Waterloo, while acknowledging in his introduction the assistance of "some of the ablest searchers of two continents into the life history of prehistoric times" (iii), sought to use *The Story of Ab* to promote the unorthodox view that there was no hiatus between the Old and New Stone Ages. The progressive force of evolution properly understood, the Neolithic Revolution[29] could have been initiated by a single innovator and accomplished quickly without a replacement of European hunter-gatherers by Asiatic invaders.

Ab, who lives in a cave in the Thames valley in an interglacial epoch, invents the bow and arrow, promotes polished stone artifacts, builds the first shelter, and domesticates the dog. Waterloo claims that the monogamous Ab and his woman Lightfoot were superior in health and morality to many modern people. Indeed, the novel is a primer in manliness and eugenics for young Americans, with particular reference to the pioneer virtues of self-reliance and ingenuity that must be preserved against atavistic and decadent tendencies. It is no coincidence that *Ab* appeared at the threshold of the new imperialist age of the Rough Riders, the Great White Fleet, and the "strenuous life" as promoted by Theodore Roosevelt.

In 1914, Waterloo's *A Son of the Ages: The Reincarnations and Adventures of Scar, the Link*, was published posthumously. It is an ambitious episodic pf novel that chronicles human development in fourteen chapters, from tree-dwelling ape-men to the Vikings, preceded by an introduction in which the geological history of earth from the Precambrian eons to the emergence of man is summarized in slightly more than three pages. At the end of each chapter the protagonist "Scar the Link" dies, to be reborn at the start of the next. This narrative strategy of preserving identity via reincarnation allows Waterloo to gain a measure of dramatic unity, while Scar's first-person narrative encourages the reader to identify closely with the quasi-immortal protagonist.

Waterloo begins his outline of hominization by rewriting the *felix culpa* of Genesis. The original Scar, a simian tree dweller combining aspects of Adam and Cain, has a "fortunate fall" in the most literal sense: his thumb, seriously injured in a tumble from a tree, heals in a manner that makes it opposable. He is thus the first primate able to wield a club—and so with him begins the human conquest of the Earth. Moreover, Scar's digital dexterity, though acquired, is inheritable. Such Lamarckism[30] appealed to Waterloo, a writer steeped in progressionist ideas, as it allowed rapid social changes to be brought about through the hereditary retention of advantageous accidental organic changes.

Rapid social change was very much part of the experience of Waterloo's contemporary American readers. Indeed, they celebrated their contemporary and compatriot Thomas Alva Edison as the paradigm of the genius whose inventions had transformed the world in his own lifetime. Waterloo himself had benefited from that quintessentially American phenomenon, meritocratic social mobility, which enabled him to rise from boyhood on a Michigan farm to the presidency of the Chicago Press Club. He used pf to celebrate the dynamism of American culture, viewing it as the culmination of a progressive evolutionary force characterized by the flowering of individualism.

Moreover, in the eugenic vein increasingly prevalent at the turn of the century, Waterloo suggested that Western civilization ought to protect its Paleolithic heritage to ensure that its bloodlines remained vigorous. At the end of *Ab*, he asserts: "Strong was primitive man; adroit, patient and faithful was primitive woman" (350). He even identifies four modern worthies, each from a different Western nation, in whose veins runs the "good blue blood" of Ab and Lightfoot: Abraham Lincoln (United States) (to whom Ab's name obviously alludes), William Ewart Gladstone (United Kingdom), Victor Hugo (France), and Otto von Bismarck (Germany) (349–351).

In the first decade of the twentieth century pf began to appear regularly in a variety of different forms in the United States. Katharine Elizabeth Dopp (1863–1944), one of the first women both to earn a Ph.D. from and to teach at the University of Chicago, produced an illustrated pf series for six- and seven-year-old children, beginning with *The Tree-Dwellers* (1904).[31] In her pedagogical notes concluding the first volume, Dopp states that her book is intended to help teachers harness children's energy in constructive ways: for example, by having them re-create aspects of prehistoric daily life in the classroom or on field trips. It will also evoke strong positive emotions in children by recounting primal "racial experiences" (158). Indeed, race memory, eugenics, and racial determinism are already evident in this product of advanced scientific and social thought mediated by first-wave feminism. The publisher's "Announcement" at the end of the volume approves Dopp's choice to write about the "early life of Aryan peoples, rather than . . . those contemporary tribes [that is, American Indians] which represent an arrested development" (159).

Some American writers of pf for adults were more ambivalent than Dopp about the modern savages forming the North American aboriginal population. In 1904, Gouverneur Morris (1876–1953), great-grandson and namesake of a statesman and diplomat who helped shape the U.S. Constitution, published *The Pagan's Progress*, probably the first pure pf novel set among Paleo-Indians. The narrative claims to trace the upward spiritual progress of the "pagans" (for example, by showing the development of romantic love from animal lust), though Morris often seems content to revel in the unregenerate violence of prehistoric tribal life. It was also his intention to reclaim an *American* prehistory, while indirectly justifying colonization as a faster and more efficient means of tempering savagery than evolution.

A Woman of the Ice Age (1906) by L(ouis) P(ope) Gratacap (1851–1917) synthesizes several of these nativist strains. For much of his professional life, Gratacap was curator in mineralogy at the American Museum of Natural History in New York City; as a trained geologist, he might have been expected to adhere closely to the "normal" paleoanthropology of his time. Scientific caution, however, was no match for Gratacap's passionate obsession to establish prehistoric man—or, rather, woman—in postglacial California 30,000 B.P.[32] To do so was essential to his teleological vision in which a divine "Doctrine of Intention" (one that strongly favored the Pacific coast) directed human evolution (13).

Gratacap's Paleo-Indians are not merely noble savages; they are more beautiful physically and morally even than the idealized European Cro-Magnons.[33] For Gratacap's own "Great Intention" (48) was to celebrate, through his heroine Lhatto, North American Woman as the source of all life, progress, and civilization. His novel is not feminist in any modern sense, even though Lhatto is refreshingly different from the pallid, passive, or masochistic savage women found in much pf of the period. Rather, it is the work of a philogynist who lavishes praise on New Eve as if to atone for how Old Eve had been for so long reviled.[34]

The first great writer in the English language to give his full sympathetic attention to pf was Jack London (1876–1916). If H. G. Wells was prospective by temperament, London was retrospective, fascinated in particular with rediscovering the primitive animal in man. Indeed, a prehistoric man makes two appearances in London's first masterpiece, *The Call of the Wild* (1903), the short novel about a dog, Buck, who shakes off millennia of domestication in the Northern forests. There a "hairy man" with a stone-tipped club, embodying the "call" of the primal wilderness before wolves were enslaved by humanity, appears in visions to Buck (86–87, 124–125).

London's major pf work, the short novel *Before Adam*, was published in 1907.[35] The first-person narrator is an old man who has been plagued since childhood with nightmares about his prehistoric past life. At college, he had discovered from his studies in evolution and psychology that he was suffering from "racial memories" (17) that were imprinted into the consciousness of humanity in prehistoric times and to which, by a "freak of heredity" (18), he was peculiarly attuned.

"Racial" or "organic" memory derived from a quasi-scientific hypothesis that emerged in the late nineteenth century in default of an understanding of the genetic mechanisms of heredity. It "proposed that memory and heredity were essentially the same and that one inherited memories from ancestors along with their physical features. . . . [J]ust as people remembered some of their own experiences consciously, they remembered their racial and ancestral experiences unconsciously, through their instincts" (Otis, 2–3). As we shall see, ancestral memory harmonized well with popular recapitulationist ideas: if the ape was still within us, and if by some atavistic quirk our inner ape became accessible to us, then so did its memories.

London's narrator channels his avatar Big-Tooth, a semi-arboreal man-ape living in the mid-Pleistocene epoch (fig. 1.9). Big-Tooth details his tribal upbringing among "the Folk," his conflict with the atavistic brute Red-Eye, his successful pursuit of his mate "the Swift One," and his encounters with members of two other closely related but hostile groups of hominids, the primitive Tree-People and the advanced Fire-People. The former tribe, who are arboreal ape-men, represent nature; the latter (our Cro-Magnon ancestors), culture. In

Figure 1.9 Big-Tooth's father swings through the trees in London's *Before Adam.*

this way, London explores the tension between atavistic and progressive tendencies in human society, suggesting that while a brutish antisocial ape survives in every man, this individualistic beast may be less dangerous than modern cooperative society, which can be coldly and murderously inhumane to those whom it views as its enemies. Ending with a casual genocide of the Folk perpetrated by the Fire-People for the sake of lebensraum, *Before Adam* chillingly anticipates some of the ugliest events of the twentieth century.

Jack London also wrote two short stories with strong prehistoric elements. "When the World Was Young" (1910) is about a modern San Francisco businessman, James G. Ward, who, as a result of a similar quirk of racial memory to the one afflicting the narrator of *Before Adam*, is transformed by night into an "uncouth, wife-stealing savage of the dark German forests" (241). This striking prehistoric sf story, which may be read as a parable of how modern masculinity must negotiate its inner caveman, is an obvious source for Edgar Rice Burroughs's Tarzan, who first appeared in print the next year. By contrast, "The Strength of the Strong" (1911), though masquerading as pure pf, is an overt apologue in the Langian vein. As his cavemen learn the advantages of communality over primeval anarchy, London preaches socialist solidarity over selfish individualism.

Jack London did not write pf primarily out of intellectual curiosity about our evolutionary past; he was compelled to do so for personal, emotional reasons. He was caught between two irreconcilable chimeras—the Socialist Utopia and the Nietzschean Superman—while waging a losing battle with alcoholism. His resort to prehistory was, as it was for his protagonist Darrell Standing in his last major novel *The Star Rover* (1915), a desperate path to self-knowledge by a man straitjacketed by society and condemned to death by his own self-destructive heredity.

London subscribed fully to Ernst Haeckel's recapitulationist approach to evolutionary theory, highly influential at the turn of the century. This approach derived from the belief that the embryonic development of an organism was an accelerated analogue of the evolutionary history over millions of years of the biological phylum (that is, the largest biological subdivision) to which the organism belonged. Haeckel considered progress a fundamental law of nature.[36] It was undoubtedly his progressionism that caused him to elevate certain suggestive embryological resemblances into a "*biogenetic fundamental principle*," expressed in the axiom, "*Ontogeny is a short and quick repetition, or recapitulation, of Phylogeny*" (1:33; emphasis in original). In this view, each human being in utero ascended through the stages of fish, reptile, bird, and so on, until reaching the pinnacle reserved for mankind.

Haeckel's recapitulationism was intellectually and emotionally appealing to London and his contemporaries probably because it smuggled back the scale of nature, human privilege, and teleology into Darwin's naturalistic universe (that is, one operating without supernatural interventions). At the same time, it gave a quasi-scientific gloss to anxieties about degeneration and the beast within that haunted the nineteenth century. Haeckel's recapitulationism gave literal force to Tennyson's lament that traces of the ape and tiger remained "in" the civilized man, explaining his continuing propensity to lust and violence. So, for London's Darrell Standing, his impending fate was proof enough that the ape and tiger were very far from dead in human society (*Star Rover*, 327).

Recapitulationism also underpinned the Italian anthropologist Cesare Lombroso's theory that criminal behavior could be explained by atavistic reversion to more primitive states of being—to prehistoric times, perhaps, when rape and murder were adaptive mechanisms. The genetic mechanisms of heredity not yet understood, vague notions of the perpetuation of the past in the present were made more "scientific" through the hypotheses of organic, ancestral, or racial memory. For Jack London, one way of coping with the discontents of civilization was to reconnect with a more authentic prehistoric self by using his imagination to tap these "memories."

London was confident enough in his grasp of recapitulationist doctrine—one hesitates to call it theory—to send a copy of *Before Adam* to Haeckel himself.[37] But pf in English began to constitute itself as a genre when its practitioners started to become influenced, positively or otherwise, by their *literary* precursors. London's correspondence reveals that he had read Waterloo's *The Story of Ab*, Morris's *The Pagan's Progress*, Wells's "The Story of the Stone Age," and Lang's "The Romance of the First Radical" (Labor 2:572, 624). And Stanley Waterloo was in no doubt that *Ab* had influenced Jack London. On 19 October 1906 in a San Francisco newspaper he accused London of plagiarism, citing similarities between descriptions of primitive arboreal hominids in the openings of *Ab* and *Before Adam*, the latter of which had just begun serialization.

Waterloo's case was weak, as London knew when he fired off a response to his accuser:

> [D]on't you think that it is mighty rash to talk that way about a whole book, on the strength of having seen only the opening installment?
>
> And don't you think that it is a case of getting your feet into the trough, when you arrogate to yourself the whole field of the primitive world for exploitation in fiction? At that rate, when one man describes a sunset, no other men are ever to describe sunsets. . . .
>
> The only resemblance between your *Story of Ab* and my *Before Adam* is that both deal with the primitive world. . . . [Y]our story and mine are as wide apart as the poles in treatment, point of view, grip, etc. Why, I wrote my story as a reply to yours because yours was unscientific. You crammed the evolution of a thousand generations into one generation—something at which I revolted from the first time I read your story. (Labor, 2:624)[38]

As all of London's points were largely true, Waterloo's reply was subdued. Without apologizing, he noted, "I read all you write with interest. I would suggest that you do not make arboreal man and the cave man contemporaneous, *in the same region*" (Labor, 2:625; emphasis in original). No litigation ensued, and from this point onward, American pf existed not as one man's fiefdom but as a territory open for exploitation to anyone who could stake a valid claim.[39]

This affair is a reminder that literary success is not gauged by originality of subject but by freshness of treatment, which in itself implies that in good work, close intertextual relationships with earlier writings in a similar vein are inevitable. Waterloo thought that the success of *The Story of Ab* had earned him the right to corner the market in fiction about human prehistory. Evidently he was either not aware of, or believed that he could ignore, his antecedents. London, writing *Before Adam* almost a decade after *Ab* was published, had read his pf precursors, understood that their work constituted an embryonic genre, and sought to make his mark by beating them at their own game.

Moreover, though both Waterloo and London accused one another of being unscientific, in the end the issue was, and remains, not one of scientific accuracy but of fictional plausibility. Waterloo was probably correct that most prehistorians in 1907, fixated on a unilinear hominization scenario, would not have scientifically approved of the idea of tree people and cave people as contemporaries, let alone neighbors. Regardless, as fiction London's scenario is far less counterintuitive than Waterloo's in *Ab*, in which one man in his lifetime is responsible for innovations that almost certainly took millennia to accomplish. As in sf, plausibility in pf is a better guarantor of aesthetic success than rigid adherence to normal science.

2.

▾ From Rosny's First Artist to
del Rey's Last Neanderthal

> Am I Randall Crone, a scientist connected with a great public
> museum, or am I Ran Kron, a youthful warrior of a savage tribe
> in the eon-old Ice Age? Is my wife, Rhoda—the gently nur-
> tured, highly cultured Rhoda Day—the modern product of this
> Twentieth Century; or is she Red Dawn, the flaming-haired
> daughter of a red-haired witch priestess of a devil-worshipping
> tribe of skin-clad Anthropophagi in that same remote Ice Age?
>
> —Nictzin Dyalhis, "The Red Witch" (1932)

Rosny and French-Language Prehistoric Fiction, 1876–1914

The most important figure in French pf is J.-H. Rosny *aîné* (Rosny the
elder; 1856–1940), who was also a leading figure in the development
of French sf. Rosny is little known in the English-speaking world,
though there is a strong argument for considering him more accomplished than Jules Verne at deriving aesthetically successful fictional
scenarios from scientific discourse. Rosny's novella "Les Xipéhuz"
(1887), which has been referred to as the first true work of French sf
(Baronian, 707), describes an alien invasion of earth—more than a
decade before Wells's *The War of the Worlds* (1898).[1] Moreover, "Les
Xipéhuz," set in Mesopotamia a thousand years before the early civi-
lizations of that region invented writing, is also a work of prehistoric
sf. Bakhoûn, the protagonist, is endowed with a rational scientific
spirit far ahead of his time. He identifies the invading aliens for what
they are and engineers their defeat, even though his people are no-
mads who worship primitive gods and have not the beginning of a notion what an extraterrestrial threat to Earth might signify.

Rosny *aîné* was born Joseph-Henri-Honoré Boëx in Brussels, Belgium, to a French father and a Flemish mother. As a young man he

spent ten years in London, and his first wife was English. He began his literary career as a disciple of the naturalist school of Zola, but in the year of "Les Xipéhuz" he and a group of four other young Zolaists broke with their master over what they considered his crude excess of realism.[2] Thereafter Rosny had a long and prolific career as a writer of adventure novels, lost-race tales, pf, sf, and their hybrids. Between 1893 and 1907, he cowrote fiction with his younger brother Séraphim-Justin-François Boëx (aka Rosny *jeune*, 1859–1948), though it is generally believed that the elder Rosny was exclusively responsible for the work with prehistoric content written during this period. Indeed, the elder Rosny is one of the very few writers before Jean M. Auel who are now best remembered for their pf.

Rosny by no means invented pf: as we have seen, he was preceded by several Francophone and at least two Anglophone writers. Moreover, by 1892, when Rosny's first pf novel was published, he could not even be considered a pioneer in imaginative prehistory; for more than a decade there had been an outpouring of French visual art on prehistoric human subjects, initiated by Bayard's engravings in Figuier's *L'Homme primitif.* This work was academic in style (that is, it was formally composed and strove for a photographic realism) but at its best it achieved powerfully dramatic effects. Exhibited in the Salon alongside paintings and sculpture on historical and mythological subjects, these images of prehistoric life, often thoroughly researched and filled with documentary detail, served to whet the public appetite for prehistory as a background for heroic or erotic fantasies. This body of work is little remembered today, as nineteenth-century French academic painting has been out of fashion for more than a century.[3]

The huge canvas entitled *Caïn* (1880) by Fernand Cormon (Fernand Anne Piestre, 1845–1924) gave "prehistoric art" an enduring icon by working out some of the revolutionary implications of the science of human origins. Cormon depicted Cain and his retinue, not as vagabonds exiled from Eden by God, but as prehistoric settlers displaced by drought and desertification (fig. 2.1). With their tangled hair, animal skin clothing, stone-tipped spears, deer carcasses, and cadaverous dogs, this ragged crew are depicted heading eastward, presumably to where they are destined to found the first city (Genesis 4:16–17).[4]

Other notable "artists of prehistory" of this period include Léon Maxime Faivre (1856-1914), whose *L'Envahisseur* (The invader) (1884) depicts a blond troglodyte struggling with a dark-haired invader for possession of his cave and woman; Paul Joseph Jamin (1853–1903),

Figure 2.1 Cormon's Cain and his retinue as a displaced prehistoric tribe.

who specialized in scenes of primal sexual violence such as *Un Rapt à l'âge de pierre* (Stone Age abduction) (1888); and Paul Richer (1849–1933), whose sculpture *Premier artiste* (The first artist) (1890) portrays a heroically built Cro-Magnon man beatifically smiling as he finishes a sculpture of a small mammoth. Richer used a cast of an actual skull found at Crô-Magnon in 1868 to dictate the shape of his First Artist's head.

Rosny's best pf derives from this fin de siècle moment in which prehistoric human life rapidly became at once an absorbing spectacle and a rejuvenated mythology.[5] Like the artists, Rosny uses existing myths to shape his prehistoric scenarios with the aim of evoking, in the deserts of modern urban life, nostalgia for the vitality of a "younger world." As J.-P. Vernier notes, "Rosny's vision is permeated with the Edenic myth, i.e. with nostalgia for an imaginary period when the universe was characterized by the organic union of opposite and contradictory elements" (161). Rosny's prehistoric worlds, which stand in for this "imaginary period," are peopled by various species of men and animals locked in life-or-death conflict, punctuated by noble gestures and unexpected alliances. The winners of the Darwinian struggle are our ancestors, and their victories fill them with unbridled hope for the future. They stand in implicit contrast to their descendants, disenchanted and demoralized by modernity.

Rosny's first pf novel, *Vamireh: roman des temps primitif* (Vamireh: a novel of primitive times) (1892), is set 20,000 B.P. in the late Magdalenian Age (just before the Neolithic Revolution), when *Homo sapiens*, represented by the Cro-Magnons, supposedly enjoyed a golden age of physical health, well-being, and artistic achievement. Like Richer's *First Artist*, the blond giant Vamireh is a combination of Hercules and Michelangelo. A warrior of superhuman strength and ferocity, he is also a sensitive mobiliary artist, not to mention a paragon of compassion in his dealings with the lower races of the forests. He loves Elem, daughter of the round-headed,[6] dark-haired Asiatic invaders who, aided by their vicious dogs, are destined to supplant Vamireh's hunters as the masters of western Europe. Nevertheless, the love of Vamireh and Elem is progressive, and their racially mixed descendants will be glorious additions to humanity.

Eyrimah (1896) Rosny's second pf novel, also celebrates exogamy. It is set 6000 B.P. among Neolithic lake dwellers, and describes the conflict between these descendants of Elem's Asiatics, and the mountain people, a remnant of Vamireh's Cro-Magnons. The eponymous heroine is a blonde mountaineer who as a child was captured by the lacustrians. She has since caught the eye of their chief's son, but the pair must negotiate an epic series of hurdles before they can unite. Rosny suggests (as Berthet had done) that these lacustrians on the threshold of the Age of Metals were as complex as the elaborate cities on stilts that they built in the lake shallows. *Eyrimah* is nothing less than "the *Iliad* transposed to Switzerland," as Phillippe Dagen has suggested (36). Flight, rescue, amorous intrigue, betrayal, and racial conflict on a grand scale culminate in a battle that determines the fate of Europe, though history bears no trace of it.

Rosny's pf novella "Nomaï" (1897) is also set among lacustrians. The uncouth giant Rochs desires the beautiful Nomaï, the Chief's daughter, but she prefers Amreh, an undistinguished warrior. Too much of a weakling to defeat Rochs in combat, Amreh collaborates with Nomaï in a successful ruse to slay his rival by ambush. The Chief signals his acceptance of his daughter's union by ritually breaking one of her teeth, and as Amreh presses his mouth to Nomaï's in sympathy, the pair both literally and figuratively consecrate their wedding in blood. While romantic love allows intense emotional identification and fosters female agency, its Neolithic birth marks the passing of the warrior virtues that formerly prevailed in the hunt for a mate.

Marvelously evocative works, *Vamireh*, *Eyrimah*, and "Nomaï" have never been translated into English. In contrast, Rosny's masterpiece, *La Guerre du feu* (1911; translated as *Quest for Fire* in 1967), is the best-known work of French pf in the English-speaking world thanks to the 1981 movie adaptation of the same title (see chapter 3). The novel is set in an unspecified place and time in Upper Paleolithic Eurasia when hominids at various levels of development might have encountered each other by accident: in this Rosny anticipates "pre-Sapiens" theory.[7]

The Oulhamrs' fire has been accidentally extinguished and they do not know how to rekindle it, so Naoh, the virile protagonist, embarks on a quest to restore living warmth to his people. In the course of his adventures he defeats savage animals, makes a mutually beneficial alliance with woolly mammoths, and daringly steals a firebrand from the camp of Neanderthaloid cannibals. Eventually he learns from an intellectually advanced but physically degenerate tribe the technique of fire-making using firestones: flint is struck against iron pyrite and the resulting sparks used to kindle tinder (fig. 2.2). Then, defeating an atavistic rival from among his own people, he triumphantly brings back the firestones to the Oulhamrs.

What elevates *La Guerre du feu* above Rosny's other pf novels is the classic simplicity of its structure as heroic quest, thematically deepened by allusions to myth. From the opening, we sympathize strongly with the Oulhamrs, helplessly bereft of comforting light and warmth in "the terrible night" (11), and unreservedly admire their enterprising hero. Naoh is as fierce as Achilles, as determined as Prometheus, as resourceful as Odysseus, and as compassionate as Androcles. He is also a prototype of the valorous knight of romance who seeks only the favor of a princess as his reward. Indeed, at the end of the novel chivalry enters the world for the first time, as the Oulhamr chief rewards Naoh with the power of life or death over his daughter: "Naoh, placing his hand on Gammla, gently raised her up, and what seemed like time without end stretched out before them" (143).

Of other French pf before 1914, several works retain interest. *Aventures d'un petit garçon préhistorique en France* (The adventures of a prehistoric boy in France) (1888) by Ernest d'Hervilly (1839-1911) was the first important pf novel for older children, human antiquity now being viewed as one of the facts of life that young French people ought to be introduced to at puberty. Framed as a modern father's frank conversation with his adolescent son, Hervilly's descriptions of prehistoric life as a perpetual struggle against rival tribes, animals, the elements, and hunger are lively and frequently gruesome; the book's realism is enhanced by striking illustrations by Félix Régamey.

Figure 2.2   Rosny's Naoh uses firestones for the first time.

A notable work by a Belgian who preceded Rosny is *Le Poignard de silex* (The flint dagger) (1889) by G(ustave) Hagemans (1830–1908), vice president of the Brussels Society of Archaeology. This episodic novella is ingeniously unified by the motif of the eponymous weapon whose lethal trail is followed from the Mammoth Age to the Bronze Age. Also in 1889, appeared the first pf by a female author, *Misère et grandeur de l'humanité primitive* (The misery and greatness of prehistoric humanity) by Mme. Stanislas Meunier (1852–?).[8] Its first part is a paean to the Magdalenians, the artistically accomplished Upper Paleolithic people that the French liked to think of as their ancestors. This imputed sense of kinship is probably why Meunier argues that the Magdalenians were not replaced but "modified" by contact with their Neolithic successors (x). The second part contains a series of "justificatory readings" (129) from scientific works, the inclusion of which undoubtedly helped the work's adoption as a textbook by the Ministry of Public Instruction.

Though pf was early appropriated in France as a blunt didactic tool, the fin de siècle aesthetic movement did not disdain the genre's potential for poetic suggestiveness. Marcel Schwob (1867–1905), friend of Oscar Wilde, produced two pf stories, both dedicated to Rosny. The first, "La Vendeuse d'ambre" (1891; translated as "The Amber-Trader" in 1982), probably influenced both *Eyrimah* and "Nomaï." It portrays the encounter between brutal, treacherous, Alpine lake villagers and the improbable but appealing figure of a Neolithic New Woman—a free-spirited blonde amber trader. Schwob's second pf story, "La Mort d'Odjigh" (1892; translated as "The Death of Odjigh" in 1982), totally eschews realism. It culminates in the Christlike self-sacrifice of a wolf hunter at the foot of a glacier to save humanity from ice age extinction. By the turn of the century, then, Francophone pf already offered a spectrum of different approaches to prehistory, written by authors of varied backgrounds for different intended readerships. In such a context the emergence of a specialist in literary pf—a Rosny—seems almost inevitable.

Jules Verne's return to pf in 1901 was driven by the need to confront the evolutionary implications of *Pithecanthropus erectus*. In 1898 Haeckel had publicly affirmed the importance of Dubois's Javan discoveries, and in 1900 Dubois had displayed his missing link to the world in the form of a lifesize statue at the Paris Universal Exposition. Verne's response was the first significant work of lost-race prehistoric sf, the novel *Le Village aérien* (1901; translated as *The Village in the Treetops* in 1964). In the modern world, a tribe of arboreal hominids, the Waggdis, are discovered to be still living in the dense jungle of the Congo basin in central Africa. Verne conforms to Dubois's *erectus* designation by allowing his "anthropopithecoids" [man-apes] an upright posture, but deliberately flouts Haeckel by granting them speech. The Waggdis are ruled by Dr. Johausen, a German anthropologist who had made an enigmatic disappearance from civilization some years before.

Verne then approaches the vexed question of the transmutation of species. On the one hand, the existence of the Waggdis might be held to support "the upwards evolution postulated by Darwin"; on the other, the Darwinian theory fails to take into account "differences of the first importance in the intellectual and moral order" (152–153). Verne firmly denies the Waggdis "the conception of a Supreme Being" (164). In his view, the exclusive human possession of revealed religion separates us entirely from the animal kingdom. Animals cannot cross this gulf at all, though we humans can cross it backward, as the case of Johausen illustrates: the anthropologist, perhaps intended as a caricature of the militant monist Haeckel, is discovered to have degenerated completely into a "human beast . . . a monkey" (184) as a result of his prolonged contact with the Waggdis. Verne thereby intends to demonstrate that reversion to animality is the inevitable consequence of a purely materialistic worldview.

In *The Village in the Treetops*, then, Verne accepts the missing link, but only under the condition that it be viewed, not as an ancestral species, but as an intermediate creation affirming human exceptionality. If Waggdi men-apes still exist in the present, then (as with the Quaternary man and the mammoth herdsman in *Journey to the Center of the Earth*), they cannot be our ancestors, and the Darwinian view of human descent is cast into doubt. However, if Verne's aim was to demonstrate his magnanimity in conditionally acknowledging the possibility of the missing link between apes and men, then his gesture now seems too tentative and belated. H. G. Wells in *The Island of Doctor Moreau* (1896) had already considered the physical and psychic gulf between man and beast and had come to the disturbing conclusion that it probably did not exist.

The young Rosny had left Brussels permanently in 1875 for metropolitan opportunities. Yet by the end of the nineteenth century his birthplace had become a center of avant-garde culture receptive to radical new ideas. Symbolism, theosophy, and art nouveau all flourished there, while the fantastic imagery of the Belgian visual artists Jean Delville, James Ensor, and Fernand Khnopff anticipate later modernist movements, surrealism in particular. Meanwhile, the discovery of two almost complete Neanderthal skeletons at Spy d'Orneau near Namur in 1886 established Belgium as an important locus of paleoanthropological research.[9]

The Belgian writer and journalist Ray Nyst (1863–1948), a habitué of avant-garde circles in Brussels, was responsible for the work in which Francophone pf attains generic self-awareness. *La Caverne* (The cavern) (1909) is preceded by a lengthy "Documentary Introduction" in which Nyst enumerates his pf predecessors (including Rosny, Hagemans, and Wells) and claims to have written the first novel about Tertiary man.[10] Conceived as European versions of Dubois's *Pithecanthropus*, Nyst's unnamed first man and woman are founders of the earliest human social group, the tribe all of whose members descend from a single breeding pair. Such a group is what Sigmund Freud would refer to in *Totem and Taboo* (1913) as "Darwin's primal horde" in which a "violent and jealous" Old Man dominates a harem of women and drives away his sons when they grow large enough to threaten his mastery (202).[11]

That Nyst's horde is a nuclear family (comprising a father, mother, and their twenty-seven children) also encourages the reader to draw analogies between prehistoric life and the modern individual's psychological development. Indeed, invoking recapitulationism, Nyst asserts, "Prehistoric man isn't dead. He lives in us" (32). Moreover, that the horde is perforce promiscuous and incestuous may also remind us of Freud's exactly contemporaneous attempts to expose, via his concepts of the Oedipus complex and the "Family Romance," the archetypal fantasies of children as they struggle to assert their self-hood against the dominant influence of their parents.[12] In parallel to Freud, indeed, Nyst claims that the Oedipal struggle of the sons to re-place the father was central to social development. He also suggests that female fecundity (191) allied to a male "instinct for domination" (280) is central to our success as a species: we can outbreed *and* over-power all rivals. And Nyst consciously rewrites Genesis: his first couple are Adam and Eve, scientifically revised; the original sins are incest and parricide; Cain is the embodiment of every son's desire to replace his father; and the biblical Flood derives from a racial mem-ory of the annual rainy season of subtropical Tertiary Europe.

Though *La Caverne* was a strikingly original work, it was quickly eclipsed by the subsequent publication of two pf masterpieces: *La Guerre du feu*, a superior aesthetic achievement; and *Daâh, le premier homme* (Daâh, the first man) (1914) by Edmond Haraucourt (1856–1941), an ambitious, brilliant novel of ideas that, like *La Caverne*, approaches major issues of hominization in both their social and psychological aspects, but with more ingenuity, vitality, and humor. *Daâh*, like *La Caverne*, is set at the transition between the Tertiary and Quaternary periods. It traces through a series of very short chapters the transformation of the ape-man who is acclimatized to the unde-manding tropical Eden of the Tertiary into the man-ape who is capa-ble of surviving the testing environment of the first Ice Age. Like Jack London and Ray Nyst, Haraucourt invokes race memory as his means of access to the mentality of our prehistoric forefathers: "I invent nothing: I try to remember" (41).

Haraucourt, covering the lifetime of a single individual, avoids the implausibility that London objected to in Waterloo's *Ab* by making no attempt to represent realistically—for example, by detailing a se-ries of inventions—the progress that his protagonist makes toward becoming human. Instead, *Daâh* is an unapologetically philosophical novel in which characters function primarily at the level of arche-types. Daâh is a prehistoric Everyman whose appetites always exceed his ever more ingenious attempts to satisfy them; as such, he is the ir-redeemable brute still lurking beneath our veneer of civilization.

Indeed, according to Haraucourt "the doctrine of interior beasts" (72) was itself one of humanity's earliest set of beliefs, used to explain such internal organic disruptions as indigestion and pregnancy. In a clever variation upon Haeckel, Haraucourt imagines Daâh as a "colossal fetus" of the being he will become, one in whom the belly and the head are the dominant features (46). It is almost scandalous that this remarkable novel has never been translated into English. Was its sexual frankness too strong for its time? Was its publication in 1914 overshadowed by the descent into global war? Whatever the case, *Daâh* is one of the small group of pf masterpieces.

Prehistoric Fiction between the Wars

In retrospect, the period between the World Wars was a golden age of paleoanthropology. Notable discoveries include: the first fossil australopithecine in the shape of Raymond Dart's Taung child (now classified as *Australopithecus africanus*) in South Africa (1925); the many findings of Louis Leakey and his team in east Africa (from 1926); numerous remains of Peking Man (now *Homo erectus*) at Zhoukoudian, China (from 1927); and Robert Broom's discovery at Kromdraai, South Africa (1938) of the stocky man-ape *Paranthropus* (now *Australopithecus robustus*). At the time, however, the significance of these discoveries was less clear because a fog of preconception and prejudice enveloped them.

Haeckel's insistence that human beings had originated in Asia, reinforced by Dubois's discovery of Java Man, had resulted in a great reluctance to accept that Africa might be a source of fossil human beings. Meanwhile, the dehumanization of Neanderthal man had been completed even before the First World War by the French paleontologist Marcellin Boule, who had assessed the almost complete skeleton of the "Old Man" of La Chapelle-aux-Saints (Corrèze) (discovered in 1908), and had concluded that Neanderthal man had been a bestial, slouching creature, not worthy of a place in the direct line of human ancestry.[13]

The expulsion of Neanderthals from the human lineage opened an awkward gap in the "man-ape" part of the scale. For many in the English-speaking world, this rung was conveniently filled after 1911 by "Piltdown Man." This all-too-literal ape-man whose remains were "found" in Sussex consisted of a modern human skull and an orangutan jaw, cunningly fabricated to make them seem as if they belonged to the same individual. The perpetrator of the Piltdown hoax—he is still unidentified, and his deception would not be exposed for forty years—craftily exploited the British determination to discover a large-brained prehistoric "Englishman" to counterbalance French pride in their Cro-Magnon ancestors and to induce German shame at their Neanderthal ones.

In 1918, the Western world, emerging from the greatest debacle in history to date, started almost immediately to lurch toward an even greater bloodbath. Pf—and there was an abundance of it in the 1920s—ought to have been a genre where writers scrutinized the violent ape in the mirror that had just trampled contemptuously upon the faith of Victorian progressionists. Instead, there was a failure of imagination, and no interwar pf reached the heights achieved by London, Rosny, or Haraucourt.

Of all the writers of the period, none tried harder to seek clues in prehistory for the disaster of the Great War than H. G. Wells. Wells had never lacked imagination, yet after 1918 it was increasingly constrained by his desire to agitate for political and educational reform. In 1920 he published *The Outline of History*, a brave and eloquent attempt to write a universal history from the beginning of life on Earth to the contemporary postwar moment. However, in the early section on the Upper Paleolithic Transition, Wells strongly suggests that our Stone Age ancestors would have been justified in deliberately ethnically cleansing the Neanderthal submen from Europe (1:88). Once the Neanderthals had been "rehumanized" after the Second World War, Wells was retrospectively cast in the role of an apologist for genocide.

For the origin of war, Wells in *The Outline of History* blamed the rise of irrational beliefs during the Neolithic period. He noted how our knowledge of the great sweep of prehistory "which fills a modern mind with humility and illimitable hope" had been "veiled by the curtain of a Sumerian legend" (2:984)—that is, the Mosaic creation myth—until very recent times. Yet "The Grisly Folk," Wells's second foray into pf, deals not with the Neolithic Revolution but with the European encounter between Neanderthal aboriginals and the "true men" (608) invading from the east (figs. 2.3 and 2.4).

Wells cannot be blamed for the demonization of the Neanderthals; as we have seen, this process had been under way in both paleoanthropology and pf since the 1870s. But in depicting Neanderthals as intolerable monsters whose only legacy are our legends of "ogres and man-eating giants" (618), Wells failed to draw a connection between his construction of the subhuman Other and the propaganda that had helped to justify what had taken place on the killing fields of Eu-

Figures 2.3 and 2.4   A Sub-Man (*left*) and a True Man (*right*) according to Wells.

rope.[14] Indeed, Wells's loathing for the Neanderthals seems too excessive to have a scientific rationale; it seems more intelligible if "The Grisly Folk" is read as a political allegory. In this light the Neanderthals represent the destructive force of selfish individualism. Our ancestors, though individually weaker, cooperated with each other in order to wipe them out. Read in this way, the story is an Langian apologue pleading, like Jack London's "The Strength of the Strong," for socialist solidarity. It has to be admitted, though, that few readers of "The Grisly Folk" have supposed that Wells's baby-stealing cannibals might be bloated plutocrats in disguise.[15]

Wells's, though perhaps the most influential, was not the only interwar failure of the pf imagination. Rosny's last two pf novels simply avoided confronting the problem of how hominization might have culminated in mechanized murder on a global scale perpetrated by the most "civilized" nations on earth. A sequel to *La Guerre du feu* featuring Naoh's son Aoûn as protagonist, *Le Félin géant* (1920; translated as *The Giant Cat* in 1924, retitled *Quest of the Dawn Man* in 1964) merely rehearses many of the earlier novel's themes in a less mythically resonant manner.

In *Helgvor du fleuve bleu* (1930; translated as *Helgvor of the Blue River* in 1932), in which a noble Stone Age hero clashes with brutal Bronze Age orientals, Rosny revisited the same territory as *Vamireh*, using the Parnassian diction that forty years earlier might have been strikingly evocative but now seemed mannered and even pretentious. His overtly nostalgic and escapist vision of prehistory was epitomized by "La Grande Enigme" (The great enigma) (1920), a short dream vision.

The modern protagonist recalls passing through a mountain fissure into a lost Edenic Tertiary landscape, where he glimpses those "vertical beasts" our ancestors, in the form of a first family glowing with youth and promise (656).

Very different in tone, "Les Hommes Sangliers" (The boar men) (1929)[16] is Rosny's one late success, a powerful novella about the dark side of the desire for the savage. A young Dutch woman in the colonial East Indies is abducted and raped by members of a lost Paleolithic tribe, the cannibalistic Boar Men of the title. After escaping their clutches, she finds herself in a state of total *dépaysement* (disorientation after being uprooted from familiar territory), unable to live in either the Modern or the Stone Age. This prehistoric sf story brings modernity and savagery together in a violent clinch, a strategy better attuned to the ominous mood of the interwar period than the escapism of Rosny's pure pf.

Two of the most interesting pf novels of the 1920s were first published in French. Possibly the best pf novel of the whole interwar period is *La Fin d'un monde* (1925; translated as *The End of a World* in 1927) by Claude Anet (1868–1931).[17] Revisiting the scenario of *Vamireh* with far more vigor than Rosny himself would be capable of in *Helgvor*, Anet imagines how the great period of Magadalenian art came to an end as the blond Cro-Magnons were replaced by more militant brunet peoples from the East. In his postscript, Anet reports consultations with a host of prehistorians, including Abbé Breuil, the leading expert on cave painting, and Denis Peyrony, the former schoolteacher who had been involved in numerous major discoveries in the Vézère valley.

Also in 1925, Max Bégouën (1893–1961), the son of Count Henri Bégouën, professor of prehistory at the University of Toulouse, published *Les Bisons d'argile* (translated as *Bison of Clay* in 1926; fig. 2.5). As a teenager in 1912 Max Bégouën had discovered the Magdalenian cave of Tuc d'Audoubert (Ariège) in the French Pyrenees containing the now-famous clay sculptures of a pair of mating bison. Bégouën's romance plot between the warrior Lynx and the female chief Spring-on-the-Prairie serves as an expedient springboard for speculations about the function of totem animals in Paleolithic shamanism, the origin of warfare in the rivalry between clans, and the meaning of cave art. The actual sculpting of the clay bisons serves as the climax of the novel (188–193).

Both Anet's and Bégouën's novels are well researched, thus serving

Figure 2.5 The cover of Bégouën's *Bison of Clay*.

to reveal the laziness or exhaustion that tarnishes other pf *entre les deux guerres*, be it French, British, or American. *Les Enchaînements* (1925; translated as *Chains* in 1925) by Henri Barbusse (French, 1873–1935) is an epic novel in which the young poet-narrator, suffering from involuntary ancestral memories, uncovers the chains of time that hold the majority in bondage for the profit of the few. Yet the protagonist and his Paleolithic alter ego are psychologically indistinguishable, a serious implausibility and one suggesting that Barbusse had no interest in exploring primitive mentality.

H(enry) Rider Haggard (British, 1856–1925) in his posthumously published romance *Allan and the Ice-Gods* (1927)[18] uses drug-induced time travel to take his recurrent hero Allan Quatermain back into the mind of Wi, his Stone Age ancestor. Wi struggles mightily to raise his tribe from savagery, but only so that the narrator can conclude that the effort was not worth it, modern civilization being "a great sham" (285).

Carnack the Life-Bringer (1928) by Oliver Marble Gale (American, 1877–?) is a completely implausible narrative about a prophet of progress in Paleolithic North America who leaves his testament in cartoonish engravings so that his contributions to spiritual progress will not be forgotten in the future. To the reader today, this work's complete failure as imaginative literature serves only to reaffirm two important truths: (1) after the Great War, nineteenth-century progressionism was dead beyond resuscitation; and (2) pf, as a post-Darwinian literary genre, is completely incompatible with traditional religious doctrine.

There was an interwar tendency to use prehistory as a thinly sketched backdrop for more traditional fantasies of power. In the popular cultural field, this trend is epitomized by the pseudo-pf of Edgar Rice Burroughs, of which *The Eternal Savage* (1925; reissued as *The Eternal Lover*) is a representative example. Mere time cannot separate the destined love between Nu, mightiest of prehistoric hunters, and Victoria Custer of Nebraska, a guest of Lord Greystoke (aka Tarzan) in central Africa. Earthquakes transport the lovers to the "Niocene" (an imaginary geological epoch) where sadism, violence, and daring rescues from fates worse than death abound.

In contrast to Burroughs, the popular "Og" series of pf stories for boys by Irving Crump (American, 1887–1979) is earnest in its concern to detail the slow growth of abstract ideas during the "childhood" of mankind. From his first volume, *Og, Son of Fire* (1922),[19]

Crump focuses on the importance of the individual innovator in mitigating the Darwinian struggle of prehistoric existence. More than his precursor Stanley Waterloo, Crump saw hominization as a series of conceptualizations that must be successively discarded if progress is to occur. Only the genius is ever prepared to abandon the superannuated myths normally used to explain the world—the myths that most people, Paleolithic or modern, cling to because they are familiar.

The orphaned cave boy Og, knapping a flint to make a tool, is astonished to find that his actions cause sparks to be thrown off the stone. He already knows how to use fire: now he has been presented with a clue about how to make it from scratch: "He sat and thought and thought and thought, until his brain grew tired. The fire was in the rock, of that he was certain, but how to get it out and in his possession, under his control, was a vexing question" (Crump, q.v., chap. 9). Regardless of its context in a story for boys, the cognitive issue raised here lies near the heart of what makes pf a genre worth reading. Crump describes our ancestral arrival at the counterintuitive epiphany that there is fire "in" certain stones that can be made to leap out on demand—counterintuitive because the stones with fire in them are not hot and will not burn. The simple phrase that Crump attributes to Og, "the fire was in the rock," encapsulates metaphorically the complex and painful struggle that precedes the conceptual breakthrough and underlies our peculiarly human way of apprehending the world. Good pf, through imaginatively recapitulating how our earliest ancestors might have begun to tame the world through language, bridges the millennial gulf and sheds light on characteristic and enduring human ways of thought.

In contrast, two half-baked British prehistoric sf novels of the 1930s fail in different ways to match Crump's sensitivity to language as the key to recapturing prehistoric thought processes. At the same time, they both suggest that hatred of the modern world is alone insufficient to justify the escape to prehistory. S(ydney) Fowler Wright (1874–1965), the author of the accomplished disaster novel *Deluge* (1927) and other works in which modernity is suddenly swept away, was temperamentally drawn to the idea of sending his characters back to the dawn of humanity and letting them sink or swim.

Wright's first prehistoric sf novel *Dream; or, The Simian Maid* (1931)[20] frames itself as the tale of a strong modern woman, Marguerite Cranleigh, who, disillusioned with weak modern men and the

"earth-wide curse" of polyphiloprogenitive humanity (22), with a ma-
gician's help dreams herself back to a simpler, more authentic age.
There she becomes Rita, a hirsute tree person trying to avoid more
advanced but spiritually corrupt cavemen and farm folk. These dream
adventures serve as a test of her chief suitor's manhood: he has followed her into the same dream, and thereupon their involvement in a
series of adventures involving subterranean crevices and giant rats
proves their compatibility for marriage in the real world.

In truth, Wright's novel suffers from either his poor grasp of the demands of pf as a developing genre, or his complete indifference to the
paleoanthropological background, or both. In presenting three different but coeval kinds of prehistoric peoples he borrows, consciously or
otherwise, from *Before Adam*, but his sympathies are far narrower than
London's. His only remedy for present ills is to imply repeatedly that it
was a mistake for humanity ever to have descended from the trees.
Also, his novel is marred by a stylistic awkwardness that comes from the
same urge to simplify. For example, Rita's thought processes are rendered in faux primitive indirect discourse, the result of which is far from
a primal lucidity: "So she had grief at a joy which might be less near
than she thought, which had been a grief of another depth, had she
known what the doubt was" (127).

Three Go Back (1932) by the Scottish writer J(ames) Leslie Mitchell
(aka Lewis Grassic Gibbon, 1910–35) has a very similar plot structure
to Wright's *Dream*. Once again, a strong female protagonist, despair-
ing at the condition of the modern world, is carried magically back to
a prehistoric age in company with two others, one of whom is a man
who must prove himself worthy of her. Once again, the protagonist
and her lover die in the past, but in the narrative's closing frame are
reborn in the present. Mitchell's novel may well have been a deliberate attempt to revise *Dream*, not from any fundamental disagreement,
just more strongly to reaffirm that "Rousseau was right . . . and the
twentieth century evolutionists all wrong" (90). Perhaps to signal the
tonal contrast to *Dream*, the diction of Mitchell's novel is marked by
extreme unrestraint: verbose, infelicitous phrases such as "blowsily
mammalian women" (49), "strange, grassy fluffment" (94), and "sier-
raed toweringness" (161) proliferate.

At the beginning of *Three Go Back*, Clair Stranlay, who has lost her
lover in action in World War I, is traveling across the Atlantic in an
airship. It crash-lands in prehistoric Atlantis where Clair and two male
survivors find naked, golden-skinned proto–Cro-Magnon hunters

living a harsh but healthy existence without "gods, chancels, and torture-chambers" (99). These noble savages are threatened by brutish Neanderthalers, "sullen, individualist beast[s]" with a "black resentment against life" from whom descend "the militarists and the hanging judges and the gloomy deans of the twentieth century" (163). Clair takes to permanent nudity and a Cro-Magnon lover, but when she is snatched back to modernity just before falling victim to the Neanderthalers, she finds that her surviving male companion is, rather conveniently, the reincarnation of *both* her prehistoric and her soldier lover.

In *Three Go Back* Mitchell reprimands H. G. Wells by name for failing to conceive of primitive men who were neither "stalking ghouls of the night" nor "flea-bitten savages" (154). Mitchell had formerly been a disciple of Wells, but by 1932 had come to feel that an extreme form of diffusionism[21] was the key to understanding humanity's problems, while their cure lay not in Wellsian education or social engineering but in neoprimitivism, anarchism, and nudism. Mankind had gone wrong when it had abandoned the nomadic hunter-gatherer lifestyle and settled in agricultural communities. This great social transformation (the Neolithic Revolution) had in Mitchell's view "diffused" from its accidental origin in the Nile valley. With it, religions invented to assuage the self-inflicted miseries of so-called Archaic Civilization had spread like a plague (91, 116).

Three Go Back does have the virtue of showing more interest than Wright's *Dream* in conducting a dialogue with paleoanthropological theory. It would seem, however, that Mitchell argued, not in order to promote one scientific hypothesis over another, but to cast himself in the role of misunderstood heretic—even if this meant assailing Grafton Elliott Smith, the godfather of hyperdiffusionism.[22] Ultimately *Three Go Back* is not so much a sophisticated cocktail of anthropological ideas as a homebrew to be knocked back before stripping off one's clothes and plunging into the wilderness.[23]

Mitchell's only other work of pf is somewhat better focused and controlled. "The Woman of Leadenhall Street" (1936) is an elegiac speculation upon the origin of a female hominid skull unearthed when the foundation of the new Lloyd's Building in the City of London was being excavated in 1925.[24] Mitchell's Woman was the last survivor of a race of pithecanthropi; in relating her death, he reminds us of the pitilessness of Nature, who quickly tires of her experiments and blots them out: our modern civilization will not be exempt. Mitchell's is the most interesting imaginative failure among interwar pf writers.

He failed not because he lacked scientific knowledge, but because he used it to construct a totally implausible prehistoric situation, as if defying existing paleoanthropological authorities would give his pf more authenticity than careful extrapolation.

The few successful works of 1930s British pf are more modest in their posture and scope. For example, the story "Isis of the Stone Age" by F(rederick) Britten Austin (1885–1941), part of his episodic fictional universal history *Tomorrow* (1930), effectively dramatizes the "accidental" discovery of agriculture by placing it in a plausible human context. Austin forges for the reader the necessary emotional connection between prehistoric and modern worlds by positing that the status of women in the 1930s was only just recovering from its collapse during the Neolithic Revolution.

The best American pf novel of the interwar period is *Ogden's Strange Story* (1934) by the versatile adventure writer, traveler, and hunter Edison Marshall (1894–1967). The self-styled intellectual superman Ogden Rutheford survives a plane crash in the wilds of the Yukon, to find himself returned to life as Og the Paleolithic savage, deprived of all but his most primal ancestral memories and instincts. Evidently Marshall despised the modern world as much as Wright and Mitchell, but his profound knowledge of the wilderness, together with his admiration for Jack London, Melville, and Hemingway, and his respect for the Emersonian tradition of self-reliance, allowed him to produce an altogether more convincing survivalist scenario than the British writers.

The key to Marshall's success is his ability to link physical survival with "survivals" in the Tylorian and recapitulationist senses. To endure his reduction to a primeval state, Og must tap into what unwittingly survives in each of us, physically and psychologically, of our long prehistoric heritage. Discovering that he must kill if he is to eat, Og hurls a rock at a ground squirrel, and as he does so,

> a sound gushed out from his tight-drawn lips. It was half a growl, half a snarl; and Ogden Rutheford would never have dreamed that it abided in his throat. It was the outburst of a savagery that lurks in the deepest wells of man's subconscious—ordinarily forgotten until, perhaps, the stabbing rush of a bayonet charge over no man's land. And this was no man's land today. Rather, it was the land of beasts, of primal forces over which man has not yet extended his reign. (33–34)

Marshall's strength is his ability to project himself into the mentality of Og the Dawn man, to use him to reveal to us the "shadow of the past" as it falls upon the present (48): to show how war, religion, and romantic love might have originated, the desperate struggles and defeats that underlie our nonchalant mastery of fire or horsemanship, and the hidden primal meanings behind such familiar gestures as the handshake and the kiss. Perhaps *Ogden's Strange Story* is above all a homage to Jack London: it is *The Call of the Wild* rewritten from a human rather than a canine point of view.

During the 1930s, the emergence in the United States of "science fiction" as a widely accepted label led to pf's generic subsumption into sf for at least the next forty years.[25] Indeed, a cluster of sf stories with prehistoric elements started to appear just as *Amazing Stories*, the original American sf pulp magazine, was changing its subtitle from "Scientific Fiction" (April 1933) to "Science Fiction" (May 1933). "The Memory Stream" by Warren E. Sanders (possibly a pseudonym of F[rederick] Orlin Tremaine, American, 1899–1956) (Bleiler, 354) is about an experiment that allows a modern couple to voyage "up" the stream of racial memory to experience the violent thrills of Paleolithic sexual politics. The illustration by Morey epitomizes the enduring erotic appeal of Courtship with a Club (see chapter 5).

"Martian and Troglodyte" by Neil R(onald) Jones (American, 1909–88) concerns a visit by advanced Martians to paleolithic Earth, where they rescue an "advanced" pair of lovers from their brutish fellow tribesmen and install them in a place where they will be able to found the modern human line. Both these stories, firmly in the progressionist vein initiated by Berthet and Wells, were perhaps intended to reassure pimply teenaged sf fans that brain was destined to triumph over brawn. The slightly more original "N'Goc" (1935) by Raymond Z(inke) Gallun (American, 1911–94) appeared in *Astounding Stories*, the magazine that under John W. Campbell's editorship from 1937 would become the leading organ of sf's golden age. However, this story's prehistoric setting is simply a convenient way of framing an ingenious speculation about the origin of spiders.

A better story than these is "The People of the Arrow" by P(eter) Schuyler Miller (American, 1912–74), published in *Amazing* in July 1935. Set in the Rhone valley, it retells "The Grisly Men" from the Cro-Magnon point of view. Kor is the new chief of the Arrow People, having killed the Old One and seized his wolf totem. To avoid a drought, Kor must lead his tribe north to a new land occupied by woman-stealing, cannibalistic ape-men (Neanderthals) who seem "hairy, grizzled beasts" (69) to the Cro-Magnons. From trails secretly left by their abducted women, the Arrow People find a Neanderthal campfire and slaughter the submen with their bows and arrows. Now Kor prepares to conquer the realm of the "gray man-things" (70), ready to fight until one of the two peoples is extinct. Miller's tale can be viewed as a missing link between Wells's story and Golding's *The Inheritors*, the final chapter of which it strongly anticipates in setting, language, and theme.

Better yet are two stories by young sf writers from the stable of John W. Campbell, both published in *Astounding* in 1939 on the threshold of global war. L(yon) Sprague de Camp's prehistoric sf story "The Gnarly Man"[26] is about an immortal Neanderthal who has lived for 50,000 years on the margins of human society until at a Coney Island freak show he is identified by another outsider—a female anthropologist. Almost forty years later de Camp (1907–2000) apologized for dehumanizing his protagonist according to the Boulean canons of the time ("Author's Afterword," 358–359). His remorse was unfounded, as his "misinterpretation" of the Neanderthal is irrelevant to the story's enduring theme: that civilized human beings frequently behave worse than savages.

A similar theme is evident in "The Day Is Done" by Lester del Rey (1915–93).[27] The narrative represents the point of view of Hwoogh, the last Neanderthal, who lives on charity at the margins of a "Talker" (Cro-Magnon) settlement. His hosts, with their fully articulate speech, alcohol, and bows and arrows, are awesome beings to Hwoogh. He is grateful to be thrown the occasional scrap of meat and to be allowed a physically handicapped Talker woman as a mate. But he is cruelly persecuted by the children of the camp and the endless humiliations of his situation cause him to lose interest in life. Though credible on the realistic level, the story is also a parable of colonization's impact on subject peoples: deprivation of dignity brings about extinction almost as efficiently as deliberate extermination. "The Day Is Done" is the finest pure pf story of its time.

3.

▼

From Fisher's "Testament of Man" to Auel's "Earth's Children"

The blood-spattered, slaughter-gutted archives of human history, from the earliest Egyptian and Sumerian records down to
the most recent unspeakable atrocities of World Wars I and II,
accord with universal cannibalism, with systematized animal
and human sacrificial practices or their substitutes in formal religions, and with the world-encircling practices of head-
hunting, scalping, body-mutilating and necrophilic practices of
mankind in proclaiming this common blood-lust differentiator,
this mark of Cain, that separates man dietetically from his anthropoid relatives

—Raymond A. Dart, *Adventures with the Missing Link* (1959)

Killer Apes and Flower Children

In September 1940 four French teenaged boys, searching for a dog
that had trapped itself in a hole on a hillside in the upper Vézère
valley, stumbled across Lascaux (Dordogne), the finest Upper Paleolithic painted cave yet discovered. Here Magdalenian artists working by lamplight circa 17,000 B.P. had decorated the walls of the various chambers and passages with polychrome images, chiefly of
animals. The parietal (wall) paintings at Lascaux reveal a composi-
tional sophistication and an ability to capture animal movement that
would be unmatched until modern times. Henceforth Lascaux would
claim from Altamira (see chapter 7) the title of the "Sistine Chapel of
Prehistory."

After Lascaux it was no longer credible to assert that human culture had progressed by slow increments since the Paleolithic. As if to
emphasize the point, an unprecedented reversion to savagery was
then under way in western Europe. Nazi troops had entered Paris three

months before Lascaux was discovered; just as the cave began to yield its secrets, Hitler, who had earlier begun his objective of world domination by invading Belgium and Holland, launched an all-out bombing campaign on London as he prepared a fleet to invade Britain. The provocative juxtaposition of Lascaux and blitzkrieg[1] raised at least two large questions in the human sciences. If hominization had not involved a slow ascent from savagery to civilization, then what course had it taken? and how might its future trajectory be plotted? In the immediate aftermath of the Second World War, the answers seemed to lurk in the still savage heart of man.

Raymond Dart, who in the 1940s had been excavating at Makapansgat, South Africa, had become convinced that the fire-using apemen (*Australopithecus prometheus*) whose remains he believed that he had found there had been brutal cannibalistic killers who had wielded weapons of bone, tooth, and horn to smash the skulls and rip the flesh of their own kind. In "The Predatory Transition from Ape to Man" (1953), Dart proposed that the "mark of Cain" distinguishing us from other apes was our carnivorous heritage: we had been a violent, bloodthirsty species from the beginning.

Dart's notion of the killer ape would be popularized by the American journalist and playwright Robert Ardrey in a series of forceful polemics. In the chapter entitled "Cain's Children" of *African Genesis* (1961), Ardrey noted: "Man is a predator whose natural instinct is to kill with a weapon. . . . Our history reveals the development and contest of superior weapons as *Homo sapiens'* single, universal cultural preoccupation" (316–318). Indeed, "the antique assumption that man had fathered the weapon" was now replaced by the harsh truth: "The weapon . . . had fathered man" (29). After Auschwitz, Dresden, and Hiroshima, Dart and Ardrey were preaching to the converted.

If "we," Wells's "true men," had been killers from the start, then the world wars of the twentieth century were not aberrations; they were the unfolding of a biological destiny. But what then of our close relatives, the cannibalistic baby killers who had taken on the role of subhuman Other in the popular imagination? As the Neanderthals had apparently died off shortly after contact with the Cro-Magnons during the Upper Paleolithic Transition circa 30,000 B.P., then did it not follow that our ancestors must have been even more murderous than the brutish "submen"? After the exposure of the Piltdown hoax in 1953, many paleoanthropological truisms suddenly became suspect.

Figure 3.1 Coon's rehumanized Neanderthal Man.

The moral balance swung back in the Neanderthals' favor; they began to be rehumanized with a vengeance.

In 1927, one authority had noted that if a female Neanderthal were to walk down London's Bond Street "the very dogs would bark at her" (Henderson, 50). By 1939, Carleton S. Coon's *The Races of Europe* was offering an image of "Neanderthal Man in Modern Dress" portraying the Old Man of La Chapelle-aux-Saints in respectable bourgeois attire (fig. 3.1), while the caption noted that "the facial features were probably essentially human" (24). A thorough reassessment of the Old Man's skeleton in 1955 led William Straus and A. J. E. Cave to conclude that if a Neanderthal man, "bathed, shaved, and dressed in modern clothing," were encountered on the New York subway, he would probably not attract any unusual attention (Trinkaus and Shipman, 303).

This rehumanization, increasingly attuned to the countercultural currents in the United States during the Vietnam War, culminated in Ralph S. Solecki's *Shanidar: The First Flower People* (1971). The author, who had been excavating Neanderthal remains in Iraq since 1953, detailed how he had found a site (Shanidar IV) in which a corpse had been scattered with flowers before burial (246–250).[2] Our hirsute cousins, it seemed, had been gentle, peace-loving creatures. In an era when shaggy-locked antiwar protesters waving flowers confronted helmeted, heavily armed militia, it seemed easy to imagine how the Neanderthals' extinction might have come about.

Prehistoric Fiction, 1940–1979

At its best, the pf of the postwar period rose imaginatively to the challenge of an age in which many of the truisms of hominization were thoroughly interrogated. Several major works of pure pf and of sf with a strong prehistoric element were published, and one masterpiece of comic pf. This broad spectrum of achievement came about partly because both writers and readers were more familiar with the pf tradition. For example, the greatest postwar pure pf novel, William Golding's *The Inheritors*, though sometimes viewed as extremely original, more consciously and deliberately incorporated elements of earlier pf than any previous work. Moreover, to make its satirical points the comic masterpiece, Roy Lewis's *What We Did to Father*, depended on readers' knowledge of pf clichés.

The postwar years saw a number of American writers hitherto associated primarily with sf publish successful prehistoric sf works, thereby broadening the genre. Three examples, all involving interactions between Neanderthals and twentieth-century scientists, appeared in consecutive years: "The Long Remembering" (1957) by Poul Anderson (1926–2001); "The Ugly Little Boy" (1958) by Isaac Asimov (1920–92); and "The Alley Man" (1959) by Philip José Farmer (b. 1918). At the same time, paleoanthropologists turned to fictional forms, perhaps as much to indulge their creative imaginations as to popularize their speculations about prehistoric human beings. In 1949, Abbé Henri Breuil (1877–1961), the foremost French expert on cave art, published *Beyond the Bounds of History: Scenes from the Old Stone Age* in English, containing thirty-one Paleolithic episodes illustrated with amateurish, fanciful pencil drawings by the Abbé himself.[3] Soon thereafter François Bordes (1919–81), later professor of geology and prehistory at the University of Bordeaux and expert on stone tools, began to produce prehistoric sf stories under the pseudonym "Francis Carsac," beginning with "Tâches de rouille" (Rust stains) in 1954. (None has yet been translated into English.)

For people reaching adulthood in the 1950s, the problem of how to negotiate human-against-human violence in the unprecedented context of the thermonuclear age loomed large. To engage this readership, pf novels intended for young adults offering parallel situations from prehistory began to appear. *The Coming of a King: A Story of the Stone Age* (1950) by I(drisyn) O(liver) Evans (British, 1894–1977) is about the effect of the Neolithic Revolution on peaceful Magdalen-

FIRE-HUNTER   SABER-TOOTH

Figure 3.2   A prehistoric idyll from Kjelgaard's *Fire-Hunter.*

ian culture, as agricultural ideas diffuse into the Vézère valley from their Egyptian origin. *Fire-Hunter* (1951) by Jim Kjelgaard (American, 1910–59) concerns a spear-maker who is banished by his conservative tribe for experimenting with weaponry but who survives by linking up with a resourceful girl and a domesticated dog (fig. 3.2). In the prehistoric sf novel *Mists of Dawn* (1952) by the American anthropologist Chad Oliver (Chadwick Oliver Symmes, 1928–93), a young orphan accidentally travels back in time to 50,000 B.P., where in combat against Neanderthals he attains an authentic manhood and sense of purpose impossible under the shadow of the Bomb.

The most ambitious pure pf project yet undertaken by any writer began to bear fruit even before the end of the Second World War. These were the first four novels of the "Testament of Man" series by the Idaho-born Vardis Fisher (1895-1968): *Darkness and the Deep* (1943), *The Golden Rooms* (1944), *Intimations of Eve* (1946), and *Adam and the Serpent* (1947). The critical truism about Fisher (with which he himself agreed) is that his reach exceeded his grasp when he embarked on this epic series of novels about the intellectual and spiritual evolution of humanity from prehistoric times.[4] Indeed, Fisher's literary reputation today is in almost complete abeyance. Nevertheless, the first two of these novels are artistic successes, even if they are not masterpieces; the other two are less compelling but contain much of interest.

Darkness and the Deep was the first sustained attempt by a writer in English since Bierbower to depict Tertiary man. As such the novel compares favorably with Nyst's *La Caverne*, though it lacks the breadth and psychological penetration of Haraucourt's *Daâh*. Fisher was heavily influenced by Freud's vision of the Oedipally conflicted primal

horde in *Totem and Taboo*. His anthropoids have no knowledge of kinship aside from maternity, no incest taboos, no shelters, fire, language, tools, weapons, nor sense of futurity. The novel's first part
deals with Ho-wha's conflicts with the junior males of his horde; the
second deals with Wuh's splinter group and how he fashions it into a
horde by developing the use of the club as a weapon. Fisher plausibly
dramatizes protohuman groping toward rationality and innovation,
and exposes with admirable frankness the destructive aspects of male
sexuality.

The Golden Rooms is the most accomplished of Fisher's four pf
novels. It deals with the Upper Paleolithic Transition, the episode of
hominization that most challenged pf writers in the postwar period
because, even before Dart's killer ape hypothesis, the "sudden" extinction of the Neanderthals seemed to suggest that modern humans
had a primal capacity for genocide. Though Fisher uses no scientific
terms in *The Golden Rooms*, he clearly proposes that our ancestors the
Cro-Magnons—ironically as a result of having achieved an unprecedentedly complex level of consciousness—deliberately exterminated
the Neanderthals.

The narrative of part 1 is limited to the point of view of Harg, the
cleverest of a tribe of several hundred Neanderthals in what is now
France. It follows Harg's rise to his tribe's leadership as a result of his
invention of fire-making and pitfall traps. In part 2, the narrative perspective shifts to that of Gode, a Cro-Magnon chief. Gode gains prestige among his tribe by domesticating a wolf, then cements his power
by leading a campaign of extermination against Harg's tribe. In spite
of the Neanderthals' greater physical strength, the Cro-Magnons are
easily able to slaughter them with a weapon that kills at a distance, the
bow and arrow. The burden of guilt that Harg assumes for directing
this politically motivated genocide leads to his moral and spiritual
development. This novel, effectively elaborating upon the final episodes in London's *Before Adam*, strongly anticipates Golding's *The Inheritors* in many positive ways. In this way it is a crucial "missing link"
in the development of pf, and does not deserve to have fallen into such
obscurity.[5]

Intimations of Eve and *Adam and the Serpent* are both about prehistoric matriarchies based on a lunar deity (Moon Woman, aka The
Mother), social structures fated to be replaced by the sun-worshipping
patriarchies with which we are familiar. *Intimations of Eve* describes a
society in which fear of the many unknown aspects of human exis-

tence, especially death, is exploited by old women who claim to have knowledge of the magic that can control the ghosts of the dead who threaten the living. *Adam and the Serpent* is set in a Neolithic community. Dove, a man tired of being cowed and humiliated by women, conceives of a male supreme deity, a father in the sky, to supplant the cult of the lunar goddess that empowers the matriarchy. In doing so, he originates the notion, later to be enthusiastically embraced by the Abrahamic religions, that all evil enters the world through women. Fisher was no sentimental philogynist: his priestesses are cruel and abusive to both men and women, and constantly jockeying for power with one another. He evidently felt, though, that the agents of the patriarchy would commit far worse atrocities than the matriarchate they had superseded.

At present, the ethical debate about how to define the boundary between the human and animal realms remains for the most part at a relatively low temperature; our closest primate relatives are of distinctly different species from ourselves. The debate would quickly come to a boil, however, if anthropoid apes capable of interbreeding with humans were suddenly to appear. Such is the scenario in the outstanding postwar work of lost-race prehistoric sf, *Les Animaux dénaturés* (1952; first translated as *You Shall Know Them* in 1953)[6] by Vercors (Jean Marcel Bruller, 1902–91).

Vercors's novel, now better known in English as *Borderline*, begins with the contemporary discovery in New Guinea of a species of missing-link hominids, *Paranthropus erectus*, or "tropis" for short. The problem of human self-definition is brought to a head by the protagonist, Douglas Templemore, who deliberately kills the hybrid infant that he has fathered by artificial insemination on a tropi mother. If his child was an ape, then he can't be considered a murderer; but if the child was human—as Templemore so believes, from the two species' evident capacity to interbreed—then he must be tried for homicide. Though Templemore may be executed if found guilty, he will have achieved his ethical goal of saving the tropis from exploitation or extermination by those who view them as mere animals. The human tendency to dehumanize the tropis allowed Vercors, a French Resistance hero during the Second World War, to draw uncomfortable but potent historical analogies: with the Nazi relegation of disfavored "races" to subhuman status, and with the colonialist exploitation of subject peoples for profit.

The Inheritors, the second novel by William Golding (1911–93), is perhaps *the* masterpiece of pf. Its reputation, however, has always been overshadowed by the enormous popular success of *Lord of the Flies*, published the previous year. This obscuring is unfortunate, as *The Inheritors* is a richer, deeper work than its predecessor—though also a more difficult one for readers unfamiliar with pf reading protocols. *The Inheritors*, like *Lord of the Flies*, raises the issue of the "civilized" human capacity for evil, particularly as manifested in the Nazi death camps that had been revealed to a shocked world in 1945. Many tried to explain these atrocities by reference to the unique psychopathology of Hitler or to the cultural specificity of Germany, but Golding insisted on locating evil, not in the Third Reich, but in human nature.[7]

While *Lord of the Flies* approaches the problem of evil by tracing the moral degeneration of the malefactors (marooned English schoolboys deprived of adult supervision), *The Inheritors* focuses primarily on the victims, namely Neanderthals at the hands of our Cro-Magnon ancestors. Lok and his family group are peaceful beings sharing an intense empathy and spiritually attuned to the surrounding natural world; their simple communitarianism, however, makes them vulnerable to being wiped out by the more complex, individualistic New People invading Europe from the south. The Neanderthals, who unwittingly embody the gentlest Christian virtues, evoke our intense sympathy, but in truth they are aliens: they are impossible role models *because* of their inhuman moral perfection. The New People, on the other hand, are clever, conflicted, cunning, cruel, corrupt—in short, they are ourselves. The meek did not inherit the earth.

Golding wove together elements from earlier pf in order to make his great statement about how humanity, even when viewed from a secular, Darwinian perspective, is a fallen species. Alerted by Golding's epigraph from *The Outline of History*, critics have long noted that *The Inheritors* began in reaction to Wells's belief that the Neanderthals were subhuman—hence Golding's reattribution of child-stealing and cannibalism to the Cro-Magnons. Few have noticed, however, how much *The Inheritors* owes to *Before Adam*. London's novel ends with the exodus of eight survivors of a simple tribe, most of whom have been brutally massacred by more advanced humans for living space. Having recast Big-Tooth's Folk as Neanderthals, Golding depicts the cruel but inevitable fate of this remnant. In doing so he also develops London's idea that a consciousness incapable of conceiving of a weapon like the bow and arrow is likely to be tragically oblivious to its dangers. Golding's debt to Vardis Fisher's *The Golden Rooms* is also considerable: one sees it in the avoidance of scientific names; in the analysis of what drives human beings to genocide; in the use of a point of view that latterly shifts from victims to perpetrators; and in the final Cro-Magnon preservation of a Neanderthal infant in belated acknowledgment of a common humanity.

In *The Inheritors* there are also many lesser borrowings from or echoes of other works of pf. Lok's thornbush weapon has its counterpart in both Roberts's *In the Morning of Time* (31) and Fisher's *Darkness and the Dawn* (206). Lok's tribe's apelike fear of water echoes a scene in George Sterling's pf serial "Babes in the Wood" (1914) (q.v.). Both Haggard's 1927 *Allan and the Ice Gods* (40) and F. Britten Austin's 1927 episodic pf *When Mankind Was Young* (31–33) are possible sources for Golding's descriptions of the worship of a Great Mother manifest in water dripping from glacial ice caves. As noted above, the final scene of *The Inheritors* is strongly reminiscent of the final scene of Miller's "The People of the Arrow." Cleve Cartmill's story "The Link" (1942), about Lok, an ape-man who is rejected as worthless by his tribe but who has useful "pictures" in his head, surely provided Golding with the name of his protagonist and a key motif concerning Neanderthal cognition. Golding may even have borrowed a typographical device suggesting silent interrogation—"?" (104, 114)—from Mitchell's *Three Go Back* (101). One of the reasons that *The Inheritors* is a great pf novel is because its author has built upon a solid foundation laid by his literary predecessors.[8]

There have been comic depictions of prehistoric human life in popular culture since the late nineteenth century. Perhaps the first notable example was "Prehistoric Peeps" (1893–96) by E(dward) T(ennyson) Reed (1860–1933), a series of cartoons first published in *Punch* showing cavemen acting out the staid rituals of Victorian life, with stone replacing iron and dinosaurs standing in for familiar domestic animals. Comic cavemen featured at the dawn of the movies: in Charlie Chaplin's silent short *His Prehistoric Past* (1914), Charlie dreams himself back into a prehistoric world when the chief has a thousand wives and "where the man with the biggest club has all the fun." In the opening Stone Age segment of Buster Keaton's first feature film, *The Three Ages* (1923), a parody of D. W. Griffith's *Intolerance: Love's Struggle throughout the Ages* (1916), Keaton defeats a burly male rival and drags off his delighted female prize by the hair. First drawn by V(incent) T(rout) Hamlin in 1932, the syndicated newspaper comic strip *Alley Oop* (still extant) recounts the adventures of a time-traveling caveman.

Most famous of all, the animated cartoon series *The Flintstones* (originally broadcast from 1960 to 1966) inherits the petrified modern artifacts and dinosaurs of "Prehistoric Peeps" but updates them to 1960s American suburbia. In all these cases, the characters depicted are modern people dressed in prehistoric outfits. Charlie Chaplin, for example, wears the caveman's standard off-one-shoulder animal skin but retains his derby hat. The function of these travesties is chiefly mild satire of modern masculinity for the purpose of comic relief. Post-Darwinian anxiety that men are primitive brutes under their civilized veneer is dissolved when they reveal themselves to be fully domesticated if immature creatures who like to play at being savages. A broader social satire may also be developed via the bathetic reduction of modern complexities to Stone Age simplicity.

In 1960, the same year that *The Flintstones* first appeared on U.S. television, the classic work of comic pf by the British journalist and economist Roy Lewis (1913–96) was first published in the United Kingdom under the title *What We Did to Father* (though it is now usually reprinted as *The Evolution Man*).⁹ Its protagonist is the patriarch of a self-styled "subhuman" family group in Paleolithic Africa. The narrator is his son Ernest, and all talk as if they were characters in an English middle-class drawing room comedy: "Looks like we may be in for an interpluvial, after all" (10). Father, a tireless revolutionary and creative thinker, is determined to drag his brood out of the Stone Age by inflicting all sorts of social improvements on them; but they, complacent or atavistic, are reluctant to accept his radical program. *What We Did to Father*'s ridiculously accelerated view of human progress was anticipated by Curwen's *Zit and Xoe*, while the ludicrous incongruity of a modern middle-class consciousness in caveman attire allies Lewis's novel to the tradition of "Prehistoric Peeps" (fig. 3.3).

There are, however, two elements that elevate *What We Did to Father* above routine examples of prehistoric comedy in popular culture. First, Lewis has studied his armchair anthropologists carefully, and satirizes them by suggesting that their ingeniously theoretical ideas are out of touch with human nature. For example, Father refuses to allow his sons to mate with their sisters, extolling the virtues of exogamy and warning about how placid domestic contentment leads to degeneration. But his mandated alternative, wife capture, itself quickly degenerates into a cozy bourgeois ritual. Second, Lewis con-

Figure 3.3 Dreams of progress from Lewis's *What We Did to Father.*

siders Father's blind progressionism—apparently it survived the world wars and remained alive and kicking in the mid-twentieth century—to blame for mankind's stampede to the brink of thermonuclear destruction. In his obsessive quest to raise humanity above nature through the mastery of fire, Father manages to set an entire tract of country ablaze.[10] He thereby oversteps the limits of tolerance of the more conservative elements in his family, who kill and eat him for his pains, thereby helping to shape "the basic social institutions of parricide and patriphagy" (165).

The short prehistoric sf story "The Doctor" (1967) by Ted Thomas (Theodore Lockard Thomas, American, b. 1920) is another, if more somber, attempt to lay the ghost of unthinking progressionism. Dr. Gant's time machine has broken down 500,000 B.P. and now the U.S. medic must make the best of his reduced circumstances. He has taken a cave wife, with whom he has a son, and seeks to improve the life of his adopted tribe (for whom a broken leg normally meant death) by applying modern medical techniques. Yet his efforts are mostly in vain, either because of linguistic inadequacy or because of primitive ideas of tit-for-tat. Ultimately his own son is murdered by a mother seeking to "avenge" a life-saving tracheotomy Gant had performed on her own son. While this story reminds us how medical advances were paid for by the sacrifices of innumerable generations of healers, it also suggests how difficult it is to artificially raise cultural development to a new level when those to be raised are not ready for it.

As Lewis and Thomas intimated, progressionism was far from dead. It had merely sloughed off its skin, to reappear in a guise appropriate to a decade of radical change. By far the most famous and influential prehistoric scenario in popular culture during the 1960s was the one depicted in the opening sections of both the works known as *2001: A Space Odyssey* (1968): in part 1, "Primeval Night," of the novel by Arthur C. Clarke (1917–2008), and in "The Dawn of Man" section of the movie directed by Stanley Kubrick. The simultaneously conceived novel and movie differ considerably in style: Clarke's narrative is prosaic, workmanlike, and thematically explicit; Kubrick's film is poetic, highly polished, and (especially for those who have not read Clarke's novel) enigmatic. In 1968, Clarke's novel, though a better-than-average example of his sf, seemed almost quaint in relation to New Wave sf of the later 1960s. By contrast, Kubrick's movie was highly innovative and was immediately hailed as a cinematic landmark. In spite of these differences, however, the two works are close enough in structure, plot, and intended meaning to be dealt with simultaneously.

Although cast as a near-future scenario, the historical point of reference in *2001* is the cold war present, just as it is in Lewis's *What We Did to Father* and Kubrick's earlier masterpiece *Dr. Strangelove* (1964). In *2001*, as in these other works, humanity is threatened with thermonuclear self-destruction because its psychological and moral evolution have not kept pace with its technological development. At the start of their respective variants, Clarke and Kubrick take us back to an analogous time in prehistory: the great Pliocene drought that drove our nonspecialized hominid ancestors to the verge of extinction. They survived (according to *2001*) only because aliens, seeing a latent potential for transcendence in a few of their number (specifically, the apeman known as Moon-Watcher), boosted the hominids' cognitive skills by reprograming their brains, an effect that was inheritable because it involved deliberate mutation at the genetic level (19). The formerly vegetarian Moon-Watcher was thereafter able to exploit a new, rich source of nutrition by developing weapons and tools that enabled him to kill, butcher, and eat animal flesh even though he lacked the attributes of the typical carnivore.

In this way, then, Clarke and Kubrick offer qualified support for the Dart-Ardrey killer ape hypothesis. They propose, however, that we became meat eaters not because we were naturally bloodthirsty, but because aliens made us so for their own ultimately inscrutable reasons.[11] Nevertheless, our carnivorous appetite and affinity for weaponry have now outlived their usefulness: in the thermonuclear age we face self-extinction unless we can modify our destructive instincts. But again we cannot do this alone: alerted by their monolithic lunar sentinel[12] that humanity has reached a critical juncture in its development, the aliens again intervene, transforming Dave Bowman into an advanced entity, the Star-Child, who will save mankind from its own weapons of mass destruction.

The enormous popular appeal of the Clarke-Kubrick scenario almost certainly resides in the elements that it inherits from Victorian progressionism. It slightly updates and restates the doctrine that human evolution is not a random or blind process but one supernaturally directed toward a transcendental end. *2001*'s neo-progressionist scenario confutes Darwinism (and buttresses our illusion of centrality) not only by suggesting that our modern human nature could not have arisen by natural means, but also by proposing that we inherited

Moon-Watcher's acquired characteristics. Yet if *2001* flatters our sense of human exceptionalism, it simultaneously avoids delivering a simplistic theological message to the secular majority among its intended audience. It does so by casting mysterious but highly advanced aliens, rather than gods, in the providential role. *2001*'s fusion of pf and sf, while far from unique in the closely entwined history of both genres,[13] achieved its unparalleled success by reassuring its audience about the cosmic centrality and supreme destiny of the human species without appearing directly to assail the grand temporal context opened up by evolutionary theory.

Of the two major pure pf novels of the 1970s, neither is from the English or French traditions and both are about the extinction of an ancient culture. In *Den Svarta Tigern* (1978; translated as *Dance of the Tiger* in 1980), the Finno-Swede Björn Kurtén (1924–88), a distinguished professor of palaeontology at the University of Helsinki, subordinates character and plot to his desire to promote his ingenious hypothesis accounting for the disappearance of the Neanderthals. Kurtén believes (like Golding) that this matriarchal, fully human subspecies was morally superior to our Cro-Magnon ancestors, but doesn't think that the Neanderthals died out because we deliberately exterminated them. There was, he speculates, much crossbreeding that produced sterile hybrids. But Neanderthal women produced relatively more hybrids as a result of their aesthetic preference for neotenous[14] sexual partners operating in tandem with the patriarchal prejudices of the Cro-Magnons. Kurtén wrote a more fluent sequel, *Mammutens Rådare* (1984; translated as *Singletusk* in 1986), dealing with the quest of the hybrid protagonist to save his adoptive Neanderthal father.

A more brutal and also more plausible replacement scenario is depicted in *O Homem do Sambaqui* (1975; translated as *Sambaqui* in 1987) by the Brazilian children's writer and journalist Stella Carr Ribeiro (b. 1932). This excellent short novel for adults is set 7,000–8,000 B.P. among the shell midden people who occupied the coast of Brazil before the Indians. Ribeiro's achievement is to expose the internally generated forces that at once bind a tribal society and hinder its progress. Animism, totemism, cannibalism, suttee, self-mutilation, couvade, and infanticide are all described unsensationally, even sympathetically, as logical responses to circumstances by the Sambaqui given the state of their knowledge.

The male protagonist, an intelligent fisherman who questions the beliefs of his tribe, dies at the hands of invading Indians and leaves no genetic or cultural legacy. In contrast, the female protagonist, who "had a nature made only to feel things" (11), is abducted but survives her brutal transplantation to bequeath her chief quality, a passive fatalism, to her new tribe. Ribeiro describes unsentimentally the cultural (if not genetic) extermination of the Sambaqui via trickery, woman-stealing, and mass murder, the last simplified by superior weaponry. Needless to say, it will be the Indians' fate to be similarly replaced by "men-of-cloth" (European colonists) (122). One of Ribeiro's great strengths is her use of striking metaphors to convey the world-view of the lost Sambaqui: to them the moon was "white-eye of night," the sea "angry-water" (1), the sun was "eye-of-fire" (11). In the end, she suggests, it is above all through language that the pf novelist can pay tribute to a vanished culture.

The end of the 1970s also saw the publication of one of the most interesting generically hybrid works about Neanderthal survival into historical times. The novella "The Treasure of Odirex" (1978) by Charles Sheffield (British/American, 1935–2002) manages harmoniously to combine motifs from prehistoric sf, historical fiction, and detective fiction while making a case for the large debt owed to Darwinism by writers in all three popular genres. The Darwin who appears as the protagonist in Sheffield's story, however, is Erasmus, Charles's grandfather, and the story is set in the eighteenth century. Ghostly "fiends" who mysteriously haunt an abandoned lead mine in a remote mountainous district of Yorkshire are revealed by Erasmus to be peaceable Neanderthals who had taken refuge there millennia before to avoid our aggressive ancestors (with whom they have nevertheless since occasionally interbred). But Erasmus can only make his deduction by formulating an evolutionary theory and accepting its logical consequence, heretical at the time: the great antiquity of the human species. Sheffield ends with an "Author's Exegesis" in which he claims that the older Darwin, a pioneering Enlightenment freethinker, "steered" Charles toward *The Origin of Species* by serving as a philosophical model (194).

"Grotto of the Dancing Deer," a story by the veteran sf master Clifford D(onald) Simak (American, 1904–88), was published in *Analog* in April 1980 and won both the Hugo and Nebula awards for short stories published that year. It's about an American archaeologist who, having discovered a major Azilian painted cave in the French Pyrenees, is faced with the more sensational revelation that the Cro-

Magnon artist responsible for the cave's bizarre animal paintings is still alive, 22,000 years later. That Simak's story, ploddingly narrated and riddled with pf clichés, should have garnered such laurels is the most interesting thing about it. Perhaps pf had become so obscure a phenomenon by 1980 that a story about an immortal caveman seemed freshly minted; if so, then American pf was in desperate need of rejuvenation. Fortunately, it only had to wait a few weeks to receive it: on 4 May of that same year, an Oregon-based mother of five without a single previous fictional publication to her name published a first novel that would not only raise the public profile of pf but also transform the genre itself.

Jean M. Auel and Prehistoric Romance after 1980

Born in Chicago of Finnish ancestry, Jean M(arie) Auel (b. 1936) had developed an amateur fascination with human prehistory that led her to complete, in six months during 1977, a 450,000-word manuscript that would serve as the basis for the entire Earth's Children series (Heltzel, 43). So far the series consists of five novels, each of which is based on extensive paleoanthropological research, makes many more demands on the reader's general knowledge and imagination than the average best seller, and is epic in scope. According to Auel's publisher her novels have sold in total more than 37 million copies globally.

The first novel in the series, *The Clan of the Cave Bear* (1980) promised to be a literary phenomenon even before publication. The totally unknown author received a record advance of $130,000 after her agent had engineered a publishers' auction for the contract. *Clan* is one of those very few works that were both original and successful enough to initiate an enduring type of popular fiction. Its predecessors include Ann Radcliffe's *The Mysteries of Udolpho* (1794), founding work of the female gothic novel; James Fenimore Cooper's *The Last of the Mohicans* (1826), of the Western novel; and J. R. R. Tolkien's *The Lord of the Rings* (1954–55), of heroic fantasy. Such works are significant as much for sociological as for aesthetic reasons; as John G. Cawelti has convincingly suggested (35–36), they are likely sources for insights into the nature of the culture that produces them. But before discussing prehistoric romance, the new subgenre that Auel founded, I shall consider *Clan* within the evolving tradition of pf.

The Clan of the Cave Bear is set in what is now the Crimean peninsula of southern Russia during a Würm interstadial, that is, a warmer spell of the last Ice Age. Its protagonist is Ayla, a Cro-Magnon girl orphaned at age five by an earthquake and adopted by a Neanderthal tribe, the Clan. It thus deals with perhaps the central issue of post-1945 pf, namely, why our ancestors in Europe survived the Upper Paleolithic Transition circa 30,000 B.P. while the Neanderthals did not. Considered in the context of the pf tradition, Auel's primary achievement in her first novel was to offer a more plausible answer to this question than had any previous pf writer.

By 1980 the Dart-Ardrey killer ape hypothesis had lost much of its credibility.[15] Moreover, the idea that sapients had ruthlessly killed off the Neanderthals seemed to take no account of the thousands of years that the two peoples had almost certainly coexisted and possibly also interbred throughout Eurasia. In the 1970s, anthropologists such as Ashley Montagu in *The Nature of Human Aggression* (1976) and Richard E. Leakey in *Origins* (1977) assailed the "innate aggressionists" (Montagu, 274) and argued that that humanity was better defined by compassion, cooperation, curiosity, art, and invention than by savagery and violence. Björn Kurtén had adopted a similar position in his two pf novels, but his Neanderthal replacement hypothesis had been too elaborate to be appealing to the nonspecialist reader. How might a nonaggressionist approach to the Upper Paleolithic Transition be reconciled with a dramatic and captivating plot?

Though Auel had no academic training in paleoanthropology, she had the capacity to undertake extensive reading in the subject, the ability to absorb it, and the imagination to extrapolate from it in ways that were both intellectually plausible and emotionally appealing. One of her most important speculative extrapolations from the fossil evidence was that Neanderthals and Cro-Magnons did not think alike: that was why their skulls (and brains) differed in shape. She proposed that Neanderthals had mental access to an extensive archive of racial memories, causing them all to think and respond to the world in a similar, predetermined manner. Consequently they had less need for a complex verbal language and had never developed much of a vocal apparatus.[16] Though capable of uttering simple words, they chiefly communicated using manual signing, a method particularly adaptive for bands of hunters required to stalk their prey silently. Most significant, the two Neanderthal sexes had each a different set of racial memories as a result of the ancient and rigid division in their society between (dominant) male hunters and (subordinate) female gatherers.

Cro-Magnons, on the other hand, had mental access to far fewer communal racial memories. Consequently they required long cultural instruction, thought more individualistically, and needed complex verbal structures to express their ideas to others. Their society was also patriarchal and divided by gender, but not so rigidly as the Neanderthals'. It was impossible for a Neanderthal woman to learn to hunt, for she had no access to the memories that would allow her to do so. But a Cro-Magnon woman under the pressure of circumstance could learn this traditionally masculine skill, as Ayla does. Moreover, sapient men like Jondalar and Ranec, Ayla's love interests, do learn such feminine crafts as weaving and cookery respectively.

Auel hypothesizes, then, that their mental flexibility, especially in relation to gender roles, would allow sapients to adapt more successfully than Neanderthals to rapidly changing postglacial conditions. *Clan* is about a young woman who becomes fully independent by learning the essential survival skill: to hunt and kill animals for sustenance. She must do so in defiance of her adoptive tribe, who have tabooed all weaponry to women. When at the end of the novel Ayla leaves her hybrid son Durc in the Clan's care and sets out in search of her own people, she is not so much being driven into exile as embarking on a literal version of the modern woman's paradigmatic quest, the one undertaken by Nora in Ibsen's *A Doll's House* (1879): to become a full human being by sacrificing a life of secure constraint for uncertain freedom.

Clan's literary sequels trace the consequences, both positive and negative, of Ayla's unusual upbringing. She finds and retains a lover worthy of her extraordinary qualities, learns to thrive among her own species, and bears a daughter, in the process developing and transmitting many innovations. But she finds that sapient prejudice against Neanderthals makes it difficult for her to be honest about her upbringing and the fact that she has borne a hybrid son. Her alienation from Durc also continues to haunt her. Though she has liberated herself from the Clan, she discovers that she owes it a large moral debt, the repaying of which gradually comes to dominate the latter part of the Earth's Children series.

In *The Valley of Horses* (1982) Ayla learns to survive on her own on the mammoth steppe. Away from the constraints of Clan life, she is able to use her sapient creativity to the full, while her solitude is made endurable by the companionship of a domesticated foal and cave lion cub. In a parallel plot, Jondalar and his brother Thonolan, young

Cro-Magnons of the Zelandonii tribe based in the Vézère valley, are on a long eastward journey of initiation. The plots converge when Thonolan is killed and Jondalar wounded by Ayla's cave lion and his mate. Ayla nurses Jondalar back to health, falling in love with the first man of her own kind that she has ever met.

In *The Mammoth Hunters* (1985) Ayla and Jondalar join the Mamutoi, a sapient tribe who hunt mammoth in what is now Ukraine. Ayla, socially inexperienced among her own kind, nevertheless impresses the Mamutoi with her remarkable abilities, and is officially inducted into the tribe. But because Jondalar is disturbed by Ayla's Clan upbringing—the Zelandonii view Neanderthals as "flathead animals" and children of "mixed spirits" (hybrids) as abominations—the pair are emotionally alienated for much of the novel, and Ranec, a dark-skinned Mamutoi carver, becomes a rival for Ayla's affections.

Ayla and Jondalar are reconciled once he comes to accept the Clan as fully human, and they set out together to return to his people. Their westward odyssey along the length of the Great Mother River (the Danube) is described in *The Plains of Passage* (1990). *The Shelters of Stone* (2002) deals with Ayla's difficulties in integrating with the Zelandonii because of their prejudice against the Clan. Nevertheless, she and Jondalar eventually are married and Ayla (now nineteen) gives birth to their daughter. A sixth and concluding novel, as yet unpublished, promises to resolve the tension between the Neanderthal and sapient cultures as embodied in Ayla herself, and to reveal the fate of Durc, her hybrid son.

Before Auel no writer of pf had been able to appeal directly to the female majority of contemporary readers of popular fiction, to most of whom the world of cavemen probably seemed forbiddingly masculine. And though Cro-Magnons had frequently been described by prehistorians as anatomically and mentally modern, few earlier pf novelists had been able to conceive of, let alone depict, Paleolithic feminism in any positive and plausible manner. But if much of Auel's success lay in her ability to draw female readers to prehistory, she also attracted a significant number of male readers. Her version of feminism in *Clan* assailed not men in general, nor even patriarchy per se, but extreme narrow-mindedness and rigidity in sexual matters. Moreover, Auel's grasp of the physical and technical demands of that traditionally masculine activity, hunting for survival, was authoritative. Few paleoanthropologists failed to be intrigued by her well-informed extrapolations, even if they didn't agree with them, and many were delighted by the new interest in their discipline that her novels generated.

The success of *Clan* and its sequels brought into being a new subgenre of popular fiction that I shall call *prehistoric romance*. With Auel, prehistoric romance is a hybrid of pure pf and postfeminist women's romance fiction, the latter of which allows copious amounts of female-centered eroticism. Prehistoric romance's classic plot formula, mapped out in Auel's first two novels, traces the fortunes of an oppressed but feisty female protagonist who must struggle against intensely patriarchal tribal traditions and terrible physical odds to find and win a worthy exogamous mate. The literary value of a prehistoric romance novel is not necessarily inversely proportionate to its adherence to the formula. Some of the works that stick most closely to the formula— for example, Sue Harrison's *Mother Earth Father Sky* (1990)—are more impressive achievements than others that diverge from it.

The Auel effect that brought mass-market prehistoric romance into being stimulated the overall growth of pf as a genre, though it did little to revive interest in earlier works.[17] According to Steve Trussel (q.v.), twenty-seven pf works were published in the period 1970–79, a small increase over the twenty that had appeared in 1920–29, the next most prolific decade. From 1980 to 1989, however, fifty-five pf works appeared (including many titles that I would categorize as prehistoric romance), while between 1990 and 1999 one hundred and twenty-eight were published. Nevertheless, prehistoric romance is not produced in sufficient quantity to merit its own section in bookstores. It may be found shelved under "Fantasy," "Science Fiction," "Historical Fiction," "Romance Fiction," or scattered under all of these labels. Most (but not all) authors of contemporary prehistoric romance are female and write chiefly for a female readership. The most popular and prolific authors after Auel herself are "William Sarabande" (Joan Lesley Hamilton Cline, b. 1942), and the married archaeologists Kathleen O'Neal Gear (b. 1954) and W. Michael Gear (b. 1955).

More ambitious authors of prehistoric romance, who rival Auel in their imaginative reconstructions of prehistoric life, include Sue Harrison (b. 1950), whose Ivory Carver trilogy (1990–94) is set among the Paleo-Aleuts of western Alaska; Megan Lindholm (Margaret Astrid Lindholm Ogden, b. 1952), whose *The Reindeer People* (1988) and its sequel *Wolf's Brother* (1988) take place in Bronze Age Lapland;[18] and Linda Lay Shuler, whose best-known novel, *She Who Remembers* (1988), is set among the Pre-Columbian Anasazi of the American

Southwest.[19] Other writers of prehistoric romance include Margaret Allan (William Thomas Quick, b. 1946), Amanda Cockrell (b. 1948), Rose Estes, Mary Mackey (b. 1945), Lynn Armistead McKee (Lynn Sholes), Charlotte Prentiss (Charles Platt, b. 1945), Judith Redman Robbins, and Joan Wolf.

Four Important Prehistoric Movies of the 1980s

One of the immediate effects of Auel's success was to encourage film-makers to try to make the "proverbial" good prehistoric movie (see Clarke, *Lost Worlds*, 17). Before 1980, the most successful films set in prehistory (with the exception of the opening section of *2001*) had been fantasies in the vein of Edgar Rice Burroughs in which "primitive" elements were mingled with a blithe disregard for scientific accuracy and chronology. Hal Roach's *One Million B.C.* (1940) was the prototype: a beautiful woman in a skimpy animal-skin costume (Carole Landis as "Loana") from an advanced cooperative tribe improves the manners of a brutish, male-dominated tribe while dodging "dinosaurs" (a lizard and doctored dwarf alligator filmed in extreme closeup). Roach's scenario was repeated, with minor variations but with much greater box office success, in Don Chaffey's *One Million Years B.C.* (1966), which had the added advantages of DeLuxe color, more realistic stop-motion dinosaurs animated by Ray Harryhausen, and above all, the nubile Raquel Welch as Loana, sporting her famous doeskin bikini.

In the aftermath of Auel, realism ruled, though it would rarely be a scientific realism, and the movement to make a worthy prehistoric film would peter out in less than a decade. Significantly, the best (and the most financially successful) prehistoric movie diverged farthest from the paleoanthropological record: Jean-Jacques Annaud's *Quest for Fire* (1981). Major changes were made to adapt the classic French pf novel to film. While Rosny's "oneiric, lyric, and grandiose" style (Cohen, *L'Homme*, 208) maintains a formal distance from the reader, Annaud strives for an earthy, authenticating realism supported by the advice of contemporary experts. The distinguished ethologist Desmond Morris served as *Quest for Fire*'s gesture coach, while the novelist and linguist Anthony Burgess invented the proto–Indo-European languages that are used, unmediated by subtitles, in the screenplay.

However, as Michael Klossner points out in his definitive survey *Prehistoric Humans in Film and Television* (2006), rather than being truly realistic, *Quest for Fire* merely gives a sufficient impression of realism (124), chiefly through its graphic documentation of the harsh, filthy, and dangerous conditions of the Paleolithic. Otherwise, the film departs from scientific accuracy in innumerable ways, not the least of which is the supposed proximate coexistence a mere 80,000 B.P. of such physiologically and culturally disparate hominids as the anatomically modern Ulams, the hairy Wagabou ape-men, the cannibalistic Kzamms, and the "advanced" Ivaka. Nevertheless, the movie works well, because the important scenes are both visually striking and offer thoughtful speculations about how major steps in hominization might have occurred in a world not yet subdued by technology.

For example, the film includes Ika (a character not in Rosny) who serves as Naoh's love interest. That she is played by a beautiful nude actress who has a graphic sex scene with Naoh certainly adds box office spice to Rosny's earnest scenario. Yet Rae Dawn Chong's blue body paint is less exploitative than than Raquel Welch's bikini. When Ika shows Naoh the missionary position (his tribesmen know only to take women animalistically from behind), the scene effectively and plausibly conveys how intimacy might have been transmitted to men by exogamously acquired women. We see how mutual pleasuring is more adaptive than the exercise of unilateral force: it conduces to pair bonding and reciprocity, leading to the willing divulgence of valuable information (such as how to use a fire drill) that furthers social progress. And the opening scene (recapitulated at the end) in which a tiny flame burns in a darkling badlands landscape, is worthy of Kubrick (to whom it is evidently indebted): it recalls the precious frailty of humanity's status in terrestrial nature and in the universe as a whole.

Fred Schepisi's *Iceman* (1984) is about Charu/Charlie, a 40,000-year-old Neanderthal hunter who is found frozen in a block of glacial ice near an Arctic research station. He is thawed out, revived, imprisoned in a vivarium, and then studied, chiefly to understand the secret of his preserved tissues. Charu looks more like a modern man than a Neanderthal, but otherwise the movie's dominant mode is kitchen-sink realism. Schepisi attempts the landscape artistry of *2001* and *Quest for Fire* only in late scenes set on a glacier; for the most part he finds magic in the sprinkler systems, mirrors, electric lights, and PA announcements of the modern world as we watch a truly primitive mind try, and fail, to comprehend these wonderful banalities.

Iceman is an effective exploration of how culture constrains the human capacity to understand unfamiliar circumstances and how science can dehumanize. The sensitive anthropologist Shepherd (Timothy Hutton) does his courageous best to communicate with Charu (a fine performance by John Lone), and there are many amusing or poignant moments when the two men find a bond of common humanity. Most of the members of the research team, however, show little willingness to consider Charu a fellow human being: their scientific materialism and self-absorption reduce him to a clinical specimen. But the more absolute failure of understanding is Charu's. The film powerfully demonstrates how impossible it is to expect that the iceman could ever grasp the reality of his predicament: to have been transported far into the future beyond all hope of reunion with his kind.

Charu was frozen while on a dream quest to encourage his gods to send favored game animals back to his tribe. After he has escaped from the research station, he begins to recast what is most unfamiliar to the Arctic landscape—a search helicopter—into a supernatural agent that, according to his people's mythology, comes as a messenger from the gods. His (long-deferred) act of self-sacrifice at the movie's end is futile and tragic, yet it is hard to see how he might have arrived at a better fate. The most obvious alternative would have been an undignified end as a clinical specimen in a laboratory, his body dissected by surgeons avid for the wealth and fame flowing from the discovery of the elixir of immortality.

Michael Chapman's 1986 movie adaptation of *The Clan of the Cave Bear* is a more than competent production. Darryl Hannah as the adult Ayla, James Remar as Creb, and Pamela Reed as Iza give strong performances; the beautifully shot outdoor locations in British Columbia plausibly suggest the unpopulated interstadial landscape; and the half-vocal, half-gestural language of the Clan is effectively conveyed with the help of a sensitive voiceover narrative and minimal subtitles. The movie's final scene drives home the novel's feminist theme of a woman who must abandon her child and domestic situation to find herself as a human being. As for fidelity to paleoanthropological knowledge, Klossner calls the film "the most accurate movie ever made about prehistoric people" (3).

Yet the movie failed with both public and critics, recouping barely $2 million of its $15 million budget. Auel herself was displeased enough with the film to remove her name from the credits and a planned sequel was never made. Ironically, the film's chief fault may have been its too respectful fidelity to its literary source: it depends on the viewer having read and absorbed the novel's nontraditional message about Paleolithic life and sexual politics. For an audience expecting either a caveman entertainment with dinosaurs and doeskin bikinis, or an exercise in *nostalgie de la boue* in the vein of *Quest for Fire*, the pacing is too slow, the Neanderthals too human, the musk-oxen hunt too unglamorous, the sexuality and violence too restrained. It should be added that when it comes to prehistoric film, even the most experienced movie critics often seem to be unable to shake off their conditioning by popular culture. For example, Roger Ebert (q.v.) protested that Chapman's film "shows us a woman winning respect from a patriarchal tribe, when, in reality, the men would have just banged her over the head real good." Ebert's "reality" is actually the enduring pop-culture fantasy of "Courtship with a Club."

The last prehistoric movie of the 1980s worthy of consideration here is the most obscure: as I write, it is not yet available on DVD. David and Carol Hughes's *Missing Link* (1988) is also perhaps the only important feature film (except for the opening sequence of *2001*) about early African hominids. It concerns the fate of the very last *Australopithecus robustus*, whose tribe has been displaced and slaughtered by our encroaching ancestors. The movie is essentially a one-man show, with Peter Elliott giving a magnificent performance as the peaceful man-ape who wanders about the desert landscape of Namibia in vain search for his kind, a journey enlivened by many striking wildlife encounters. That the movie announces its setting as one million years ago is undoubtedly intended as a realistic corrective to the pop-culture caveman movie tradition.

At the end of the film, the australopithecine comes to the ocean, the end of the road in both literal and figurative terms. For most of the action, he has been clutching a stone ax stained with blood that he found lying by the bodies of his murdered mate and child. He has kept the ax as a memento of his family, and it is clear by the way that he holds it that he does not understand its function as a weapon. Slowly he begins to experiment with it as a tool and learns its power. Nonetheless, at the movie's end the camera follows the whirling flight of the ax after the man-ape hurls it into the ocean. He, and the filmmakers, are thereby rejecting the legacy of violence that the stone ax, and its bone counterpart in *2001*, represents. *Missing Link*, sentimental moments notwithstanding, is a powerful movie, reminding us, like much good pf from *Before Adam* to *The Inheritors*, of an unresolvable paradox in human desire. We yearn for an Edenic innocence close to nature, yet our hominid cousins who failed to separate themselves from nature by the aggressive adoption of tools and weapons met extinction, very possibly at our ancestors' hands.

Recent Prehistoric Fiction

Some 1980s pf was not directly influenced by Auel or prehistoric romance. In the United Kingdom, three writers revived the episodic narrative common in earlier pf in order to emphasize the unbroken cultural links between the present and the prehistoric past. In so doing they were contributing to the growth of regional awareness, even of resurgent nationalism, in the United Kingdom's constituent parts, a phenomenon probably stimulated by the nation's membership in the European Union after 1973.[20] These writers were undoubtedly aware, too, that a literal prehistoric link with the European continent was about to be reforged: the Channel Tunnel (constructed 1987–94) would physically join the island of Great Britain to France for the first time since the end of the last Ice Age.

The Scottish novelist and social activist Naomi Mitchison (1897–1999) published *Early in Orcadia* (1987) in her ninetieth year. Tracking several generations of emigrants from the Scottish mainland to found a new life in the Orkney Islands 5,000–6,000 B.P., this ambitious novel is an elderly woman's attempt at emotional reconnection with her remote ancestors "who did not have to think, as we must, in terms of total world destruction, but who could concentrate on living" (8). Mitchison conceives their society at the threshold of history as one composed of male and female "persons" (66) who are considered equally valuable, though they are not so individualized as they have become under our present patriarchal dispensation. She ends her narrative with an admonitory vision of social harmony under threat as Sun Man supersedes Moon Woman as the ruling divine principle.

Also in 1987, Edward Rutherfurd (Francis Edward Wintle, b. 1948) published *Sarum: The Novel of England*, the first of his popular episodic historical novels rooted in a particular location in the tradition of James A. Michener.[21] *Sarum* is an epic spanning 20,000 years that begins with three prehistoric sections, dealing respectively with moon-worshipping postglacial hunter-gatherers, sun-worshipping Neolithic makers of long barrows,[22] and the astronomer-priests who built Stonehenge. Rutherfurd uses each of these episodes to advance his thesis that there is a positive "Englishness" connecting the earliest times to the present. According to him, the earliest inhabitants of what is now England were of ethnically mixed origin, by temperament pragmatic, independent, hospitable to strangers, and reluctant to go to war. He convincingly suggests that folk memory is long in this insular but not remote land, and that the modern English landscape is a palimpsest concealing manifold layers of settlement.

Perhaps in response to these visions of primal Scottishness and Englishness, Raymond Williams (1921–88), the literary scholar and cultural critic, attempted an even more ambitious episodic pf novel in the form of a prose epic of the evolution of Welsh nationhood. The two completed parts of *People of the Black Mountains* (1989, 1990) trace the formation of Welsh culture and identity from 25,000 B.P. to A.D. 1415 and, with the help of a modern frame, identify ancient survivals in contemporary mid-Wales.[23] For Williams, mountainous Wales (unlike England, the "White Land" or Albion of open plains) has always been "a strange, difficult, unknown country" (96). Against the chaotic turbulence brought about by waves of invaders, Williams counterposes the human drive for order that he terms "measuring" and that first manifests itself in the "counter bones" (15) used as a crude calendar by Paleolithic horse hunters. Embodied as Dal Mered the Measurer who brings advanced mensuration to Wales from Stonehenge in 2000 B.C., the technique allows human beings to gain control over nature by predicting the future (seasons, tides, eclipses) in a nonmagical way.

Episodic pf that aims to track a specific culture's evolution over long periods of time must renounce unity of action and hence tends to dissolve into a collection of short stories. Perhaps the most aesthetically successful British pf novel of the recent past retains this unity while sacrificing the geographical specificity of the three works just mentioned. *The Gift of Stones* (1988) by Jim Crace (b. 1946) is set in an unidentified location at the end of the Neolithic Age. It is about "stoneys," the inhabitants of a nameless village who make a comfortable living from trading their expertly knapped flints. The narrator is the adopted daughter of the protagonist, to whom she simply refers as "my father." When a boy, father lost an arm after being shot by a strange horseman's poisoned arrow; unable to work flints, he gradually assumed a new role as the village storyteller. Wandering afield in search of material for good stories, he comes across Doe, a woman abandoned by her husband who survives by exchanging sex for food from passing men. Father brings Doe to his village, but she allows him no intimate role in her life save that of baby-sitter to her small daughter. Later, Doe is killed by an arrow with a bronze head shot by the same horsemen that had wounded father years before. The Age of Metal has begun, the stoneys' means of livelihood has disappeared, and their settlement near the flint mine has lost its raison d'être.

While many pf writers after Auel felt obliged to display, even to flaunt, their paleoanthropological research, Crace makes little attempt to achieve verisimilitude or narrative authenticity in this way. Instead, by being deliberately vague about prehistoric details, he is able to generate a rich array of symbolic levels of meaning. One of his most striking strategies is to associate the tactile craft of flint knapping metaphorically with the more abstract art of narrative: "The ship had formed the rough and tidy core from which my father could detach at will his patterned blades of fable, romance, lies" (57). Indeed, Crace's novel is perhaps best approached as an allegory about the nature and function of the writer of fiction. The storyteller, of whom father is a typical example, is a wounded personality, incapable of quotidian work, too damaged to forge satisfactory close relationships. His social role is to transmute his pain and emotional isolation into stories that make "stony" lives bearable. Indeed, when radical change is forced upon people, as it always will be, their shared hoard of fantastic stories—myths, legends, fairy tales—that evoke wonder and hope may be all that will hold them together until they find the resources to adapt to transformed circumstances. At the end of the novel, it is the narrator's father who leads the villagers away in search of a new life, his task now being "to invent a future for us all" (169).

Perhaps the most impressive recent works of American pf are the two novels by Elizabeth Marshall Thomas (b. 1931), the anthropologist and ethologist. *Reindeer Moon* (1987) is set in Paleolithic Siberia circa 20,000 B.P., and narrated by Yanan, a young woman who has died in childbirth but whose spirit lives on in various metamorphosed animal forms. The novel, strongly influenced by Joseph Campbell's *The Way of Animal Powers* (1988), paints a plausible picture of how animistic beliefs derive from the hunter-gatherer lifestyle and in turn shape the characters' worldview. Thomas also deals effectively with the very harsh realities of life for prehistoric women, notwithstanding the matrilineal structure of their society.[24] As a professional anthropologist writing pf in the 1980s, Thomas perhaps wished to distance herself from Auel and prehistoric romance.[25] Her female protagonist is already dead; thus readers' expectations about a romance plot are undermined from the start. Her passages on canine domestication are highly informed and more credible than Ayla's achievements with the horse and cave lion in *The Valley of Horses* and with the wolf cub in *The Mammoth Hunters*. And Thomas's first-person narrative, owing something to Björn Kurtén's pf,[26] makes few concessions to the nonspecialist reader, who must patiently reconstruct from hints and clues how an unfamiliar all-encompassing belief system operates.

Thomas's second pf novel *The Animal Wife* (1990) is an even more impressive achievement, partly because its stronger plot is a variant of the universally popular type of folktale referred to in the title. "Animal Wife" tales are about a man who marries a woman who is really an animal; they often end when, because of his failure to understand her nature, she reassumes her animal skin and disappears from his life along with their children. *The Animal Wife's* first-person narrator is a young man, Kori, the son of a shaman / mammoth hunter first encountered in *Reindeer Moon*. Kori abducts a woman whom he calls Muskrat from a tribe who are more advanced than his own; nonetheless, because she is a foreigner he thinks of her as a lesser being—an animal (fig. 3.4). Thomas cleverly uses Kori's callowness to highlight the complex roles, and especially the covert power, of women in Upper Paleolithic society. Her novel also reveals the dangerous consequences of the almost universal human tendency to structure the world as a rigid hierarchy of power arranged according to the schema

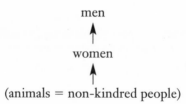

men

↑

women

↑

(animals = non-kindred people)

I shall end this survey where I began it, with French pf. Two recent but very different achievements indicate that the oldest national pf tradition continues to generate innovative work, even if the Anglosphere takes too little account of it. Pierre Pelot (b. 1945) was known as a prolific author of routine fiction in various popular genres until in collaboration with the distinguished French paleoanthropologist Yves Coppens and the Italian comic artist Tanino Liberatore he produced *Le Rêve de Lucy* (Lucy's dream) (1990). This excellent short

Figure 3.4 Artwork by Geoff Taylor from Thomas's *Animal Wife.*

novel set 3,000,000 B.P. is about an *Australopithecus afarensis* female from a beleaguered vegetarian tribe who encounters a larger, more confident tribe of carnivorous habilines (that is, members of the hominid species *Homo habilis*), who function as our ancestors. Fascinated, she leaves her own people to follow them—but at a distance, fearful lest they reject her. Her infatuation with or love for this new people ends only when she is accidentally drowned in a swollen river. She is, of course, the famous "Lucy" whose remains were found at Hadar, Ethiopia, in 1974.

But *Le Rêve de Lucy* was only the prelude to what may be the most ambitious pf project yet undertaken anywhere: Pelot's series of five novels entitled "Sous le vent du monde" (Under the wind of the world), written under the aegis of Coppens and depicting our ancestors at key stages of human evolution. The first, *Qui regarde la montagne au loin* (He who watches the distant mountain) (1996), deals with contact between two varieties of australopithecines in east Africa 1,700,000 B.P.; the last, *Ceux qui parlent au bord de la pierre* (Those who speak at the edge of the stone) (2001), is set in the Upper Paleolithic Transition 34,000 B.P.[27] Throughout the series, Pelot powerfully evokes *dépaysement* in the reader, sometimes by using the characters'

Figure 3.5 Roudier's Vo'Hounâ tends to a wounded Cro-Magnon warrior.

own vocabulary in unglossed, riddle-like combinations. In this way he is able to suggest an ancestral worldview that at first seems entirely alien but that slowly becomes more familiar as we learn to decode the meanings from their contexts.

The graphic novel has a venerable tradition in France—where it is known as *la bande-dessinée*, or *BD* for short—and the *Rahan* series of prehistoric comics for children written by Roger Lécureux (1925–99) and drawn by André Chéret (b. 1937) has remained popular since 1969. Yet there had never been a pf *BD* for adults that had managed to exploit the large body of paleoanthropological knowledge amassed since 1945—until the young graphic artist Emmanuel Roudier (b. 1971) produced his first album, *La Saison d'Ao* (2002), in the ongoing series entitled "Vo'Hounâ." Suitably enough, this series, currently comprising three albums, is set in prehistoric southern France in the Upper Paleolithic Transition, and centers on a love affair between a male Cro-Magnon hunter of the Aurignacian culture, and a female Neanderthal shaman, one of the last survivors of her Châtelperronian culture (fig. 3.5). Roudier writes as well as he draws, and his books are evidently painstakingly researched: one finishes them entirely convinced that Cro-Magnons and Neanderthals interbred willingly! The endpapers of the albums feature reproductions of some of the exquisite animal images from Rouffignac and Lascaux Caves, indicating that Roudier's admirable ambition is to produce drawings worthy of an graphic tradition 35,000 years old.

II

Thematic Evolution

4.

▼   Nature and Human Nature

> Human nature is ... a hodgepodge of special genetic adaptations to an environment largely vanished, the world of the Ice-Age hunter-gatherer.
>
> —Edward O. Wilson, *On Human Nature* (1978)

> No animal was ever intended to steal fire from the tops of mountains. You have transgressed the established laws of nature. I'll have a little of that antelope now, Oswald.
>
> —Roy Lewis, *What We Did to Father* (1960)

Human Nature in Literature

Many of those great literary works that succeed in offering profound insights into human nature, such as Shakespeare's *Hamlet* (1603–4), Dostoyevsky's *Crime and Punishment* (1866), or Ibsen's *Hedda Gabler* (1890), do so very indirectly. Such works provide elaborate psychological portraits of protagonists whose difference from the average person is striking. We are likely to gauge from contact with such works our own unrealized potential by analogy, or our own shallowness by contrast, but little about, for example, how the human species in general differs from its nearest nonhuman relatives.

Milton's *Paradise Lost* (1667), on the other hand, approaches the question of the specificity of human nature more directly. Moreover, it does so by using a stratagem rather similar to pf, namely, by providing an account of our origin in order to explain or "justify" how we are in the present. It does so, however, from a theological, dogmatic perspective that is unlikely to be shared in a secular, skeptical age, notwithstanding the grandeur of Milton's vision and the brilliance of his execution. And even here, it is an exceptional individual (Satan), one who is not even himself human, who offers (again very indirectly) the deepest insights into human nature.

Works of good sf, emerging from an age in which the scientific method had become the dominant epistemology, can offer more direct insights into human nature. One of sf's most typical strategies is to bring mankind, represented by one or more everyman characters, into contact with nonhuman aliens. This encounter allows the reader to observe the significant differences between "us" and "them" and thereby to infer something of the characteristic nature of our species beyond individual differences. Notable works in this vein include H. G. Wells's *The War of the Worlds* (1898), Stanisław Lem's *Solaris* (1961), and Ursula K. Le Guin's *The Left Hand of Darkness* (1969).

Good pf, of the kind that plausibly dramatizes one or more phases of hominization, can enable us to confront more directly than any other kind of literature our human nature viewed as the result of an evolved process. Indeed, perhaps pf's highest function as a literary genre is to cast light on human nature in our post-Darwinian age. But how is human nature to be defined? For current purposes, it will be understood to include those innate qualities that all human beings share as a result of our genetic membership in the species that immodestly denominates itself *Homo sapiens sapiens*.

In fact, there are surely two distinct, if overlapping, human natures—a male and a female. This chapter will confine itself for the most part to the overlap, while the next will focus on the sexes' differing natures. Furthermore, human nature will here be supposed *not* to include the cultural elements that divide people, namely, those differences that we acquire and transmit through education. Attention to such differences will be deferred until chapter 7, which devotes itself to some central elements of culture. Hereafter, when I seek to represent the perspective of early writers operating in a more uncritically patriarchal age, I shall use "Man" with an uppercase M. These writers often used "Man" to refer to our whole species, usually under the assumption that a male protagonist—an every*man*—would better represent human virtues or embody our nobler flaws.

All this said, with our species it is almost impossible to separate nature from culture. After all, human nature is often supposed to have been determined by our separation from "nonhuman" Nature (hereafter spelled with an uppercase N), and in particular from the animal kingdom—a separation given a positive emphasis in Judeo-Christian Scripture and in the ethics derived from it. To take two examples: according to the Bible, God created Man in His image and gave him dominion over animals (Genesis 1:26–27); in law, to kill another human being deliberately is usually considered an act of murder, but it is not possible to "murder" a nonhuman animal.

While geneticists have estimated that at least 94 percent of our DNA is identical to that of our closest nonhuman relative (the chimpanzee), hominization scenarios in paleoanthropology typically emphasize the growing distance of our separation from Nature. We boldly descended from our ancestral trees, left our less enterprising primate cousins behind in the receding Tertiary forests, put distance between our minds and the earth by assuming an upright posture, used our freed hands to make tools and weapons that liberated us from animal servility to Nature, and mastered fire to escape the tyranny of the elements. Whatever nature we all share, it is apparently quite different from the Nature that we first turned our back on when we decided to become human, the Nature that we later "conquered" to prove that we had made the correct decision.

Pf is aware of the many paradoxes generated when "nature" is used in relation to humanity. The genre is a quintessentially post-Darwinian phenomenon, and most writers do not accept, any more than Darwin himself did, that there is an unbridgeable gulf between ourselves and animals,[1] however much we stand upon our dignity and strive to remain aloof. Yet pf is not deluded enough to treat Man— the almost hairless, big-headed, slow-developing, neotenous, omnivorous, anestrous, gregarious, adaptable, vertical primate—as merely one creature among many. It knows that we, all 6.5 billion of us, constitute an extraordinary case in Nature, and sees its particular duty to imagine how we came to be so unusual, even as it tries as much as humanly possible to resist the blandishments of homocentrism.

Hominization as Narrative

Before looking at those works of pf that have offered the most interesting insights into human nature, we should note that the human sciences are not unaware of the particular difficulty of attaining objectivity in a discipline in which all the subjects under scrutiny are long dead and have left no written testament, but among whom we count our direct ancestors. Paleoanthropologists typically aim to understand our present human circumstances by constructing a coherent evolutionary narrative that links our ancestors to ourselves. Those evolutionary narratives that have a familiar, satisfying plot are more likely to be quickly adopted by popular culture and bring fame (and occasionally fortune) to their creators. But under such circumstances, does science always shape the plot, or does the plot sometimes shape the science? Some commentators have gone so far as to suggest that myths and fairy tales have been unconscious structuring principles in most if not all scientific narratives of hominization.

For example, Niles Eldredge and Ian Tattersall in *The Myths of Human Evolution* (1982) show how the "myth of constant adaptive change" (29)—it is a myth because most species are morphologically conservative—operated powerfully in early paleoanthropological thought because it accorded with Victorian progressionism. By way of a countermyth, they propose that the Kubrick-Clarke *2001* screenplay, in which ape-man is rapidly transformed into man-ape, may offer a more accurate gauge of how quickly changes actually occurred in human evolution (if, presumably, alien intervention is discounted!) Alluding to Karl Popper's well-known criterion of falsifiability in *The Logic of Scientific Discovery* (1959), they also offer the sobering reminder that statements about human ancestry based on the fossil record "are not susceptible to disproof, and are thus essentially nonscientific" (128).

For Misia Landau in *Narratives of Human Evolution* (1991), paleoanthropology is "the most intimate of the narrative sciences" (ix). She shows how descriptions of hominization by some of the most distinguished figures in the field have been influenced, indeed distorted, by the unwitting superimposition of narrative functions of the kind found in the common European folk-tale tradition as codified by Vladimir Propp in his *Morphology of the Folktale* (1928). Landau provocatively compares Darwin's *The Descent of Man* with that perennially popular narrative, the Cinderella tale. She suggests that Darwin casts humanity in the role of the protagonist who rises, thanks to the providential intervention of Natural Selection as fairy godmother, to the highest position on the organic scale (60).[2] If Victorians felt humbled by *The Descent*'s revelation of their lowly origin, they could also feel a compensatory pride in how high Man had since ascended by his own initiative—or, even more to the point, in how far civilized Englishmen had outstripped modern savages.

Wiktor Stoczkowski's *Explaining Human Origins: Myth, Imagination, and Conjecture* (1994) identifies an even closer link between paleoanthropology and fictional narrative. He introduces the concept of the "conditioned imagination" (3–28), according to which new scientific discoveries come to be defined by preestablished assumptions.

Because of serious deficiencies in hard evidence about how hominization occurred, an "imaginary" human prehistory (6) is constructed
using the pseudologic of common sense applied to stock narrative
models. For example, in the post-Darwinian age, theories of the origin of culture involved recasting Nature, formerly a good mother, in
the role of the wicked stepmother.

Stoczkowski, comparing two dozen descriptions of human development from Lamarck to the present, suggests that they are as formu-
laic as Western movies: "'Human' characteristics are the ingredients
of the hominization scenario, just as the sheriff and the outlaw are of
the Western, and we can bring them together in a list, in which
stereotyped positions mark the 'principal roles,' such as *bipedalism*,
tools or *free hands*, and the place of the secondary characters, such as
prolonged infancy or *disappearance of oestrus*" (46; emphasis in original).
In Stoczkowski's eyes, a naïve anthropologist is one who is unaware
that most supposedly quintessential human characteristics are shared
by nonhuman animals, and that there is no actual evidence in the paleoanthropological archive that one human adaptation (for example,
bipedalism) caused the next (for example, tool-making). He concludes
that while stock fictional narratives are built to last, scientific theory
is built up in order to be demolished. Lacking hard evidence, anthropologists inevitably borrow the almost indestructible fictions to
strengthen the tenuous logical structure of "objective" scientific hypotheses about hominization.

My aim in citing these commentators is not to suggest that all pa-
leoanthopology is equally contaminated by fiction, hence unscientific. It is instead to raise the possibility that human beings may require
a coherent narrative if they are at all to conceptualize their evolution
as a species. Moreover, as narrative coherence is frequently a function
of plot familiarity, hominization narratives are likely to "stick" only
if they are based on existing models. These points are conceded by
Mark Pluciennik early in his important theoretical essay "Archaeological Narratives and Other Ways of Telling" (1999).[3] Pluciennik goes
on to argue that archaeologists should use narrative with more consciousness of its importance in cognition, and analyze its existing man-
ifestations in the discipline with more sophistication and flexibility.

We turn from these theorists back to pf with further support for
our introductory position that the genre's relation to paleoanthropology is not parasitic and supplementary but parallel and complemen-
tary. As the authors of a recent article in the leading archaeological

journal *Antiquity* put it, "Narrative—both as novels and in more academic syntheses—is the prime means of explaining the past. We are inherent story-tellers, and in lectures, papers, syntheses and novels, we tell and re-tell stories about the past with a greater or lesser reliance on hard-won factual detail" (Hackett and Dennell, 824).[4] If it is in our human nature to understand the world chiefly through stories, then pf viewed in this light is no longer a supplement, frill, or airy tree-dwelling far from the ground of hard facts. The genre offers instead a virtual world where the mind is allowed more freedom to produce speculative narratives about its origins than is possible under the constraints controlling the release of new scientific knowledge in the real world.

Monkey Gone Wrong?

While individual myths and fairy tales are cultural products, the narrative types to which they belong are so ubiquitous and so ancient that they seem to emanate from a universal human nature. Pf writers who revise the story of the Fall of Adam and Eve, for example, are not necessarily betraying their post-Darwinian scientific inheritance by alluding to an narrative that science has "proved" to be literally untrue. Rather, in their concern with exploring the ongoing problem of human moral frailty, they construct a revised Eden partly in homage to the author of that powerful and enduring fantasy known as the Book of Genesis, and partly because it is a more efficient cognitive strategy to reframe a potent existing narrative than to sweep it away and start from scratch.[5]

If there is a single key to the radical revision of Man's place in nature brought about by Darwinism, it may be in the latter's inversion of the trajectory of hominization described in Scripture. Simply put, according to the Bible, Man is a fallen creature, but according to Darwin he is a risen one. This revision is nowhere more emphatically expressed than at the beginning of the last paragraph of *The Descent of Man*: "Man may be excused for feeling some pride at having *risen*, though not through his own exertions, to the very summit of the organic scale; and the fact of his having thus *risen*, instead of having been aboriginally placed there, may give him hopes for a still higher destiny in the distant future" (2:405; emphasis added).

It is important to note, however, that the title of Darwin's book contains the word *descent*. In this context the word signifies "genealogy" or "derivation," but this meaning is inevitably colored by associations with the word's primary meaning, "a downward or earthward movement." By this significant choice of diction, Darwin declines to participate in the triumphalist progressionism of his contemporaries such as Herbert Spencer and Ernst Haeckel, to whom *The Ascent of Man* would surely have been a more congenial title. Indeed, Darwin's concluding sentence, "Man still bears in his bodily frame the indelible stamp of his lowly origin" (2:405), is an unequivocal assertion that it is not in Man's power to expunge the "ape and tiger" within, for they are woven into the fabric of his being. For Darwin, Man is not Adam, nor (*pace* Misia Landau) is he Cinderella: the "indelible stamp" that he bears is strongly reminiscent of the mark of Cain (fig. 4.1).

Much early pf attempted to delineate the lowliness of Man's origin in order to remind readers how far they had risen. In so doing, the writers assumed that our modern human nature had come about as a result of a severance from nonhuman Nature. Some, like Pierre Boitard, simply inverted the Eden scenario, depicting the "solitary, poor, nasty, brutish, and short" life of Natural Man as specified by Thomas Hobbes in *Leviathan* (1651) (82) as a way of promoting science at the expense of clericalism.[6] But more ambitious pf writers began quite early to explore the more complex and vexatious idea that human beings could never completely cast off their animal Nature, just as Darwin had implied in *The Descent*.

Elie Berthet noted that a savage struggle for existence prevailed among the wild beasts encircling Quaternary Paris: "The most feeble became the prey of the strongest; the large devoured the small, according to the primordial law of Nature. Cries of pain and death arose every hour." How did Man survive, "cast helpless and naked into the midst of these carnivorous animals" (15)? Berthet's answer is to describe a two-stage hominization process. First, thanks to his powerful muscles and his crude club, primitive Man—embodied by Red the Neanderthal—became the most formidable carnivore of all. Second, our Cro-Magnon ancestors, whose brains were developing at the expense of their musculature, invented a means of killing at a distance. The second adaptive strategy easily defeated the first. But Fair-Hair's success in disposing of his stronger rival was in a sense an "unnatural" trick that broke our animal contract with Nature. In Berthet's revision of Genesis, feeble Cain shoots his hairy rival Esau[7] and gains the girl and the meat. Our ancestors engineered their own exemption from Nature's "primordial law," and human nature, founded on the

Figure 4.1 Waterloo's prehistoric Cain and Abel.

corpse of Natural Man, began to set the agenda for the future development of the species.

One of the most lively passages in Wells's "A Story of the Stone Age" explores this "unnatural" aspect of human nature by adopting an animal point of view in the manner of Rudyard Kipling's *The Jungle Books* (1893–94). Andoo the cave bear, "greatest of all meat-eaters"[8] (673) is king of the Paleolithic Thames valley. To him, the two hairless bipeds (Ugh-Lomi and Eudena) who have trespassed on his realm resemble a tasty hybrid of monkey and young pig. Shortly thereafter, smarting from the edge of Ugh-Lomi's ax, Andoo confides his bafflement to his mate:

> "A feebler sort of beast I *never* saw. I can't think what the world is coming to. Scraggy, weedy legs. . . . Wonder how they keep warm in winter?"
>
> "Very likely they don't," said the she-bear.
>
> "I suppose it's a sort of monkey gone wrong." (681)

From the perspective of Nature, indeed, a human being might well seem a "monkey gone wrong," a post-Darwinian notion even less flattering to ourselves than the biblical one of a creature made in God's image but disobedient and fallen. This Wellsian bout between a titanic masterpiece of Nature and one of her half-baked miscreations will end with Andoo lying dead from a fractured skull while the she-bear, left to ponder the inconceivable, is filled with "a novel feeling as of imminent strange evils" (683). In truth it is Nature's reign that is over, dethroned by the product of her own apparently botched experiment.

The first pf writer to theorize human nature in full as the product of an alienation from Nature in the context of Darwinian struggle was Ray Nyst, for whom human ferocity, rather than intelligence, was what chiefly conduced to our ascent. For Nyst, primitive Man inhabited a *"marâtre univers"* (89); that is to say, for him, Mother Nature was really an evil stepmother. To survive, the "disdained monkey" of the forest (11) had to become the "fiercest animal on earth" (231). And so he did: it was the caveman, not our civilized selves, who invented the essential arts and techniques of survival. Given his innate deficiencies of body, prehistoric Man deserves to be styled a hero for what he achieved. Indeed, this club-wielding Hercules who dared to dress himself in a lion's skin was a kind of genius (50–55). At the same time, Nyst insists we acknowledge that Man went in for homicide from the start. His first human victims were his sexual rivals; we are descended from this primal killer, not from those he massacred. To admire Man today, then, is to congratulate our murderous ancestors. And because murder was so central to the formation of our nature, it remains the source of all our inspiration and symbol of all our joys (303–304). In short, we are children, not of Adam, but of Cain.

Edmond Haraucourt invokes Hobbes to emphasize that Natural Man was at first glance a contemptible creature: small, solitary, naked, deprived of claws or fangs in the "immense meat-safe" (39) of the Pleistocene forest. But appearances are deceptive: like Nyst's unnamed hero, Daâh with his club is a formidable opponent from the start. But Haraucourt's protagonist is more than the killer ape that Dart and Ardrey would later envisage. Conscious of his vulnerability, Daâh turns a badge of dishonor into a virtue: he proudly denominates himself The One Who Walks Upright (97). Moreover, Daâh's simian power of imitation is as important as his talent for innovative weaponry as an agent of hominization. By performing mimicry in front of his mate and watching her reaction, Daâh speaks to himself, and in this form of soliloquy is the origin of thought. Indeed, Daâh is even capable of imitating himself imitating an animal, the origin of self-reflection. But there is a price to pay for this transformation of *cervelle* (brain) into *cerveau* (intelligence) (213). The horde's shock when a cataclysmic earthquake occurs contrasts starkly with the preparedness of all the other animals, showing that the human faculties, so admirably developed as cognitive instruments, are no longer attuned to the external world. Self-absorbed, Man loses his apprehension of Nature.

Fire and Ice

Early pf often depicted our ancestors as dwellers in a subtropical Edenic forest until the climate suddenly worsened with the Quaternary onset of the Ice Age. To survive, Tertiary Man (usually conceived as a European) had a choice. He could migrate to the warmer south, thereby "deciding" to remain an ape. Or he could take up Nature's challenge, stay put, and begin to sharpen his wits on the "grindstone of pain and necessity," as Wells's Time Traveler refers to the Darwinian stuggle (*Time Machine*, 92–93). These are precisely the alternatives sketched in Bierbower's *From Monkey to Man*, the first American pf novel. A hairless primate accustomed to the warm Tertiary forest certainly rose to Nature's challenge in using animal skins to cover its own nakedness as the climate cooled. But what actually altered the balance of power between Man and Nature, at least in the majority view of early pf, was the mastery of fire.

Fire, more than any other invention or innovation, gave Man the upper hand over Nature. In *Longhead: The Story of the First Fire* (1913) by C(harles) H(enry) Robinson (American, 1843–1925), fire-making is described as simply "the greatest [discovery] in all time" (33). Trying to describe a campfire to his mate, Andoo the cave bear in Wells's "The Story of the Stone Age" can only explain what he has seen indirectly through metaphor and analogy: "The bright thing, too, they seem to have—like that glare that comes in the sky in daytime—only it jumps about—it's really worth seeing. It's a thing with a root, too—like grass when it is windy" (681). Here, through the apparent inadequacy of the cave bear's ordinary vocabulary to describe the phenomenon perceived, Wells suggests just how unprecedented in Nature was the process of hominization. Indeed, Man-made fire seems conceived in the image of its brilliant, restless, fascinating creator.

Other pf writers similarly associate the mastery of fire with emergent human nature. In *The Story of Ab* we learn that carnivores dislike "the queer thing, man" (26) and seek to devour him to rid the world of him, but they find themselves in outer darkness prowling vainly around his settlement, not daring to breach the barrier of flame at the cave mouth. Even as he is sleeping warm, safe, and fully fed in his cave, Man remains a "disturbing element" to the rest of Nature (26). Rosny, too, suggests that the nocturnal fire was the wedge driven by Man between himself and Nature. At the beginning of *Quest for Fire*, the Oulhamrs, deprived of their fire cages, "felt naked and defenceless before the crushing mass of the dark" (51). Their fiery guardian extinguished, they are reduced to a state of Nature, a condition that their human nature, forged beside the tribal hearth, now finds unendurable. In this context, we may recall not Hobbesian Man, who has never known comfort, but "unaccommodated man" evoked by Shakespeare's King Lear exiled on the bare heath—a once proud lord of Nature now reduced to "a poor, bare, fork'd animal" (III.iv.106–108).

Book 1, "Fire," of *The Long Journey* by Johannes V(ilhelm) Jensen (1873–1950) elaborates fire's crucial role in hominization as though to compensate for Scripture's unaccountable silence on the matter. Man had his origin in "the wild joyous forests" of the Tertiary, "where existence was bound by no laws but Nature's own" (10), where there was "only to-day, the summer day without beginning or end [. . .], eternal sunshine and the world a larder" (17).[9] Man's remote ancestor was a tree dweller in the subtropical Garden of Eden that is now southern Sweden. But he became so comfortable and well fed that he grew too heavy for branches to bear him and "a gradual descent, through generation after generation" brought him down to earth (38). (This is a striking elaboration of Darwin's central metaphor of hominization.) The prehuman Forest Folk, filled with the tree dwellers' ancestral dread of fire, now find themselves squatting at the foot of an active volcano.

Jensen's protagonist, significantly named "Fyr" [Fire], must learn to overcome his instinctive terror of fire if he is to alleviate the hardships of terrestrial life for the more progressive of his horde. What Fyr does is simply to take a branch up the volcano, light it, and bring fire back down to his people. This precipitates the irrevocable split between Man and Nature, one cast in terms of primate speciation: "those who followed Nature remained her dependents and had to migrate in order to retain the conditions they required; those who followed [Fyr] rose superior to the restraints of existence and became changed men" (42). Our ancestors, who followed Fyr, were thereafter "masters of the night and its ancient abyss of terrors" (53). Fyr is a Moses who brought something far more useful than stone tablets down from a mountain. More important, he is the prototype of the Titan Prometheus, one who defied the elemental powers to benefit Man. Fyr, whose very name suggests a human appropriation of Nature's energy, did not merely benefit the human race; in a sense, he actually created it (as by some mythological accounts Prometheus also did).

In science as in pf, a hypothetical hominization narrative that relates climatic change to Man's fallen/risen state will be appealing because of its compatibility with the Miltonic myth of disobedience, with the Promethean one of defiance, or with both at once. Robert Ardrey in *The Hunting Hypothesis* (1976) describes the Miocene, heyday of the ape,[10] as "our" paradise lost (24–46). In his view, however, it was the nonhuman primates, not ourselves, who were doomed when the climate changed. Unfallen innocents, they couldn't thrive outside the affluent environment of the eternal forest. Those who fell to earth, however, learned to become human by honing their survival skills in the "fickle, changeful Pleistocene" (107).

There is more than a trace of Ardrey's scenario in Yves Coppens's more scientifically respectable "East Side Story" hypothesis as dramatized by Pierre Pelot in *Le Rêve de Lucy*. According to Coppens, a tectonic, climatic, and ecological chain of events in the Rift valley of east Africa five million years ago led a population of the common ancestor of apes and humans to diverge and speciate. The apes and Lucy's prehuman australopithecines preferred the humid forests west of the Rift, while the more progressive habilines (the earliest species of *Homo*) evolved in the dry savannah to the east (Pelot and Coppens, 169–170; see also Stringer and McKie, 24–25). In Africa, the lost Eden of modern paleoanthropology, aridity replaces ice as the catalyst for *encephalization*, namely, the rapid development of the higher centers of the human brain.

The Fire in the Stone

In *Le Totémisme aujourd'hui* (1962; translated as *Totemism* in 1969), Claude Lévi-Strauss noted that people have attributed symbolic functions to certain species of animals, "not because they are 'good to eat' but because they are 'good to think'" (162). We may find animals "good to think" because of what they, regardless of their reality in Nature, can reveal about ourselves after we have used them to embody our own concerns. Wells's cave bear Andoo, who cannot even conceive of a controlled fire, is an example of an animal used in this way. The bear's bewilderment at Man's apparently supernatural powers of artifice functions primarily to reawaken us to our extraordinariness as a species. At the heart of good pf are narrative strategies that help us reexamine our own nature in relation to, or in contradistinction to, Nature.

So completely today do we depend upon our ability to control fire that it is difficult to envisage the immense mental distance our ancestors must have traveled before attaining this effortless mastery. Most animals instinctively fear and shun fire; yet Paleolithic peoples discovered that the unpredictable destroyer could be tamed, domesticated, used to mitigate cold and darkness, to keep predators at bay, to harden the points of weapons, even to improve the edibility and flavor of food. Like Jensen's Fyr, they must have learned to resist their animal instinct to flee from fires started by volcanism or lightning, and discovered how to capture, tend, preserve, and transport the flames. Later they attained true mastery of fire and thus the highest level of independence from Nature: the capacity to make a flame where none before existed. The ability to teach that capacity to others is a fundamental pillar of human culture.

One of good sf's great strengths is its ability to evoke a sense of wonder or enchantment by imagining advanced technologies. Magic enchants us most, and as Arthur C. Clarke has pointed out, "Any sufficiently advanced technology is indistinguishable from magic" (*Profiles* 39) to those encountering it for the first time.[11] An equivalent sense of wonder can be evoked by pf when it enables us to identify with Natural Man confronted with a form of apparent magic that will transform his relation to the universe. Here pf may generate wonder very effectively through the conjectural reconstruction of prehistoric thought processes, so that what seems simple and obvious to us today is revealed to be the product of a long cognitive struggle that may have required the abandonment of intuition, habitual wisdom, and even natural logic.

A classic episode occurs in Rosny's *Quest for Fire*. The Oulhamrs keep their fire, which they consider to be "the source of all delights . . . father, guardian and savior" (11), in three portable cages, in the form of glowing embers that can be nursed for days and used to kindle a new fire when required. But when two of their cages are destroyed and the flame in the third goes out, the survival of the tribe is threatened, for they do not know how to make fire afresh. The Oulhamrs' questing hero Naoh, son of the Leopard, having failed to regain fire by theft, encounters the Thin Men, a feeble and torpid race. He guesses correctly that they are more knowledgeable than his own tribe, and soon observes a Thin Woman striking two stones together: "At first sparks flew; then a little red dot danced along a blade of grass that was very tiny and dry; other blades flamed, which the woman kept up softly with her breath: the fire spread to leaves and twigs. The son of the Leopard stood motionless in awe" (110).

Naoh's state of enchantment is brief; it is human nature not to be content with effects, but to seek causes, to demand explanations, to strive to understand. The woman holds out her firestones to Naoh: "He felt them; they were cold. . . . When he was able to discover no fissure in them, his surprise grew. Anxiously he wondered, 'How does the fire get into the stones, and why are they not hot?' With fear and mistrust he returned them to the woman" (111). Anxious because his understanding of the material world is under threat, Naoh rationalizes: perhaps the Thin Men had somehow "imprisoned the fire in the stones" (113)? Soon, however, he is reassured to discover that "the secret had to do with the things themselves and not with any power of men" (113) and that two different kinds of stones (flint and iron pyrite) must be struck together to produce a spark. When he first makes fire in this way himself "he experienced the greatest joy. He realized that he had just won something more potent than any of his ancestors had possessed and that now the fire would be forever his" (114). Naoh's cognitive journey here dramatizes Frazer's suggestion in *The Golden Bough* that, because magic and science share so many intellectual characteristics, magical thinking is the preliminary stage of Man's conquest of Nature via scientific understanding (1:32).

If Rosny deals best with the *transmission* of fire-making techniques, it is Jensen in book 2, "Ice," of *The Long Journey* who offers the most resonant description in all pf of the *discovery* of the technique. The protagonist Carl, lineal descendant of Fyr, now struggles against the deteriorating conditions produced by the oncoming Quaternary glaciation. The volcano that was the Forest Folk's only renewable source of fire has been extinguished by the Deluge preceding the first glacial winter. But Carl's inherited spirit of defiance will turn him into "the first man" (90); Jensen implies that true humanity is only attained upon Nature's acquiescence to Man.[12] As he knaps his stone tools, however, Carl senses that "in some way unknown to him fire was present in flint or in the air about it" (134). So he starts to break every stone he can find: "If the fire was there, there must be a way of driving it out. It must be sitting in *one* of the stones" (135). His persistence pays off when he eventually discovers iron pyrite: "Never had Carl felt anything lie so weightily and richly in his hand as this stone. It bred a wholly new joy of possession, roused a mighty desire and satisfied it at the same time, since he had it. It gave him unbounded power, it was the first treasure of his race and of mankind" (138). And given the cultural significance of this discovery, it is appropriate that shortly thereafter, Carl is vouchsafed a future vision (beyond his own understanding) of an early twentieth-century Chicago street (142). The great midwestern metropolis is made habitable for millions on frigid winter nights only by electricity, the direct legacy of Carl's discovery of how to release the fire in the stone.

Episodes of first fire-making occur in many other works of pf, but no other writers deal so effectively with its momentous effect upon hominization as Jensen and Rosny. Sometimes, indeed, the opportunity is entirely lost. In Harry Harrison's prehistoric sf novel *West of Eden* (1984), for example, the protagonist Kerrick learns fire-making from a Neolithic farming people, but when he demonstrates the use of the stones to his chief, the latter blandly comments: "There is fire captured in this rock . . . and the other stone releases it. The Sasku do indeed have strange and powerful secrets" (439). To make so little of this episode is to fail to comprehend the characteristic spirit of pf. To put it another way: no fire will ever come from this stone.

Jean M. Auel in *The Shelters of Stone* (2002) deals with the transmission of fire-making by flint and pyrite firestones at length and in detail, but what she makes of these episodes reveals a problem characteristic of the later volumes of the Earth's Children series. Ayla shows her adopted tribe, Jondalar's Zelandonii, the use of firestones, recalling that she discovered this technique because she was not bound by tradition: she was alone in the Valley of Horses, "with no one to show me how to do things, or to tell me what couldn't be done" (192). Ayla's knowledge of firestones certainly elevates her prestige in the eyes of the Zelandonii. But Auel, fixated on demonstrating her heroine's exceptionality, fails to attach enough weight to how the transmitted technique might affect the Zelandonii. Auel is able to focus on Ayla's status because she (Auel) has constructed the Zelandonii as already fully modern in mentality. But is it really possible that any people could be mentally fully modern without the immense boost in confidence, and the consequent transformation in their relation with Nature, conferred by the knowledge of how to use firestones?[13]

Rosny, on the other hand, is more aware even than Jensen of the ambiguous consequences for humanity of this powerful new technique. The firestones brought back by Naoh evoke in the Oulhamrs an enormous optimism for the future and they celebrate him as a hero and chief-in-waiting. Yet their true benefactors, the Thin Men, whose lives have been eased by their mastery of fire, are a declining race, having lost their vigor as a result of their alienation from Nature. In the short term, learning the secret of fire-making rescues the Oulhamrs from what Rosny in *Quest of the Dawn Man* memorably terms "the approach of carnivorous night" (18). But ultimately the firestones will not be able to save them from the self-generated consequences of Man's unilateral divorce from Nature.

The film adaptation of *Quest for Fire* contains a prolonged scene in which Naoh observes fire being started with a fire drill by one of the Ivaka, a tribe who are more advanced than the Oulhamrs but—unlike the Thin Men, their counterparts in the novel—show no degenerative traits. While Annaud strikingly reveals the physical effort and dexterity that went into prehistoric firemaking, and effectively shows Naoh's awe at the process, he misses Rosny's subtler point: it is the *simplicity* of making fire by striking two stones together—the careless *ease* with which Man learns to use Nature against itself—that may well lead to his undoing.

Domestication and Its Discontents

In Genesis God grants Adam dominion over the animals, but in pf, imbued with Darwinian doubt, Man's relationship with nonhuman Nature is more complex and fraught with ambiguity. Many pf writers have tried to depict the primal scene of domestication when Man first tamed wolf or horse, but the results are often implausible or ludicrous. Perhaps such scenes are tainted by ethical distaste at our ability to impose our will upon other, physically more powerful, species. In *Dream*, the misanthropic S. Fowler Wright frankly confessed his disgust for the ignoble cunning that degrades both master and slave: "Men have won to be first of all beasts by the practice of fraud and trick. . . . If there be anything which is stronger than fraud it is a lesson which is still to learn" (98–99).

Domestication and its discontents are a major theme in Wells's "A Story of the Stone Age." Fleet, powerful wild horses then roamed in herds on the open grasslands. From the paleo-equine point of view, Men seemed contemptible "pink monkey things" (686) that lacked even the benefit of hind legs: "No whisper of prophetic intelligence told the species of the terrible slavery that was to come, of the whip and spur and bearing-rein, the clumsy load and the slippery street, the insufficient food, and the knacker's yard" (684). Ugh-Lomi drops from a tree onto the back of the Master Horse, and clings on by his still prehensile limbs as the stallion bolts off at a tremendous pace, outstripping even a rhinoceros. Yet while Ugh-Lomi's defeat of the cave bear was heroic, his first horseback ride seems gratuitous and undignified. The episode confirms Andoo's intuition that there is something of the "monkey gone wrong" about our species, and it almost comes as a relief to the reader when the horse finally throws Ugh-Lomi off in sight of his bewildered tribe. Nevertheless, Man has gotten his first exhilarating taste of speed and power, an experience worth any temporary humiliation: from now on, the horse's days of freedom are numbered. The episode suggests that the moment that Man ceases to fear Nature, his awe is transformed into self-regard.

In London's *Before Adam*, Big-Tooth and his friend Lop-Ear admire—because they fear—the packs of wild dogs that tear apart any of the Folk who cannot reach a safe tree in time. One day the two boys come across some orphaned wild pups and decide to steal them. Their motives are simply to show off their new possessions to the Folk and to impose their will on creatures weaker than themselves. Big-Tooth takes his pup home and over the next week begins to care for it, even catching animals for it to eat. We expect that this new sense of responsibility will mark a significant stage in his, and our, hominization. But alone one day, Lop-Ear gets hungry, kills the pup and is just about to eat it when Big-Tooth returns. Outraged at his pet's fate, Big-Tooth attacks his friend; the boys fight, sulk for a while . . . then reconsecrate their friendship by each devouring half of the puppy raw. London hereby suggests that canines, social predators like ourselves, seem predisposed to fidelity and trust; it is we, insatiable of appetite, who seem incapable of becoming properly domesticated.

For Rosny, domestication is tarnished by association with disfavored racial attributes. In *Vamireh* the Asiatic invaders of Magdalenian Europe have begun to domesticate horses and cattle, to control which they must employ trained dogs. The dogs are also used for martial purposes, and their typically "Asiatic" fighting spirit suggests their training in blind obedience and subordination of individual to communal values. In contrast, Vamireh, the blond occidental protagonist who fights solo epic battles against hordes of them, represents individualism and the artistic temperament. Nevertheless, the orientals' dogs will ultimately enable them to conquer western Europe.[14]

While domestication was a function of human estrangement from Nature, the human-animal alliance was in Rosny's view more harmonious—not a relationship of dominance/submission but a partnership based on reciprocity and trust. In *Quest for Fire* Naoh forges an alliance with the mammoths by feeding them water lily stems in exchange for protection against the cannibalistic Kzamms (fig. 4.2). It requires extraordinary bravery for a mere man to dare to parley with such huge creatures, but the alliance is forged because the intelligent mammoths recognize this courage. In *Quest of the Dawn Man*, in contrast, unheroic Zouhr's alliance with the giant sabertooth cat comes about because of the feline's preference for any sort of company over solitude. Whatever the motivation for the alliance, if the result is mutual obligation and cooperation between species, then this, for Rosny, characterizes a fruitful relation between Man and animal Nature.[15]

Figure 4.2 Rosny's Naoh forges an alliance with the mammoths.

One of the most shocking and powerful scenes in pf associated with domestication occurs at the end of Claude Anet's novel of the Reindeer Age, *The End of a World*. Set in the Vézère valley 12,000 B.P., this work is a revisitation, in the light of a generation of new paleoanthropological discoveries, of Rosny's scenario in *Vamireh* of the invasion of western Europe by Neolithic Asiatics. Anet's Magdalenian protagonist, Nô, fearing that his people, like the reindeer upon which they depend, will be wiped out by the Round Heads and their hunting dogs, decides that he must learn to "cast a spell" (256) over an animal, too, so that his people would also have an ally that "they would be able to eat without being obliged to hunt" (254). He decides on the wild horse, which has always had a prominent place in the art and rituals of his people, and receives appropriate esoteric knowledge from the tribe's shaman. With great difficulty, he manages to lasso a wild colt and render it immobile by tying its legs. Slowly, patiently, repeating the shaman's spell, Nô attempts to gain the animal's trust until the colt is eating out of his hand. Taking this as a sign of alliance, Nô unties the colt's legs to make a halter of the rope. But the colt, realizing it is free, spins round and kicks repeatedly Nô in the head, fracturing his skull. Nô dies because he has failed to understand that Nature will not be charmed by spells but must be beaten into submission. His people, too noble for the harsh new reality of the Neolithic age, are doomed, and Rosny's romantic vision of alliance between Man and Nature is extinguished.

If Man's attempts at domestication in pf are often doomed to failure, Woman has more success. As early as 1895, the anthropologist Otis Tufton Mason had suggested that primitive women might have first tamed wild animals not through brute force but by becoming substitute mothers: "the first domestication is simply adoption of helpless infancy. The young wolf, or kid, or lamb, or calf, is brought to the home of the hunter. It is fed and caressed by the mother and her children, and even nourished at her breast" (151). Although Auel was not the first to dramatize this insight in pf,[16] she developed the scenario to an unprecedented degree in the lengthy episodes in *The Valley of Horses* when Ayla learns to survive alone on the Eurasian steppe.

Ayla first adopts Whinney, a young wild horse whose mother has been killed in a pitfall trap. Later, she rescues and tames a wounded cave lion cub, Baby, that has been trampled by reindeer and left to die. Aware that it seems at first glance highly implausible that a carnivore and its prey might be persuaded to live together in harmony, Auel rises to the challenge and persuades the reader of its possibility. Ayla's circumstances as a solitary outcast, her thwarted desire to nurture as a result of her surrender of her infant son Durc to the Clan, the young animals' desperate need to be mothered, Ayla's vocation as a healer, her human yearning for companionship, the fact that the cave lion is her totem animal and has given her a "sign of approval" by allowing her to devise a working travois—all serve to increase the likelihood of Ayla's success, especially as failure will lead to death for them all. These episodes constitute a narrative tour de force in which Auel makes a powerful plea to view domestication not as the imposition of Man's will on an animal but as the fulfillment of a set of complex reciprocal needs between "the animal called human" (187) and other animals. Humans are "puny compared with their carnivorous competitors"; that is why they "depended on cooperation and compassion to survive" (187). Lacking a social network, the human animal (or at least its female version) has the intelligence and imagination to cast nonhuman animals in social roles—and to succeed not by force but by fulfilling mutual needs.

In *Reindeer Moon* Elizabeth Marshall Thomas sets up an apparently similar domestication situation to Auel's. The protagonist Yanan and her dependent younger sister Meri get lost in the snow and find themselves sharing an abandoned hunting lodge with a female wolf and her pup for the rest of the winter. But this remarkable episode, "The Wolf" (81–122) though it comes to similar conclusions to Auel's about domestication and human nature, may also be intended by Thomas as a realistic corrective to the more exceptional aspects of Auel's scenario in *The Valley of Horses* as well as to Ayla's rather too easy adoption and training of "Wolf," the abandoned cub in *The Mammoth Hunters* that thereafter becomes her faithful ally.

At first Yanan entertains the preconceptions about wolves typical of her hunting culture. Wolf cubs are easy meat; an adult she-wolf, on the other hand, is a competing carnivore and a terrifying enemy when one has no weapons to protect oneself. Yet Yanan soon realizes why the mother wolf does not attack the girls: she needs them to babysit her cub while she goes out hunting! Yanan also begins to grasp the underlying politics of this close encounter between two highly social species, and senses that the wolf may be ahead of her in strategic thinking: "If I killed the pup . . . would the wolf leave? She might, but she also might kill Meri so that I would feel pain as she felt pain. I dropped the idea" (94). The ability to imagine another's pain leads to sympathy and compassion, but it also enables one to manipulate others by hypothetical threats. Neither capacity is evidently an exclusive human preserve, and it is only our anthropocentrism that deludes us into thinking that it is.

Soon, in return for childminding duties, the wolf is feeding Meri in the same way that she feeds her own cub, by vomiting up already masticated meat for her. Yanan, whose hunger overcomes her disgust, also quickly adapts to this method of being fed. The wolf then "suggests" to Yanan how to improve their hunting success: she will chase wild horses toward where the girl waits with a spear.[17] Though this stratagem fails because of Yanan's incompetence with weaponry, it is clear that the mature wolf has much to teach the immature girls. Indeed, Meri soon learns to howl like a wolf to call her adoptive mother, who has replaced her biological parents in the role of provider. But if the wolf requires the girls to play the role of a surrogate family, why is this social predator not part of a pack? Yanan begins to wonder if the animal may not be banished for some sexual transgression, as happens to human females. By this stage, thoroughly convinced of the continuities between the human and animal realms, we are hesitant to accuse Yanan of anthropomorphism. Eventually, however, the wolf does leave to rejoin her pack, but the cub remains with the girls to grow up as a dog among humans.

The dog was probably the first creature to be domesticated, and would have surely been essential in helping hunters and pastoralists maintain control of fast-running herd animals such as horses and reindeer when these animals were still in a predomesticated state.[18] Thomas and Auel both conjecture, however, that domestication probably did not begin as part of Man's relentless program to subordinate Nature to his will. Because humans and nonhuman mammals shared the fundamental interests of food gathering, shelter, reproduction, and the care of young, alliances that furthered these common interests would almost inevitably have evolved. And it is likely that prehistoric women, whose biological and social roles were centered on these fundamental interests, would have been better than men at forging mutually sustaining alliances with their fellow mammals. Men, by contrast, would have been likely to form alliances only to further exclusively human political or military ends—of which, with due respect to Rosny's mammoths, animals can have little understanding. Men would surely also have been more likely to demand, and enforce, subordination or even slavery in their domestic relations with nonhuman animals, as this was how they typically treated their women. But as gender refuses to be excluded any longer from the discussion of human nature, it is time to grant it fuller attention.

5.
▼
Sex and Gender

[T]he human family is the result of the reciprocity of hunting, the addition of a male to the mother-plus-young social group of the monkeys and apes.

—Sherwood L. Washburn and C. S. Lancaster, "The Evolution of Hunting" (1968)

More efficient hunting permitted the women to stay more often at home instead of following the hunters to get their share of the kill. "Woman's place is in the cave," Father began to say.

—Roy Lewis, *What We Did to Father* (1960)

Revising Genesis

The biblical account of human origin, while vague about many other aspects of the divine creation, is unequivocal about how there came to be two human sexes and what the difference between them signifies. A male God first created from the dust of the earth a male human being in his image to tend Eden. Later, as an afterthought, he created a woman out of an inessential part of Adam's body (a rib) to be his companion (Genesis 2:20–23). The human sexes, then, were created at different times out of different substances for different purposes, and the male had seniority, and retains priority, over the female.

Once created, Eve immediately displays the weakness to be expected of a secondary being made from disposable material. There is only one divine interdiction in Eden, but she breaks it and uses her naked charms to ensure that Adam breaks it too. The future mother of Cain is gullible, fickle, disobedient, and manipulative from the beginning; her first significant act is to use her sexual power to damage male integrity. Genesis could hardly be more explicit: God punishes Eve with painful childbearing and mandates that for humanity's good she must in future be ruled by Adam (Genesis 3:16). Scripture implies that subsequent generations of men will be justified in blaming Eve's daughters for everything that has gone wrong in their lives.

One of the first joint tasks of Darwinism and paleoanthropology after 1859 was to revise Genesis so as to tell a new story about how, why, from when, and to what extent men and women differed. Darwinism provided a credible naturalistic theory of human origin. It reduced the role of a supernatural Creator to providing, at best, the "vital spark" that set the evolutionary process unfolding at the beginning of time; for many, it simply disposed of him altogether. But to get rid of God was also to dispose of the divine anathema on womanhood. Even the obstetric "curse" could be naturalistically explained by evolutionary theory. Babies' heads had expanded at a rate too fast for mothers' pelvic openings to accommodate comfortably. Indeed, labor pains affirmed that evolution by natural selection was an imperfect and contingent process. What kind of omniscient Designer could have failed to anticipate, chosen to ignore, or refused to remedy one of the more obvious consequences of our increasing braininess?

Darwinism, then, tended to restore Woman to the primary status that observation and natural logic demanded: Man came out of her, not the other way around. But how, in the new naturalistic universe, to account for the universal fact of women's social subordination to men, into which relative size, physical strength, and intellectual attainment all seemed to factor? The answers surely lay in human evolutionary history, but human fossils were tantalizingly silent on the question of prehistoric gender roles. Early paleoanthropology had consequently to extrapolate from the behavior of modern savages and of nonhuman primates.

There is a strong argument to be made for locating the origin of first-wave feminism in the perceived need to revise Genesis in the Darwinian aftermath. If there was no divine mandate for female social subordination, then it could well be a human phenomenon, and if it was, humans could change it. In such an insight lay the embryo of the current usage of *gender* to emphasize the constructedness and transformability of human sexual politics in contrast to the relative fixity of biological *sex*. At the same time there was a rapid growth after 1859 in what we now call scientific sexism. Most theorists in the new discipline of sexology were male, and had the vested interest in preserving the status quo typical of all dominant groups. Many of them proposed that there were essential biological or physiological reasons for female subordination. If not eternal in the theological sense, sexual asymmetry had been prevalent in human affairs from earliest prehistory. Precisely this asymmetry explained and justified the extant sexual-political hierarchy.

The Darwinian worldview accords to reproductive success an importance that theology formerly granted to personal salvation. Prose fiction has always granted a central role to the sexual drama. It is not surprising, then, that from pf's beginnings, the sexually dimorphic human species and its unbalanced sexual politics have provided an inexhaustible well of fascinated speculation. Pf promised to offer insights into the origin and development of human mating practices, including courtship rituals, sexual taboos, romantic love, and marriage, and sometimes it delivered them. Of course, descriptions of the brutish or uninhibited mating practices of our ancestors were also capable of providing many varieties of erotic stimulation. But one question underlay much of the early speculation: Were the prehistoric relations between the sexes worse, or better, than they are today?

Aboriginal Sexual Politics

Early writers of pf, almost all male, got no definitive answers from the scientific literature about how and why men and women differed, but they found plenty of fertile opportunities for speculation. For example, Darwin noted that human males had a great advantage over females in physical strength (*Descent*, 2:325), and suggested that this imbalance might have been originally a by-product of female selection of the fittest males (2:372–375). Did this mean that women like to be dominated? And, if so, didn't that prove that the New Women agitating for equality were unwomanly? Darwin had also noted that "in the savage state" Man keeps his women "in a far more abject state of bondage than does the male of any other animal" (2:371). Some early pf writers of strongly progressionist cast were eager to show how far we had come from the brutish Adam who dominated his harem of Eves like a male gorilla.[1] Others, alarmed by the slight shifting of the sexual balance of power in women's favor in the later nineteenth century, envisioned a natural order now under threat from modern tendencies. Darwinian passages that, taken out of context, essentialized difference—"Man is more powerful in body and mind than woman" (2:371)—could be used to suggest that there had been a dangerous falling away from a natural state in which Eve knew her place and was soundly thrashed by Adam if she forgot it.

Zit and Xoe, the first attempt in pf to revise the Adam and Eve scenario, is a mildly satirical work. Curwen's targets are probably those among his contemporaries dissuaded by "Mrs. Grundy," the embodiment of Victorian prudery, from fully accepting that the human species had a lowly origin. His strategy was indirect: to show that Mrs. Grundy's reconciliation of Scripture and Darwinism was ludicrous by rewriting Genesis as an evolutionary scenario censored by genteel prejudices. The narrator Zit is a freak among his arboreal folk: a tailless, bipedal ape with opposable thumbs. Kicked out of the trees by his father, he finds himself alone, "unarmed and innocent and naked" (461) in the struggle for existence. Now he encounters the woman Xoe, who advises him primly to get dressed: "You would feel much more comfortable, and you would really look ever so much nicer" (464). Along with clothing and cookery, Xoe has invented mid-Victorian feminine morality, in which sexual hypocrisy ("a girl never says what she thinks" [469]) is mixed with protofeminism ("I will be no man's slave" [477]). Too ladylike herself, she "allows" Zit to do the dirty work of killing animals, while her coyness at bedtime almost drives him crazy with frustration.

In the end, Mrs. Grundy's influence was too strong to allow Curwen to speculate more seriously on the origin of sexual differences. Indeed, only one nineteenth-century British work, now very obscure, did try to confront this issue directly: *The New Eden* (1892) by C(harles) J(ohn) Cutcliffe Hyne (1866–1944).[2] This short novel, set in the present, describes an experiment in which a boy and girl, too young to retain any memory of external humanity, are placed on two adjacent uninhabited South Sea islands so their "evolution" (17) can be secretly monitored over the long term. Hyne describes how the biological difference between new Adam and Eve expresses itself in sex-specific behavior; how, when the pair finally meet, their differences generate a potentially fatal conflict; how they resolve their conflict and unite; and what they each contribute to the new society. He is particularly interested in whether or not his quasi-primal pair are fated to recapitulate the biblical Fall of Man.

Like Curwen, Hyne suggests that Woman is more innately gifted than Man, though she is also more conservative and narcissistic. Hyne's new Eve is quite Adam's equal in aggression if not in strength, and patriarchy evolves collaboratively rather than being imposed by male main force. The constraints of maternity, amplified by Eve's comfort-seeking nature, cause her willingly to hand the responsibility for providing for the family to Adam. By ingeniously attempting to restage hominization as a controlled experiment, Hyne in *The New Eden* dealt as frankly as was then possible with human sexuality as the supreme generator of both tension and pleasure.

By the turn of the twentieth century American women had made the most progress of any of their sex toward equality. However, several male American pf writers maintained that women were only then beginning to approach the high status that they had *lost* in prehistoric times. In so doing they implied that the United States was where sexual harmony would first be reinstated. Bierbower in *From Monkey to Man* noted, "There were amazons before there were belles. Woman's equality in public affairs was recognized before her inferiority, and equal rights were as yet the law of the race" (90). In London's *Before Adam*, the Swift One is "very wise, very strong, and no clinging skirts impeded her movements" (140). Stanley Waterloo was even more emphatic: Ab's cave-dwelling mother "had a certain unhampered swing of movement which the modern woman often lacks" (*Story of Ab*, 11). Unconstrained by a corset, she was "lithe as the panther," her figure as "healthfully symmetrical" as the Venus de Medici's, her hair glossy, her chin "well defined and firm," her teeth "strong and even, and as white as any ivory ever seen," her biceps "tremendous," her feet "beautiful"; in short, though she might have been a little too hairy-faced to benefit from modern cosmetics, she was "as healthy a creature . . . as ever trod a path in the world's history" (11–14).

The best clue to what was motivating this American recuperation of Eve may be found in Gratacap's extraordinary *A Woman of the Ice Age*. Here the prehistoric Eternal Feminine finds its embodiment in Lhatto, the Paleo-Indian heroine:

> Ageless woman! . . . the origin of human life, the vast procreative source of all civilization and all progress, and from her bosoms, clutched by the fixed hand of infancy, flows the milk that has formed the tissues of all known human annals.
>
> Prophecy dwells upon her head, for from her proceed the nations of the earth. Poetry and Drama surround her, for she, in her evocative charm, haunts the innermost chambers of Desire, and it is her touch that lights the fires, else unseen, upon each altar of Passion, of Aspiration, of Revelry, of Joy. (40–41)

Though Lhatto has a "superb physique" and "steel-like muscles" (50), her function is not so much to represent female agency as to be an

embodied object of male desire for the fulfillment of the divine intention. She is a eugenic American Eve fully restored to Nature, purged
of physical weakness and sexual shame. Posed nude on a Pacific beach,
standing in "the waves that were now lapping with soft kisses her
knees and thrusting out innumerable tongues upon her smooth and
sculptured thighs" (52), she anticipates nothing so much as an air-
brushed *Playboy* centerfold.

For Jack London, too, Woman was not so much Man's equal or
helpmeet as his sexual inspiration or distraction. At the end of *The
Star Rover*, the protagonist, shortly to be executed for the murder of
a sexual rival, mentally travels back in time to connect with his prehistoric forebears. The earliest, a hunter, is distracted from trapping
the mighty sabertooth by his "savage mate" whose "arms chained
me, and her twining legs and heart beating to mine seduced me
from . . . my man's achievement" (304). The next, an archer, transmits
his knowledge of bows to our Aryan ancestors thanks to his "mate-
woman" Igar: "a race-mother . . . broad-built and full-dugged . . . she
could not but draw to the man heavy-muscled, deep-chested, who
sang of his prowess in man-slaying and in meat-getting, and so, promised food and protection to her in her weakness whilst she mothered
the seed that was to hunt the meat and live after her" (304–305). Primal Woman's main achievement was to nurture strength in her sons.

European writers of early pf, identifying the same sex-based dis-
tinction in social function, were less idealistic than their American
counterparts. For them, aboriginal humanity was defined by Woman's
primal and absolute subordination to Man. For Ray Nyst, Adam was
from the first "hunter of herds, enemy of beasts, giant of Nature, in-
domitable conqueror of all" (145). Eve attached herself to him not
from love or admiration but because of the meat he provided (148).
In return, she would offer her teeming womb to him, and his aggression complemented by her fertility would, reduplicated, conquer the
earth. For Jensen, the primal horde was nomadic and the order in
which it proceeded and even the objects it carried reflected an essential sexual hierarchy: "the Man in front with spear and stone, ready to
thrust or strike, the Woman in the rear with the fruit of her body and
her sex, a never-healing wound which the Man keeps open" (31). If
this injurious relationship is lamentable, it is also supposedly "natural" and ineluctable: the sexual metaphors of "fruit" and "wound" es-
sentialize both female suffering and male sadism.

Haraucourt is even more explicit in rewriting Genesis from a naturalistic perspective. His Eden is the great European forest at the transition between the Tertiary and Quaternary, in which solitary ape-people wander alone like orangutans. Only when male and female meet by chance does the reproductive process begin: Daâh simply overpowers Hock and rapes her. The timid Hock is used to predators trying to kill and eat her, but this one spares her and remains with her after the attack. For the first time she notices her solitude and attaches herself to the male. The primal sexual arrangement, then, is Woman as Man's dependent slave. Daâh walks ahead, carrying his club; Hock walks behind, bearing her infant whose relationship to Daâh neither of them suspect, for paternity is as yet unimagined. It is Man's weapon—his club—that was his first true partner and love object (116).

Courtship with a Club

One of the few things that everyone knows about sex in prehistory is how a caveman chooses a wife: he creeps up on an unsuspecting maiden who has caught his eye, stuns her with a blow of his club, and drags her back to his cave by the hair. This scenario, which I have denominated "Courtship with a Club" (q.v.), has been milked for comedy in popular culture since the early twentieth century (fig. 5.1). The motif itself, however, dates from the beginning of paleoanthropology itself. In fact, it was once an orthodox scientific opinion that Courtship with a Club had been the usual mating practice of our ancestors, that its brutality was justified by prevailing circumstances, and that it represented a moral advance over earlier practices.

The origin of Courtship with a Club can be traced to *Primitive Marriage: An Inquiry into the Origin of the Form of Capture in Marriage Ceremonies* (1865) by John F. McLennan, a Scottish-born anthropologist. McLennan set himself the problem of imagining from what original conditions the genteel customs associated with Victorian courtship and marriage might have evolved. A progressionist like most of his contemporaries, he started from the premise that if civilized sexual relations were typified by monogamous fidelity, then the most primitive human social group (the horde) must have been totally promiscuous. By similar progressionist logic, McLennan argued if the Victorian empire was characterized by the Pax Britannica, then the primal horde must have lived in a Hobbesian state of perpetual war with its neighbors. In this context, savages would have viewed infant

Figure 5.1   Courtship with a Club, 1930 style.

sons as potential food providers and warriors in the perpetual struggle for existence. Daughters, by contrast, would have represented only
bouches inutiles (useless mouths) and the potential for reproducing
more of the same. Consequently, female infanticide was universally
practiced, savages being unable to foresee the inevitable consequence:
too few women to ensure the horde's reproductive survival. This
scarcity in turn increased inbreeding and the physiological and mental (not to mention moral) retrogression resulting from it.

The prehistoric solution to the dangers of incest was a system of
exogamy (23)—a term invented by McLennan—according to which
young men were constrained to seek wives from outside their own
horde. As a horde's neighbors were all hostile, peaceable matrimonial
arrangements were out of the question: exogamy necessitated wife
capture. Meanwhile, contemporary ethnological reports suggested
that among Australian aborigines, clubbing a woman unconscious and
dragging her off was a standard courtship practice. If the lowest of
modern savages acted this way today, then our ancestors probably behaved likewise before they had been able to rise from their primal
degradation. Indeed, evidence that our ancestors *had* behaved in this
manner was surely to be found in familiar myths and legends such as

the Trojan abduction of Helen and the Rape of the Sabine Women, as well as in such modern survivals as the custom of carrying a new bride across the threshold. Darwin himself, noting that "almost all civilised nations still retain some traces of such rude habits as the forcible capture of wives" (*Descent*, 1:182), gave McLennan's theory a qualified endorsement. A prehistoric system of wife capture supported Darwin's view that men had used their physical dominance over women to appropriate to themselves the power of sexual selection that female animals usually have in nature (2:371).

Early pf writers found the motif irresistible. In an age of long engagements, the sheer directness of Courtship with a Club was no doubt refreshing to male authors and readers. Perhaps, too, men in that era when the machine and the New Woman seemed to be conspiring to undermine traditional virility were nostalgic for a well-defined, dominant gender role. The courting caveman played the quintessential masculine role of hunter, while woman was cast as his most desirable prey. He wielded the phallic club, she bore the flowing locks of femininity that he seized as a sign that he had claimed possession of her body. The caveman's success at capturing a mate proved his manhood while his victim's temporary loss of consciousness and transportation to a strange cave marked her initiation into wifehood. Moreover, the morally progressive nature of exogamic wife capture became clear once it was realized that the alternative was incest. There was even a eugenic element to Courtship with a Club: the "hunter" undoubtedly chose his "prey" for her beauty—a Darwinian mark of reproductive fitness—while a successful capture indicated his fitness to beget offspring upon his victim.

It was both titillating and shocking to Victorians to imagine that their forefathers could have behaved in such a way. The mixture of arousal and horror evoked by wife capture found its embodiment in the sculpture by Emmanuel Frémiet known as *Gorille enlevant une femme* (Gorilla carrying off a woman) (1887). A male gorilla bares his fangs, a struggling nude woman wedged horizontally under his right arm, while in his left he wields a Paleolithic hand ax (fig. 5.2). This fin de siècle icon, incarnating an exaggerated sexual dimorphism, seethes with animal eroticism. Frémiet's gorilla embodies an primeval male sexual principle in which unrestrained desire is legitimized by irresistible physical strength, while his stone tool or weapon collapses the boundary between animality and humanity. The captive represents Woman as totally vulnerable in her weakness, nakedness, and help-

Figure 5.2 The ape in man: Frémiet's *Gorilla*.

lessness to bestial male desire. Frémiet's gorilla is both the ape from which Man has descended and that which still inhabits him, agitating for release.

Most early writers of pf found such a sexually charged motif acceptable only in a context that emphasized its atavism. That is to say, they preferred to associate violent wife capture with male antagonists who "threw back" to the ape, thereby suggesting that more progressive male protagonists, those who were more truly the ancestors of the modern bourgeoisie, had since developed more chivalrous methods of courtship. By a kind of triangulation, Courtship with a Club could be assimilated into the romance tradition: a fair maiden, abducted by a brutish villain, would be rescued by a gentler hero from a fate worse than death. The seminal episode of Courtship with a Club in pf is in the first, Paleolithic episode of Berthet's *The Pre-Historic World*. Red the atavistic ogre, annoyed by Deer's preference for her proto-Celtic sweetheart Fair-Hair, "seized the coquettish beauty by the waist, raised her from the ground, and began to carry her away" (33). When her parents try to intervene, Red smashes the skull of her father and stuns her mother with his "formidable club," tosses aside her two younger brothers, and, utterly disregarding her struggles, "turned toward the forest, carrying Deer as a wolf carries a sheep" (34). Berthet spells out Paleolithic sexual politics: "Respect for woman did not exist at that period, and the dominion of the stronger over the weaker sex was exercised without limit" (48). Fortunately for the future of civilization, Fair-Hair, no match for Red in animal strength, kills the ogre from a safe distance with his bow and arrow, and rescues the maiden before her virtue is damaged.

This scene is recapitulated in *Before Adam*, with the large difference that Jack London seriously interrogates Berthet's progressionist assumptions. Red-Eye, the most atavistic of the Folk, is a serial wife killer. Having beaten his last mate to death, he then lights upon the Singing One, wife of the diminutive Crooked-Leg. Red-Eye breaks the little husband's neck, seizes the victim "by the hair of her head, and he drag[s] and haul[s] her up into the cave" (181) (fig. 5.3). Although the rest of the Folk are outraged, they are incapable of combining to bring Red-Eye to justice. Instead, working themselves into a "sensuous frenzy" through a dance to the drum, their anger is "soothed away by art" (184). Red-Eye remains unpunished, and indeed ultimately survives the genocide of the Folk to bequeath his violent nature to posterity. In London's view, Red-Eye, "in spite of his tremendous atavistic tendencies, foreshadowed the coming of man, for it is the males of the human species only that murder their mates" (179). Modern sexual violence against women has not been reduced to harmless symbolic survivals, nor can it cannot be explained away eugenically. It remains an unreconstructed part of male human nature.

London's loss of confidence in progress became much more widely reflected in Western society after the First World War. In the political realm, some nations' desperate search for credible forms of au-

Figure 5.3 A prehistoric man-beast drags off his victim.

thority resulted in their willing submission to authoritarianism. Likewise, in the realm of sexual politics there developed a new interest in demonstrating that more extreme forms of male dominance and female submission were natural or essential patterns of behavior. Some pf writers answered Freud's notorious question of 1925, "What does Woman want?" by slightly altering the even more notorious advice given to Nietzsche's Zarathustra so that it read, "Thou goest to women? Do not forget thy club!"[3]

The prehistoric sf novel *In the Beginning* (1927) by the Canadian popular novelist Alan Sullivan (1868–1947), for example, begins with a conversation between Jean Caxton and her father, an explorer and anthropologist, about her problems deciding between two suitors, the big-game hunter Gregory Burden or the botanist Phil Sylvester. Caxton asks his daughter whom she prefers, to which she replies, "That's the queer part of it . . . I can't be sure yet. Sometimes it's Gregory— he's so big and strong and confident. And yet at other times he frightens me a little. Am I quite mad?" (2). To this, he replies: "No, that's not mad, but atavistic. Your progenitors, a good many centuries back, simply adored the hairy men who hit them on the head with a club, threw them across their shoulders, and made their lives miserable ever after" (2). Sullivan's implication here is that modern woman has an atavistic tendency to revert to a submissive, even masochistic role. But how should she negotiate it? Caxton goes to Patagonia to investigate a sighting of a megatherium (an extinct giant ground sloth), taking along Jean and her two suitors with the idea of testing them to see which will be worthy to win her hand. In the Pleistocene lost world, Gregory atavistically reverts, taking a primitive woman for his mate, while Jean and Phil prove their compatibility because in them civilization is stronger than savagery.

Rosny's powerful prehistoric sf novella "Les Hommes Sangliers" is more subtle in its account of female forms of atavistic reversion, and less optimistic in its conclusion. Set among Dutch colonists in southeast Asia, its protagonist is Suzanne Dejongh, an orphaned young woman living under the protection of her uncle. One night she is abducted by cannibalistic Boar Men, prehistoric missing links who live in the depths of the jungle. When the chief of the Boar Men leads her away from the camp, she fears that he will kill and eat her. Instead he throws her to the ground and does something to her of which she, the product of a strict Calvinist upbringing, had been totally ignorant and which evokes in her a mixture of fear and intoxication (676–677).

This brutal violation is repeated daily and each time she experiences a strange exaltation. Eventually Suzanne manages to escape by raft, enduring the hardships of the journey only because the savage who has entered her body has now colonized her soul. Restored to her uncle, she now feels the emotional poverty of her mild Dutch upbringing in opposition to the power of the carnivorous jungle. A savage desire has awoken in her (683), and she hardly resists when a Boar Man comes to her window at night, silences her dog with one pass of his hand over its head, and takes her back to the jungle. But now, caught between two worlds and unable to live in either, she escapes by drowning herself in a marsh pool.

One of the least ambivalent occurrences of Courtship with a Club occurs in one of the few early pf works by a woman. New Zealand–born Dulcie Deamer (1890–1972) was known as the "Queen of Bohemia" in 1920s Sydney, Australia. Deamer's *As It Was in the Beginning* (1909), a slender volume illustrated by the celebrated Australian artist Norman Lindsay, is a series of pf stories set in a vaguely imagined prehistoric Europe.[4] Four of the stories deal with the Strong Man (aka the Lion-Slayer), a club-wielding brute from a cliff-dwelling tribe who steals the nubile Red-Haired Woman from a more advanced, but effete, group of cattle herders and takes her back to his cave. There she endures his brutal treatment until circumstances conspire to cause her to save his life by spearing a lioness (fig. 5.4). Now his gratitude salves her resentment and she prostrates herself willingly before him. He becomes "her man—the man who had reived her with the violence of a beast, who had beaten her sullenly, savagely, to break the wild-cat hate of him that he had roused . . .—whose heel she licked in self-abasement before the dominance of his strong manhood" (51). He respects her strength only because he dominates her, and she is pleased to submit. As he is dying he cuts her throat so that she will never be possessed by another man, whereupon she contentedly lies down to die too. Deamer here celebrates an authentic caveman masculinity to which the strong woman craves to submit. Obviously, Courtship with a Club was an erotic fantasy enjoyed not only by men.

What ended serious treatments of wife capture in pf (though Courtship with a Club still survives in comic form) was not feminism but satire. In Lewis's *What We Did to Father*, Father is determined to impose exogamy on his sons as part of his progressive project. When Oswald, the oldest, protests that "People *always* mate with their sisters. . . . It's the done thing," Father, evidently saturated in Darwin,

Figure 5.4 Prehistoric sexual politics from a female perspective.

McLennan, and Freud, retorts that sisters "provide too uninhibited
an outlet for the undisciplined libido. No; if we want any cultural development, we must put the emotions of the individual under stress.
In short, a young man must go out and find his mate, court her, capture her, fight for her. Natural selection" (82). But Father's mandated
alternative, wife capture, itself quickly degenerates into a cozy bourgeois ritual. In this story, most girls are eager to let themselves get
caught by eligible young men and hence be rescued from the tyranny
of "a straitlaced, domineering sire who exacted utter submission from

his terrorized women-folk and who was even then preparing to expel his growing sons from the horde" (108). What might such a monster be, if not any average modern middle-class father viewed from the perspective of his teenaged children?

When Women Ruled

The notion that in prehistoric times there was originally a matriarchy that was later replaced by the now-universal patriarchy was first developed in *Das Mutterrecht* (1861; partially translated as *Myth, Religion and Mother Right* in 1967) by the Swiss anthropologist Johann Jakob Bachofen. This idea, which found considerable academic support at the time, was not a feminist one; its champions believed that patriarchy was an evolutionary advance over matriarchy: a hierarchically organized rule of the masculine mind had superseded the anarchic rule of the feminine body.[5]

As Cynthia Eller has persuasively argued in *The Myth of Matriarchal Prehistory* (2000), the primal matriarchate was almost certainly a nineteenth-century anthropological fantasy. But it continues to be invoked for feminist purposes, as for example in Marilyn French's *From Eve to Dawn: A History of Women* (2002), which begins:

> At some point in the distant past, but probably not much further back than twelve or ten thousand years, men rose in rebellion against women. They felt dominated by women, even though there were probably no political structures of domination. Women were central to society and they supported men; men may have felt marginal or left out, but they wanted children to be theirs instead of women's. To accomplish this transfer, they had to push aside mother-right (the right to name the child and control its labor) and so they invented patrilineality, naming the children for their fathers. But this connection is tricky, since fatherhood, before DNA testing, could never be assured. To guarantee paternity they had to control women, keep them under surveillance, and, in effect, own them. The revolution was a violent one. (7)

In spite of her reference to the "distant past," French is here suggesting that patriarchy was imposed toward the end of prehistory—perhaps during the Neolithic Revolution. This makes it a relatively recent phenomenon, given the approximately 100,000 years since anatomically modern human beings first appeared.

There is evidence that hunter-gatherer cultures that have survived into modern times are more sexually egalitarian than pastoral or agricultural cultures. But such does not prove that Stone Age women once effectively held power over men. The Paleolithic lasted an immensely long time over a huge swath of territory and there is simply too little hard evidence of any kind from which to generalize about prehistoric sexual politics. The appeal of the primal matriarchate, however, is utopian and nostalgic and is little diminished by lack of evidence. It is based upon the thoroughly conditioned intuition that in the past humanity fell from an Edenic state of uterine peace into the testosterone-fueled nightmare of history. Given pf's characteristic urge to revise Genesis, one might imagine that the supersession of matriarchy would have become a recurrent topic for feminist exploration in the genre. Yet, only one pf writer has attempted to dramatize in any sustained way the "revolution" alluded to by French, and that writer was male.

For Vardis Fisher, anarchy was the primal human condition. It was succeeded by matriarchy only when humans had reached a certain level of intelligence and social organization. Then matriarchy was in turn superseded by patriarchy as the result of a male insurrection. Fisher believed that the typically asymmetrical sexual balance of power in human society derived from the fact that the biological roles of men and women were (and still are) incompatible: "A woman's unconscious desire was to be impregnated; and then, with her hunger stilled, she was content. A man's unconscious desire was to impregnate every adult female he could find, and from this blind drive in him he found no rest except in physical exhaustion" (*Darkness*, 259). Deprived of the corporeal and spiritual satisfaction endowed by motherhood, men are restless seekers, their endlessly unfulfilled sexual desire mutating easily into aggression and lust for conquest.

Wuh, Fisher's most primitive male protagonist, watches an army of ants methodically destroy a nest of wasps, and becomes violently aroused by the revelation that organized numbers of warriors can defeat a much larger individual foe:

> While Wuh was swinging his club and shouting and looking vainly for an enemy, Murah came out in a tantrum and scolded him and made him go away. She thought he was a stupid fellow to trumpet a war cry when there was nothing in sight to cry at. She did not understand her man, and Wuh did not understand his woman. While she had been nursing an infant, he had watched an army of ants destroy

an army of wasps. That was the difference between them, the difference between birth and murder, between peace and war. (258)

In the remainder of his pf quartet, Fisher anatomizes the incompati-
bility of Mars and Venus with admirable objectivity. His aim is to suggest how the Judeo-Christian myth of Adam and Eve, nonsensical if
read literally, but extremely powerful if understood as a parable justifying the patriarchal status quo, came to be generated.

In *The Golden Rooms*, our ancestors the Cro-Magnons consider the
Neanderthals to be subhuman and have no compunction in annihilat-
ing them, even though the two peoples are very similar, especially in
their ignorance. For example, neither understands the male role in
conception and both have a set of anxiety-driven beliefs and rituals
about menstruation. But certain small differences between the peoples
will have great consequences. In Harg's Neanderthal tribe of nomadic
scavengers, the women are almost of the same size and strength as the
men, and are even more savage when threatened by enemies. They all
live an animalistic existence with "very little sense of the future and
almost no memory of the past" (36). Consequently they live shame-
lessly in a state of almost total promiscuity. When Harg becomes
chief he celebrates by having sex with both his twin sister and his
mother, the latter of whom does not recognize Harg as her son as he
is no longer her dependent child. Gode's Cro-Magnons, in contrast,
have a brain much more capable of storing and retrieving memories.
Superior encephalization has led to the development of a moral law
among them, one ironic consequence being "more repression of the
rights of the weaker members" (174). Cro-Magnon men and women
are equally jealous and status-conscious, but their greater sexual dimorphism reflects a wider separation of social roles than that found
among the Neanderthals. Cro-Magnon men hunt while their women
are reduced to domestic tasks. More important, a Cro-Magnon woman
and her children are under the protection of—and are essentially the
possessions of—one man.

In *Intimations of Eve*, pastoralism starts to supervene over hunting
and gathering; now the developing notions of the ghost and the soul
mark the start of a human spiritual bondage, "the end of which is not
yet" (23). Lacking an understanding of paternity, humans' most important relationship is the one between mother and child. The balance of power has now tipped toward women; they hold the key to the
set of supernatural beliefs and rituals that supposedly assure female

fertility—and hence species continuity—because of their menstrual kinship with that unearthly entity, the moon:

> [Women] completed their cycle every time the Moon Woman completed her cycle from youth to age; and so they knew that the moon was a woman and was like all women except in her discovery of the secret of youth. Because she had discovered this secret and now lived above the earth, eternally in her own special home, it was in her power to fertilize the earth's women or to make them barren, to give babies or deny them, and to control, in ways wholly mysterious and unpredictable, the whole pattern of human life. (13)

Because of their lunar connection, "all women, but especially old ones, were in possession of mysterious and dreadful magic" (31). "[B]ecause hate is a blind and unreasoning defense against a fearful object that is not understood" (143), men instinctively have come to hate women. In other words, misogyny originated in men's fear at women's uncanny power, a power expressed in the mystery of birth and reproduction that is symbolically reenacted in the heavens by the moon as it goes through its phases. Raven, a man spiritually restless and humiliated by his sense of inferiority to women, will invent the idea of a witch and tie all the evil in the world to her. This strategy cannot be successful, however, until Moon Woman, the goddess upon whom all good fortune depends, is replaced by a male deity.

The development of agriculture during the early Neolithic age, one of the most important of all social revolutions, was according to Fisher in *Adam and the Serpent* entirely initiated by women. Nevertheless, this was also the period when men regained their social dominance by what Fisher considers the greatest revolution of all. Dove, the male protagonist, discovers in the sun a symbol of spiritual power that *must* be male because, as the source of daylight, it stands in symbolic opposition to the female moon that wanders abroad only at night. Dove then becomes a solar wizard (his descendants will be priests) whose chief doctrine will be to attribute all the world's evil to his usurped counterpart, the lunar witch. Under the new patriarchate, the Great Mother, the female supreme deity once known as Moon Woman, will be reincarnated as fallen Eve. Motifs formerly held sacred by women are now invested with evil: they include the serpent, an erstwhile symbol of the object of women's sexual passion because it resembles the male organ and "reincarnates" itself by sloughing its skin; and the apple, once made by women into an alcoholic beverage that stimulated sexual desire and hence encouraged men to impregnate them. Inspired by Dove's revelation of how sin entered the world, a man for the first time savagely beats a woman, "and this furious lunatic was giving a foretaste of the horrors to come—of all the incredible agonies to be suffered by millions in flame, on the rack, in dungeons, on the cross, because a mad prophet, shamed by his low estate and hating women, had boldly decided that they were the source of evil." (327–328).

For Fisher, then, the rule of women had been tyrannical, but the patriarchy would be even crueler. Men feared women's sexual power, envied their reproductive power, and harbored resentment for their own long political eclipse during the matriarchate. Even if the notion of the ancient rule of women is a fantasy, Fisher's quartet remains a rigorous and impressive attempt to infer from the Judeo-Christian account of human origin the unsavory prehistoric sexual politics that might have shaped this myth. Fisher's aim in his "Testament of Man" was nothing less than to discredit the story of Adam and Eve in Genesis as a source of moral guidance for the modern world.

Feminism

As Lori D. Hager has noted, the science of paleoanthropology itself "has traditionally been a male domain" (15), one in which women have not been encouraged to participate in fieldwork. Those few women who have made major discoveries, such as Mary Leakey (she brought to light both *Zinjanthropus* and the Laetoli footprints), have often had their contributions undervalued as a result of the sexist assumption that they were playing merely an ancillary role to their male colleagues. In paleoanthropology, moreover, there has always been a close connection between theories of prehistoric gender roles and the sociohistorical context in which the theorizing takes place. For example, in the 1960s, the highly influential "Man the Hunter" hypothesis[6] "suggested that the pursuit and acquisition of meat by males accounted for *all* morphological, technological, and social innovations that were the hallmark of 'mankind'"; females, who stayed at home, minded babies, and traded sex for meat, "were seen as peripheral to our evolutionary history" (5).

During the Second World War, in the enforced absence of servicemen from civilian life, many traditionally male jobs were taken by women. After the war, demobilized soldiers returned to the work-

force, ousting these women. To justify returning women to domestic-
ity, it became necessary to rationalize it theoretically. Hager suggests
that "Man the Hunter" not only "gave *credibility* to . . . late forties,
fifties and sixties sex roles of women as mothers and homemakers,"
but also "pointed to the *inevitability* of these roles because they were
'natural' or 'inherent' to our species" (5; emphasis in original). Even
some feminists of the period wrote off prehistoric women's lives. For
example, Simone de Beauvoir in *Le deuxième sexe* (1949; translated as
The Second Sex in 1952) stated that Paleolithic Woman, terribly handicapped by her reproductive function, was not even capable of engaging in what we would now call "activities"; she merely "submitted
passively to her biologic fate"—to give birth, to suckle infants (63).
The lot of women in the primitive horde was very hard; they were essentially domestic animals exploited to the death by men for their
labor and their reproductive capacities. Only man—*Homo faber* with
his club—was capable of transcending the animal condition and fur-
thering hominization (63).

It was not until the 1970s that female paleoanthropologists, their
confidence buoyed by cresting second-wave feminism, attempted to
restore full humanity to Paleolithic women by offering a counterblast
to "Man the Hunter." This rebuttal took the form of the "Woman the
Gatherer" hypothesis proposed by Sally Slocum in 1971.[7] Among
other points, Slocum argued that male bias in anthropology gave
prominence to activities associated with males, but that the evidence
from primatology suggested that hominid society centered on mothers and their offspring, while males, whose chief function was protec-
tive, were relatively peripheral. She further postulated that female
gathering was the primary mode of subsistence among primates; and
that the first hominid technological innovations were likely to have
been baby carriers devised by mothers so that their hands could be
freed to gather.

In 1975, Patricia Draper revealed that the women of the nomadic,
foraging !Kung tribe of the Kalahari Desert were highly knowledgeable about food sources and autonomously gathered the majority of
their tribe's food supplies. She concluded, however, that the state of
relative egalitarianism between the sexes in this hunter-gatherer society was quickly replaced by female subordination when a tribe settled
in a village to raise livestock and plant crops (109).[8] From such evidence, Adrienne Zihlman would later conclude, "custom, not nature,
makes women sedentary and dependent" (97). Though "Woman the

Gatherer" never became a mainstream paleoanthropological theory, it effectively demonstrated that those who summarily denied the possibility that females had been as important as males "as active agents of change" (Hager, 6) in hominization were impelled by sexism, not by scientific evidence.

For the greater part of its relatively short history, the science that brought pf into being was certainly male-dominated and androcentric. It frequently conceived of human prehistory as a time when women were as a matter of course brutalized, enslaved, sexually abused, and traded or exchanged by men as commodities, while female infants and old women were killed off as *bouches inutiles*. It is not unreasonable to conclude that early pf attracted few women authors or readers because paleoanthropology found little room for female interests or concerns. Yet this conclusion would be too great a simplification. Anglophone pf, though written mostly by men, had emerged at the same time as first-wave feminism and was often positively influenced by it. Wells, Waterloo, and London all provided active female characters who were the source of progressive tendencies in human evolution. Gratacap's Lhatto was nothing less than the embodiment of Goethe's "das ewige Weibliche" (The eternal feminine) even if her pedestalization may be read as an unconscious strategy of reducing Woman to Other. Few men before 1910 had ever written a more overtly feminist fiction of any kind than Ashton Hilliers's *The Master-Girl*. In it the Cro-Magnon female protagonist saves her man from a bear, kills her enemies and rivals with her invented bow, discovers firestones, rises to the leadership of her adopted tribe and, because she is barren herself, handpicks the women fit to bear her man's children. And in the aftermath of the Second World War, Vardis Fisher was evidently impelled by a desire to register the horrors to which unbridled patriarchy could lead, while William Golding in *The Inheritors* sympathetically gendered Neanderthals as gentle "feminine" victims of our brutal masculinist ancestors.[9]

Moreover, in a later, little-known work, Golding used early hominids to represent an essentialist vision of gender difference colored, if not by feminism, then certainly by philogyny. His pf novella "Clonk Clonk" (1971), set in East Africa 100,000 B.P., describes a protohuman society in which social harmony prevails because females make the important decisions while allowing the males to think they are in charge. Palm, a mature woman, decides that she is not too old to bear another child. Aided by her Bee Women she gets a male drunk and "rapes" him, later assuring him that the episode was all a dream. Through this story, Golding suggests that women's pragmatic realism is greatly preferable to men's comically deluded idealism.

Male pf had, then, often been sympathetic to women even if it had not been much read by them. Auel's *The Clan of the Cave Bear* marked a new phase in pf not in its subject matter but in its authorship, its intended readership, its aesthetic success, and its appearance at a key historical moment. Its unprecedented popularity as a pf novel derived from its being a highly imaginative work by a female author from a feminist perspective with a primarily female intended readership appearing just as liberal feminism was becoming mainstream. Indeed, Auel has placed on record that she had been a feminist as early as 1964: "I was 'the generation,' that Betty Friedan spoke to in *The Feminine Mystique*. And her book was a catalyst for me. . . . I wanted to be a person! I wanted to do something myself! And her book convinced me that I could *be* whatever I wanted to be" (Hitchcock, q.v.).

Auel's feminism is driven primarily by her aspiration toward liberation, not by ideological resentment. Of *Clan*, she states, "I had absolutely no intention of writing a feminist book. I was just writing a book that said, 'This is the book I always wanted to read.' 'This is the heroine that I didn't have when I was growing up,' because when I read books very often, if there were woman, or girls in them, they were kind of sitting around in the background being *Heroines! Waiting for someone to come and save them!* And I was always with the *protagonist*" (Hitchcock, q.v.; emphasis in original). Consequently, Ayla is a female protagonist who does not merely engage in "activities" but has adventures. She not only has all the main qualities—courage, physical strength, stoicism, independence—associated with traditional male heroes, but is also beautiful and feminine, making it easy for the typical female reader of romance fiction to identify with her.

The Clan of the Cave Bear (more than the later volumes in the Earth's Children series) has a strongly feminist agenda. Through Ayla, who teaches herself to hunt with a sling in spite of Clan interdiction, Auel is making a deliberate assault on the sexism underlying the "Man the Hunter" scenario. But Auel did not begin to shape her narrative with a prehistoric setting in mind. Rather, it would seem that she discovered that the vast lacuna of prehistory allowed her the imaginative latitude to create a credible female adventure hero, while history, with its grim documentation of female subordination, did not. If from a paleoanthropological perspective Auel's greatest achievement in *Clan* was to envisage perhaps the most plausible Neanderthal replacement scenario yet devised in fiction, for the common reader the strength of her novel was in Ayla's determination not merely to survive and endure, but actually to defeat and surmount patriarchy at its most repressive.

As individuals, most of the Clan are sympathetic characters; indeed, one of the ongoing themes of Earth's Children is that Neanderthals are not "flathead animals" (as the Cro-Magnon slur has it) but fully human beings. Still, the Clan is oppressively rigid in its gender roles. Clan women are supposed to be docile and incurious. They must look down when men speak, request permission from men before speaking themselves, avoid men during menstruation, favor their male infants, and assume a receptive position whenever men want to relieve their sexual needs. Moreover, until the advent of Ayla, Clan women do not understand that they are oppressed because they simply cannot conceive of a more balanced sexual politics.

Clan, then, may be read as a parable in which the deficiencies of an alien society in the remote past alert us to similar weaknesses in our own. Though Clan women may not acknowledge their oppression, we certainly do, thanks to the successful consciousness-raising of the second-wave feminist movement about the connection between sexuality and power in our own society. We recognize that Broud repeatedly rapes Ayla not from animal lust but because he is an insecure male exercising his power to suppress a female whom he perceives as a threat to his dominance. Indeed, no aspect of the Clan's oppressive sexual politics is truly unfamiliar to us, including its response to Ayla's perceived transgressions: "[Ayla] was living proof of what they had always maintained: if men were too lenient, women became lazy and insolent. Women needed the firm guidance of a strong hand. They were weak, willful creatures, unable to exert the self-control of men. They wanted men to command them, to keep them under control" (179).

In *Clan*, Auel eternalizes the sexual imbalance of power evident—albeit in different degrees—in all modern human societies by internalizing it within the brain structure of the Clan members. Her novel may in fact be read as a feminist dystopia. With the Clan, it is as though the fictional Sons of Jacob—that is, the patriarchal elite in Margaret Atwood's *The Handmaid's Tale* (1986)—or the real Taliban had been in power so long that female subordination had become literally innate. As Ayla by her nature cannot yield to Clan values, and the Clan by its nature cannot adapt to hers, in the end she must leave or die. (She leaves.) Auel suggests, then, that though the circumscribed gender roles among the Clan preclude conflict between the sexes, the Clan is doomed to extinction for its rigidity—as are all modern human societies that follow the Clan path. On the other hand, we who are truly Ayla's descendants will be saved by our "flexibility in gender roles" (Pollak, 299), even though the fact that these roles are less well defined may cause perpetual tension among us.

As formulated by Auel in *Clan* and its sequel *The Valley of Horses*, the quintessential prehistoric romance plot concerns a woman of independent mind who has been raped, impregnated, and outcast. Autonomous and self-sufficient by necessity, understandably wary of all men, she will eventually encounter a man from a different tribe who earns her trust and with whom she learns to enjoy the mutual pleasures of sexual intimacy. The male love interest in prehistoric romance, exemplified by Auel's Jondalar, tends to be more insipid than the rugged antiheroes who must be tamed by the heroines of conventional romance fiction. In the better prehistoric romances, however, the blandness of the male lovers is not a serious aesthetic defect: the female protagonist's struggle against patriarchy itself replaces the romance heroine's struggle to win a recalcitrant male love object. In this way, then, prehistoric romance as it descends from *The Clan of the Cave Bear* is not merely a feminism-influenced popular genre, but a feminism-inspired one.

To some readers, the most striking episode in *The Plains of Passage*, the fourth novel in the Earth's Children series, might seem to indicate that Auel herself subsequently changed her mind about feminism. Ayla and Jondalar encounter a tribe, the S'Armunai, led by the female chief Attaroa, who imposes her tyrannical will on her people with the help of her Amazonian guard, the Wolf Women. The males of her tribe are Attaroa's chief victims: she deliberately weakens the men by semistarvation and keeps them imprisoned and enslaved, while she mutilates male children or even has them killed. The S'Armunai are the most dysfunctional tribe in the Earth's Children series, and they are led by a woman. Has Auel come around to the view that female leadership is a recipe for social chaos?

It would be a perverse misreading of Auel's intention so to conclude, as Clyde Wilcox has effectively demonstrated in his essay "The Not-So-Failed Feminism of Jean Auel" (1994). Auel's point is not that patriarchy is the only successful social structure; it is that female leaders can be just as monstrous as male ones if they refuse to share power and allow hatred and the desire for revenge to direct their actions. Attaroa was neglected and abused as a child, and later beaten by her sadistic mate. She responded by cultivating a perverted sexuality in which the infliction of pain became her only true pleasure. Her cruelty to all males in revenge for her suffering at the hands of one man is a sign of a mind seriously unbalanced: in fact, Attaroa is nothing less than "evil" (601, 623, 663) according to Auel's moral system. She is evil because she has *chosen* her moral path rather than being merely a victim of misfortune. Ayla recognizes in Attaroa a strong and once beautiful woman whose past hardships were not unlike her own. Ayla too was a motherless child who after puberty was frequently sexually abused. But Ayla did not blame all males for what Broud did to her, nor determine to avenge herself upon them by humiliating, torturing, or killing them. Indeed, Ayla believes that Attaroa (who had suffered abuse) is more morally delinquent than Broud (who had not), in that, unlike Attaroa, Broud "never purposely hurt children" (663).

In Auel's prehistoric world, tribes can be effectively led by either men or women, or co-led by both, as long as the individuals have appropriate leadership qualities. For society to function effectively, the sexes must at least "cooperate apart" (as among the Clan). Far more preferably, however, they should cooperate together as individuals of equal potential worth who, regardless of gender, strengthen their tribes by pooling their natural talents. Wilcox correctly concludes that a consistent "egalitarian feminism" (68) pervades Auel's work.

Megan Lindholm's *The Reindeer People* and its sequel, *Wolf's Brother*, set among Paleo-Lappish reindeer herders, closely reprise many elements of Auel's romance plot. Before the action begins, the protagonist, Tillu, was abducted from a southerly farming settlement and sexually enslaved by atavistic raiders. As a result, she gave birth to Kerlew, a boy with a series of physical and mental disorders resulting from his hybrid heritage. Indeed, Kerlew sometimes seems like an alien to his mother. A self-taught healer, Tillu finds a niche among Northern reindeer herders, whom she first thinks of as primitive. The novels track the tortuous course of her romance with the herdsman Heckram, a paragon of manhood who proves his trustworthiness by his fatherly care of her difficult son.

The strength of Lindholm's saga is not in the twists of the mating drama, but in the way that it traces the flowering of Tillu's selfhood, even though she is an outsider in a society apparently less advanced than the one into which she was born. Carefully balancing her own needs with those of her dependent son, ignored as a mere female un-worthy of male attention, Tillu must stoically accept the severe con-straints on her freedom. Slowly she realizes that the women of this primitive herdfolk are not so downtrodden as she had assumed them to be: they retain their property after marriage and take quiet pride in their independence. Indeed, the herdlord's daughter, Keri, seems to express a radical independence of thought far in advance of Tillu's own aspirations. But the self-mutilating Keri is also not what she seems. Her apparent protofeminism turns out to be psychopatholog-ical, a symptom consequent upon the sexual abuse that she suffered as a child. Tillu's ultimate triumph, then, is not so much in her success-ful union with a worthy lover, or even in helping Kerlew to find his place in herder society. It is in coming to terms with a traumatic past and making the best of very difficult present circumstances rather than being broken by them, as Keri will be. In this way Lindholm foreshadows Auel's similar theme as it is expressed through the con-trast between Attaroa and Ayla in *The Plains of Passage*.

Good prehistoric romance like Auel's and Lindholm's does not assume that prehistoric life was easier for women than life in the mod-ern world. Nor does it contrive scenes in which the Paleolithic patri-archy has its consciousness raised by a precociously feminist protag-onist. Instead, it suggests that female autonomy, independence, and creativity could have been compatible with strongly male-dominated prehistoric social structures. It assumes, with some reason, that these female capacities must surely have remained adaptive for a long time or the rapid transformation of Western women's lives by feminism over the course of the past century would never have been possible. Had women's sphere been separate from and subordinate to men's throughout hominization, the fictional Ayla and her real daughters today might very well resemble the women of the Clan, unable to act autonomously and mentally incapable of learning privileged mascu-line pursuits like hunting. Good prehistoric romance, expanding on feminist paleoanthropologists' spirited rebuke to the formulators of the "Man the Hunter" scenario, refreshingly reminds the reader today that, in Claudine Cohen's phrase, "Prehistoric Man was a Woman too" (*La Femme des origines*, 7).

6.

▼
Race or the Human Race

> The combination of swarthiness with stature above the average
> and a long skull, confer upon me the serene impartiality of a
> mongrel; and, having given this pledge of fair dealing, I proceed
> to state the case for the hypothesis I am inclined to adopt.
>
> —T. H. Huxley, "The Aryan Question and
> Prehistoric Man" (1890)

> "I wonder just when they left the parent anthropoid stem,"
> mused Father. . . . "Are unions with them fertile, do you know?"
> "I won't be certain till I get back," said Uncle Ian cautiously.
>
> —Roy Lewis, *What We Did to Father* (1960)

Race or Races?

No nineteenth-century thinker was more committed to demolishing
the prejudices generated by the scriptural account of human origins
nor more eloquent in his appeal to educated people to subscribe to the
Darwinian "New Reformation" than T. H. Huxley. It was Huxley who
in *Evidence as to Man's Place in Nature* concluded that there was no
"cerebral barrier" (89) between man and ape. Even the human brain
does not render our species preternatural; we are part of the continuum connecting all the animal kingdom.

In the same work, Huxley eloquently summarized how much was at
stake as the greatest of modern intellectual revolutions was unfolding:

> The question of questions for mankind—the problem which under-
> lies all others, and is more deeply interesting than any other—is the
> ascertainment of the place which Man occupies in nature and of his
> relations to the universe of things. Whence our race has come; what
> are the limits of our power over nature, and of nature's power over
> us; to what goal we are tending; are the problems which present

themselves anew and with undiminished interest to every man born into the world. (52)

No less than the whole genre of pf has its seed in the phrase, "Whence our race has come," while the embryo of sf lies in "to what goal we are tending." Yet to the reader today the passage may be as striking for its blindness as for its insight. Huxley's use of the terms "mankind," "Man," and "his relations," and his reference to "every man born into the world," suggest that this eminent Victorian was incapable of imagining a world in which women were as equally human as men and might be equally interested in the question of our place in nature.

To accuse Huxley of sexism, however, is about as useful as blaming the Wright brothers for the September 11, 2001, terrorist attacks: it is to display an inadequate sensitivity to both Huxley's historical context and his probable intention. Still, Huxley, master of rhetoric, was not always so sensitive to nuance as he should have been. His use of "our race" in this passage was probably intended to be *inclusive;* that is, to refer to the human race, aka the biological species *Homo sapiens sapiens.* But many of Huxley's contemporaries will certainly have construed "our race" as an *exclusive* reference to "the English," "Anglo-Saxondom," or similar quasi-ethnological entity.[1] The modern conception of humanity as a single biological species owes much to Huxley. Nevertheless, from our current perspective he suffered from an impercipience about race that is analogous to his insensitivity to gender. For example, in *Man's Place in Nature* he notes, "Since the revival of learning . . . the Western races of Europe were enabled to enter upon th[e] progress towards true knowledge" (53). We may interpret these (plural) "Western races of Europe" as groups of people differentiated from each other by cultural markers such as language, religion, or national boundaries, and who are in turn distinct from the putative "Eastern races of Europe," "African races," and so forth. Yet Huxley knew as well as any of his contemporaries that all members of these distinct "races" belong to the (singular) "human race" because they are potentially capable of producing fertile offspring by mating with other members of our species. In this context, his nonchalant addition of a terminal "s" to "race" has the unfortunate consequence of dissolving biological unity into a chaos of competing interests.

When under an external threat that is real or perceived, there would seem to be a universal human tendency to identify aggressively with one's tribal group as though it were an extension of oneself, while demonizing strangers or relegating them to subhumanity. During such episodes, markers of difference that are physiologically trivial, such as height, skin color, or nose shape, are inflated into quasi-biological determinants of hostile otherness. Such would seem to be the basis of racism in its most virulent, genocidal form, and the history of the twentieth century indicates that the cultural sophistication claimed by developed nations provides no immunity against it. In this light, we deem Huxley naïve in his confidence in the progress of "the Western races of Europe" toward "true knowledge."

As one of the cultural products of these "Western races," pf in its short history has inevitably reflected and promoted many of the fallacious ideas deriving from the confusion between biological species and ethnological group. Berthet and Wells, for example, both assumed that there was a "racial" continuity between Paleolithic peoples living on the banks of the Seine or Thames and modern Parisians or Londoners. Such an error, more forgivable in an era when absolute dating was impossible, arises chiefly from a failure to comprehend just how fleeting is the whole of recorded history in comparison to the millennial timescale of the Stone Age.

The error was not entirely harmless, however. When mated with progressionism it often gave birth to the idea of a prehistoric master race (typically the Aryans) destined to prevail at the expense of lesser races. The atavistic Neanderthal used in racial opposition to the progressive Aryan is often found in early pf and, though purged of its cruder elements, the binary motif remains important in Auel's Earth's Children series. The eugenic movement, based on an illusion whose dangers were not fully exposed until the Nazi era, influenced much pf before 1945. Polygenism, which claimed that modern human ethnic groups originated in a very ancient divergence (and consequently are very different from one another), strongly influenced Jules Verne. In the modified shape of the "Multiregional Evolution" hypothesis it continued to have major supporters until recently.

At present monogenist ideas seem to be prevailing as a result of genetic research tracing mitochondrial DNA. The "Out of Africa" hypothesis of Christopher Stringer, for example, holds that all living human beings descend from a small number of African women who lived a mere 100,000–200,000 B.P.[2] Though the popular embodiment of our common ancestor, "Mitochondrial Eve,"[3] is probably as mythical as the unlamented Aryans, monogenism does promote the essential unity of humanity and thus is in harmony with the humanities as a cultural project. Whether the monogenists are correct or not remains to be seen; we can, however, say that the truth that humanity is one species is more likely to conduce to our survival—and is therefore more important and valuable—than the truth that individual human beings show great phenotypic diversity. Similarly, pf (or indeed any artistic product) that affirms that, despite our differences, all human beings are united in their fundamental humanity, is likely to be more culturally valuable and aesthetically praiseworthy than counterclaims that our differences are unbridgeable because of primal racial incompatibilities.

The Rise and Fall of Prehistoric White Supremacism

The history of pf demonstrates very clearly the remarkable shift in attitudes toward race that came about after the Second World War, when after the defeat of Nazism it was almost impossible not to acknowledge the disastrous consequences of a supremacist ideology. From its beginning through 1945, pf had sought explanations in prehistory for the rise of nations consisting largely of white people of European ancestry to a position of global hegemony. During this period it was usually taken for granted that a white skin indicated the possessor's physical, intellectual, and moral superiority over those with darker skins. After 1945, when it became clear that a racist ideology could lead to genocidal insanity, there was a sharp revulsion against white supremacism in pf. The assumptions that the prehistoric ancestors of Huxley's "Western races of Europe" were both white and morally superior to their now-extinct contemporaries came under interrogation.

Many authors of early pf had not been immune from racial determinism, as it was seemingly supported by orthodox Darwinism and hence needed no supernatural validation. For example, a scenario "explaining" the prehistoric origin of Nordic supremacy may be found in "Ice," book 2 of Jensen's *The Long Journey*. According to Jensen, northern Europe was once subtropical forest, but the coming of the Pleistocene ice rapidly transformed the landscape. The aboriginal Europeans, apelike jungle dwellers, were forced to make a choice. Some retreated southward, thereby retaining their lifestyle. Others, under their leader Carl, chose to stay in the north and adapt to the new subglacial conditions. Hence humanity subdivided. Geographical separation, compounded by time, led to divergence, and "the gulf between the two races parted by the Ice became a profound eternal chasm" (147).

The Ice Folk (aka the sons of Carl) found it hard to adapt to their new harsher conditions, but the ensuing Darwinian struggle quickly winnowed out the weaklings:

> The sons of Carl grew big and strong as bears in their toilsome hunters' life on the ice-sheet. The clothes they wore made their own coat of hair superfluous, their skins became red and white from living in the shade. The everlasting wet weather bleached their hair, and their massive-browed eyes, which once had been as dark as the confines of the forest, took their color from the crevasses of the glacier and from the open, blue-green blink of the horizon between ice and sky. (147)

Their human nature also differed profoundly from that of their lazy cousins of the tropics: "they had to remember and think ahead if they were to survive the seasons. In place of the passion, harmless enough, of primitive man, they had assumed a self-command which might have an air of coldness" (148). So, in Jensen's sons of Carl we recognize the prehistoric origin of the Aryans. This Nordic master race, supposedly improved and purified by natural selection, bore in its pallid features the signs of its long and inevitable path to political ascendancy.

After 1945, those who were no longer convinced by the association between Nordicity and moral superiority began to expose the flaws in Jensen's racial logic. Perhaps the most obvious lay in the fact that the aboriginal inhabitants of western Europe who lived below the Pleistocene ice sheets were not Paleo-Vikings but the apelike troglodytes of the popular imagination—Neanderthals. The rehabilitation of the Neanderthals in both science and fiction began with the acknowledgment that their dehumanization had been motivated by a prejudice indistinguishable from racism.

In Poul Anderson's prehistoric sf story "The Long Remembering" (1957), an impecunious graduate student volunteers to return to the Upper Paleolithic as part of an experiment enabling him to inhabit the mind of his Cro-Magnon ancestor. He becomes the hunter Argnach, whose blonde and blue-eyed woman Evavy has been stolen by Neanderthals, viewed by the Cro-Magnons as demonic goblins. But Argnach's heroic rescue of the damsel in distress quickly assumes a unexpected poignancy when he discovers that the Neanderthals are a fair-skinned, blue-eyed, peaceable people who had reclaimed the hybrid Evavy as one of their own. Argnach comes to realize that Evavy was more comfortable with the Neanderthals than among the darker-skinned, aggressive Cro-Magnons.

Similarly, in Björn Kurtén's *Dance of the Tiger*, the Cro-Magnon interlopers in northern Europe carry "the inheritance of a long line of ancestors from sun-scorched steppes far away. They called themselves Men; others called them Black" (28). Intensely patriarchal and violent, they owe their ascendancy not to moral superiority but to the ruthless use of advanced weaponry. In contrast, the Neanderthal aboriginals are kindly, vegetarian, and fair-skinned. As skin color has always been a vexed issue when dealing with racial questions, Kurtén is careful to justify his choices in his author's note, "As a rule . . . people living at high latitudes have lighter pigmentation than the inhabitants of tropical and subtropical regions. . . . As the Neandertals had lived in Europe for a very long time, the inference that they were light-skinned is obvious" (251).

In truth, there is currently no evidence from which the skin, eye, or hair color of Paleolithic human beings, be they Neanderthal or Cro-Magnon, can be determined. Nevertheless, Kurtén's ironic reattribution of positive racial characteristics to a disfavored Other is typical of the postwar attempt to revise dangerous racial stereotypes. Such a strategy was naturally based on the realization, in the light of recent history, of the sad untruth of claims that white skin conferred a moral superiority on its possessors. In the knowledge that Africa was now the accepted cradle of mankind, Lewis in *What We Did to Father* amusingly satirizes the fallacious logic of white supremacists. The peripatetic Uncle Ian notes that some fellow Africans are "going in for black skins" to keep off the sun, to which Father replies: "No good will come of that. The only sensible colour for human skin is dark brown or serviceable khaki—the colour of the veldt, the colour of lions. I regard that as settled from an evolutionary point of view. [Next thing you will be telling me you met with some hominid species going in for *white* skins!]" (72). Father's witticism is greeted with a gale of laughter by the assembled company.[4]

The Neanderthal as Racial Other

Neanderthals were the first fossil hominids to be identified because they had inhabited western Europe for millennia and left their remains where the first paleoanthropologists, all western Europeans, were likely to find them. Neanderthal limb bones are relatively more massive than most modern humans' and the brow ridges of Neanderthal skulls are more prominent. In the Darwinian aftermath it was almost inevitable that these features would recall the gorilla, the most massive living ape and the one with the largest superciliary ridge. In the 1860s the gorilla was very much in the news; indeed, a "Great Gorilla Controversy," incited by the writings and specimens of the American explorer Paul Du Chaillu, was raging.[5] At issue was the nature of the relation between ape and man in the light of new evolutionary theory.

In 1863 Huxley had carefully argued that there was "no absolute structural line of demarcation" (*Evidence*, 102) between man and the great apes; that man was closer to apes than apes were to monkeys; and that from the limited fossil evidence, Neanderthals were much closer to us than to the ape. But his fine distinctions or nondistinctions were frequently ignored in the emotive light of the "self-evident" similarities between gorillas and Neanderthals and the equally "obvious" differences between both of them and ourselves. Huxley emphasized the continuum between ape and man to demonstrate the strong evidence for our descent as an evolved animal rather than as a being specially created by God in his image. But many who could accept evolutionism in theory balked at embracing their inner gorilla or Neanderthal; Stevenson's Mr. Hyde and Frémiet's "Gorilla" sculpture both embodied the horror generated by such an idea. So the unacceptable beast within was expelled by reconfiguring Huxley's horizontal continuum as a vertical hierarchy that was based on an apartheid (racial separation) principle (see, for example, Blake, cxli). The following schema underlying modern "scientific" racism was generated:

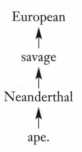

European

↑

savage

↑

Neanderthal

↑

ape.

After the physically impressive, modern-looking Cro-Magnon fossil remains were first found in 1868, the dawning realization that they and the now-extinct Neanderthals had inhabited the same western European territory generated early attempts in pf to imagine a racial conflict between these peoples. The underlying assumption, difficult at the time to resist, was that the victors of this prehistoric battle were our ancestors, who in superseding a "lower race" proved the inevitability of progress in general, the transcendent destiny of whichever European "race" one identified as victorious, or both. Moreover, if one began from the assumption that Neanderthals had been of all humans "closest to the ape," their "conquerors" would surely be identifiable by features demonstrating their remoteness from the ape. Because the ape was construed as a gorilla, that is, as a squat, brutish, hairy, dark-colored inhabitant of central Africa, so the conquering master race must have been tall, elegant, smooth-skinned, blond, and Nordic.

In *An Essay on the Inequality of the Human Races* (1853–55), the French aristocrat and white supremacist Arthur de Gobineau had identified Nordic features with the Aryans, a people who spoke the hypothetical language that was the common ancestor of the Indo-European family of languages. There was no archaeological evidence that the Aryans had actually existed, but that did not stop post-Darwinian pseudoscience from bringing them back to life. The theosophist Helena Blavatsky in *The Secret Doctrine* (1888) would attribute a privileged essence to the Aryans and contrast their virtues with the defects of their supposedly degenerate offshoot, the equally mythic "Semitic race."[6] Blavatsky's idea was twisted further into a pseudoscientific doctrine of racial supremacy by the Pan-Germanist Houston Stewart Chamberlain in *The Foundations of the Nineteenth Century* (1899), and would later find its apotheosis in the genocidal policies of Nazi Germany.

Aware of how easily biological and cultural features of humanity can be confused when a short historical timescale is ignorantly superimposed upon an almost inconceivably long evolutionary one, Huxley warned in his important late essay "The Aryan Question and Pre-Historic Man" that language and ethnic origin have no necessary correlation with each other. He went on to carefully define a race as a subdivision of the human species containing certain distinct but physiologically trivial heritable characters—essentially what we now call an ethnic group. In the light of the 1886 discoveries of Neanderthal remains at Spy, Belgium, he suggested, too, that as such a vast period of time separates us from the Neanderthals, they might have subsequently evolved into modern human beings and thus have been our direct ancestors. But Huxley's scientific caution was no match for the euphoric appeal in identifying with a victorious race, especially as the imperialist tide of the late nineteenth century encouraged white Europeans to believe that it was their destiny to dominate the globe.

The case of "Le Vieillard" (The old man) suggests how difficult it was to maintain scientific objectivity once the hierarchical structure of scientific racism had been firmly implanted in people's minds. In 1908 an almost complete skeleton of a male Neanderthal was found at La Chapelle-aux-Saints in France. This "Old Man" had been more than fifty years old at his death and had been intentionally buried. Marcellin Boule, France's leading paleontologist, began work on describing and interpreting the remains, and between 1911 and 1913 produced a monograph that was "of such thoroughness and merit that it established the paleontology of humans—paleoanthropology, as it would later be called—as a scientific discipline" (Trinkaus and Shipman, 190). Yet experts have since concluded that Boule's "objective" description was seriously distorted and led to a false image of Neanderthals, one that persists even today in popular culture.

It is now suspected that Neanderthals became extinct in Europe as recently as 24,000 B.P.[7] Before then, they certainly coexisted for millennia with our ancestors and may have interbred with them. In 1908, however, Boule was "inclined to believe that Neandertals had nothing to do with human ancestry, and his anatomical analysis succeeded in expelling these brutish forms from the human family tree" (194). The Old Man had been arthritic and his skeleton bore many signs of a hard life. From this Boule generalized that all Neanderthals had been stooped, slouching, brutish ape-men. Evidently he was temperamentally unable to identify this former inhabitant of the upper Dordogne valley as an ancestral Frenchman of whom he could be proud.

The evidence from the earliest pf suggests that Boule's dehumanization of the Neanderthal was not so much a product of rational deduction as the consequence of an emotional reaction already thoroughly conditioned by scientific racism. As we have seen, as early as 1876 Berthet, extrapolating from "the fact . . . that in those remote ages two different races of men inhabited the banks of the Seine" (36),[8] had used the site of Paris as the stage for a contest to the death between Red, an atavistic ogre, and Fair-Hair, a progressive proto-Celt, for the hand of the maiden Deer. Berthet attributes to Red hairiness, massive strength, a solitary condition, nonexistent social graces, and brutality toward women: he is indeed a "Neanderthal" in the current informal sense of the word.[9] Fair-Hair, on the other hand, has bright eyes, a good-humored expression, long silky blond hair, and a complexion "fair as that of the Celtic race from which we have descended" (36). Moreover, Fair-Hair has fallen in love with Deer, wooed her with gifts of his skillful ivory carvings, and "become engaged with the consent of the parents" (37). As befits a respectable Paleo-Parisian with good prospects, he is prepared to postpone marriage until he can find a cave of his own. Through Fair-Hair's defeat of Red and union with Deer, Berthet suggests that our racial destiny was secured by the elimination of the Neanderthal.

Berthet's characterization of Red as a fairy-tale ogre is unsurprising given the Neanderthals' early notoriety as devourers of human flesh. The Neanderthal-as-cannibal hypothesis seems to have derived from a series of misunderstandings and mistranslations in discussions about the discovery of the La Naulette jaw in 1866. It would later be reinforced by interpretations of the many fragmentary Neanderthal remains found at Krapina, Croatia, from 1899. By 1939 the broken fossil skull of a Neanderthal found in the Grotta Guattari in Italy was interpreted as having been deliberately opened so the brain could be extracted and eaten.[10] But the cannibalism hypothesis probably has less to do with actual evidence than with the way that the human imagination is conditioned by prejudice: "there is no more universally common way of distancing oneself from other people than to call them cannibals. It is one of the ultimate insults, one of the definitive signs of nonhumanity" (Trinkaus and Shipman, 105). Few imputed habits tend to dehumanize more than the enthusiastic consumption of babies and human brains.

The work of pf that probably did most to dehumanize—and demonize—the Neanderthals was H. G. Wells's "The Grisly Folk," a short fictionalized dramatization of material in two consecutive chapters of his *Outline of History*. In "A Story of the Stone Age," Wells, following Berthet, had identified the Neanderthal as an atavistic strain within humanity that had been eliminated, or at least suppressed, by the victory of our more progressive ancestors. But after Boule's definitive dehumanization of the Old Man, Wells now promoted a scenario in which "so-called men" who were "not of our blood, not our ancestors" came into conflict with "the true men" as the latter "came wandering into Europe" (607–608). Though Wells knew that Neanderthals had teeth that were "less like the apes' than ours," as well as a brain "big as a modern man's" (609), he nevertheless emphasized differences that were (and still are) largely speculative. Neanderthals were "probably" speechless; they were "perhaps bristly or hairy in some queer inhuman fashion" (609); they "must have been almost solitary creatures" (610); they were "stupid" (618); and they "thought the little children of men fair game and pleasant eating" (619).

Of all his contemporaries, the author of *The Time Machine* might have been expected to have acknowledged the incommensurability between the timescales associated with, on the one hand, cultural production and, on the other, biological evolution. Yet Wells now suggested that "[t]he legends of ogres and man-eating giants that haunt the childhood of the world may descend to us from those ancient days of fear" (618), thereby compressing almost to a vanishing point the vast chasm of time between ourselves and the end of the Pleistocene. In so doing he ignored a far likelier explanation: that Neanderthal man had been cast in the conveniently preexisting role occupied by legendary monsters in order to serve the cultural function of subhuman Other whose menacing presence serves to heighten "racial" solidarity.

In truth, Wells was no more a racist than his intellectual hero Huxley, and "The Grisly Folk" is free from many aspects of the pervasive racial determinism of its period. Wells's "true men," the ones who were "our ancestors," are not idealized Aryans, for "the fairness of the European" had not yet evolved; they were "brownish brown-eyed people with wavy dark hair" who painted their naked bodies with colored ochre (612). As is clear from *The Outline of History*, Wells conceived them rather as Arcelin had depicted his Solutreans, even noting that their "pictorial . . . disposition" suggests their affinities with American Indians (1:90).[11]

Wells was not personally responsible for expelling the Neanderthals from humanity. He merely collaborated in a process long under way, one in which cultural conditioning had always gotten the better of scientific objectivity. That the dehumanization of the Neanderthal in "The Grisly Folk" had been fueled by sentiments identical to those responsible for scientific racism only became fully evident a generation after Wells's story was published. William Golding, writing with Wells in mind in the aftermath of the Second World War, would suggest in *The Inheritors* that there was a human disposition to genocide that long predated Nazi Germany. Be it in the Upper Paleolithic or today, our inhibitions against murder can be overridden if we can be persuaded to view our victims as biologically subhuman. After

Auschwitz, the claim of the long-extinct Neanderthals to a common humanity rebuked us, perhaps because we were better attuned to their bones' mute appeal.

In "The Grisly Folk," a Cro-Magnon girl who had ventured too far from the tribe is stolen by a gray, hairy ogre and subsequently killed and eaten. Click, the chief of the true men, will henceforth be stirred into righteous anger by "the cry of the lost girl" in his imagination (617). After this primal atrocity, the true men, whose instinct was to recognize the Neanderthals as fellow human beings, would now deal with them as though they were dangerous animals to be ruthlessly exterminated.[12] So humanity has always dealt with competing predators who will not learn to avoid us and cannot be domesticated. Wells, then, affixes cannibalism, the "definitive sign of nonhumanity," to the Grisly Folk, thereby exonerating us for their extinction.

Cannibalism subsequently played a central role in Golding's project to expose the unwitting but dangerous prejudices that govern how we define who is or is not human. In *The Inheritors*, the Neanderthals are chiefly vegetarian and have a taboo against killing living creatures. They do practice ritual intratribal cannibalism, but only for a noble motive, namely, to internalize the virtues of their deceased fellows. When Mal, the oldest of the tribe, is dying, he warns the others, "Do not open my head and my bones. You would only taste weakness" (87), thereby modestly indicating that he no longer possesses qualities worth absorbing.[13]

By contrast, the New People, the conquering Cro-Magnon invaders from whom we are descended, are gratuitous devourers of extratribal human flesh. In a precise inversion of the scene in "The Grisly Folk," the Neanderthal girl Liku is abducted by the New People. Though Tanakil, the daughter of one of the New People, finds Liku quite human enough to befriend, the Neanderthal girl will soon be killed and eaten during a drunken orgy. Golding conveys the full horror of this episode through indirection: first, through the desperate stratagems of Fa, Liku's mother, to shield Lok, Liku's naïvely trusting father, from knowledge of the atrocity; and second, through the catastrophic physical and mental decline of Tanakil as a result of her own tribe's actions. After butchering her playmate, the Cro-Magnons—in vain, as it turns out—offer Tanakil herself to the uncomprehending Neanderthals to assuage their guilt.

Our revulsion at these events is compounded by our sense of complicity in them. As the inheritors of the New People's dark, complex genetic legacy, we seem as incapable as they were of retaining our moral innocence, and are just as likely to project our burden of guilt and shame at our fallen state onto a racial Other. Then, having demonized the Other as sub- or nonhuman, we proceed to annihilate the intolerable monster of our own creation. To further his ironic inversion of "racial" stereotypes, Golding's peaceful Neanderthals are covered with ogrish red hair, while our ancestors have skin as white and smooth as bone (106).

Multiculturalism, Exogamy, and the Neanderthals

The genetic evidence currently suggests that there was probably little interbreeding between western European Neanderthals and modern human beings of European ancestry, so the former are unlikely to be our lineal ancestors: Boule was right, but for the wrong reasons. Nevertheless, in recent pf the moral rehabilitation of the Neanderthal has continued apace; after Golding, the Neanderthal was much likelier to figure as a sympathetic character, or as a positive internalized genetic heritage, than as a grisly monster.[14] It is as though recent pf writers have felt obliged both to atone for past sins and to affirm contemporary racially inclusive or multicultural values.

In *Child of Time* by Isaac Asimov and Robert Silverberg (b. 1935),[15] Timmie, a three-year-old Neanderthal boy, is snatched from 40,000 B.P. to our time, where he is caged in a temporal bubble called the Stasis. His nurse, Miss Edith Fellowes, considers Neanderthals to be primitive brutish creatures. Only after prolonged contact with Timmie does she learn to distrust the voices of her human education. Timmie's playmate, the human boy Jerry, constructs neater pyramids of wooden blocks than Timmie. Miss Fellowes reasons that perhaps this aptitude has less to do with innate differences, and more with social circumstances. Jerry has a physicist father who coaches him in block construction techniques, while Timmie had no blocks or father when growing up in the Middle Paleolithic. Soon thereafter, Miss Fellowes, who had believed it pointless to try to teach Timmie to read, is shaken to discover that he has mastered the rudiments of literacy on his own. In this work Asimov and Silverberg have produced an overt parable in which the Neanderthal boy in his Stasis represents the disfavored racial Other who cannot join the modern world, not because he is unable to but because we won't let him.[16]

In a scene in the Paleolithic narrative frame of *Child of Time*, a Neanderthal woman offers herself sexually to a Cro-Magnon man but is rejected (41–42). The authors, perhaps with "The Grisly Folk" in mind, here suggest that our willingness to exterminate Neanderthals derived from our construction of them as uglier than they constructed us. But such an idea, in which the exogamic urge is trumped by racially based aesthetics, seems unconvincing, if only because the coauthors offer no plausible evolutionary reason why modern humans should have been sexually·attractive to Neanderthals but not vice versa. Kurtén, who describes much interbreeding in *Dance of the Tiger*, at least attempts to remedy this omission: invoking neoteny, he argues that "the 'childlike' features of the sapient face appeal[ed] to the tender emotions of the Neandertals"·(254).

In *The Clan of the Cave Bear*, Auel at first blush seems to be exploiting traditional aesthetic stereotypes in her construction of Ayla as a tall, blonde, blue-eyed, beautiful Aryan among squat, dark, beetle-browed Neanderthals. However, though Auel certainly uses a conventional ideal of feminine pulchritude to increase identification between her protagonist and readership, she avoids tying beauty and race too closely together because she wants to ensure that the Clan, as individuals, mostly retain our sympathy. Broud, however, is firmly excluded from that sympathy. Because he does *not* find Ayla beautiful, we understand more clearly that he rapes her purely to humiliate her, and these repeated violations seem therefore the more unforgivable, because they are motivated by no other passion than hatred.

Ayla is not beautiful in Clan eyes because she diverges markedly from the Neanderthal female aesthetic standard. (Because of her upbringing among the Clan, she is ugly in her own eyes too, and must readjust her aesthetic criteria when she joins her own kind; here Auel plays an extended variation on Andersen's fairy tale "The Ugly Duckling" [1844].) Yet most of the Clan treat with compassion a child whom they consider to be ugly and alien; they probably behave more humanely in this respect than most modern humans would if the roles had been reversed. While Broud is the only Clan member who is overtly prejudiced against Ayla, Cro-Magnon bigotry against Neanderthal "flathead animals" pervades the later books of the Earth's Children series. It will be one of Ayla's major tasks to try disabuse her congeners of what we recognize as nothing less than racism fueled by ignorance.

The *plot* function of Ranec of the Mamutoi in *The Mammoth Hunters*, the third novel in Auel's series, is to serve as Jondalar's rival for Ayla's affections. After much agonizing, Ayla eventually chooses

Jondalar, and sets off with him on the long journey (recounted in the sequel, *The Plains of Passage*) back to his people, the Zelandonii. What Ayla has learned from her liaison with Ranec is that physical attraction and sexual compatibility are not equivalent to love. With Ranec, there is something missing from the Pleasures that she can only find with Jondalar. Yet Ranec, a talented mobiliary artist, loves Ayla and treats her impeccably, and we sympathize with his devastation when Ayla rejects him for Jondalar.

But Ranec's chief *thematic* function has little to do with love. Wymez, a white Mamutoi man, fathered Ranec upon an African woman that he had met on a Journey of Initiation; he then brought the brown-skinned child back to live among the Mamutoi after Ranec's mother had died. The adult Ranec is strikingly different in appearance from all the other Mamutoi, yet he seems completely accepted by the tribe and Ayla immediately finds him physically attractive. Is Auel suggesting that our ancestors were blind or indifferent to differences of skin color, and that therefore racism in its most characteristic form is a modern invention?

The answer is certainly in the negative. Auel's Cro-Magnons immediately notice differences of skin color. When they are not under emotional stress, they tend to find these differences exotic and attractive: Wymez thought that Ranec's mother "was the most exciting woman I ever met" (*Mammoth Hunters*, 42), and Ranec feels the same way about Ayla. Prejudices quickly emerge, however, when the stress level rises. Under territorial pressure from rival tribes, the Africans had started to fear and hate Wymez and his child because of their lighter skins. The Mamutoi tribesman Frebec, insecure by temperament, dislikes the confident Ranec and thinks that there is "probably something unnatural about such dark skin" (227).

What keeps racism among Auel's Cro-Magnons at a low temperature is not that they do not notice or care about Ranec's visible difference, but that there are other markers than skin color that absorb most of their attention; namely, whatever factors differentiate themselves from the Neanderthals to their own advantage. The flatheads lead harsh lives on the margins of Cro-Magnon territory. The Cro-Magnons refer to them as animals (that is, as nonhumans), yet they know it is possible to interbreed with them. Indeed, in *The Plains of Passage* troublemakers like Charoli of the Losadunai and his gang go deliberately into Neanderthal territory to rape flathead women and beat and humiliate their men.

Yet racism among the Cro-Magnons is not only an ideology of delinquents. The Zelandonii, the most culturally advanced people in interstadial Europe, are among the most prejudiced against Neanderthals. The reason for this is suggested in *The Shelters of Stone*: the Zelandonii drove out the Neanderthal former occupants of their caves, an ugly task but one easier to accept ethically if they could pretend that their victims were animals ("little different from cave bears, perhaps even related to them" [174]). The Zelandonii's repressed communal guilt is a major source of their racist animus against Neanderthals. (Here is a parallel with the aftereffects of slavery in the United States.) Jondalar is all too aware that if his people find out that Ayla has borne a child of "mixed spirits, half-animal and half-human," they will view her as "an unspeakable abomination" (*Mammoth Hunters*, 213). In short, mainstream Cro-Magnon attitudes to Neanderthals are very similar to contemporary white racist attitudes to African Americans.

Jondalar's anxiety in *The Mammoth Hunters* about how his people will react to knowledge of Ayla's miscegenation underlies his emotional difficulties in responding to her and sets the thematic agenda for the later novels. In the course of her short life Ayla has invented the travois, the sewing needle, and surgical sutures, perfected the use of the sling as a weapon, helped Jondalar develop the spear thrower, has developed her own unprecedented ability to heal the sick, domesticate animals, and master languages, and has discovered firestones, Lascaux Cave, and the male role in conception. She even uses a contraceptive tea that allows her to have plenty of recreational sex with two different men, as well as participate in many other kinds of "adventures" unhampered by pregnancy. But the problems that she is able to solve seem almost incidental compared to the one looming as she and Jondalar head toward his home in the Vézère valley.

In Earth's Children, then, racism gradually replaces sexism as the greater threat to Ayla's human integrity, and by implication to our own. The series began with the Clan representing an oppressive patriarchy that Ayla had to free herself from if she was going to become "one of us." By its later stages, however, Neanderthals have mutated into the victims of "our" racist determination to dehumanize whomever we choose to cast in the role of Other. Yorga, the female flathead victim of Charoli's gang of rapists (*Plains of Passage*, 755) is blonde, and Ayla is stunned by this reminder of the Self in the Other, crying out not only for acknowledgment but also for justice.

Ayla's task, the moral equivalent of raising to manhood her lost son of mixed spirits, is now to plead the case to our ancestors for according full humanity to Neanderthals, including proper respect for their differences. That is why Ayla assumes the posture of female deference at the feet of Guban, the male flathead whose leg has been broken in his attempt to save Yorga from Charoli's gang, and waits for his tap on her shoulder allowing her to speak (761). This vignette might be from *The Clan of the Cave Bear*; placed in a very different context near the end of *The Plains of Passage*, it serves as a better indicator than mere mileage of the great distance that Ayla has traveled from her starting point among the Clan.

Monogenism versus Polygenism, Tropis versus Waggdis

Typically, nineteenth-century monogenists "championed the common origin of all humans from a single apelike ancestor"; polygenists, on the other hand, "believed the races had been created (or had arisen) separately and were thus as different as, say, robins and pelicans" (Shipman, *Evolution of Racism*, 76). But the debate between monogenists and polygenists in the post-Darwinian period was not strictly a scientific one. It was founded on a set of beliefs—or better, prejudices—not on a body of evidence, and one's affiliation was determined more by temperament than by the rational adjudication of facts.

The Bible would at first glance seem to uphold a monogenetic origin of humanity, in that everyone descends from Adam and Eve. But if it is assumed that Noah's Flood wiped out all the antediluvian human population not secured in the Ark, then modern humanity derives from one of Noah's three sons, Shem, Ham, and Japheth, from whom "was the whole earth overspread" after the Flood (Genesis 9:19). If these three sons are supposed to have begotten three different human races, then the Bible favors polygenesis. But by the later nineteenth century, it was scientists' ideological relation to Darwinism, as much as their scriptural beliefs, that determined their affiliation. Darwin was a monogenist; the leading anti-Darwinians Richard Owen in England and Rudolf Virchow in Germany were both polygenists.

So was Jules Verne: *The Village in the Treetops* constitutes his rearguard action against Darwinism as a theory promoting the unity of humanity. By 1901, Verne was prepared to concede continuity between human beings and the rest of animal creation, including apes. But he was only prepared to do so if this continuity were conceived as a "ladder" (100), the rungs of which were each fully occupied by different entities in ascending order, with the upper rungs occupied by the races of man, also in ascending order. Once this ladder was in place, what began as a species question, How are men different from apes? reformulated itself as a race question, Which kind of men are farthest from apes? In answering this question, Verne the pious Catholic invoked the theories of an anticlerical German disciple of Darwin who had differed from his master precisely over the question of the racial unity of mankind.

In 1867 Verne had revised *Journey to the Center of Earth* with the aim of casting doubt on the existence of extinct races of human beings by proposing that they might still be alive in the subterranean world. By 1901, however, Cuvierian catastrophism could no longer explain away the many intervening discoveries of fossil men. Verne himself acknowledged that Eugène Dubois had discovered in Java the remains of a creature who "really appeared to be an intermediary between the ape and man" (*Village*, 143; author's footnote). So in 1901 Verne adapted his strategy of 1867 to the changed paleoanthropological context, and thereby invented a new subgenre of pf. *The Village in the Treetops* is the first important work in which a lost race of prehistoric hominids survive into the modern age. By this new narrative strategy, Verne's aim was now not so much to deny the antiquity of man as to affirm that the chasm between his own race and people with darker skins was unbridgeable.

In describing the Waggdis, Verne refers to the claims of Carl Christoph Vogt as expressed in his once popular *Vorlesungen über den Menschen* (1863; translated as *Lectures on Man* in 1864), one of the first post-Darwinian works to deal with human evolutionary origins. Vogt was indebted to Darwin for the idea of human descent from apes, but diverged from his master by propounding a view that the human races originated in three different species of living ape. Verne summarizes Vogt's polygenetic hypothesis thus: "The Orang, a brachycephalic type with long brown hair, would . . . be an ancestor of the Negritos.[17] The Chimpanzee, a dolichocephalic type, with less massive jaws, would be the ancestor of the Negroes. Finally from the Gorilla, specialised by the development of the chest, the form of the foot, the gait, and the osteological character of body and limbs, had descended the White Man" (152–153). For Vogt, the human races were either already different species or originated in different species.[18] Unfortunately, both alternatives are equally wrong. All modern human beings can interbreed with all others, so cannot be of different species. And if there were three original human "races" evolving in parallel from different ape species, then they could not interbreed in the first place, let alone later undo speciation and converge. But Verne was only interested in the way that Vogt supported his vision of the ladder of creation.

The Waggdis do not represent a missing link between man and ape; they represent the missing link between black Africans and chimpanzees. The Waggdis are African; they live in treetop nests but have the "fleecy wool [that is, hair] of the natives of equatorial Africa" (151). They have very small heads like the microcephalic idiots that Vogt had invoked to "prove," by reference to the theory of atavism, a missing link between man and ape. The Waggdis walk upright, have no tail or prehensile foot, have identical dentition to ourselves, can speak, make fire, and build boats. They are gentle, have moral ideas and a sense of property, and exhibit family affection.

However, when the French ivory hunter Max Huber asks his American colleague John Cort why the Waggdis, in spite of all their similarities to ourselves, are not admissable into the ranks of humanity, Cort replies that they lack an idea "which is common to all men. . . . The conception of a Supreme Being. In one word, religion, which is found among the most savage tribes" (164). The Waggdis, then, have been constructed by Verne to demonstrate by default what defines true humanity. These missing links occupy the rung immediately below black Africans, when the latter are conceived of as the lowest human race. The Waggdi rung lies immediately above the one holding chimpanzees, which according to Vogt were the apes from which the black races derived. Verne thereby implies that black Africans occupy a place on the ladder of creation several rungs below whites, so that even if their full humanity is conceded, black Africans are still more biologically proximate to their ape progenitor than whites are to theirs. He has compressed Vogt's parallel but convergent evolution into an equally incoherent linear hierarchy based on race.

Having dehumanized the Waggdis in order to better define humanity, Verne then uses them to dehumanize people who have willingly abandoned the defining human feature that the Waggdis naturally lack: belief in a divinity. Such a one is the mad scientist Johausen, who has become the Waggdis' king. Johausen evidently suffers from a form of biological degeneration that either causes or is caused by loss of faith in God. In Verne's view, though a man can never ascend the ladder of race, he can fall by his own actions from civilization not merely into savagery but even into that state of godless subhumanity represented by the Waggdis.

Verne's recourse to Vogtian polygenism in *The Village in the Tree-tops* probably had little to do with any scientific objection to Darwinian monogenism. It is more likely that Verne felt that Darwin took offensively too little account of the width of the gulf between Jules Verne and his primate relatives. In 1944, Vardis Fisher in *The Golden Rooms* speculated on the prehistoric origin of race prejudice. His Cro-Magnons smear themselves with red ochre and knap arrowheads as they prepare the first-ever mass mobilization to exterminate the Neanderthals: "they were going to kill, not for the pleasure of killing, but to rid the world of a repulsive imposter who was trying to look like them. The emotion they felt was obscurely righteous in its intensity and fervor. In their simple and primitive way they were undertaking a crusade in an effort to make the world conform to their notions of what it should be" (261). More than forty years earlier, Jules Verne in *The Village in the Treetops* had expressed a similar sense of outraged privilege.

For Verne, the lower races demonstrated their inferiority biologically. Huber's and Cort's guide, Khamis the Cameroonian foreloper, "had that amazing calmness of the African of Arab blood, a blood thicker than that of the white man, which blunts the feelings and is less susceptible of physical pain" (34–35). Vercors, writing after the Second World War, felt that it was urgent to demonstrate how Verne's racist assumptions, typical of his time, came to be exploited by "those criminal racial hierarchies which we still have in odious memory" (138). For example, the ethical inhibitions of doctors about experimenting on living human subjects were removed by the Nazi recategorization of their patients as *Untermenschen* (subhumans).

At the beginning of *Borderline* the protagonist, Douglas Templemore, expresses views on the continuity of species that are identical to Jules Verne's: "Between the ape and man . . . or rather, d'you see, between an ape and an individual—and even, if you like, between the human animal and the individual—there I see a gulf" (37). But the tropis, as gentle as the Waggdis, seem to bridge this "gulf." Like apes they are covered with hair and have receding foreheads, almost no noses, and long fanglike canine teeth; but like humans they make fire, bury their dead, and speak a protolanguage (48). While the discovery of the tropis plunges Templemore into profound introspection about what constitutes his own humanity, others are less reflective. The capitalist sharks Vancruysen and Granett, arbitrarily deciding that tropis are livestock, draw up plans to use them as a cheap form of labor in woolen mills, having first gelded the males to make them more docile.

Meanwhile the anthropologist Julius Drexler, corrupted by his connections with big business, produces a scholarly article that justifies the capitalist exploitation of the tropis on "scientific" grounds:

> *The appearance of the tropis . . . proves that the oversimple notion of the oneness of the human species is inept. There is no human species, there is only a vast family of hominids, in a descending color scale, with the White Man— the true Man—at the top of the ladder, and at the bottom the tropi and the chimpanzee. We must abandon our old sentimental notions, and at last establish scientifically the hierarchy of the intermediate groups "improperly called human."* (83; emphasis in original)

Drexler, using the same pseudoscientific "ladder" trope as Verne, relegates the tropis to subhumanity, a state that will enable them to be exploited or killed at the will of a white supremacist political elite. It is Drexler's article that impels Douglas to perform the shocking act that he views as the only way of precipitating the ethical crisis that will force humanity to define itself inclusively in a way that will forever lay the *"grimacing ghost of racial discrimination . . . with its hellish attendants"* (83; emphasis in original).

For Vercors, the kind of racism that masquerades as cool, unsentimental, objective science had proved itself to be the most dangerous. But the close intertextual relationship between *The Village in the Treetops* and *Borderline* suggests that Vercors was certainly aware that the ghost that he was trying to lay was one that had manifested itself a long time before "those loathsome doctors in the camps of death" had made their claims "that the heinous experiments they had perpetrated were of great profit to human knowledge" (139). As William Golding would revise "The Grisly Folk" in order to subvert Wells's assumptions, so Vercors re-created Verne's scenario of the survival of a missing link, then used the species question arising from it to try to dissolve rather than reinforce ideas of racial difference.

7.

▼ ## A Cultural Triad
Language, Religion, Art

> Humans become human through intense learning not just of
> survival skills but of customs and social mores, kinship and social
> laws—that is, culture. . . . Culture can be said to be *the* human
> adaptation.
>
> —Richard Leakey, *The Origin of Humankind* (1994)

Language: Transitional Speech and the Ursprache

> "[I]t is really little more than a courtesy to call a language the few hundred sub-
> stantives we possess, the score of all-purpose verbs, the poverty of prepositions and
> postpositions, the continued reliance upon emphasis, gesture and onomatopoeia to
> eke out shortages of cases and tenses.
>
> —Roy Lewis, *What We Did to Father* (1960)

In Huxley's view, Victorian man's humiliation at his discovery of his
cousinship to the lower animals might be partly assuaged by the realization that he is a member of a uniquely gifted species: "He alone
possesses the marvelous endowment of intelligible and rational
speech, whereby . . . he has slowly accumulated and organized the experience which is almost wholly lost with the cessation of every individual life in other animals; so that now he stands raised upon it as on
a mountain top, far above the level of his humble fellows, and trans-
figured from his grosser nature by reflecting, here and there, a ray
from the infinite source of truth." (*Evidence*, 104). After Darwin, if
culture was the key to human nature, then language, our chief means
of accumulating, organizing, and transmitting knowledge, was surely
the key to culture. But how was human language different in kind
from the communication systems of our "humble fellows," and how
did it originate?

Huxley's admission that human language was a "marvelous endowment" was seized upon by creationists. The anti-Darwinian biologist

St. George Mivart, for example, noted that even among the lowest savages no example could be found of "men in a nascent state as to the power of speech" (50), proving that man's linguistic gift had not evolved but had come to us fully formed from the Creator. Consequently Darwin, when addressing the origin of human language, was far more circumspect than Huxley had been. On the one hand, "Articulate language is . . . peculiar to man" (*Descent*, 1:54); it "is an art, like brewing or baking"; and "[i]t certainly is not a true instinct, as every language has to be learnt" (1:55). On the other, parrots are also capable of articulate speech; the inarticulate cries that we make in common with the lower animals "are more expressive than any words" (1:54); and "man has an instinctive tendency to speak . . . whilst no child has an instinctive tendency to brew, bake, or write" (1:55).

Darwin's apparently self-contradictory musings reveal his extraordinary care to take into account all possible approaches to the remarkable phenomenon of human language. But for many of his disciples, the manifest fact of linguistic evolution proved not only that humans had evolved from lower creatures but also that some humans had evolved more than others. The record of extinct languages was much fuller than the fossil record,[1] so detailed linguistic genealogies could be constructed. The philologists who did so tended to work from two faulty assumptions: that there had been an exact correspondence in prehistory between language and race; and that their own language was the most perfect. Consequently, they concluded that those languages farthest from their own on the evolutionary tree were the most imperfect, and those languages' speakers the most racially inferior.

In 1848 the German philologist August Schleicher had divided all languages into three groups of unequal status. Isolating languages (for example, Chinese) were the simplest, consisting of unchanging monosyllabic root words. Agglutinating languages (for example, Turkish) affixed relational elements to these roots. Inflecting languages (for example, German) were the most complex, with an "organic" relation between a transformable root and affixes that allowed flexibility and subtlety of expression. Moreover, there was a direct relation between the complexity of a language and how far the "race" that spoke it could develop culturally. That languages could be arranged in families of different orders of complexity supported polygenism. Schleicher "believed that there was no one *Ursprache* [original language] whence the other languages descended; rather there were many *Ursprachen*, each having developed in different geographical regions out of cries of emotion, imitation, and ejaculation. Since language and thought were two sides of the same process, as language groups developed and evolved independently of one another, so did the different groups of human beings who spoke them." (Richards, 26–27) .

Schleicher's ideas were taken up by Ernst Haeckel, his colleague at the University of Jena. For Haeckel, the development of speech was "the most important stage in the process of the development of Man . . . which above all others helped to create the deep chasm between man and animal, and which also caused the most important progress in the mental activity and the perfecting of the brain connected with it" (2:300). Haeckel's famous missing link was an ape-man (*Pithecanthropus*) who was speechless (*alalus*). The historical analysis of language, however, demonstrated that the living human races did not descend equally from this link: "As, according to the unanimous opinion of most eminent philologists, all human languages are not derived from a common primaeval language, we must assume a polyphyletic [that is, polygenetic] origin of language, and in accordance with this a polyphyletic transition from speechless Ape-like Men to Genuine Men" (2:294).

Early pf writers were naturally eager to explore the idea that there were prehistoric "transitional" languages that served as missing links between animal sounds and human speech. Berthet, interested in the relation between linguistic "fitness" and racial extinction, was the first to explore transitional languages. His Paleolithic Parisians are not great conversationalists: "Language at that period . . . must have consisted of only a few hundred words, for there were no complex ideas to express. Most of the time they talked in monosyllables, or even by signs" (21). Nevertheless, Deer's taciturn family are linguistically more advanced than the subhuman Red, who announces his arrival with a "guttural cry . . . so harsh in its intonations that it might have been uttered by some animal in the forest" (22).

Red can speak, but like most dimwitted cavemen thereafter, he tends to omit verbs ("Fair-Hair bad hunter") and uses third person both to address an interlocutor ("Deer shall eat") and to refer to himself ("Red was the strongest") (30, 51, 54).[2] By making solecisms typical of small children or pidgin-speaking savages, he reveals his low mental powers. He has a poor grasp of higher abstractions—verbs being generally less concrete than substantives and demanding complex qualifications of number and tense—and he has little use for the first-person pronoun because of his animal lack of self-consciousness. When Deer, trying to defend her virtue, tells him that "the Great Spirit" punishes the wicked after death, Red, bursting into laughter, replies with unassailable logic, "Red is alive" (54). Ironically, these are his last words: too stupid to conceive of supernaturally ordained morality, he and his kind are fated to be swept away by our ancestors.

Other early pf writers, interested in the idea of transitional speech, lacked Berthet's narrative resources to represent it. Stanley Waterloo in his pf story "Christmas 200,000 B.C."(1899)[3] refers to the "queer 'clucking' sort of language, something like that of the Bushmen" (231) of his characters, but he actually represents their speech in standard English. Jules Verne in *The Village in the Treetops* wonders sardonically why, if Darwin's claim that we had monkeys for ancestors were true, scientists have so signally failed to interpret simian speech (84). Though his Waggdis flout Haeckel by being able to speak, Verne never allows us to hear what they have to say. Moreover, Dr. Johausen, their human "king," is no help as an interpreter: he has degenerated to the extent that, when addressed by John Cort, his "only response was to scratch himself in a very monkey-like fashion" (184).

In contrast, Louis A. Gratacap, who aimed to rehabilitate primeval man as a nobler version of our degenerate modern selves, implies in his opening "Apology" to *A Woman of the Ice Age* that he started from the assumption that his prehistoric characters spoke with modern fluency: "speech has necessitated structural modifications in the human brain *totally absent* from the brain of the Anthropoid Ape" (8; emphasis in original). In other words, for Gratacap it was part of the original divine intention to distinguish humanity from the rest of the animal creation, and Lhatto's fully formed speech is part of the evidence for this. Indeed, Lhatto is able to compose imagistic lyrics, which she sings to the sea:

> The fish swims in the deep water,
> The clouds swim with the fish,
> The sun buries his head there too.

(47)

Lhatto's natural poetic gift suggests that hers is not speech in transition between ape and man, but language fully attuned to nature in a way that has since been lost as art became ever more formalized.[4]

Pf writers in a more orthodox Darwinian vein found that they needed to develop appropriate conventions of representing transitional speech. The "guttural" name of Wells's hero Ugh-Lomi in "A Story of the Stone Age," and his and Eudena's tender exchange of "Waugh!" (678) as a greeting suggest the half-animal qualities of the protagonists. But inarticulate grunts do not make for absorbing dialogue. So Wells allows animals to converse among themselves and with human beings so as to suggest that the modern gulf between man and nature had not yet fully opened up. A squirrel scolds the exiled Eudena, "'What are you doing here . . . away from the other men beasts?' 'Peace,' said Eudena, but he only chattered more" (659). The pair of cave bears discuss the mystery of human fire while hyenas jeer at them from a safe distance: "Ya-ha! . . . Who eats roots like a pig?" (673).

Occasionally, pf writers have offered ingenious speculations on the origin and nature of the *Ursprache*. In Haraucourt's *Daâh*, the newly widowed Ta invents the affirmative concept "Yes" by bowing her head as a gesture of submission to her new master, while Daâh's first wife Hock, displeased at having to share meat with another woman, moves her head violently from side to side "as if she were trying to shake off something troublesome": "No!" (127). In *Borderline*, when one of Vercors's tropis refers to himself,

> he made a sort of inner murmur, a *mmm* which seemed embedded in the depth of his lungs. When, on the contrary, he wished to indicate someone else, he would eject between his teeth a very hard sound, a *ttt*, which he spat violently outwards. Pop wondered whether those two sounds . . . might not be at the origin of the words *me* and *thou*, which, in almost all the languages of the world, start with an *m* or with a *t* or *d* respectively. (65)

Jack London was the first pf writer to suggest that the conceptual poverty of a transitional language might have a tragic consequence for its speakers, rather than merely attest to their unfitness to survive. The peaceable Folk in *Before Adam* have a proto-isolating language with a vocabulary of thirty or forty sounds. Each sound refers to an object, but its meaning is qualified by context, intonation, quantity, pitch, and speed of delivery. Any new thing has to be expressed by a new sound whose meaning must be laboriously conveyed to others by repetition and supplementary pantomime. With such a limited linguistic instrument, would-be innovators are doomed to frustration: "Sometimes . . . we thought too long a distance in advance of our sounds, managed to achieve abstractions . . . which we failed utterly to make known to other folk" (41). Lacking the "thought-symbols" to coordinate their actions, the Folk are unable to expel the murderous atavism Red-Eye from their midst, and are easily exterminated when the cooperative Fire People, who have "speech that enabled them more effectively to reason" (197), decide to appropriate their territory.

In William Golding's *The Inheritors* the encounter between transitional speech and articulate language is raised into a major tragic theme. For Lok's Neanderthals, silence seems "so much more natural than speech" (34) and they do not suffer from their taciturnity. On the contrary, they commune and empathize with one another with an intensity impossible for modern human beings.[5] Their ability to share "pictures" (that is, ideas in the form of visual images) is not strictly telepathic because some pictures cannot be shared. Rather, the "mindless peace of their accord" (38) seems to enhance their nonverbal intersensitivity, allowing them to operate as a gestalt entity, rather like a flock of birds who all simultaneously "know" that they should wheel in the same direction. This ability depends on a sensorium more acute in some respects than that possessed by modern humans, whose sophisticated language allows more complex (and therefore less direct) messaging. So Lok is able to perform "miracles of perception in the cavern of his nose" (50)—as a dog might—but gains little useful insight into the world through the manipulation and interchange of words in spite of his own verbosity.

As among London's Folk, Golding's Neanderthals' lack of verbal skills make it difficult for them to innovate. Of her small band, Fa is the most intelligent or creative in the modern sense. Early in the novel, she has a "picture" in which the succulent shoots that she is eating are growing close to the tribal hearth on the terrace by the waterfall (49). When she tries to make Lok "see" this picture, he laughs at her, telling her that such shoots do not grow on the terrace. But we can "see" that Fa is visualizing a first step toward agriculture; in her imagination she has relocated edible plants so that they grow closer to home. Lok, however, is unable to conceive of such a hypothetical situation and "presently Fa forgot her picture" (50) as she could not share it.

Lok is characterized by the Old Woman (his mother) as a man of "many words and no pictures" (70); in short, in Neanderthal terms he is an intellectual lightweight. His predilection for words does allow him to understand better than the rest of his band the mentality of the New People. Nonetheless, his rapid linguistic acculturation cannot save him. Having accepted the reality of these unprecedented Others who do not look or behave like himself, Lok, returning to his tribal hearth, starts to feel that he has become "Lok-other" (77). Because he is aware that it is beyond his ability to convey to his people the meaning of his contact with the Others, he feels already slightly alienated from his band, because they "understand each other" (72) fully. But to be alienated from his band is to be self-alienated, and indeed Lok has now split into "inside" Lok" and "outside" Lok (141). He has experienced the painful dawning of self-consciousness as a consequence of the acquisition of modern human language.

Later, after he believes himself to be entirely bereft of his band, the self-divided Lok comes to an even fuller understanding of how human language works. He discovers the concept "Like," and through it the power of language to impose, or rather reimpose, order on a world that language has itself atomized: "Now, in a convulsion of the understanding Lok found himself using likeness as a tool as surely as ever he had used a stone to hack at sticks or meat. Likeness could grasp the white-faced hunters with a hand, could put them into the world where they were thinkable and not a random and unrelated irruption" (194). But Lok's insight allows him only to articulate the new circumstances, not to resist them: the New People "are like the river and the fall, they are a people of the fall; nothing stands against them" (195). "Like" an irresistible force of nature even though they are unnatural, the New People sweep Lok and his people into extinction. For Golding, sapient language alienates us from all that is not-Self to the point where, should we so wish it, we are always able to destroy not-Self by naming it as inimical Other. The tragedy of humanity is that our marvelous linguistic capacity has turned us into a species capable of liquidating even our closest relatives or neighbors as though they were deadly enemies.

In *The Clan of the Cave Bear* Auel wants her Neanderthals to seem as human as possible in both social and biological terms. Ayla is adopted and raised by the Clan as one of their own and is later impregnated by one of its members. But Auel also wants the Neanderthals to exhibit a specific nonadapative trait that explains why they died out. Their extreme rigidity in sexual roles must serve as a warning to us to avoid similar tendencies in ourselves. The lack of innovation in their tool kit over millennia had suggested to Solecki that the real Neanderthals "did not develop a fully articulate and precise language" (260). But because it was important to her humanist agenda that her fictional Neanderthals be unjustly stigmatized by

Cro-Magnons as subhuman, Auel did not want the Clan to speak a crude transitional language.

She resolved the problem by extrapolating from Neanderthal fossil remains. Their skulls indicate that Neanderthals had brains at least as large as ours but differently constructed. If the Neanderthal extinction was caused by their inferior mental capacity relative to the sapients who replaced them, then their large brains must have had some capacities that were superior to those of our ancestors but less adaptive. Auel's Neanderthals have an equal (but different) ability to communicate sophisticated ideas, and they have a memory that is in some ways superior to our own. To speak they use sophisticated hand signals and body language supplemented by the occasional sound. As this method resembles the sign language of the deaf, the Clan, though articulate and precise communicators, seem handicapped from the perspective of modern human speakers.

The Clan's adaptive deficiencies ironically stem from the way that their superb memories generate linguistic concepts. When they see a large woody perennial plant, they remember it as *an oak* or *a pine*, not as *tree*. In fact, they have no word or gesture for *tree* (126). This is not because they have a small vocabulary (as was the case with London's Folk), but because they have no need for more abstract general terms: they remember specific objects too well. Moreover, their culture is innate; when growing up, instead of being taught, they need only to be "reminded" of what is already in their memory. They have also have communal access to racial memory and can "join their minds, telepathically" (29) in recollection of events that did not occur in their own individual experience.

Nevertheless, the Clan's superbly accessible cultural archive, together with their inability to conceive higher-level abstractions, make them less adaptable to rapidly changing conditions than our sapient ancestors. Clan members are fixed in social roles predetermined by sex, and male and female cultures are too different to conduce toward empathy between the sexes. Moreover, the Clan are unable to conceptualize a changed future and are poor at innovation. Again, this deficiency is not because their vocabulary is small, but because their imaginations are limited by their brain structure. Particularly significant in this context is the fact that they cannot lie and have no concept of untruth: "Their form of communication, dependent for subtle nuance on barely perceptible changes in expressions, gestures, and postures, made any attempt [to lie] immediately detectable" (65).

In contrast, our habitual mendacity might be viewed as one of the costs of our ability to use language in the service of our creative imaginations. But our sapient facility with untruth is also adaptive: by telling ourselves stories about people who never existed and events that never happened we can generate empathy that is capable of embracing both sexes, all peoples, even all living things, and express via the fiction the truths of a higher order that are obscured by local or contingent circumstances. Good pf, such as Jean M. Auel's, offers a sterling example of the process in action.

Religion: Darwin's Otherwise Sensible Dog

> I satisfied myself that a significant correlation between shadow-capture, shadow-spearing and subsequent kill could be demonstrated. It was immediately obvious to me that this had implications of great practical value—stupendous possibilities, in fact.
>
> —Roy Lewis, *What We Did to Father* (1960)

When dealing with the question of the origin of religion, Darwin attempted to distinguish between two issues that he claimed were wholly distinct: man's *belief* in gods or God, and the *actual existence* of "a Creator and Ruler of the universe" (*Descent*, 1:65). About the latter, he noted diplomatically, "this has been answered in the affirmative by the highest intellects that have ever lived" (1:65). Nevertheless, Darwin felt that he could state with some certainty that this "Creator" never "aboriginally endowed" man "with the ennobling belief in [his] existence," as many savages do not have a word for God, even though almost all of them have a belief in "unseen or spiritual agencies" (1:65). Of course, in suggesting that antediluvian Adam had no awareness of his maker, Darwin had already flatly contradicted the scriptural authority.

Darwin's references to canine behavior in this context suggest that he may have been somewhat disingenuous in his determination to decouple the question of man's belief in God from the question of God's actual existence. Recalling that his own "very sensible" dog growled at an open parasol shifting in the wind as it lay on the lawn, Darwin suggests that the dog would probably not have acted thus had the parasol made similar movements in a person's hand (1:67). Just as it was the inexplicability of the parasol's movements that evoked anxiety in the dog, so it was Man's fear of the unknown that was at the root of religion.

Darwin then notes that a dog may feel for his owner "love, complete submission to an exalted and mysterious superior, a strong sense of dependence, fear, reverence, gratitude, [and] hope for the future," and cites approvingly the idea "that a dog looks on his master as on a god" (1:68). He implies that the dog's deification of his master seems rational and even dignified when contrasted with the human tendency to worship an imaginary being created out of our doglike need for reassurance in the face of what we do not understand and cannot control.

With a few exceptions, pf is agnostic and anticlerical, in the spirit of its post-Darwinian origins. From the beginning it was interested in exploring the cultural evolution of religion and of the idea of the divine because such scenarios tended to promote the scientific worldview at the expense of theology and dogma. Typically, pf views Abrahamic monotheism as a recent human invention, exactly as Darwin himself suggested: "The idea of a universal and beneficent Creator of the universe does not seem to arise in the mind of man, until he has been elevated by long-continued culture" (2:395). Darwin's strong implication is that God's existence is not so much discovered as a result of cultural elaboration, as actually brought into being by it. Moreover, Christianity is often viewed in pf not as a revelation of something new, but as a survival (in the Tylorian sense) of something very old, with the corollary that those who continue to believe in it are prehistoric savages at heart.

Hyne's *The New Eden* is a case in point. On the island where the Archduke is conducting his experimental attempt to recapitulate human social evolution, monotheism evolves from the same psychosexual roots that gave rise to patriarchy. Hyne's new Adam only embarks on a spiritual quest after he has been displaced by the infant Cain from the focus of Eve's attention. Now, suddenly unsure of his status and purpose, he becomes consumed with the search for an "evasive something" (221), namely, life's metaphysical meaning. He places an idealized clay image of himself in a crude temple while spouting innuendoes that impress Eve with their nebulosity. She, more easily satisfied at the spiritual level because motherhood has made her more certain of her ontological function, needs to placate the man upon whom she and her child are dependent. So she treats the idol as though it were an embodiment of her husband's importance to her, making it the focus of comforting rituals that affirm her bond with him.

But soon the idol crumbles, confirming to Adam that it was not a satisfactory sublimation of his yearnings, and, disillusioned, he takes to alcohol. The little society is threatened by moral collapse and it is saved only by a deus ex machina. Smoke from a distant volcanic eruption darkens the sky and Adam realizes that the light and heat that they have all taken for granted can be taken away. As he tries to rationalize the deprivation, the transcendent Something that he has been struggling to conceive suddenly comes into focus. He explains to Eve that the sun "had been hurled headlong from its midday perch, had been drowned when immature, and so no new sun could now be born. They were doomed henceforward to an endless night—perchance as a punishment" (250).

But soon the clouds begin to disperse, and finally Adam "saw his god and worshipped" (253): he has identified the sun as the source and guarantor of his small community's existence on earth. Here Hyne confirms two interlocking post-Darwinian sets of ideas: those of the physicist John Tyndall in *Heat* (1863) about the sun as the source of all life on earth, and those of the philologist Friedrich Max Müller in *Comparative Mythology* (1865) about solar mythology as the foundation of human culture. And simultaneously Hyne disconfirms Scripture: his neo-Edenic scenario, culminating in the invention of solar-based proto-monotheism, entirely inverts the aboriginal priority of God over Adam in Genesis by suggesting how prehistoric man might have thought God into existence.

Other early pf writers were in agreement that religion came into being very early in human prehistory as the result of imagination stimulated by fear of the unknown. For example, Bierbower in *From Monkey to Man* speculates that the extreme geological instability of the Tertiary, during when a whole mountain ridge would suddenly have arisen causing devastating earthquakes, floods, and fire, might have generated a mythology, and later a religion, rooted in fear. First, however, the ape-man Shoozoo, a notorious liar, must "invent" the fictional imagination. Shoozoo's tall tales, such as the one in which he recounts how he would have brought home a piece of the moon had an alligator not swallowed it, have hardened into doctrine over a number of generations.

After each natural catastrophe, the ape-men have come to believe that elemental forces, embodied as a great winged Alligator, were punishing them for a moral infraction and hence must be appeased with a sacrifice. The ape-men view fire as a snake that cannot be strangled, the sun as a monstrous fire-snake in the sky, the thunder as its voice, and the lightning as its occasional descent to earth to feed:

There was, in short, so much that the early race did not understand that they were perpetually in awe. Every convulsion of nature was a subject of worship to them. . . . Earth-quakes soon got a name, and were placed among the divinities. Thunder, Lightning, Rain, Hail, and subsequently Snow were canonized as heavenly spirits. The wind was the breath of Shoozoo, or of his great Alligator. . . . A spirit world had dawned upon them, and the supernatural began to rule the race. All the unknown was fashioned into gods, and the realm of ignorance became one of terror and devotion. (104–105)

Haraucourt, too, traces the origin of religion back to the Tertiary ape-man trying fearfully to cope with a world in transition. For Daâh, the inanimate world is animated by his fear: the mud where his foot sticks is the earth "hungry" for his flesh (89). The creation of such a metaphor indicates that man, for whom animism was the first belief system, "was a poet before he was a reasoner, since he subjectivized the world . . . ; before giving himself a soul that was his exclusive privilege, he gave a soul to the universe, and already arrogated to himself the role of handing out the punishments deserved by those souls that only existed in himself" (95).

In *Daâh*, faith and science are twins born from the same womb. They owe their conception to the human discovery that a flung stone can strike a distant object if properly aimed. This ability to act at a distance, immediately turned by our poetic imagination into a trope, gave us the idea, fundamental to our humanity, of projecting our thought into invisible realms: beyond the distant horizon, upward into the heavens, or forward into the future. To colonize these realms, "Man will invent the gods fashioned in his own image, peopling the empyrean with images of himself and his passions. . . . Beyond, always beyond, ever since that marvelous and symbolic moment when the first stone was thrown by a hand which, from that moment, was a human hand!" (165).

But if the prehistoric foundation of religion was viewed sympathetically by early pf writers as an imaginative project to master fear, there was from the inception of the pf genre a very strong parallel anti-clerical strain. The prehistoric priesthood—shamans and their ilk—are typically portrayed as men who exploited their tribes' credulity for their own aggrandizement and hence served as a major impediment to social progress. In Andrew Lang's "The Romance of the First Radical," Why-Why wages a continual battle with "medicine-men or clerical wizards" (294), who, together with their chief conservative constituency, the old women of the tribe, hate him because his public contempt for irrational superstitions and ceremonies threatens their own ascendancy. Lang is also determined to show that survivals of prehistoric superstitions still inhabit progress in the later nineteenth century. So, the weekly "'tabu-days,' when the rest of the people in the cave were all silent, sedentary, and miserable" (295) bring to mind the Lord's Day observance legislation that barred pleasurable activities on Victorian Sundays, the one day of the week when people were free from work. On these days Why-Why defiantly walks about whistling, chipping flints, or setting nets.

It is in the tribal wizard's vested interest to attribute all deaths among his people to evil spirits, because such an explanation enables him to blame his enemies for having invoked the demons and thereby consolidate his own power. When the wizard, using divination from beetles, denounces Why-Why for his radical skepticism, rather than vainly argue against unreason and prejudice, Why-Why simply pins the shaman to a tree with his spear. But Why-Why understands that sometimes a more subtle iconoclasm is called for. When another wizard refuses to feed him during a long enforced vigil over a corpse, Why-Why kicks the shaman into a ravine. Suffering no adverse consequences for this act, Why-Why thereby demonstrates to his tribe that he has committed no sacrilege. Even so, Why-Why cannot escape the fate of the reformer too far ahead of his time. Mortally wounded by his own tribesmen, he proclaims with his dying breath that a day will come when they will be free of priestcraft. Lang concludes his apologue by expatiating on this theme to his liberal, secularist contemporaries: "Our advance in liberty is due to an army of forgotten Radical martyrs of whom we know less than we do of [the leading Victorian freethinker] Mr. Bradlaugh" (300).

A fine later pf story, "Man o' Dreams" (1929) by Will McMorrow, takes up Lang's anticlerical theme and develops it less dogmatically and more dramatically. The dreamer of McMorrow's title is the Cro-Magnon protagonist, Jal. He is intelligent and progressive, having used his dreaming creatively to produce fine cave paintings, domesticate a wild pony, and invent a stringed musical instrument. He heroically saves the shaman Sho-Sho from cannibalistic Neanderthals, so now according to tribal law he may demand the hand of Sho-Sho's beautiful daughter Leth, with whom he is in love. But the shaman hates Jal because the latter's innovations are a more powerful magic than his own necromantic mumblings. Jal even dares to engage Sho-

Sho in a doctrinal debate and defeat him by logic. The soul cannot be a shadow, as the shaman claims, because a dead body still casts a shadow, while men do not die just because their shadows disappear at sunset (118).

The false visionary intends to foil the true one by claiming that Jal only imagined that he saved Sho-Sho's life, and that the latter was actually saved by the shaman's spirit protectors. Indeed, Sho-Sho plans to sacrifice Leth to these nonexistent spirits to ensure that Jal will never have her. Sho-Sho breaks tribal protocol by displaying his daughter naked to the men of the tribe, whereby the narrative suggests that the clergy have always outraged the most fundamental moral laws to protect their own interests. As was the case with Why-Why, Jal can never single-handedly defeat the retrogressive spirit that shamans have inculcated in his tribe; nevertheless McMorrow allows room for a little more optimism than does Lang. Having speared the shaman to death, Jal escapes with Leth in a boat of his own invention. If the lovers can survive their exile, they will found a new race that is likely to flourish, being no longer under the heel of dogma and obscurantism.

While earlier pf writers, freshly under the influence of Tylor and Frazer, were often concerned with condemning religion as an irrational survival from prehistory, later writers were more willing to explore the possibility that Paleolithic religion was a genuine response to circumstances (sometimes with the proviso that religion had become degraded and corrupted in more recent times). Such exploration was further stimulated by theories that the great parietal cave art of southwest France and northeast Spain had a religious function, and that the post-Magdalenian disappearance of this art represented a profound spiritual loss in hominization.

In the French Pyrenean cave of Trois-Frères (Ariège) discovered in 1914, the most famous of the many parietal engravings is the image known as "Le Sorcier" (The sorcerer). It depicts a dancing therianthrope (beast-man) with a human body, stag's head, bear's paws, and horse's tail; the engraving seems to stare owlishly into the viewer's eyes.[6] Inspired by this powerful icon and by the two sculpted clay bison that he had discovered at the nearby Tuc d'Audoubert, Max Bégouën in his novel *Bison of Clay* describes how the Magdalenian hunter-gatherers who had occupied the caves had created a set of beliefs and rituals based on the interaction between natural forces and the animals upon which the tribe were dependent.

The shaman Eye-of-Fire is a central figure in the totem clan of the

Red Bison. Bégouën identifies him with The Sorcerer, to the extent of describing the inspired shaman actually creating this image as a kind of spiritual self-portrait (144–145). Eye-of-Fire knows "how to communicate with all the spirits, good and evil, which were to be found alike in living beings and inanimate objects" (27). He can lay spells and make charms that avert bad luck. His completed self-portrait causes the warriors of the Red Bison to abase themselves before it in awe and terror. Eye-of-Fire is no charlatan. His power derives from his training in the observation and interpretation of natural signs during incessant wanderings that have familiarized him with the wider world. His educated eye has enabled him to become an accomplished artist who "had studied the animals and could draw them in a lifelike manner" (26). His self-imposed asceticism, including fasting, enables him to enter visionary states of "sacred delirium" (31) in which he mediates between his tribe and the elemental powers that confer good or bad luck.

When a hunter is killed by a fearsome bison bull, Eye-of-Fire must allay the clan's fear that, if the animal has been able to kill a man, an "evil spirit" (22) must have entered its body, and that if nothing were done, they would forever be haunted by the hunter's unquiet ghost. Eye-of-Fire performs an elaborate funeral ceremony, orchestrating the clan's grief and then expelling it cathartically through a combination of dance, song, and drama. The hunters, having worked themselves into an ecstatic state, ritually plunge their javelins into a bison skin. Eye-of-Fire then draws the outline of the "possessed" bull in blood on the cave wall, thereby demonstrating through his art that he has the power to capture the beast and hence ensure its death at the hands of the hunters of the tribe. In this way the shaman, archetype of the initiate into the supernatural mysteries, restores confidence to his people.

Later the shaman will fashion the clay images of the male and female bison to ensure the continuing fertility, both human and animal, of the region. He will then seal them up in the narrow cavern so that "the spirits of fecundity," drawn to the altar where the bison stand, cannot escape (193). (These are the clay bison that would be found intact more than 20,000 years later by the young Max Bégouën.) As the tribesmen dance wildly to celebrate the sealing of the cave, Bégouën notes, "The Shaman dominated everything: it was he who conversed with the spirits and it was his power which gave life to inert clay" (192). In this way he links the human religious impulse with artistic creativity. As an artist, man seems not merely to attune himself with the supernatural world but actually to become a god, creating new life out of the inanimate earth.

Art: The Haft of Tuami's Dagger

"What is it?" demanded Uncle Vanya in a terrible voice. . . .
"R-representational art," squeaked Alexander.
"Horrible child," Uncle Vanya yelled. "What have you done to my shadow?"
—Roy Lewis, *What We Did to Father* (1960)

Altamira Cave is in northeast Spain near the coastal city of Santander. In November 1879, Maria, the five-year-old daughter of Don Marcelino de Sautuola, the local landowner and an amateur archaeologist, pointed out to her father what she called "bueyes" (oxen)—they are actually bison—painted on the cave's ceiling (Kühn, 54, Bahn and Vertut, 20). Sautuola immediately brought the discovery of these magnificent polychrome paintings to the attention of the scientific community. The story about that community's refusal to accept the antiquity of the paintings for more than twenty years (Sautuola died disappointed in 1888) is often retold to demonstrate the civilized world's extreme reluctance to accept that Stone Age savages could have produced art. It was not until 1902 that the leading French prehistorian Emile Cartailhac published the recantation "Mea culpa d'une sceptique" (A skeptic admits his error), in which he accepted the authenticity of the parietal art at Altamira and elsewhere.

It had been clear from the 1860s that people of the Reindeer Age had made mobiliary art. But the prehistoric artist had been viewed as a primitive who scratched crude designs onto his tools and weapons during whatever brief respite from the struggle for existence he was able to enjoy. In 1865 the pf pioneer Berthoud reproduced pictures of decorated bones in *L'Homme depuis cinq milles ans*, noting that the images of animals "are easily recognizable by species, the clumsiness of the work notwithstanding" (22). After 1902, however, the cult of the Paleolithic cave artist as mystic genius began to grow, regardless of the very variable quality of the artwork. Picasso, who visited the cave in 1902, is supposed to have remarked that "after Altamira, all is decadence." Ever more elaborate hypotheses about the meaning of the images have since been constructed, under the assumption that they offer profound clues to the culture of the people who made them.

As early as 1903, Salomon Reinach in "L'Art et la magie" (Art and magic) suggested that the depiction of animals in the parietal art of the Reindeer Age was a form of sympathetic magic (Ucko and Rosenfeld, 123–130.) Cave artists "captured" animal images on the wall and depicted them being speared in the belief that such improved the chances of hunters doing the same in real life. Abbé Breuil, who documented and reproduced thousands of parietal images between 1901 and 1961, extended and popularized this approach. For Breuil, there was hunting magic in depictions of game animals, reproductive magic in depictions of pregnant or mating animals, and destructive magic in depictions of competing predators such as carnivores (Sieveking, 55).

One of the problems with Breuil's interpretation of the animals that dominate French and Spanish cave art was that reindeer, the preferred game animal of the artists' tribes, was rarely depicted. In *Préhistoire de l'art occidental* (1965; translated as *The Art of Western Man in Prehistoric Europe* in 1968) the structuralist anthropologist André Leroi-Gourhan, following Lévi-Strauss's interpretation of totem animals, argued that the animals depicted in Paleolithic cave murals had nothing to do with diet. Instead they were a symbolic bestiary representing spiritual beliefs, an elaborate code based on the division of gender that one must learn to decipher by the frequency and distribution of animals depicted in each cave. Of the most commonly represented animals, horses and associated images represented the male principle, while bison and their constellation represented the female (Ucko and Rosenfeld, 140–143).

More recently, the South African rock art expert David Lewis-Williams in his fascinating study *The Mind in the Cave* (2002) has proposed that parietal art, experienced by flickering lamplight in subterranean gloom under altered states of consciousness, served as gateway to new levels of awareness. The artwork represents an emergent metacognitive level of human consciousness; in producing it Cro-Magnons affirmed their mental superiority to Neanderthals. It will probably remain impossible to prove Lewis-Williams's ingenious hypothesis, though it has to be said that his ideas harmonize well with Golding's and Auel's speculative distinctions between Neanderthal and sapient mentalities. Indeed, in Auel's *The Shelters of Stone*, Ayla in a painted cave experiences a visionary episode that seems directly drawn from Lewis-Williams's theories (395–398).

There is no doubt that interpretations of the motives for and meaning of Paleolithic art have become increasingly elaborate over the past century, though it does not necessarily follow that Paleolithic cultures were far more complex than we first thought. In her study *The Cave Artists* (1979), Ann Sieveking concluded that we will probably never understand Paleolithic art as it is "a language for which we have no vocabulary" (209). Such an attitude may seem too defeatist to endorse with enthusiasm, but it is harder to disagree with the anthropologist Margaret Conkey, who concludes her survey "A Century of Palaeolithic Cave Art" (1981) by admitting that "a monolithic explanation for at least 20,000 years of artistic activity is no longer satisfactory" (24).

In nineteenth-century pf, written at a time when the only Paleolithic art that was recognized as such was mobiliary, the artist is not usually explicitly connected with religious beliefs or rituals. The prehistoric sf novel *The New Eden* does provide an interesting exception, however. Hyne's Adam latterly takes to carving "sacred" images of himself in his quest for psychological compensation for having been displaced from Eve's attention by the infant Cain (228–229). The Archduke's experiment, then, suggests that sculptural representation of the body and the shaping of theology are closely related symptoms of a specifically male quest to fill an emotional deficit caused by ontological insecurity.

Usually, however, the Paleolithic artists in early pf are associated with progressive tendencies that are by definition secular rather than spiritual. Vamireh, Rosny's Cro-Magnon protagonist, is a sensitive artist who periodically retreats to an island solitude to painstakingly etch a floral motif into a cave lion's fang (33). In Arcelin's *Solutré*, I-ka-eh, the female chief of the Solutreans, lives in a reindeer-skin hut that is covered with her colored paintings of animals (42–43). Born into a superior race and freed from the struggle of existence as tribal leader, she has the ability and leisure to develop her artistic talent. And lest we assume that the Neanderthal cognitive incapacity for art is a recent notion, one of the ways that Berthet distinguished his advanced hero Fair-Hair from the atavistic Red was by characterizing the former as a mobiliary artist who carves images of animals into bone and mammoth ivory (30) and fashions a *bâton de commandement* (commander's baton)[7] from the antler of a reindeer (83). But what Berthet intuited from very little evidence in 1879 seems to hold true today: the Neanderthals with whom our ancestors shared western Europe did not make art.[8] As we survived and they didn't, that might suggest that art was adaptive.

With the exception of the independent-minded Arcelin, early pf writers assumed that Paleolithic artists were male. After all, they were writing in the aftermath of the 1864 discovery at Laugerie-Basse (Dordogne) of the "Vénus impudique" (Immodest Venus), first of the many feminine figurines to be unearthed in the nineteenth century. Curwen's *Zit and Xoe* was one of the first pf works to suggest that the artistic impulse may have originated in man's desire to express his erotic response to woman. Fascinated by the graceful curves of her beautiful body, Zit carves Xoe's image on his tools and later, in tracing her shadow, invents portraiture (614). But it was not only eroticism in the archeological remains that conduced to the masculine gendering of Paleolithic art. In the first children's pf novel, Hervilly's artists are male hunters who, on their travels, carve in bone or stone images of the strange animals and plants that they have seen as aide-mémoires that they will show to their children on their return to enlarge their understanding of the world.[9]

Waterloo in *Ab* introduces the idea of the artist's needful exemption from the social struggle for existence so that he can produce objects or images of cultural value. Little Mok, Ab's youngest son, is born weak and crippled, and only Lightfoot's maternal devotion is able to save him at infancy from the stern law of survival of the fittest. The child has an innate manual dexterity inherited from his flint-knapping grandfather, while his freedom from the usual male hunting duties allows him to hone his observational skills. The result is that his physical incapacity is compensated for by an unprecedented technical ability. The little cripple, "of the world, yet not in it," develops into an artistic genius who draws on the wall of his cave reindeer so "wonderfully life-like" (312) that everyone admires them. Though Little Mok's paintings have no evident purpose, utilitarian or spiritual, their value as art is apparently self-evident to his tribe. In this way the paintings reflect Little Mok himself, who is also highly valued though he is unable to fulfil his normal tribal duties. Little Mok dies at twelve, but his precocious accomplishments teach his father that brute strength and warrior courage are not the only masculine virtues. Indeed, Little Mok's brief life has been the trigger for the emergence of a new humane social ethics. And in tracing this process, Waterloo, perhaps surprisingly for a writer in an American culture imbued with social Darwinism, identifies aestheticism (art for art's sake) as a stage in moral progress.

By the 1920s, neither the quality nor authenticity of Upper Paleolithic art was at issue. Instead, people wondered why the pictorial achievements of the Reindeer Age had suddenly ceased, to be unequaled for millennia. The first pf novel to focus specifically on the cave artist as representative of a culture in crisis was *The End of a World*, set in the Vézère valley during the late Magdalenian age. Anet's novel is illustrated with many reproductions of Upper Paleolithic art, including a rendering by the modernist painter Pierre Bonnard of the "Dame à la capuche" (Lady with the hood) figurine (20), which inspired Anet's representation of his female protagonist Mah[10] (fig. 7.1). Through this direct juxtaposition of "authentic" prehistoric images and fictional text Anet suggests not only that Magdalenian art speaks directly to the present—it is "modern"—but also that it can be used to remind us, at a critical time for Western culture, of the true meaning and function of pictorial art.

Anet's People of the River are Cro-Magnons with a highly sophisticated industry. The abundance of game and lack of competition have ushered in an era of leisure and peace during which the arts have flourished. Now, however, the same arts are used chiefly to shore up the tribe's increasingly unsustainable totemistic beliefs. In an overt allusion to the Judeo-Christian myth of origin, Nô's tribe nostalgically recall a vegetarian Eden in which men once "lived happily in peace with their brothers the animals" (46). Later, the myth continues, men erred by murdering and devouring their totemic Ancestor, a cave bear. They recur often to this mythological parricide to explain the increasingly imperfect world in which they live. Now the People hunt animals for their flesh, and must placate their blood guilt, appease the slaughtered animal spirits, and control living animals through elaborate religious rituals. The cave artist's role is to depict as accurately as possible the needful game animal, so that "the beast's spirit, deceived by the resemblance, would elect to dwell in this accurate image of itself" (47). In this way, realism has become an essential criterion of artistic merit. Once the animal is "captured" on the cave wall, the appropriate spell is uttered and the image magically comes to symbolize an equivalent living animal that will be delivered into the hunter's power.

Now the great herds of reindeer are thinning out, the cave bear is nearly extinct, and there are fears that that women's fertility is waning. The sages of the People try to stop the rot: "They caused to be carved on ivory or horn little female figures, emblematic of fecundity, powerful matrons with wide hips and wombs capable of bearing a vigorous child, and with heavy breasts that were inexhaustible fountains" (55).[11] Nô the artist must do his part to save the tribe; even though he

Figure 7.1 *The Lady with the Hood* as a portrait of Anet's Mah.

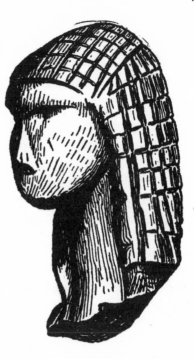

has never seen a cave bear, he produces a large polychrome image of the Ancestor on a cave wall. While his art is primarily motivated by the pious desire to put his own son under the Ancestor's protection, he simultaneously experiences the "strange joy" of the creative artist: "There, where nothing had previously existed, sprang forth suddenly an animal which he, Nô, had called to life!" (165).

But the People, devastated by a diphtheria epidemic, are doomed to be replaced by invading Asiatic Round Heads, who have domesticated the dog and can outcompete the Cro-Magnons at hunting. Nô eventually abandons painting because its magic is too weak: it fails to produce the required sympathetic effect. Instead he and his tribe invest all their remaining energy in the pursuit and capture of a cave bear, in the hope that a sacrifice of the ancestral Father will allow his sons to live. In a scene that powerfully suggests the desperation underlying all rituals of communion, the bear's living heart is ripped out of its chest and devoured raw by the people (242–243). But all is in vain: the Round Heads continue to prosper at the Cro-Magnons' expense, and Nô will soon die in a futile attempt to appropriate the stronger magic of the invaders.

Anet's explanation for the disappearance of Magdalenian art, then, is that its aesthetic elements, although superb, were entirely sub-ordinated to its religious function. Its creators had placed too much confidence in its efficacy as sympathetic magic to adapt to changing circumstances. Moreover, Anet suggests that our valuation of cave art—and of our own art—should not be based on the realism of the representation, but rather on whether the images evoke the "strange joy" of the aesthetic experience. Anet's high modernist sophistication seems a world away from Waterloo's unquestioning acceptance of the canons of academic realism.

The aesthetic richness of Anet's novel—its literary success—has little to do with its dependence upon, and rigorous extrapolation from, the now-superannuated Reinach-Breuil theory of art as hunt-ing magic. Instead, it resides in the plausibility and coherence of its evocation of the disappearing world of the cave artist. Anet's achieve-ment can be gauged when *The End of a World* is compared to the epi-sode "In the Days of the Mammoth" in F. Britten Austin's *When Man-kind was Young*. Austin is as knowledgeable as Anet about the cultural context in which Rock-Lizard, his artist-protagonist, was working, and agrees with the French novelist that animal images had a "com-munal and purely utilitarian" purpose (53). But he is unable to explain why a culture that produced the wonderful art of the Reindeer Age would be superseded by the "grossly inferior" Azilian-Tardenoisian industry (59). Instead he indulges in routine nostalgia for the extinc-tion of the handsome and supremely gifted Magdalenians.

Golding was equally as indebted as Anet and Austin to the now-outdated theory of art as sympathetic magic. Moreover, he often seems to be unaware of, or to ignore, contemporary research into Pa-leolithic cultures.[12] But *The Inheritors'* profound insights into the meaning and value of art are unaffected by Golding's failure to adhere to the normal paleoanthropology of his time. In the novel, our Cro-Magnon ancestors' capacity to make artificial images in order to in-vest them with symbolic meaning is perhaps the central difference between themselves and the "unfallen" Neanderthals. This capacity is brilliantly expressed by Golding via episodes in which the New People perform actions that are incomprehensible from a nonsapient perspective. The reader, trying to read between the lines of the Neanderthal-focalized narrative, experiences the confusion and stress caused by Neanderthal cognitive deficiency in the face of the mortal threat posed by the Cro-Magnons.

Lok's tribe make and share mental pictures and draw lines in the earth to indicate where a corpse is to be buried (87–88). They are capable of apprehending morphological analogy: Liku's little Oa, her "doll" representing the fertility goddess, is an "old root, twisted and bulged and smoothed away by age into the likeness of a great-bellied woman" (33). But little Oa is a found object, not an artifact such as a Venus figurine. Though they are aware that external nature sometimes reflects their internal desires, the Neanderthals are not capable of shaping nature to fit those desires, thereby gaining a measure of control over the world. They cannot make art.

At the end of chapter 7 Lok and Fa, hidden in ivy leaves atop a dead tree, watch rituals performed by the New People in the clearing below them. As the New People clap and chant, a shaman in a stag's-head outfit dances and imitates a stag's mating call, while lots are drawn and the artist named Tuami paints a polychrome image of a stag on the ground. Then Tuami cuts off one of the fingers from the left hand of his fellow tribesman ("Pine-Tree") and lets the severed digit fall on the image of the stag,[13] after which two arrows are shot into its "heart." Finally Tuami erases all but the head and eye of the painted stag. As this sequence of events is incomprehensible to Lok and Fa, it is described without logical copulas by the narrator. It is with considerable difficulty that the reader assembles the events into a sequence that makes sense: a narrative recounting a ritual of sympathetic magic. The Neanderthals do recognize the image as a "flat stag" (146), after which it becomes in their eyes a "real" stag, as does the shaman in the stag costume. Indeed, the painted image is as frightful to Lok as a real stag: he imagines that its eye sees him in his hiding place and will give him away. It is left to Fa, more intelligent than Lok, to make sense of what they have observed. The best that she can do is to imply that the flat stag went away (that is, was erased) because it was frightened of the other stag (the disguised shaman) (149). How could these Neanderthals make art when they cannot distinguish a real object from its symbolic representation?

The incomprehension of the Neanderthals suggests either the innocence that we associate with very small children or the stupidity of the mentally defective. Viewed from the estranged Neanderthal perspective, however, the episode of the flat stag also suggests that sapient consciousness frequently takes the form of an extreme irrationality bordering on insanity. The Neanderthals' interpretation of the ritual of hunting magic is determined by their low order of reason, a kind of animal logic of natural cause and effect according to which sympathetic magic makes no sense. From the perspective of our higher-order reason, the New People's elaborate and violent ritual is utterly futile as an effective means of determining the course of events in the real world. The New People (who represent ourselves) have abandoned natural logic; in contrast to this abdication the Neanderthal inability to distinguish among a real stag, a painted stag, and a man in a stag costume seems a minor deficiency of perception.

Nevertheless, it is the New People—ourselves—who have inherited the earth. And the key to our adaptive "superiority" resides in our art. The mental apparatus of the New People, for all its tendency to irrational delusion, allows them not merely to envisage but actually to create an alternative world to which they can migrate in their imaginations, and from which the real world can be viewed as if from an alien perspective and then reshaped in the image of the object of their desire.

Finally, art offers to the New People the difficult freedom that comes with enhanced choice. Tuami has been sharpening a dagger of ivory with the aim of using it to assassinate the shaman Marlan to avenge the hardship and stress consequent upon Marlan's abduction of the woman Vivani. As a result of Marlan's actions, the New People have been forced into exile, have assumed a burden of blood guilt, have suffered persecution by the "forest devils" (the Neanderthals) (224), and must endure the madness of the girl Tanakil after her traumatic abortive sacrifice to these devils. Finally, though, calmed by the sight of the intimacy between Vivani and her stolen Neanderthal infant, Tuami decides to carve an image of mother and child in the haft rather than use the blade against Marlan: "They were waiting in the rough ivory of the knife-haft that was so much more important than the blade. They were an answer, the frightened, angry love of the woman and the ridiculous, intimidating rump that was wagging at her head, they were a password. His hands felt for the ivory in the bilges and he could feel in his fingers how Vivani and her devil fitted it" (233). Golding here reminds us that while murder must be avenged ad infinitum, art offers us perhaps the only fertile resolution of the tension between the contraries in our human nature.

What has survived from our prehistoric past that more definitively affirms our continuing and irreducible humanity than art? To make bare bones live again is a potent magic, but if there are images engraved on those bones, they have never been entirely dead. Only art can resolve, if temporarily, the opposition between the ape in man and the god he aspires to be. It is the key to negotiating the conflict between our "Neanderthal" and "Cro-Magnon" legacies that pf has made into its central binary opposition. As art, good pf is like the carving in the haft of Tuami's dagger: it represents our hybrid nature more fruitfully than the blade, as we, the inheritors of the earth, paddle unceasingly toward the line of darkness that marks the unknown future.

Coda

Baxter's EVOLUTION *and Post-Hominization*

> The whole history of the world . . . although of a length quite
> incomprehensible by us, will hereafter be recognised as a mere
> fragment of time, compared with the ages which have elapsed
> since the first creature, the progenitor of innumerable extinct
> and living descendants, was created.
>
> —Charles Darwin, *On the Origin of Species* (1859)

Our highly adaptable species has, to adapt Darwin's preferred terminology, descended with many modifications, some of them possibly unprecedented in Nature. If we are to survive into futurity, then further
modifications must surely occur. What they will be is unforeseeable,
but it is safe to say that if we endure, it will likely be in a posthuman
form. While it is pf's task to dramatize our hominization, we are likely
to turn to sf for plausible speculations about our *post*-hominization.

In his masterly episodic novel *Evolution* (2002), Stephen Baxter offers a epic vision of hominization past and future. In the insights that
this work offers into our human nature and how it might have developed, *Evolution* is a paradigm of good pf. At the same time the novel's
structure suggests that pf and sf, though apparently concerned with
opposed temporalities, can (and indeed *must*) collaborate if we are to
think seriously about our destiny as a species.

To use a chemical analogy, while most prehistoric science fiction is
a compound represented by the formula PSf, *Evolution* is a mixture
with the formula Pf + Sf. Instead of using literal or virtual time travel
to place the theme of human origin in a sf frame, Baxter begins the
narrative with chronologically arranged episodes of pure pf. Then,
once time's arrow traverses the line of the present day, he concludes
with episodes of pure sf. This structure is not unprecedented: an early
French pf work, Berthoud's *L'Homme depuis cinq mille ans*, is a prototype.

However, two far better known works—both of which foreground humanity's uncertain present position on the temporal continuum between the prehistoric past and posthuman future—are a likelier influence on *Evolution*. Indeed, in his novel Baxter pays overt homage to them: Wells's *The Time Machine* and Clarke's *2001: A Space Odyssey*. Simultaneously, *Evolution* alludes at the structural level to the most familiar mythological cycle dealing with human origin and destiny: that traced in the Bible from Genesis to Revelation.

Baxter unequivocally acknowledges pf's debt to Darwinian theory. His epigraph and postgraph are both quotations from the first edition of *On the Origin of Species* published in the annus mirabilis 1859. That was the year when the scientific acknowledgment of human antiquity coincided with Darwin's first published statement that all species change with time, sometimes becoming unrecognizable, and that "very few will transmit progeny of any kind to a far distant futurity" (*Origin*, 397). Darwin's implication, affirmed by Baxter, is that our own species will not be exempt from further modifications—nor ultimately, indeed, from extinction. The great naturalist, offering consolation to his fellow Victorians, concluded that there is "grandeur" in the evolutionist perspective; the simplest of organisms need only time to become prolific of beauty (398). *Evolution* is instinct with Darwinian grandeur and beauty.

Baxter's narrative opens with a section of an external temporal frame: a Prologue set in A.D. 2031. This temporal setting serves as a baseline, returned to at three later points: in a median Interlude, in chapter 16, and in an Epilogue. Baxter's choice of this baseline makes it evident that we, the heirs to the near future, are at the focus of his grand evolutionary scenario. The 2031 framing narrative itself centers on the turbulent events at a conference called to address the question, How will we avoid the impending self-induced disasters that may lead to our extinction as a species? The conference convenor feels that the key to our survival lies in "*the globalization of empathy*" (5; emphasis in original). Baxter's project raises our consciousness toward a similar end. What we are today is the product of millions of years of successful adaptations that deep time has encoded in our genes. Whether and how we survive into the future is also encoded there, though it is accessible only as an imaginative reality: as a work of pf + sf.

Baxter's framed narrative consists of nineteen speculative episodes following the course of our development: fourteen are set in prehistory, one in historic time, and four (including chapter 16) in the future. The episodes form three larger groups: "Ancestors" (eight episodes, from 145 million to 5 million B.P.); "Humans" (eight episodes, from 1.5 million B.P. to the A.D. 2031 baseline); and "Descendants" (three episodes from the far future, the last of which is set 500 million years after the present). Its enormous temporal range makes this novel perhaps the grandest fictional vision yet offered of our hominization—and post-hominization.

Awe and humility are associated with religious feeling, but that which Baxter evokes in us does not require the existence of a supernatural designer. We feel awe at the mighty continuity of the river of genes that flows both in us and through us, connecting us to the very beginning of terrestrial life.[1] We feel humility at the sheer contingency of our existence. Our lineage began with a nondescript mammal that luckily survived the Cretaceous-Tertiary cometary extinction of 65 million years B.P.; our ancestors included one obscure, unspecialized species among many Miocene arboreal primates; and around 60,000 B.P. we came perhaps accidentally to consciousness as anatomically modern humans. The reader emerges from *Evolution* with a rejuvenated sense of the preciousness, not just of human, but of all life on earth. The novel helps us to see that we really are profoundly related to all other living things and, like them, absolutely dependent upon our mother planet. *Evolution* is good pf that works, one reader at a time, toward the globalization of empathy.

A discussion of three chapters of *Evolution*, one from each of the three sections, will suffice as a reminder of how the fraternal twins pf and sf, working in collaboration, can offer us unequaled insights into ourselves. The first chapter that I shall analyze, the only one out of chronological order, does not actually deal with our direct ancestors, but approaches hominization via nonhuman analogy. The second suggests how our modern human mentality—brilliant but flawed— might have emerged suddenly thanks to a single insane genius. The third deals with our posthuman destiny: a sf scenario of the almost unimaginably far future is rendered plausible because it is inferred logically from what has unfolded over the course of deep time.

Chapter 2, "The Hunters of Pangaea," is the episode set earliest in time. Baxter proposes that 145 million years B.P. in the single earth-spanning continent of Jurassic Pangaea, ornitholestes, a bipedal carnivorous dinosaur about human size, developed a big brain, language, and tool use by a similar "virtuous spiral" (50) to the one later responsible for rapid hominid encephalization. Such an archaic reptilian blossoming, though it might seem at first glance bizarre, is not impossible. Evolutionary relay, a form of parallel evolution whereby different species (for example, ichthyosaurs and dolphins) at different eras (Mesozoic and Cenozoic) from different classes (reptiles and mammals) may adapt in similar ways to similar ecosystems, is a well-attested phenomenon.

The rise and fall of the ornitholestes was relatively short: they died out from starvation after carelessly and needlessly hunting to extinction their chief game animal, the gigantic vegetarian dinosaur diplodocus. Baxter here aims to make us question whether those qualities we reserve to ourselves as the privileges of a unique species are really not a set of adaptations that could potentially have occurred among other species of bipedal social predators. The episode reminds us that a special providence has played no part in hominization, and that our good judgment has probably had little to do with making us the clever creatures that we undoubtedly are. Above all we have been lucky, and if we are truly clever we will not take our luck for granted. Instead, we should try to think ahead and thereby avoid the inevitable outcome of squandering the resources upon which we depend.

Chapter 11, "Mother's People," is set 60,000 B.P. among anatomically modern humans in North Africa. These people are our ancestors but, though fully encephalized, they have made few innovations for millennia and are under pressure from an increasingly unstable Pleistocene climate. In this remarkable chapter Baxter offers a plausible explanation of how language, art, and religion as we now understand them might all have come into being as the result of a single wayward genius, a woman whose dying act was to name herself "Mother."

Mother suffers from one symptom of the too rapid encephalization that characterizes her people: she is subject to migraines, and these attacks cause her to "see" geometrical shapes. Moreover, her slightly mutated brain is not quite so rigidly compartmentalized as those of her congeners. When Mother's only child dies of sleeping sickness, her anguish triggers a form of schizophrenia that, eroding her mental barriers, leads her into new forms of cognition that are easily and quickly transmissible. Mother's innovations constitute an enormous advance in hominization but they will have dangerous repercussions for her descendants (ourselves).

Mother has a talent for seeing "patterns and connections, networks of causes and effects" (288). She conceives the spear thrower as an extension of the arm's leverage, but she must communicate to others how to use it successfully. To do so she constructs, from her people's crude protolanguage of substantives and verbs, the first true sentence, "*Stick throw spear*" (293; emphasis in original), in which a causal relationship is economically represented by a syntactical structure. But the sentence, while unprecedentedly meaningful, attributes agency to the stick rather than to the thrower. Such a distortion of reality is a characteristic by-product of Mother's cognitive advance. Because to her there must be a reason for everything, she begins to attribute causes (via personification) to inanimate objects. Soon she is accusing people of causing bad outcomes that are really attributable to chance, and demanding their punishment—the sacrifice of their lives to appease nonexistent entities—as a remedy.

Mother's ability to make mental connections derives from the involuntary shapes that she sees during a migraine attack. She discovers that she can reproduce these shapes by scratching them onto a rock. Soon thereafter she finds that objects in the external world are starting to resemble her internal shapes: her spirals recur in shells, her lattices in honeycombs, her zigzags in lightning. She feels "as if the contents of her dark skull were mapping themselves on to the world outside" (298). We recognize that she has reversed cause and effect; the shapes were "in" the objects before they were in her head. But we also recognize that this inversion is a symptom of solipsism, a delusion in which the mind recasts itself as the center and origin of all phenomena. It is a universal human delusion.

Mother's form of solipsism gives simultaneous birth to language, art, and religion. All spread from her conviction that every cause must have an effect, and that she is herself "at the focus of the global web of causality and control" (308). Charismatic because of her claimed insight into mysterious forces, she becomes high priestess of her own cult, convincing most of her tribe that, for example, rains will come if a human sacrifice is made. Those she cannot sway she disposes of as sacrificial victims. Skeptics are thus weeded out and only believers remain to pass on their genes. Mother is no hypocrite: the essence of her genius is in her ability to believe "many contradictory things at once" (314). For Mother's "children," the world is entirely meaningful, gods lie at "the end of all causal chains" (323), and its ambiguous symbology is endlessly fascinating to reproduce and interpret. Moreover, Mother's heirs are formidable warriors, who fight in the belief that they cannot die and who conceive of their enemies as "objects, animals, something less than themselves" (322).

Baxter suggests that 60,000 years ago, Mother's insane mentality was highly contagious because it was adaptive: it conduced to the survival and reproductive advantage of those afflicted. Mother's descendants include everyone who has ever believed in the existence of supernatural entities (among whom are the vast majority of people alive today), not to mention those truest children of Mother, people who are eager to die in the cause of these imaginary beings. By this episode's relation to the narrative's overarching frame of 2031, Baxter tacitly invites us to ask ourselves whether Mother's mentality is still adaptive, given the current global challenges to our survival.

Chapter 19, "A Far Distant Futurity," is set circa 500 million years after the present. This far futurity in some ways resembles prehistory: New Pangaea forms Earth's single supercontinent, just as Old Pangaea once did. Ultimate, the posthuman protagonist, resembles a small monkey; the archaic primate body plan persists. The gender binary, however, has disappeared as unnecessary to reproduction: Ultimate and all her neotenous kind are functionally female, in that they bear (but do not nurture) infants. Mother and child live in a symbiotic relation with a tree, which takes care of most of their bodily needs in exchange for assistance with nourishment and reproduction. The tree's branches tap directly into the stomachs of the symbiotes when they are swaddled in their leaf cocoons.

This grim scenario of posthuman regression takes place in an arid and almost featureless landscape baked by a sun much hotter than today's. Only once a century is there a rainstorm, and then there is a grotesquely accelerated burst of life. Much of the time, New Pangaea resembles the surface of Mars as conceived of by Stanley G. Weinbaum in his classic sf story "A Martian Odyssey" (1934). As in that tale, there are bizarre creatures afoot in New Pangaea who have adapted to the unforgiving terrain, including a perambulating vegetable, rats who bury themselves in sand and wait for prey to fall into their mouths, and even an invisible predator.

Essentially, though, this chapter is a freeze-frame study of humanity at its vanishing point. What, Baxter asks, will be the last recognizable human trait, consequently the one in which we might identify our irreducible humanity? His answer is maternal love. Ultimate discovers that the tree, starved for nutrients, is attempting to absorb the body of her infant and decides to save her even though this will mean breaking the symbiotic bond upon which their common survival has so far depended. Ultimate undertakes "the last significant journey ever undertaken by any of her ancient, wandering lineage" (553), a far-future analogue of our primal descent from the safety of the tree-tops to the open, predator-haunted savanna. But she soon finds that there is simply nowhere to run, and so she returns her infant and herself to the uterine darkness of the tree and the painless transit into oblivion. Evolutionary time has completed a great cycle: Darwin's tree of life from which we all spring has become the tree of death to which we all return and which will mark our common grave. But, as in the biblical myth, the hope of resurrection in another place, time, and bodily form remains. Though all terrestrial life will soon follow Ultimate to her end, seeds shaken from Earth's life tree, in the form of almost indestructible bacteria, will seed themselves among the stars, and evolution will begin again elsewhere.

Ultimate's odyssey was a short and apparently futile one, terminating on a "desolate, silent beach" (553) of an ocean now dried up into a salt plain. Weinbaum's Mars has mutated into an imagined landscape even more central to sf. Baxter here alludes to the beach upon which Wells's Time Traveler comes to rest, thirty million years into the future, the place where he witnesses the death throes of terrestrial life. In this way Baxter, near the end of his epic of the human journey through biological time, pays homage to the time machine, the fantastic device that delivered the fraternal twin genres of sf and pf.

In Wells's *The Time Machine*, the Time Traveler in the far future watches devolved humanity in the form of a "round thing . . . hopping fitfully about" (148) in the shallows of an arid sea. In Clarke's *2001*, Tertiary ape-men are boosted to the next evolutionary level by a mysterious alien artifact. Baxter conflates and inverts these scenarios for ironic effect. An artificial sphere that is far more complex than Ultimate observes her futile actions. It is a Von Neumann machine, the descendant of a self-replicating robot that humans in the 2031 frame had constructed and sent out to colonize, first Mars, then the galaxy. Now it has returned to the obscure planet that is the putative origin of its species in the hope of finding an answer to a metaphysical question: Did its kind evolve randomly, or was it designed? (550)

At first we think we know the answer to the sphere's question: its species was designed—though not supernaturally—by ourselves. Yet further reflection may give us pause. This sphere was actually made by another sphere very like it but not identical. As Darwin's great theory suggests, adaptive changes must somehow have been incorporated into each new generation of spheres or their kind would not have survived. In the long perspective, it is perhaps truer to view the spherical species as having evolved from an extinct creature, the common ancestor that it shares with Ultimate—ourselves.

Now one sphere has returned to Earth in search of its origins. This sphere is not one that humans made, and to the sphere it is inconceivable that Earth's feeble remnant of posthumanity could have been in any way responsible for its existence. Its journey has been futile, and "with the equivalent of a sigh" (551) it leaves for the stars. Yet through the desire impelling its quest the sphere has revealed its human descent. It is profoundly in our nature to seek to understand ourselves and our destiny by returning to our mysterious beginnings. And it is always in this hope that we mount our imaginary time machines, fueled by unquenchable primate curiosity, and vanish into the unknown past or future.

A Prehistoric Chronology

Authors and works of pf and prehistoric sf are in **boldface.**

1812	Cuvier states that there are no fossilized human bones
1836	Thomsen distinguishes the Stone, Bronze, and Iron Ages
1847–64	Boucher de Perthes, *Antiquités celtiques et antédiluviennes*
1853	Discovery of Swiss lake dwellings
1856	Discovery of fossilized human bones in the Neanderthal valley
1858	Excavation of Brixham Cave by Pengelly leads to favorable reexamination of Boucher de Perthes's evidence of human antiquity
1859	Prestwich and Evans publicly endorse Boucher de Perthes
	Darwin, *On the Origin of Species*
1861	Bachofen, *Das Mutterrecht*
	Boitard, *Paris avant les hommes*
1863	Huxley, *Evidence as to Man's Place in Nature*
	Lyell, *The Geological Evidences of the Antiquity of Man*
	Vogt, *Vorlesungen über den Menschen*
1864	E. Lartet discovers an engraving of a mammoth on fossil mammoth ivory at La Madeleine
	Discovery of "Vénus impudique," the first "Venus" figurine
	Verne, *Voyage au centre de la Terre* (revised 1867)
1865	Lubbock, in *Pre-Historic Times*, coins terms "Paleolithic" and "Neolithic"
	Figuier, *La Terre avant le Déluge*
	McLennan, *Primitive Marriage*
	Berthoud, *L'Homme depuis cinq milles ans*
1866	L. Lartet names cultural phases of the Paleolithic
1867	Prehistoric displays at the Paris International Exhibition include the mammoth engraving from La Madeleine
	The issue of Tertiary man raised at International Congress for Prehistoric Anthropology and Archeology, Paris
1867–68	Mortillet subdivides Paleolithic industries
1868	L. Lartet discovers five skeletons of anatomically modern humans at Crô-Magnon
	Haeckel, in *Natürliche Schöpfungsgeschichte*, names *Pithecanthropus alalus* as the missing link

1870	Figuier, *L'Homme primitif*
1871	Tylor, *Primitive Culture*
	Darwin, *The Descent of Man*
1872	**Arcelin, *Solutré***
1876	**Berthet, *Romans préhistoriques***
1879	M. and M. de Sautuola discover the Altamira Cave paintings
1880	Cormon's painting *Caïn*
	Lang, "The Romance of the First Radical"
1883	**Berthet, "Un Rêve"**
1886	Neanderthal skeletons discovered at Spy d'Orneau
	Curwen, "Zit and Xoe: Their Early Experiences"
1887	Frémiet's sculpture *Gorille enlevant une femme*
	Rosny, "Les Xipéhuz"
1888	**Hervilly, *Aventures d'un petit garçon préhistorique en France***
1889	**Hagemans, *Le Poignard de silex***
	Meunier, *Misère et grandeur de l'humanité primitive*
1889–90	Reconstruction of scenes from prehistoric life at Universal Exhibition, Paris
1890	Frazer, *The Golden Bough*
	Huxley, "The Aryan Question and Prehistoric Man"
	Richer's sculpture *Le premier artiste*
1891	Dubois discovers *Pithecanthropus erectus* at Trinil
	Schwob, "La Vendeuse d'ambre"
1892	**Hyne, *The New Eden***
	Rosny, *Vamireh*
	Schwob, "La Mort d'Odjigh"
1893–96	**Reed's "Prehistoric Peeps" cartoons**
1894	**Bierbower, *From Monkey to Man***
1895	Rosny, *Les Origines*
1896	**Rosny, *Eyrimah***
1897	**Rosny, "Nomaï"**
	Waterloo, *The Story of Ab*
	Wells, "Stories of the Stone Age"
1899	**Waterloo, "Christmas 200,000 B.C."**
1900	Dubois's reconstruction of *Pithecanthropus* at Universal Exhibition, Paris
1901	Anatomically modern human skeletons discovered at Grimaldi
	Verne, *Le Village aérien*
1902	Official recognition of the authenticity of Paleolithic parietal art

1903	Reinach, "L'art et la magie"
1904	**Dopp, *The Tree-Dwellers***
	Morris, *The Pagan's Progress*
1906	**Gratacap, *A Woman of the Ice Age***
1907	**London, *Before Adam***
1908	Complete Neanderthal skeleton ("Le Vieillard") discovered at La Chapelle-aux-Saints
	Jensen, *Bræen*
1909	**Nyst, *La Caverne***
1910	**Hilliers, *The Master-Girl***
	London, "When the World Was Young"
1911	**London, "The Strength of the Strong"**
	Rosny, *La Guerre du feu*
1911–13	Boule publishes four-part work on Neanderthal man
	Piltdown "discoveries" by Arthur Smith Woodward
1912	M. Bégouën and friends discover Tuc d'Audoubert Cave
	Doyle, *The Lost World*
1912–19	**Roberts, *In the Morning of Time***
1913	Freud, *Totem und Tabu*
	Robinson, *Longhead*
1914	Image of "Le Sorcier" discovered in Trois-Frères Cave
	Chaplin's movie *His Prehistoric Past*
	Haraucourt, *Daâh, le premier homme*
	Sterling, "The Babes in the Wood"
	Waterloo, *A Son of the Ages*
1915	**London, *The Star Rover***
1919	**Jensen, *Det tabte Land***
1920	Wells, *The Outline of History*
	Rosny, "La grande énigme"; *Le Félin géant*
1921	**Wells, "The Grisly Folk"**
1922	**Crump, *Og, Son of Fire***
1923	**Keaton's movie *The Three Ages***
1925	Dart announces discovery of *Australopithecus africanus*
	Anet, *La Fin d'un monde*
	Barbusse, *Les Enchaînements*
	Bégouën, *Les Bisons d'argile*
	Burroughs, *The Eternal Savage*
1926	L. Leakey begins excavations in east Africa
1927	Discovery announced of Peking Man (*Sinanthropus pekinensis*) at Zhoukoudian

Austin, *When Mankind Was Young*
Haggard, *Allan and the Ice-Gods*
Sullivan, *In the Beginning*
1928 Gale, *Carnack the Life-Bringer*
1929 McMorrow, "Man o'Dreams"
Rosny, "Les Hommes sangliers"
Rosny, *Les Conquérants du feu*
1930 Austin, *Tomorrow*
Rosny, *Helgvor du fleuve bleu*
1931 Wright, *Dream, or The Simian Maid*
1932 Mitchell, *Three Go Back*
1932–72 Hamlin's *Alley Oop* comic strip
1933 Sanders, "The Memory Stream"
Brown, "Martian and Troglodyte"
1934 Marshall, *Ogden's Strange Story*
1935 Gallun, "N'Goc"
Miller, "People of the Arrow"
1938 Broom discovers *Paranthropus* at Kromdraai
1939 Coon, *The Races of Europe*
del Rey, "The Day Is Done"
De Camp, "The Gnarly Man"
1940 Lascaux Cave paintings discovered
Roach's movie *One Million B.C.*
1942 Cartmill, "The Link"
1943 Fisher, *Darkness and the Deep*
1944 Fisher, *The Golden Rooms*
1946 Fisher, *Intimations of Eve*
1947 Broom discovers skull of gracile *Australopithecus* at Sterkfontein
Dart discovers *Australopithecus prometheus* at Makapansgat
Fisher, *Adam and the Serpent*
1949 Beauvoir, *Le deuxième sexe*
Breuil, *Beyond the Bounds of History*
1950 Evans, *The Coming of a King*
1951 Kjelgaard, *Fire-Hunter*
1952 Oliver, *Mists of Dawn*
Vercors, *Les Animaux dénaturés*
1953 Piltdown hoax uncovered
Dart, "The Predatory Transition from Ape to Man"
1954 Carsac, "Tâches de rouille"
1955 Golding, *The Inheritors*

1956 Straus and Cave rehumanize Neanderthals
1957 **Anderson, "The Long Remembering"**
1958 **Asimov, "The Ugly Litle Boy"**
1959 M. Leakey discovers *Zinjanthropus boisei* at Olduvai
     Farmer, "The Alley Man"
1960 **Lewis, *What We Did to Father***
1960–66 ***The Flintstones* TV cartoon series**
1961 Ardrey, *African Genesis*
1962 Lévi-Strauss, *Le Totémisme aujourd'hui*
1964 L. Leakey announces discovery of *Homo habilis*
1965 Leroi-Gourhan, *Préhistoire de l'art occidental*
1966 "Man the Hunter" anthropological gathering
     Chaffey's movie *One Million Years B.C.*
1967 Wilson and Sarich propose that the genetic distance between humans
     and apes indicates a common ancestor at 5 million years B.P.
     Thomas, "The Doctor"
1968 **Clarke, *2001: A Space Odyssey***
     Kubrick's movie *2001: A Space Odyssey*
1969– **Lécureux and Cheret, *Rahan* series of comics**
1971 Solecki, *Shanidar: The First Flower People*
     Slocum's "Woman the Gatherer" hypothesis
     Golding, "Clonk Clonk"
1974 Johanson and Taieb find "Lucy" (*Australopithecus afarensis*) at Hadar
1975 **Ribeiro, *O Homem do Sambaqui***
1976–78 M. Leakey discovers hominid footprints at Laetoli
1978 **Kurtén, *Den Svarta Tigern***
     Sheffield, "The Treasure of Odirex"
1980 **Simak, "Grotto of the Dancing Deer"**
     Auel, *The Clan of the Cave Bear*
1981 **Annaud's movie *Quest for Fire***
1982 Stringer's "Out of Africa" hypothesis
     Auel, *The Valley of Horses*
     Bishop, *No Enemy but Time*
1984 **Kurtén, *Mammutens Rådare***
     Harrison, *West of Eden*
     Schepisi's movie *Iceman*
1985 **Auel, *The Mammoth Hunters***
1986 **Chapman's movie *The Clan of the Cave Bear***
1987 Wilson, Cann, and Stoneking's "Mitochondrial Eve" hypothesis
     Mitchison, *Early in Orcadia*

Rutherfurd, *Sarum*

Thomas, *Reindeer Moon*

1988   Crace, *The Gift of Stones*

D. Hughes and C. Hughes's movie *Missing Link*

Lindholm, *The Reindeer People*; *Wolf's Brother*

Shuler, *She Who Remembers*

1989   Williams, *The People of the Black Mountains I*

1990   Auel, *The Plains of Passage*

Harrison, *Mother Earth Father Sky*

Pelot, *Le Rêve de Lucy*

Thomas, *The Animal Wife*

1991   Asimov and Silverberg, *Child of Time*

1997–2003   Pelot, *Sous le vent du monde* series of novels

2002   Lewis-Williams, *The Mind in the Cave*

Auel, *The Shelters of Stone*

Baxter, *Evolution*

2002–   Roudier, *Vo'Hounâ* series of graphic novels

Notes

▼

Introduction: The Fiction of Hominization (pages 1–13)

1. To keep the human focus sharp I exclude from current consideration (with one exception, see Coda) the small body of prehistoric fiction with nonhuman characters, the usual aim of which is to reflect our predicament indirectly by conveying harsh truths about the evolutionary process. A notable example is *Before the Dawn* (1934) by John Taine (pseud. of Eric Temple Bell, 1883–1960), whose protagonist is a carnivorous dinosaur named Belshazzar. For a similar reason I also exclude narratives of time travel to prehuman times.

2. The "present" is fixed by archaeological convention at A.D. 1950. Strictly speaking, the Stone Age *began* to end from 10,000 B.P., as until recently there lived peoples whose technologies were similar to those associated with Paleolithic Europeans.

3. This term was popularized by Lubbock in 1865 (342–343). By the 1890s it had acquired the popular figurative meaning that it retains today: "men uncivilized in behavior, especially toward women."

4. For a narratological discussion of the status of the narrator in pure pf, see Felici, "Le Roman," 266–70.

5. Cuvier has often been misquoted. His actual words in the "Discours préliminaire" (Preliminary discourse) of *Recherches sur les ossemens fossiles de quadrupèdes* (Investigations into quadruped fossil bones) (1812) were "Il n'y a point d'os humains fossiles" (Rudwick, 232).

6. This phrase, used by Charles Murchison in 1868 (Grayson, 208), alluded ironically to Cuvier's use of "great and sudden revolution" to describe the "most recent" catastrophe of 5,000–6,000 B.P., thought to be the Noachic deluge in Genesis (Rudwick, 248).

7. The Vézère River, whose valley in Périgord contains the greatest concentration of major Paleolithic sites in Europe, is a tributary of the Dordogne. It provides the setting for many works of pf, Jean M. Auel's *The Shelters of Stone* being a notable recent example.

8. Boucher de Perthes's three-volume *Antiquités celtiques et antédiluviennes* (Celtic and antediluvian Antiquities) (1847–64) "appealed in a unique way to French patriotism. The Gallic race, he declared in these books, was of high antiquity. Picardy had been the cradle of human civilization" (Wendt, 237–238).

9. According to Marc Guillaumie ("Le Roman préhistorique," 207 n. 1) the first significant use of this term was by the Goncourt brothers in their *Journal* (in 1891, about Rosny's *Vamireh*). It was certainly current by the early twentieth century (Nyst, 8). However, neither Versins's nor Lofficier's standard reference works on French sf have entries headed "Le Roman préhistorique." The former has a lengthy entry entitled "Prehistory" (693–695) while the latter includes early pf under the rubric "Other Lands and Mad Science" (345).

10. Jensen's *Det tabte Land: Mennesket før Istiden* (literally, The lost land: man before the Ice Age) was published eleven years after *Bræen: Myter om Istiden og det første Menneske* (literally, The glacier: myths of the Ice Age and the first man). But in *Den lange Rejse* (The long journey), the completed chronologically arranged cycle of six novels, *Det tabte Land* (Fire) precedes *Bræen* (Ice). Thanks to Britt Holmström for her help with Danish translations.

11. The manuscript of this book was finished in all essential details before I was able to read Guillaumie's new study, *Le Roman préhistorique* (2006), a comprehensive scholarly analysis from a structuralist perspective of French pf from Berthet to Haraucourt. There is some overlap between our discussions of the French texts and the genre of which they are a part. We differ greatly, however, in our focus, approach, methods, aims, and perhaps even in our intended readership. Here is not an appropriate forum to debate these differences. I register my sincere admiration at Guillaumie's achievement, noting that I arrived at my readings of the French works independently of his study.

12. That is, the c. 1932 discoveries by Dorothy Garrod of anatomically more modern Neanderthal remains at Tabun and Skhul Caves, Palestine.

1. From Boitard's *Paris before Man* to London's *Before Adam* (pages 17–47)

1. This issue never similarly engaged British discourse, perhaps because of native pride in Lyell's role in undermining Cuvier's prestige, in tandem with the success of the formidable T. H. Huxley in converting educated Britons to the Darwinian cause.

2. Fossilized human bones in association with those of extinct animals were found at Souvignargues (Gard) near Nîmes as early as 1827, though Cuvier's influence long inhibited recognition of this fact (Lyon, 80–83).

3. According to the title page of *Paris avant les hommes*, the illustrations were engraved from Boitard's own drawings.

4. Though such artworks had been found since at least the 1830s, they were then thought to be Celtic. Edouard Lartet (in 1861) was the first to suggest that they were prehistoric.

5. Identification of our foremother would have to wait for a less patriarchal age and the discovery of mitochondrial DNA.

6. As Stephanie Moser has noted vis-à-vis visual representations (125), after

Darwin the episodic, hetereogeneous narrative such as those in Figuier's works (q.v.) replaced the single image of Eden as a better means of representing the new, expanded vision of human prehistory.

7. This was then a vaguely derogatory term for nonmiraculous explanations of the origin of terrestrial life. Haeckel proposed replacing it with "Monism" (1:37), thereby suggesting that there was a singular, natural explanation for life's origin that superseded the dualistic scriptural one in which supernature vitalized nature.

8. For amplification of Verne's approach to evolutionary science in *Voyage*, see Debus, 405–408, and Ruddick, "Jules Verne," 156–158.

9. Here in 1864 Lartet discovered a piece of fossil mammoth ivory engraved with the image of a mammoth, thereby demonstrating conclusively both that prehistoric man had made mobiliary art and that he had coexisted with extinct animals.

10. The Tertiary was then used to refer to the geological period before the first (Quaternary) Ice Age. In 1833 Lyell had subdivided the Tertiary into the Eocene, Miocene, and Pliocene epochs. At the 1867 congress, Abbé Louis Alexis Bourgeois presented what he claimed were worked flints that he had found in Miocene strata at Thenay (Loir-et-Cher). See also the discussion of Elie Berthet's "Un Rêve" below.

11. The action of Verne's novel begins, as the first sentence states, on 23 May 1863. Laborers working for Boucher de Perthes had "found" the Moulin-Quignon jaw on 28 March 1863, as the 1867 edition precisely reminds us (210). In May 1863, an international panel of experts had been convened to rule on the authenticity of the jaw. There was a split between the English members, who pronounced it a fake, and most of the French, who resisted this verdict, chiefly out of pride (Prestwich, 178–191). As Verne's 1867 revision indicates, Lidenbrock and Otto had left for Iceland before the affair had been resolved. By 1867, however, most experts had tacitly accepted that the jaw had almost certainly been fabricated by the workmen in order to claim a reward from Boucher de Perthes who, though unanimously deemed innocent of fraud, would die in 1868 refusing to admit that he had been duped. Lidenbrock's defense of the jaw in 1863 would be adjudged by a reader in 1867 as admirably patriotic but naïve and misguided. For a modern account of "L'Affaire Moulin-Quignon," see Trinkaus and Shipman, 90–97.

12. For example, in Nyst, 330–350; Jensen, 69; Fisher, *Golden Rooms*, 175; and Auel, *Plains of Passage*, 486–488. In Gratacap, 127–130, North American wild horses stampede themselves into extinction.

13. As Jean Combier, Arcelin's modern editor, has suggested (Arcelin, 9). For further evidence of this connection, see Rosny's comments on George Catlin in *Les Origines* (89–90).

14. The world's first pf novel remains virtually unknown outside France. It was reprinted in 1977 under the title *Chasseurs de rennes à Solutré: roman préhistorique* (Reindeer hunters at Solutré: a prehistoric novel).

15. In 1869, the Swiss ethnologist Franz Pruner-Bey had declared that the aboriginal inhabitants of France in the Reindeer Age were of the primitive mongoloid type. This new "fact" had necessitated an immediate revision of the relevant plates

in Figuier's *L'Homme primitif* so that, when its second edition appeared, the people depicted looked less European (vii).

16. For a full discussion of the Aryans as a supposed master race, see chapter 6.

17. Chellean (now Olduwan) was named for Chelles (Seine-et-Marne); Mousterian (the classic Neanderthal industry) for Le Moustier (Dordogne); Solutrean for Solutré; Magdalenian (the artistically accomplished industry associated with the Cro-Magnons) for La Madeleine. More industries (for example, Acheulian, Aurignacian, Azilian) would subsequently be added to the list.

18. According to the *OED*, Spencer himself coined the term "Progressionist" in 1859. Gould has shown how the word "evolution" has always had progressionist connotations (*Ever Since Darwin*, 34–38). Darwin's thought was inevitably inflected by progressionism, though by the late nineteenth century many of his British heirs, including Huxley, had lost confidence in the doctrine. In 1891 Huxley's disciple H. G. Wells dismissed progressionism as a popular delusion, referring to it mockingly as "excelsior biology" ("Zoological Retrogression," 159).

19. Berthet (q.v.) cites Mortillet's estimate in *Le Préhistorique* (1882) that this was 230,000–240,000 B.P.

20. The story is told with great verve by Pat Shipman in her outstanding biography of Dubois, *The Man Who Found the Missing Link* (2001).

21. The discoveries by Villeneuve at Baoussé-Roussé were so described by René Verneau in 1906. Pf has taken a long time to come to terms with the "racial" implications of this discovery, though Ranec, Ayla's dark-skinned lover, embodies one notable recent attempt; see Auel, *Shelters of Stone*, 868, where Baoussé-Roussé is alluded to.

22. It was later collected in *In the Wrong Paradise and Other Stories* (1886).

23. Survivals are "processes, customs, opinions, and so forth which have been carried on by force of habit into a new state of society different from that in which they had their original home, and they thus remain as proofs and examples of an older condition of culture out of which a newer has been evolved" (Tylor, 16). In *XXII Ballades in Blue China* (1880), Lang included a witty pf poem, "Double Ballade of Primitive Man," the latter half of which (including the stanza forming the epigraph to this chapter) was actually written by Tylor.

24. For further discussion see Sparks, who concludes her article with a telling observation on what paleoanthropologists and pf writers have in common: "they are motivated not so much by idle curiosity about what happened to our remote ancestors as by concern about what will happen to us and our descendants" (140).

25. *Zit and Xoe* was serialized anonymously in *Blackwood's* (April–May 1886), then published in book form in 1887 in the United Kingdom and 1889 in the United States. I cite the *Blackwood's* version as it is the more accessible.

26. "A Story of the Stone Age" was first serialized as "Stories of the Stone Age" in the *Idler* (May–September 1897) with illustrations by Cosmo Rowe, then collected in a slightly revised form in *Tales of Space and Time* (1899). It was reprinted by Hugo Gernsback in his pioneering sf pulp magazine *Amazing Stories* (November 1927). Unlike "A Story of the Days to Come," "Stone Age" has never been re-

printed as a separate volume. The intertextual relationship between the novellas is clarified at the end of "Days to Come" (804–805), when the protagonist in the future imagines the course of human development in the Thames valley from the Stone Age to his own time and is struck by its sheer contingency.

27. The first four chapters appeared in the *London Magazine* in 1912. Six more chapters, which continue the adventures of Grôm and A-ya, were added to the book version published in 1919. According to his correspondence, in 1923 Roberts began but never completed a pf sequel to *In the Morning of Time* to be called *Overlords of Earth* (Boone, 319–320). He also wrote a pf story called "The Guardian of the Cave Mouth," published c. 1925, though this has not been located (366).

28. Roberts grew up in bilingual New Brunswick and certainly read French. However, David Ketterer identifies climate, not culture, as the reason for what he discerns as an early Canadian fascination with the prehistoric in fiction (22).

29. This term, referring to the lifestyle transition between nomadic hunting-and-gathering and settled crop cultivation and livestock raising, did not become current until the 1920s.

30. The pioneering evolutionist Jean Lamarck argued in 1809 that an organism could initiate adaptive transformations that were heritable by its progeny; for example, the giraffe gradually acquired a long neck from generations of stretching to eat leaves from trees. Though Darwin's theory of natural selection should have made Lamarckism obsolete, it didn't, perhaps because humans are imbued with the sense that culture, normally a far stronger adaptive force in our lives than natural selection, *is* acquired and transmitted to the next generation. As Edmund O. Wilson puts it, "Cultural evolution is Lamarckian and very fast, whereas biological evolution is Darwinian and usually very slow" (*On Human Nature*, 78).

31. Roveland (q.v.) provides a useful survey of children's pf from Dopp through 1990.

32. The only material evidence at the time that such beings had ever existed was the Calaveras skull (Gratacap 23) found in 1866 in auriferous gravel in California. Even in 1906 it was considered of very dubious authenticity, and it was later exposed as a hoax.

33. Here Gratacap shows the influence of the father of American anthropology, Lewis Henry Morgan, who believed that "the history and experience of the American Indian tribes represent, more or less nearly, the history and experience of our own remote ancestors when in corresponding conditions," and that their rich cultural legacy was endangered by "American civilization." Morgan appealed to American anthropologists "to enter this great field and gather its abundant harvest" (vi–vii).

34. "There are philogynists as fanatical as any 'miscegynists' who, reversing our antiquated notions, bid the man look upon the woman as the higher type of humanity; who ask us to regard the female intellect as the clearer and the quicker, if not the stronger; who desire us to look up to the feminine moral sense as the purer and the nobler; and bid man abdicate his usurped sovereignty over nature in favour of the female line" (Huxley, "Emancipation," 68).

35. It had previously been serialized in *Everybody's Magazine* (October 1906–February 1907). The book version is copiously illustrated by Charles Livingston Bull, a wildlife artist who specialized in "primitive" subjects. Bull also illustrated London's *The Call of the Wild* (1903) and three other pf novels: Robinson's *Longhead* and Crump's *Og, Son of Fire* and *Og, Boy of Battle*.

36. The "law of *Progress* (progressus), or *Perfecting* (teleosis)" establishes that "in successive periods of this earth's history, a continual increase in the perfection of organic formations has taken place"; organisms have become ever "more perfectly and highly developed," though there are "exceptions which are due to the process of degeneration" (1:277–278; emphasis in original).

37. On 8 July 1907 London received a postcard from Haeckel thanking him for the gift (Labor, 2:709, 711 n. 2).

38. As John R. Hensley (q.v.) has shown, the two writers also differed markedly in their views on eugenics. Unlike Waterloo, London doubted the value of racial exclusiveness to engineer the "fittest" human beings, as suggested by his construction of the Swift One as hybrid.

39. The affair had further ramifications. Waterloo's novel was successfully adapted for children by William Lewis Nida as *Ab the Cave Man* (1911). With London's approval, Charles F. Lowrie tried to do the same with *Before Adam*, producing a manuscript "Big-Tooth and the Cave People," in 1910 (Labor, 2:875). Lowrie sent this to Katharine Dopp for her endorsement, only to discover that Dopp felt seriously aggrieved. She believed that London, having interviewed her personally, had used *her* ideas without suitable acknowledgment in *Before Adam*, and was now trespassing on her turf as a writer of pf for children (2:961–962). To Lowrie, London first claimed never to have met Dopp, then retracted this claim, excusing himself by having confused Dopp with Mary E. Marcy, another Chicago-based socialist New Woman. In 1917 Marcy published a children's pf novel, *Stories of the Cave People*, with a strong eugenic theme. Lowrie's manuscript was never published.

2. From Rosny's First Artist to del Rey's Last Neanderthal (pages 48–68)

1. Rosny noted, "I was the first in France . . . who produced in 'Les Xipéhuz' a new kind of fantastic motif, namely the extraterrestrial alien" (Baronian, 687). The January–February 1986 issue of the French literary journal *Europe* (3–122) (see Couegnas entry in Works Cited) offers a series of comparative studies of Rosny and Wells as founders of the sf and pf traditions in France and Britain respectively.

2. Erik Lysøe (q.v.) in his section entitled "An End-of-the-Century Inspiration" offers valuable observations on the continuing influence of Zola's naturalism on Rosny's pf after this break.

3. A 2003 international touring art exhibition, "Vénus et Caïn: Figures de la Préhistoire 1830–1930" (Venus and Cain: faces of prehistory, 1830–1930), and its

excellent accompanying catalogue (ed. Lafont-Couturier et al.), did much to rescue these fascinating artistic visions of imaginary prehistory from oblivion.

4. For more on the iconography of Cormon's *Caïn*, see Berman, 296–297.

5. Daniel Couegnas notes that Rosny, in this respect unlike his English contemporary Wells, has "a rather academic approach to representation" (un sculptural un peu pompier) (25). "Pompier" alludes to the approved formal style of the nineteenth-century French Academy.

6. In the nineteenth century, elaborate theories of the origin of civilization were constructed upon "racial" tendencies to either round-headedness (brachycephalism) or long-headedness (dolichocephalism) as determined by scientific measurements of the skull (craniometry). The supposed long-headedness (and hence greater brain capacity) of the Cro-Magnons or Aryans was used as evidence of their racial superiority, though the subsequent disappearance of these groups made this "superiority" difficult to define. Craniometry's misleading central binary opposition—in practice, there is often a great variance in cranial index among members of any given ethnic group—became toxic when allied to scientific racism. For a succinct introduction to this subject, see Gould, *Mismeasure of Man*, 98–100.

7. This long-lived theory, emerging from a synthesis of Marcellin Boule's misrepresentation of the "Old Man" (see below, this chapter) and the Piltdown hoax, held that "there had been an ancient split in the human lineage which led to the early appearance of a relatively modern skeletal form alongside a more archaic hominid, represented in the fossil record by the Neanderthals" (qtd. in Lewin, *Origin*, 51). The theory seemed chiefly motivated by the desire to expel Neanderthals entirely from human ancestry (Trinkaus and Shipman, 195).

8. Mme. Meunier, née Léonie Levallois, was a prolific popular author and the wife of the geologist Stanislas Meunier, professor at the Museum of Natural History in Paris from 1892.

9. Belgium was also the source of the Engis skull, the first Neanderthal fossil ever to be discovered (c. 1830)—though it was not recognized to be Neanderthal until 1936.

10. Evidently Nyst had not read Bierbower or London. He had earlier published two pf novels obscurely in Brussels, *Notre père des bois* (Our father of the woods) (1899) and *La Forêt nuptiale* (The nuptial forest) (1900).

11. Freud's view of the horde derives chiefly from J. J. Atkinson's posthumous *Primal Law* (1903). Atkinson in turn derived his hypothesis about social origins from observations of the natives of New Caledonia (where he died in 1899) and from Darwin's comments on the behavior of the gorilla (*Descent*, 2:362–363). Wells's *Outline of History* on Neanderthals shows strong traces of Atkinson's influence (1:76–79).

12. Guillaumie suggests that pf as a genre may be viewed as a kind of cultural version of the Freudian Family Romance, one in which we apply our imaginations to the mystery of our origin as a species ("Roman préhistorique," 217).

13. That Boule's examination was conducted with unprecedented rigor suggests

that scientific objectivity in paleoanthropology will always be difficult to attain be-cause of researchers' a priori assumptions about what is "truly" human. However, the reassessment of the Old Man in the early 1950s revealed that Boule had also been influenced by features of this individual's remains that, having no point of comparison, he could not have known were abnormal: for example, the Old Man had legs bowed by rickets. Perhaps ironically, recent genetic tests have indicated that Neanderthals probably were different enough from Cro-Magnons to have functioned as a separate subspecies.

14. One anthropologist who did draw the connection was Otto Klaatsch. Begin-ning in 1899, a huge number of fragmented Neanderthal bones had been discov-ered at Krapina in Croatia, suggesting to some that Neanderthals had cannibalized their own kind. But in 1923 Klaatsch, probably in light of what the Great War had revealed about *Homo sapiens*, proposed that the Neanderthals had been massacred in battle and eaten by our Aurignacian ancestors. Though Klaatsch's "Battle of Krapina" would be dismissed as a "legend" (Brace, 34), the idea of a violent war of extermination between ourselves and Neanderthals, with our ancestors proving themselves to be more barbaric than the submen, would be developed in pf by Vardis Fisher and William Golding.

15. J. Leslie Mitchell was one of these few readers. See the discussion below, this chapter, of his use of Neanderthals in *Three Go Back*.

16. Rosny later expanded this story into the novel *La sauvage aventure* (The sav-age adventure) (1935).

17. "Claude Anet" was the pen name of the Swiss-born Jean Schopfer, tennis champion, novelist, and travel writer, whose best known work was *Mayerling* (1930).

18. David Pringle notes that this novel was "actually plotted in collaboration with Rudyard Kipling" (v). Kipling's solo contributions to pf were two of the face-tious *Just So Stories for Little Children* (1902), "How the First Letter Was Written" (95–103) and "How the Alphabet Was Made" (107–121), and a story for older chil-dren, "The Knife and the Naked Chalk" (1910), a dream vision set in Sussex of the transition between the Neolithic and the Bronze Age.

19. Crump's other pf novels were *Og, Boy of Battle* (1925), *Mog the Mound Builder* (1931), *Og of the Cave People* (1935), and *Og, Son of Og* (1965), all first serialized in the scouting periodical *Boys' Life*. Trussel (q.v.) provides much interesting informa-tion about the series and its author.

20. There are two quasi-sequels—*The Vengeance of Gwa* (by "Anthony Win-grave") (1935) and *Spider's War* (1954)—though the former was published without a modern frame connecting it to *Dream*, and the latter is not pf but set in a neo-primitive far future. Much information about Wright, including the full texts of most of his novels, can be found at http://www.sfw.org/index.html.

21. In anthropology, diffusionist theories explain the spread of cultural innova-tions by the radiation of people or artifacts from an original center. What Daniel calls "hyperdiffusionism" (88) is any extreme variant of these theories, especially

that associated with Grafton Elliott Smith and W. J. Perry in Britain, who argued that all civilization as we know it originated in Egypt. Crackpot hyperdiffusionist ideas, especially entertained in association with "lost continents" like Atlantis and Lemuria, can be traced back to the mid-nineteenth century and were often fueled by racism, imperialism, or both. One master race (say, the Atlanteans) might be viewed as responsible for inventing and spreading civilization, which had a tendency to develop impurities as it diffused. Though Mitchell in *Three Go Back* did not explain how his version of diffusionism actually might have played itself out in (pre)history, he evidently felt that "Archaic Civilization" grew increasingly corrupt the farther it spread from its Nilotic origin, and took its most corrupt form in modern Western culture. (This was by no means an orthodox diffusionist view; see Kuklick, 127). He seems also to suggest that the unfortunate accident of Archaic Civilization came about because its founders were not of the "pure" Cro-Magnon racial strain (which still exists, though in abeyance, in the modern world, see *Three Go Back*, 100, 194) but were tarnished by intermixture with Neanderthals (163). It is not clear if Mitchell believed that miscegenation came about as a result of an enforced migration of both races to Egypt when Atlantis was destroyed.

22. For Mitchell's own position on diffusionism, see his "The Diffusionist Heresy" (1931); for his correspondence with Elliott Smith, see Munro, 62–70.

23. François Bordes calls *Three Go Back* "frankly execrable," and not just because it violates paleoanthropological plausibility. Responding to Clair's claims to have drunk Moselle on a picnic at Crô-Magnon, he snorts: "To drink Moselle in Périgord! It's one of those sins that are their own punishment!" (883–884).

24. This was the "London skull," aka the "Lady of Lloyds," later described by Elliott Smith as "a rather primitive type of the species *sapiens*" (Young, 280).

25. That is, until the subgeneric divergence of prehistoric romance after 1980. In the 1940s, the U.S. pulp magazine *Famous Fantastic Mysteries*, edited by Mary Gnaedinger, helped sustain the pf tradition by reprinting such pf and prehistoric sf novels as J. Leslie Mitchell's *Three Go Back* in December 1943, Richard Tooker's *The Day of the Brown Horde* in September 1944, John Taine's *Before the Dawn* in February 1946, Jack London's *The Star Rover* in February 1947, H. Rider Haggard's *Allan and the Ice Gods* in April 1947, and Edison Marshall's two novels *Dian of the Lost Land* in April 1949 and *Ogden's Strange Story* (as "Ogden's Strange Stories") in December 1949.

26. First published in *Unknown* (June 1939). This short-lived magazine specializing in fantasy stories was a companion to *Astounding* and was also edited by John W. Campbell. De Camp's idea of an immortal Neanderthal man was simultaneously developed by P. Schuyler Miller in his story "Old Man Mulligan" published in *Astounding* (December 1940). Both stories update the legend of the Wandering Jew.

27. Evidently this story was realistic enough to be considered "true" sf by Campbell, as it was first published in *Astounding* (May 1939).

3. From Fisher's "Testament of Man" to Auel's "Earth Children" (pages 69–99)

1. The ambitious partly pf novel *The Caves of Périgord* (2002) by the veteran British journalist Martin Walker (b. 1949) is a recent attempt to mine this seam. Walker interleaves Nazi atrocities in occupied France in 1943–44 with the tribulations of the young Magdalenian artist who decorated Lascaux Cave 17,000 B.P. The narrator notes that the Dordogne and Vézère valleys "said more about the ancient history and glorious achievement of humankind than any other spot on earth. And just as much about the evil that humans could wreak upon each other" (313).

2. *Shanidar* was also an important influence on Auel's *The Clan of the Cave Bear* (xii).

3. In a similar vein, but with more professional production values, Donald C. Johanson, the discoverer of "Lucy," in collaboration with the illustrator Kevin O'Farrell, published *Journey from the Dawn* (1990), which offers speculative scenes from the life of *Australopithecus afarensis*.

4. Of *The Testament of Man*, Fisher noted, "Now that the task is completed I feel, in looking back, that it was too big for me. I think that if a writer were to attempt what I attempted his preparation should begin early and his education should be directed toward his goal. I started late, very late, and so abused my eyes and health and drove myself at a pace that only my wife was ever allowed to see, realizing more clearly as the years passed that I'd never had enough time to assimilate and reflect on the countless wonderful facts and implications in the learned articles and more than two thousand books that I read. I developed a case of chronic mental indigestion. . . . I knew from the first that I'd want to write a novel about the ape-man. I think I was not half so successful as I had wished to be in projecting myself into the small dim world of those stooped short-legged hairy ancestors, who were learning to walk in an upright position" ("Vardis," q.v.).

5. Kirby L. Duncan (q.v.) has noted the influence of Fisher on Golding. The lurid packaging of the paperback reprints of Fisher's pf novels has not improved their literary reputation. The cover blurb of the Pyramid paperback (1960) of *The Golden Rooms* shrieks, "The primitive men & women who lusted, loved, hunted, & killed with wild animal abandon & no sense of SIN! Brutal, gory, realistic & intense adventure! They sated their lust in SEXUAL ORGIES. They DRANK THE BLOOD of their enemies. They walked NAKED and unashamed," etc, etc.

6. The superb translation was by Vercors's wife Rita Barisse. It is perhaps best known under the U.K. title *Borderline* (1954). The novel was later reissued as *The Murder of the Missing Link* (1958) in the United States. No more recently published French pf or prehistoric sf novel has been translated into English.

7. That is, primarily (but not exclusively) in *male* human nature, just as Fisher had done in *Adam and the Serpent*.

8. There is no direct evidence from Golding's published work that he had read any earlier pf aside from Wells's, though circumstantial evidence is very strong.

One suspects that, as with Jack London, Golding's is the case of a great writer who subconsciously filed away useful aspects of his extensive reading in lesser writers, later to reshape them for his own purposes.

9. *What We Did to Father* was reprinted as *The Evolution Man* (1963), as *Once upon an Ice Age (What We Did to Father)* (1979), and as *The Evolution Man; or, How I Ate My Father* (1993). A French translation by Vercors and Rita Barisse, *Pourquoi j'ai mangé mon père*, appeared in 1990.

10. Leon E. Stover claims that *What We Did to Father* "evidently is a novelization of the first three chapters of Coon's *The Story of Man* (1954)" (362). This is an exaggeration, though there are some similarities between the works. Both, for example, contain minatory images of mushroom clouds (Coon, 409; Lewis, 133) as reminders of the dangers of unrestrained technological development.

11. In *The Lost Worlds of 2001* (1972) Clarke reveals that while working on the screenplay of *2001* he had read Ardrey's *African Genesis* and that he and Kubrick had subsequently debated whether early man was a vegetarian or carnivore: "Stan wants our visitors [that is, the aliens] to turn Man into a carnivore; I argued that he always was" (34).

12. The motif of the alien monolith—crystalline in the novel, black in the movie—has its origin in the shiny pyramid, serving a similar "fire alarm" function, found on the Moon in Clarke's story "The Sentinel" (1951).

13. Possibly the first prehistoric sf scenario of prehistoric men being raised to a new level of technological expertise by alien intervention is an episode (146–149) in the rambling antireligious scientific romance *Willmoth the Wanderer* (1890) by the Kansan writer C(harles) C(urtis) Dail (1851–1902).

14. That is, retaining juvenile traits into adulthood. Modern humans are highly neotenous primates, retaining long past sexual maturity such juvenile traits as hairlessness, curiosity, playfulness, the taste for milk, and the desire to be cuddled.

15. The rehumanization of the Neanderthals caused problems for the killer ape hypothesis. If we had descended from murderous australopithecines, then our close Neanderthal relatives had almost certainly done so too. Neanderthals were carnivorous, had slightly bigger brains than us, and were more powerfully built—formidable killer apes indeed. So why were our ancestors able to replace them so easily?

16. Auel was influenced by the Phillip Lieberman–Edmund Crelin hypothesis, based on a reconstruction of the vocal tract of the Old Man of La Chapelle-aux-Saints, as proposed in their article "On the Speech of Neanderthal Man" (1971). They surmised that Neanderthals did not have a hyoid bone (which allows free movement of the tongue) and hence lacked the ability to produce the full range of modern human vowels. The 1983 discovery of a Neanderthal hyoid bone, very similar to our own, in Kebara Cave, Israel, undermined this hypothesis (Trinkaus and Shipman, 353–355, 391–394).

17. With one (indirect) exception: the success in 1981 of the movie *Quest for Fire* led to the mass-market reissue of the rather unsatisfactory 1967 English translation of Rosny's novel.

18. Lindholm's two novels were also published together in an omnibus edition entitled *A Saga of the Reindeer People* (1988).

19. This novel is set as recently as A.D. 1270, reminding us that prehistory is a relative term rather than a defined period.

20. This "devolutionary" trend is thought to be caused by the growth of pan-European government bureaucracies, leading to the weakening of centralized authority in London.

21. Rutherfurd is frank about his indebtedness to Michener, noting that he kept *Chesapeake* (1978) at his side "as an example and an inspiration" during the composition of *Sarum* ("James A. Michener").

22. The replacement of the latter by the former is the subject of the bloodthirsty saga *The Golden Strangers* (1956) by Henry Treece (British, 1911–66), a work that may also have influenced the earlier episodes of Williams's *The People of the Black Hill* (q.v.).

23. Two volumes of the projected trilogy were completed at Williams's death; the prehistoric episodes constitute most of the first volume.

24. In an afterword to *Reindeer Moon*, Thomas notes that her fictional Siberian hunter-gatherers were partly based on modern Namibian Ju/wa Bushmen, among whom she has done extensive fieldwork (334).

25. "Thomas says she began *Reindeer Moon* before Jean M. Auel's *Clan of the Cave Bear* appeared in 1980. She describes *Cave Bear* as fun to read and says, 'I don't have any ax to grind about what other people think Paleolithic people did. . . . If [Auel] wants to think they had video games and used silverware and handkerchiefs, that's OK. For all I know, they did'" (McCarthy, q.v.).

26. In a postscript to *The Animal Wife* Thomas praises Kurtén for his insights into Paleolithic animal life (316).

27. The others are *Le Nom perdu du soleil* (The lost name of the sun) (1998), set 1,000,000 B.P.; *Debout dans le ventre blanc du silence* (standing in the white belly of silence) (1999), set 380,000 B.P.; and *Avant la fin du ciel* (Before the end of the sky) (2000), set 65,000 B.P.

4. Nature and Human Nature (pages 103–124)

1. Darwin nowhere makes this argument more strongly than in *The Expression of the Emotions in Man and Animals* (1872), long suspected to be contaminated by anthropomorphism but rediscovered as a masterwork once the genetic unity of the human species and its close genetic continuity with related species had been affirmed.

2. Landau is thinking of "Cinderella" as the rags-to-riches romance of modern popular culture. In truth, traditional tales of the Cinderella type are riches-to-rags-to-riches narratives in which a high-born protagonist is humbled but later *regains* her status through marriage to the prince.

3. In this regard, Pluciennik quotes literary theorist Hayden White's axiom, "Comprehension is nothing other than the recognition of the form of the narrative" (655).

4. A reviewer in *American Anthropologist* notes that "narrative form has a new epistemological dignity in social science" and goes so far as to suggest that Thomas's *Reindeer Moon*, "our first deeply informed ethnobiological novel," may ultimately be a more memorable contribution to anthropology than supposedly "realist" (that is, objective, factual) documentation (Biesele 230).

5. A good example of this strategy can be found in the young adult pf novel *Dom and Va* (1973) by John Christopher (Christopher Samuel Youd, British, b. 1922). It is a love story between a boy from a tribe of Dartian killer apes and a girl from a peaceful group of tool-making habilines. This revised Adam ("Dom") and Eve ("Va") are ultimately revealed as "our father" and "our mother" (142), and are responsible for bequeathing to us the opposed sides of our modern human nature.

6. The Hobbesian view of Natural Man persisted for a long time in pf, as Hobbes's "war . . . of every man, against every man" (82), or *bellum omnium contra omnes*, seemed to echo Darwin's "struggle for existence." More recently, however, the Hobbesian solitaire has been shown to be as much a myth as Rousseau's noble savage. As Richard Leakey has noted, "Hobbes's view that non-agricultural people have 'no society' and are 'solitary' could hardly be more wrong. To be a hunter-gatherer is to experience a life that is intensely social" (*Making of Mankind*, 101).

7. The story of Esau the hunter tricked out of his birthright by Jacob the pastoralist (Genesis 27) is the cultural paradigm for the association in pf between male hairiness and primitive (simple, animal, virile) qualities. These would be later superseded by the "smooth," "feminine" qualities required by advancing civilization. Berman (q.v.) offers an extensive analysis of the symbolism of male hair in visual representations of the caveman.

8. It is now known that the European cave bear (*Ursus spelaeus*) was primarily a vegetarian.

9. Cf. Nyst: "man in the great freedom of the golden age of forests before he became subject to the phantoms of his imagination, customs, prejudices, social practices and laws" (30).

10. Between 1932 and 1955, Louis Leakey discovered a rich variety of fossil Miocene apes near Lake Victoria (Johanson, *Lucy*, 108, 361–367).

11. Before it was formulated as his "Third Law," Clarke (134) dramatized this idea through the encounter between advanced aliens and a Paleolithic hunter in his 1953 prehistoric sf story "Expedition to Earth" (aka "Encounter at Dawn" and "Encounter in the Dawn").

12. Left one-eyed after a fight with a bear, Carl will be the prototype of the Norse God Odin.

13. This is even more true of the shorter episodes in *The Mammoth Hunters* when Ayla demonstrates her firestones to the Mamutoi (232–235, 659).

14. In his 1929 anthropological work *Les Conquérants du feu* (The conquerors of fire), Rosny suggests that the Neolithic invention of the concept of the human ownership of animals, ushering in religions in which self-regarding anthropomor-

phism replaced animal worship, put paid to the great animal art of the Magdalenians (156).

15. In his brilliant explication of *La Guerre du feu*, Lysøe (q.v.) reads the mammoth and giant feline (now both extinct) as representing for Rosny extreme feminine and masculine principles respectively, the offspring of whose "fabulous marriage" is the hero Naoh. As our ancestor, Naoh's legacy to us is a harmonious balance between sexual principles, one we must strive to maintain if we are not also to become extinct.

16. Curwen's Xoe is perhaps the first woman in pf to domesticate the horse (464).

17. Hervilly had suggested that wild dogs may well have deliberately shown reindeer hunters how useful they could be in the capture of herd animals (219–220).

18. See Arcelin (69) on the necessity of dogs among reindeer herders.

5. Sex and Gender (pages 125–151)

1. When used to model prehistoric sexual practices, apes in early pf, even if referred to as gorillas or orangutans, tend to be as mythic as Edgar Rice Burroughs's Kerchak or Merian C. Cooper's King Kong. Few knew then that the fearsome gorilla was a peaceable vegetarian.

2. See Ruddick, "Sexual Paradise Regained?" for a full analysis of this work.

3. Freud's reported words were, "Was will das Weib?"; Nietzsche's (or Zarathustra's) actual words were, "Du gehst zu Frauen? Vergiss die Peitsche [whip] nicht."

4. Deamer's first published pf story, "As It Was in the Beginning," written under the influence of Wells's "A Story of the Stone Age," won a national competition in Australia and appeared in the periodical *Lone Hand* in January 1908, when she was only seventeen years old. Three more pf stories were published in *Lone Hand* that year, and these four were first collected with two other stories as *In the Beginning* (1909). There was a deluxe edition reprinted in 1929 including a new final story (Kirkpatrick, 181–182). Deamer was notorious for the leopard-skin cavewoman costume that she wore at parties in the 1920s.

5. Elizabeth Fee (q.v.) gives a succinct account of how patriarchal monogamy was viewed by Victorian anthropologists as a late and unnatural—yet inevitable and welcome—stage of human social development.

6. As expressed in the article "The Evolution of Hunting" (1968) by Sherwood L. Washburn and C. S. Lancaster.

7. In "Woman the Gatherer: Male Bias in Anthropology" (as by Sally Linton), reprinted (by Slocum, q.v.) in 1975.

8. There was what was perceived as an antifeminist backlash to "Woman the Gatherer" in the form of the 1981 hypothesis of C. O. Lovejoy (q.v.) that males, not females, were the original gatherers.

9. With the "flower burial" of Shanidar transposed to an alien planet, this binary opposition was developed by James Tiptree, Jr. (Alice Bradley Sheldon, American, 1915–87) in her prehistoric sf story "The Color of Neanderthal Eyes" (1988).

6. Race or the Human Race (pages 152–172)

1. As Montagu notes, Huxley himself in 1865 "decried the loose usage of classificatory terms, particularly as applied to man" because each term (for example, stock, variety, or species) invokes some prejudice that does not conduce to scientific objectivity (*Idea of Race*, 84).

2. Both Stringer and Donald Johanson, two of the most distinguished living paleoanthropologists, respect the power of existing mythology to shape their discipline's theory. Stringer's *African Exodus* (1996) contains brief discussions of several key works of pf, including *2001, La Guerre du feu*, "The Grisly Folk," and *The Inheritors* (30, 54–55, 72). Johanson's *Ancestors* (1994) mentions "The Grisly Folk," *The Inheritors*, and *The Clan of the Cave Bear* (257–258).

3. For a balanced discussion of the "Out of Africa" and Multiregional hypotheses, and an evaluation of "Mitochondrial Eve," see Lewin, *The Origin of Modern Humans*, 63–113.

4. The previous, bracketed sentence and the description of the laughter following it was added to later editions of Lewis's novel; see, for example, *The Evolution Man* (1993), 89.

5. Du Chaillu's *Explorations and Adventures in Tropical Africa* (1861) contains a description of an enraged gorilla as a "hellish dream creature—a being of that hideous order, half-man half-beast" (quoted in Blunt, 138). In the same year Du Chaillu exhibited gorilla skins and stuffed gorillas at London's Royal Geographical Society. London Zoo did not acquire a living gorilla until 1887.

6. "Semitic," like "Aryan," originally referred to a family of languages. Olender (13–20) explains how the fictitious Aryan-Semitic binary opposition migrated from philology into ethnology during the nineteenth century.

7. Remains from Gorham's Cave, Gibraltar, have been dated to 28,000–24,000 B.P., suggesting that Neanderthals lived in Europe more recently than had previously been suspected.

8. Berthet backs this "fact" up with a footnote invoking "the most recent works" of Lartet, Mortillet, et al. (36).

9. "A primitive, uncivilized, or loutish person; *spec.* a reactionary, a male chauvinist" (*OED*). As Brace notes (4), it was Boule who was chiefly responsible for the continuation of the "Neanderthal" motif in popular culture.

10. Recent analysis has pointed to animal predators as the likely cause of the nature of the skull breakage (Tattersall, 101).

11. The hypothesis that Magdalenians, driven from Eurasia by Neolithic invaders, came to North America via Siberia and were the ancestors of the Algonquin and Athabascan Indians was proposed by W. J. Sollas in *Ancient Hunters* (1911), 378–383.

12. Wells exploits the fact that "grisly" (frightful, ugly) has merged semantically with its homonym "grizzly" (which originally meant "gray") through the association with a terrifying animal (a bear), even though the words have quite different etymologies.

13. Miriam Allen deFord's prehistoric sf story "The Apotheosis of Ki" (1956), published the year after *The Inheritors*, develops Golding's idea of noble cannibalism through Neanderthals who have a proto-Christian consciousness. They are physically and spiritually refreshed after devouring the body of an alien under the misapprehension that he is a god whose divine powers they are absorbing.

14. Of recent prehistoric sf works, for example, Eric Brown's novella "The Inheritors of Earth" (1990) proposes that Neanderthals will be better fitted to inherit a future earth once we have destroyed civilization; Robert J. Sawyer's novel *Hominids* (2002) brings back the Neanderthal as a *homo superior* from a parallel universe; while both Brian Aldiss's novella "Neanderthal Planet" (1960) and John Darnton's novel *Neanderthal* (1996) suggest that peaceable Neanderthal genes remain a valuable part of our biological heritage.

15. This novel is an expansion of Asimov's 1958 novella "The Ugly Little Boy." Silverberg has written no solo pf, though his nonfiction book *Man before Adam* (1964) remains an good popular introduction to paleoanthropology for young adults.

16. The coauthors' heavy moralizing hand is lightened a little when we learn that, from the Neanderthal point of view, Cro-Magnon "Other Ones" seem ugly and stupid (237–238).

17. The indigenous people of southeast Asia, here representing the "yellow races."

18. Vogt also believed that there was a human convergence toward racial unity in spite of our polygenetic origin: "The innumerable mongrel races gradually fill up the spaces between originally so distinct types, and, notwithstanding the constancy of characters, in spite of the tenacity with which the primitive races resist alteration, they are by fusion slowly led towards unity" (468). Verne does not mention this.

7. A Cultural Triad: Language, Religion, Art (pages 173–197)

1. The analogy between these records quickly breaks down as a result of incommensurable timescales. Those extinct languages of which we have written traces are by definition products of historical time; the languages of prehistory have left no traces.

2. Felici offers an interesting summary of the conventions that pf writers have developed to represent prehistoric speech ("Emotions," 253–257).

3. This facetious story is about a girl whose will makes her more formidable than the club-wielding brute whom her father has picked as her mate. Here again in Waterloo the force of evolutionary progressionism proves irresistible.

4. Here Rousseau was probably in Gratacap's mind: "As the first motives that made man speak were the passions, his first expressions were Tropes. . . . At first, only poetry was spoken" (294).

5. The first installment of Wells's "Stories of the Stone Age" in the *Idler* serialization has a passage in the first sentence that was left out of the book version: "This story is of a time beyond the memory of man, before the beginning of history, [before the beginning of speech almost, when men still eked out their scarce words by

gestures, and talked together as the animals do, by the passing of simple thoughts from mind to mind—being themselves indeed still of the brotherhood of the beasts]" ("Stories," 418; brackets added). In this bracketed passage is the embryo of Golding's (romantic) idea of telepathic communion preceding alienating language, an idea later picked up by Auel.

6. This, "the most powerful, sinister, and diabolical of all Ice Age pictures" (Wendt, 386) was evidently the inspiration for the stag totemism of the New People in Golding's *The Inheritors* (145–146).

7. Sections of reindeer antler pierced with a hole and engraved with horses were discovered by Lartet and Christy at La Madeleine in 1865. Lartet, who so named them, thought that they might be symbols of a chief's authority, while others have supposed them to be spear straighteners.

8. Artistic objects associated with Neanderthals have been discovered, such as the "face-mask" of La Roche-Cotard (Indre-et-Loire), France, in 2002, though these tend to be minimally modified objects closer to the "found" than the "shaped" variety. Such was Liku's little Oa doll in *The Inheritors*.

9. Each of Hervilly's chapters has as its headpiece the motif of a stone ax crossed with a *bâton de commandement*; each ends with a reproduction of a different piece of mobiliary art.

10. This tiny bust in mammoth ivory of a delicate featured woman was discovered at Brassempouy (Landes) by Edouard Piette in 1894. Gravettian not Magdalenian and from the Pyrenees not Périgord, it is one of the oldest realistic representations of the human face. The "Venus of Brassempouy," as it is also called, probably inspired the description of the carving of Ayla by Jondalar in Auel's *The Mammoth Hunters* (547–548).

11. This episode is illustrated with a drawing of the steatopygic Venus of Lespugue (Anet, 56), a Gravettian figurine carved from mammoth ivory and discovered in 1922.

12. For example, it is very unlikely that Golding's Cro-Magnons would have been as white-skinned as he depicts them to be, or that they would have used sailboats of the kind normally associated with the Bronze Age. Moreover, his Neanderthals are unreconstructed Bouleans in physique (if not in temperament).

13. The allusion here is to the handprints, several of which seem to have abbreviated digits, discovered by Félix Régnault in Gargas Cave (Vaucluse) in the French Pyrenees in 1906. According to Breuil, these images of hands with severed fingers were the products of ritual mutilation associated with hunting magic.

Coda: Baxter's *Evolution* and Post-Hominization (pages 198–205)

1. Richard Dawkins's remarkable *The Ancestor's Tale* (2004), also an epic episodic narrative, is a recent nonfictional attempt to trace this "river" back to its source.

Works Cited

▼

Aldiss, Brian. "Neanderthal Planet." 1960. In Aldiss, *Neanderthal Planet*, 9–56. New York: Avon, 1970.

Anderson, Poul. "The Long Remembering." 1957. In Silverberg et al., eds., *Neanderthals*, 91–105.

Anet, Claude. *The End of a World*. Translated by Jeffery E. Jeffery. New York: Knopf, 1927.

Angenot, Marc. "Science Fiction in France before Verne." Translated by J. M. Gouvanic and D. Suvin. *Science-Fiction Studies* 5 (March 1978): 58–66.

———, and Nadia Khouri. "An International Bibliography of Prehistoric Fiction." *Science-Fiction Studies* 8 (March 1981): 38–53.

Arcelin, Adrien. *Chasseurs de rennes à Solutré: roman préhistorique*. 1872. Reprint of *Solutré; ou, Les chasseurs de rennes de la France centrale. Histoire préhistorique*, as by "Adrien Cranile." 2nd ed., ed. Jean Combier. Mâcon, France: Editions Bourgogne-Rhône-Alpes, 1977.

Ardrey, Robert. *African Genesis: A Personal Investigation into the Animal Origins and Nature of Man*. New York: Delta, 1961.

———. *The Hunting Hypothesis: A Personal Conclusion Concerning the Evolutionary Nature of Man*. 1976. New York: Bantam, 1977.

Asimov, Isaac. "The Ugly Little Boy." 1958 [as "Lastborn"]. In Silverberg et al., eds., *Neanderthals*, 39–90.

———, and Robert Silverberg. *Child of Time*. 1991. London: Pan, 1992.

Atkinson, J. J. *Primal Law*. With *Social Origins* by Andrew Lang, 209–94. London: Longmans, Green, 1903.

Auel, Jean M. *The Clan of the Cave Bear*. 1980. New York: Bantam, 1981.

———. *The Mammoth Hunters*. 1985. New York: Bantam, 1986.

———. *The Plains of Passage*. 1990. New York: Bantam, 1991.

———. *The Shelters of Stone*. 2002. New York: Bantam, 2003.

———. *The Valley of Horses*. 1982. New York: Bantam, 1983.

Austin, F. Britten. "Isis of the Stone Age." In Austin, *Tomorrow*, 1–30. London: Eyre and Spottiswoode, 1930.

———. *When Mankind Was Young*. Garden City, N.Y.: Doubleday, Page, 1927.

Bachofen, Johann Jakob. *Myth, Religion, and Mother Right: Selected Writings of J. J. Bachofen*. Translated by Ralph Manheim. Princeton, N.J.: Princeton University Press, 1967.

Bahn, Paul G., and Jean Vertut. *Images of the Ice Age*. London: Windward, 1988.

Barbusse, Henri. *Chains*. 2 vols. Translated by Stephen Haden Guest. New York: International, 1925.

Baronian, Jean-Baptiste, ed. *La Guerre du feu, et autres romans préhistoriques*. By J.-H. Rosny aîné. 1985. Paris: Robert Laffont, 2002.

Baxter, Stephen. *Evolution: A Novel*. New York: Ballantine, 2002.

Beauvoir, Simone de. *The Second Sex*. Translated by H. M. Parshley. 1952. New York: Vintage, 1989.

Bégouën, Max. *Bison of Clay*. Translated by Robert Luther Duffus. New York: Longmans, Green, 1926.

Berman, Judith C. "Bad Hair Days in the Paleolithic: Modern (Re)Constructions of the Cave Man." *American Anthropologist* 101 (June 1999): 288–304.

Berthet, Elie. *The Pre-Historic World*. Translated by Mary J. Safford. Philadelphia: Porter and Coates, 1879.

———. "Un Rêve: l'homme tertiaire.—l'anthropopithèque." 1883. http://www.trussel.com/prehist/reve.htm.

Berthoud, S. Henry. "L'Age de pierre en Europe" and "Les premiers habitants de Paris." In Berthoud, *L'Homme depuis cinq mille ans*, 16–72. Paris: Garnier frères, 1865.

Bierbower, Austin. *From Monkey to Man; or, Society in the Tertiary Age: A Story of the Missing Link, Showing the First Steps in Industry, Commerce, Government, Religion and the Arts, with an Account of the Great Expedition from Cocoa-Nut Hill and the Wars in Alligator Swamp*. Chicago: Dibble, 1894.

Biesele, Megan. Review of *Reindeer Moon*, by Elizabeth Marshall Thomas. *American Anthropologist* 90 (March 1988): 229–230.

Bishop, Michael. *No Enemy but Time*. 1982. New York: Bantam, 1989.

Blake, C. Carter. "On the Alleged Peculiar Characters, and Assumed Antiquity of the Human Cranium from the Neanderthal." *Journal of the Anthropological Society of London* 2 (1864): cxxxix–clvii.

Bleiler, Everett F., with the assistance of Richard J. Bleiler. *Science-Fiction: The Gernsback Years. A Complete Coverage of the Genre Magazines* Amazing, Astounding, Wonder, *and Others from 1926 through 1936*. Kent, Ohio: Kent State University Press, 1998.

Blunt, Wilfrid. *The Ark in the Park: The Zoo in the Nineteenth Century*. London: Hamish Hamilton, 1976.

Boitard, Pierre. *Paris avant les hommes. L'Univers avant les hommes. L'Homme fossile, etc. Histoire naturelle du globe terrestre*. Paris: Passard, 1861.

Boone, Laurel, ed. *The Collected Letters of Charles G. D. Roberts*. Fredericton, New Brunswick: Goose Lane, 1989.

Bordes, François [see also Carsac, Francis]. "Science fiction et préhistoire." 1959. In Carsac, *Oeuvres complètes*, 2:881–897. Brussels: Claude Lefrancq, 1997.

Brace, C. Loring. "The Fate of the 'Classic' Neanderthals: A Consideration of Hominid Catastrophism." *Current Anthropology* 5 (February 1964): 3–38.

Breuil, Henri. *Beyond the Bounds of History: Scenes from the Old Stone Age*. Translated by Mary E. Boyle. 1949. Reprint, New York: AMS Press, 1979.

Brown, Eric. "The Inheritors of Earth." In Brown, *The Time-Lapsed Man and Other Stories*, 151–216. London: Pan, 1990.

Burroughs, Edgar Rice. *The Eternal Savage*. 1925 [as *The Eternal Lover*]. New York: Ace, 1964.

Carroll, Joseph. "Adaptationist Criteria of Literary Value: Assessing Kurtén's *Dance of the Tiger*, Auel's *The Clan of the Cave Bear*, and Golding's *The Inheritors*." In Carroll, *Literary Darwinism: Evolution, Human Nature, and Literature*, 163–185. New York: Routledge, 2004.

Carsac, Francis. "Taches de rouille." 1954. In Carsac, *Oeuvres complètes*, 2:651–663. Brussels: Claude Lefrancq, 1997.

Cartmill, Cleve. "The Link." 1942. In Greenberg et al., eds., 100–114.

Cawelti, John G. *Adventure, Mystery, and Romance: Formula Stories as Art and Popular Culture*. Chicago: University of Chicago Press, 1976.

Chamberlain, Gordon B. "The Angenot-Khouri Bibliography of Prehistoric Fiction: Additions, Corrections, and Comment." *Science-Fiction Studies* 9 (November 1982): 342–346.

Christopher, John. *Dom and Va*. London: Hamish Hamilton, 1973.

Clan of the Cave Bear, The. Directed by Michael Chapman. 98 minutes. Warner Brothers, 1986. DVD.

Clareson, Thomas D. *Some Kind of Paradise: The Emergence of American Science Fiction*. Westport, Conn.: Greenwood, 1985.

Clarke, Arthur C. "Expedition to Earth." In Clarke, *Expedition to Earth: Eleven Science-Fiction Stories*, 125–137. New York: Ballantine, 1953.

———. *The Lost Worlds of 2001*. New York: Signet, 1972.

———. *Profiles of the Future: An Inquiry into the Limits of the Possible*. 1962. London: Pan, 1973.

———. "The Sentinel." 1951. In Clarke, *Expedition to Earth*, 155–165.

———. *2001: A Space Odyssey*. 1968. New York: Roc, 2000.

Clute, John, and Peter Nicholls, eds. *The Encyclopedia of Science Fiction*. 1993. London: Orbit, 1999.

Cohen, Claudine. *La Femme des origines: images de la femme dans la préhistoire occidentale*. 2003. Paris: Belin-Herscher, 2006.

———. *L'Homme des origines: savoirs et fictions en préhistoire*. Paris: Seuil, 1999.

Conkey, Margaret W. "A Century of Palaeolithic Cave Art." *Archaeology* 34 (July–August 1981): 20–28.

Coon, Carleton Stevens. *The Races of Europe*. New York: Macmillan, 1939.

———. *The Story of Man: From the First Human to Primitive Culture and Beyond*. 1954. 2nd ed., revised. New York: Knopf, 1967.

Couegnas, Daniel. "Préhistoire et récit 'préhistorique' chez Rosny et Wells." *Europe: revue littéraire mensuelle* 681/682 (January–February 1986): 18–29.

Crace, Jim. *The Gift of Stones*. 1988. London: Penguin, 2003.

Crump, Irving. *Og, Boy of Battle*. New York: Dodd, Mead, 1925.

———. *Og of the Cave People*. New York: Dodd, Mead, 1935.

———. *Og, Son of Fire*. New York: Dodd Mead, 1922. http://www.trussel.com/prehist/crump/ogs.htm#T213.

Curwen, Henry [as Anon.] "Zit and Xoe: Their Early Experiences." *Blackwood's Edinburgh Magazine* 139 (April 1886): 457–478; (May 1886): 612–634.

Dagen, Philippe. "Images et légendes de la préhistoire." In Lafont-Couturier et al., eds., 16–42.

Dail, C. C. *Willmoth the Wanderer; or, The Man from Saturn*. Atchison, Kans.: Haskell, 1890.

Daniel, Glyn. *The Idea of Prehistory*. 1962. Harmondsworth, Middlesex, Eng.: Penguin, 1964.

Darnton, John. *Neanderthal*. 1996. New York: St. Martin's, 1997.

Dart, Raymond A., with Dennis Craig. *Adventures with the Missing Link*. New York: Harper, 1959.

———. "The Predatory Transition from Ape to Man." *International Anthropological and Linguistic Review* 1 (1953): 201–219.

Darwin, Charles. *The Descent of Man, and Selection in Relation to Sex*. 1871. Reprint, Princeton, N.J.: Princeton University Press, 1981.

———. *The Expression of the Emotions in Man and Animals*. 1872. 3rd ed. Edited by Paul Ekman. Oxford: Oxford University Press, 1998.

———. *On the Origin of Species by Means of Natural Selection*. 1859. Edited by Joseph Carroll. Peterborough, Ontario: Broadview, 2003.

Dawkins, Richard. *The Ancestor's Tale: A Pilgrimage to the Dawn of Life*. London: Weidenfeld and Nicolson, 2004.

Deamer, Dulcie. *As It Was in the Beginning*. 1909. Melbourne: Frank Wilmot, 1929.

Debus, Allen A. "Re-Framing the Science in Jules Verne's *Journey to the Center of the Earth*." *Science Fiction Studies* 33 (November 2006): 405–420.

De Camp, L. Sprague. "Author's Afterword." In De Camp, *The Best of L. Sprague de Camp*, 355–362. New York: Ballantine, 1978.

———. "The Gnarly Man." 1939. In De Camp, *The Best of L. Sprague de Camp*, 87–111. New York: Ballantine, 1978.

deFord, Miriam Allen. "The Apotheosis of Ki." 1956. In Silverberg et al., eds., *Neanderthals*, 106–112.

del Rey, Lester. "The Day Is Done." 1939. In del Rey, *The Best of Lester del Rey*, 14–30. New York: Ballantine, 1978.

De Paolo, Charles. *Human Prehistory in Fiction*. Jefferson, N.C.: McFarland, 2003.

———. "Wells, Golding, and Auel: Representing the Neanderthal." *Science Fiction Studies* 27 (November 2000): 418–438.

Dopp, Katharine Elizabeth. *The Tree-Dwellers*. Chicago: Rand McNally, 1904.

Doyle, Sir Arthur Conan. *The Lost World*. 1912. In *The Professor Challenger* Stories, 3–213. London: John Murray, 1952.

Draper, Patricia. "!Kung Women: Contrasts in Sexual Egalitarianism in Foraging and Sedentary Contexts." In *Toward an Anthropology of Women*, ed. Rayna R. Reiter, 77–109. New York: Monthly Review Press, 1975.

Duncan, Kirby L. "William Golding and Vardis Fisher: A Study in Parallels and Extensions." *College English* 27 (December 1965): 232–235.

Dyalhis, Nictzin. "The Red Witch." *Weird Tales* 19 (April 1932): 440–458, 575–576.

Ebert, Roger. Review of Michael Chapman's film *The Clan of the Cave Bear. Chicago Sun-Times*, 21 February 1986. http://rogerebert.suntimes.com/apps/pbcs.dll/article?AID=/19860221/REVIEWS/602210302/1023.

Eiseley, Loren. *Darwin's Century: Evolution and the Men Who Discovered It*. 1958. Garden City, N.Y.: Anchor, 1961.

Eldredge, Niles, and Ian Tattersall. *The Myths of Human Evolution*. New York: Columbia University Press, 1982.

Eller, Cynthia. *The Myth of Matriarchal Prehistory: Why an Invented Past Won't Give Women a Future*. Boston: Beacon, 2000.

Evans, I. O. *The Coming of a King: A Story of the Stone Age*. London: Warne, 1950.

Farmer, Philip José. "The Alley Man." 1959. In Silverberg, et al., eds., *Neanderthals*, 263–318.

Fee, Elizabeth. "The Sexual Politics of Victorian Social Anthropology." *Feminist Studies* 1 (Winter–Spring 1973): 23–39.

Felici, Roberta de. "Emotions et langages dans le roman préhistorique de J.-H. Rosny Aîné." In *L'Homme préhistorique: images et imaginaire*, eds. Albert and Jacqueline Ducros, 243–271. Paris: L'Harmattan, 2000.

———. "Le Roman préhistorique de Rosny Aîné: 'roman scientifique' ou genre 'didactique' et de 'vulgarisation'?" *Revue d'histoire littéraire de la France* (March–April 1997): 244–273.

Figuier, Louis. *L'Homme primitif*. 2nd ed. Paris: Hachette, 1870.

———. *La Terre avant le Déluge*. 1863. 6th ed. Paris: Hachette, 1872.

Fisher, Vardis. *Adam and the Serpent*. New York: Vanguard, 1947.

———. *Darkness and the Deep*. New York: Vanguard, 1943.

———. *The Golden Rooms*. New York: Vanguard, 1944.

———. *Intimations of Eve*. New York: Vanguard, 1946.

Frazer, James G. *The Golden Bough: A Study in Comparative Religion*. 1890. Reprint, New York: Gramercy, 1981.

French, Marilyn. *From Eve to Dawn: A History of Women*. Vol. 1, *Origins*. Toronto: McArthur, 2002.

Freud, Sigmund. *Totem and Taboo: Some Points of Agreement between the Mental Lives of Savages and Neurotics*. 1913. In Freud, *Penguin Freud Library*; vol. 13, *The Origins of Religion*, translated by James Strachey, edited by Albert Dickson, 43–224. London: Penguin, 1985.

Gale, Oliver Marble. *Carnack the Life-Bringer: The Story of a Dawn Man Told by Himself*. New York: Wm. H. Wise, 1928.

Gallun, Raymond Z. "N'Goc." *Astounding Stories* 54 (May 1935): 145–152.

Gibbon, Lewis Grassic. *See* Mitchell, J. Leslie.

Golding, William. "Clonk Clonk." 1971. In *The Scorpion God: Three Short Novels*, 63–114. San Diego, Calif.: Harcourt Brace Jovanovich, 1984.

———. *The Inheritors*. 1955. London: Faber, 1961.

Gould, Stephen Jay. *Ever Since Darwin: Reflections in Natural History*. New York: Norton, 1977.

———. *The Mismeasure of Man*. New York: Norton, 1981.

———. *The Panda's Thumb: More Reflections in Natural History*. 1980. New York: Norton, 1982.

Gratacap, L. P. *A Woman of the Ice Age*. New York: Brentano's, 1906.

Grayson, Donald K. *The Establishment of Human Antiquity*. New York: Academic, 1983.

Greenberg, Martin Harry, Joseph Olander, and Robert Silverberg, eds. *Dawn of Time: Prehistory through Science Fiction*. New York: Elsevier/Nelson, 1979.

Guillaumie, Marc. *Le Roman préhistorique: essai de définition d'un genre, essai d'histoire d'un mythe*. Limoges: PULIM, 2006.

———. "Le Roman préhistorique, un roman pour les enfants?" In *Le Roman populaire en question(s): actes du colloque international de mai 1995 à Limoges*, ed. Jacques Migozzi, 207–221. Limoges: PULIM, 1997.

Hackett, Abigail, and Robin Dennell. "Neanderthals as Fiction in Archaeological Narrative." *Antiquity* 77 (December 2003): 816–827.

Haeckel, Ernst. *The History of Creation; or, The Development of the Earth and Its Inhabitants by the Action of Natural Causes: A Popular Exposition of the Doctrine of Evolution in General, and That of Darwin, Goethe, and Lamarck in Particular*. 2 vols. Translated "by a young lady." Revised by E. Ray Lankester. New York: D. Appleton, 1876.

Hagemans, G. *Le Poignard de silex: étude de moeurs préhistoriques*. Brussels: H. Manceux, 1889.

Hager, Lori D. "Sex and Gender in Paleoanthropology." In *Women in Human Evolution*, ed. Lori D. Hager, 1–28. London: Routledge, 1997.

Haggard, H. Rider. *Allan and the Ice-Gods: A Tale of Beginnings*. 1927. Reprint, Polegate, U.K.: Pulp Fictions, 1999.

Haraucourt, Edmond. *Daâh, le premier homme*. 1914. Paris: Arléa, 1996.

Harrison, Harry. *West of Eden*. 1984. London: Panther, 1985.

Harrison, Sue. *Mother Earth Father Sky*. New York: Doubleday, 1990.

Heizer, Robert F., ed. *Man's Discovery of His Past: Literary Landmarks in Archaeology*. Englewood Cliffs, N.J.: Prentice-Hall, 1962.

Heltzel, Ellen Emry. "The Return of Jean Auel." *Book* (May–June 2002): 40–46.

Henderson, Keith. *Prehistoric Man*. London: Chatto and Windus, 1927.

Henkin, Leo J. *Darwinism in the English Novel, 1860–1910: The Impact of Evolution on Victorian Fiction*. 1940. New York: Russell and Russell, 1963.

Hensley, John R. "Eugenics and Social Darwinism in Stanley Waterloo's *The Story of Ab* and Jack London's *Before Adam.*" *Studies in Popular Culture* 25 (October 2002): 23–37. http://www.pcasacas.org/SPC/.

Hervilly, Ernest d'. *Aventures d'un petit garçon préhistorique en France.* Paris: Librarie mondaine, 1888.

Hilliers, Ashton. *The Master-Girl: A Romance.* New York: Putnam, 1910.

His Prehistoric Past. Directed by Charles Chaplin. 10 minutes. Keystone Film Co., 1914. http://tesla.liketelevision.com.

Hitchcock, Don. "An Evening with Jean Auel." http://donsmaps.com/auel.html.

Hobbes, Thomas. *Leviathan; or, The Matter, Forme and Power of a Commonwealth Ecclesiasticall and Civil.* 1651. Edited by Michael Oakeshott. Oxford: Blackwell, 1946.

Huxley, Thomas Henry. "The Aryan Question and Prehistoric Man." 1890. In Huxley, *Collected Essays*, vol. 7, *Man's Place in Nature, and Other Anthropological Essays*, 271–328. Reprint, New York: Greenwood, 1968.

———. "Emancipation—Black and White." 1865. In Huxley, *Collected Essays*, vol. 3, *Science and Education*, 66–75. Reprint, New York: Greenwood, 1968.

———. *Evidence as to Man's Place in Nature.* 1863. As *Man's Place in Nature*, in Huxley, *Collected Essays*, vol. 7, *Man's Place in Nature, and Other Anthropological Essays*, 1–208. Reprint, New York: Greenwood, 1968.

———. "Further Remarks upon the Human Remains from the Neanderthal." 1864. In Huxley, *The Scientific Memoirs of Thomas Henry Huxley*, ed. Michael Foster and E. Ray Lankester, 2:573–590. London: Macmillan, 1899.

Hyne, C. J. Cutcliffe. *The New Eden.* London: Longmans, Green, 1892.

Iceman. Directed by Fred Schepisi. 101 minutes. Universal Studios, 1984. DVD.

Jensen, Johannes V. *Fire and Ice.* Translated by A. G. Chater. In *The Long Journey* (1923), 1–224. New York: Knopf, 1961.

Johanson, Donald C., Lenora Johanson, and Blake Edgar. *Ancestors: In Search of Human Origins.* New York: Villard, 1994.

———, and Kevin O'Farrell. *Journey from the Dawn: Life with the World's First Family.* New York: Villard, 1990.

———, and Maitland A. Edey. *Lucy: The Beginnings of Humankind.* New York: Simon and Schuster, 1981.

Jones, Neil R. "Martian and Troglodyte." *Amazing Stories* 8 (May 1933): 124–141.

Ketterer, David. *Canadian Science Fiction and Fantasy.* Bloomington: Indiana University Press, 1992.

Kipling, Rudyard. *Just So Stories for Little Children.* 1902. Harmondsworth, Middlesex, Eng.: Penguin, 2000.

———. "The Knife and the Naked Chalk." In Kipling, *Rewards and Fairies*, 115–142. London: Macmillan, 1910.

Kirkpatrick, Peter, ed. *The Queen of Bohemia: The Autobiography of Dulcie Deamer.* St. Lucia, Australia: University of Queensland Press, 1998.

Kjelgaard, Jim. *Fire-Hunter.* New York: Holiday House, 1951.

Klossner, Michael. *Prehistoric Humans in Film and Television: 581 Dramas, Comedies and Documentaries, 1905–2004.* Jefferson, N.C.: McFarland, 2006.

Kühn, Herbert. *On the Track of Prehistoric Man.* Translated by Alan Houghton Brodrick. 1955. New York: Vintage, 1961.

Kuhn, Thomas S. *The Structure of Scientific Revolutions.* 1962. 2nd ed., enlarged. Chicago: University of Chicago Press, 1970.

Kuklick, Henrika. *The Savage within: The Social History of British Anthropology, 1885–1945.* Cambridge: Cambridge University Press, 1991.

Kurtén, Björn. *Dance of the Tiger: A Novel of the Ice Age.* Translated by Björn Kurtén. 1980. London: Abacus, 1982.

————. *Singletusk: A Novel of the Ice Age.* Translated by Björn Kurtén. New York: Pantheon, 1986.

Labor, Earle, Robert C. Leitz III, and I. Milo Shepard, eds. *The Letters of Jack London.* Vol. 2, *1906–1912.* Stanford, Calif.: Stanford University Press, 1988.

Lafont-Couturier, Hélène, et al., eds. *Vénus et Caïn: figures de la préhistoire, 1830–1930.* Paris: Réunion des musées nationaux; Bordeaux: Musée d'Aquitaine, 2003.

Landau, Misia. *Narratives of Human Evolution.* New Haven, Conn.: Yale University Press, 1991.

Lang, Andrew. "Dedication." In Lang, *In the Wrong Paradise and Other Stories,* v–vi. London: Kegan Paul, Trench, 1886.

————. "The Romance of the First Radical: A Prehistoric Apologue." *Fraser's Magazine* 22 (September 1880): 289–300.

————. *XXII Ballades in Blue China.* London: Kegan Paul, 1880.

Leakey, Richard E. *The Making of Mankind.* New York: Dutton, 1981.

————. *The Origin of Humankind.* New York: BasicBooks, 1994.

————, and Roger Lewin. *Origins Reconsidered: In Search of What Makes Us Human.* New York: Doubleday, 1992.

————, and Roger Lewin. *Origins: What New Discoveries Reveal about the Emergence of Our Species and Its Possible Future.* New York: Dutton, 1977.

Lécureux, Roger, and André Chéret. *Rahan, fils des âges farouches.* 1969. L'Intégrale, vol. 1. Paris: Soleil, 1998.

Lévi-Strauss, Claude. *Totemism.* Translated by Rodney Needham. Harmondsworth, Middlesex, Eng.: Penguin, 1969.

Lewin, Roger. *Bones of Contention: Controversies in the Search for Human Origins.* New York: Simon and Schuster, 1987.

————. *The Origin of Modern Humans.* 1993. New York: Scientific American Library, 1998.

Lewis, Roy, *The Evolution Man. See* Lewis, *What We Did to Father.*

————. *What We Did to Father.* London: Hutchinson, 1960.

Lewis, R. W. B. *The American Adam: Innocence, Tragedy, and Tradition in the Nineteenth Century.* Chicago: University of Chicago Press, 1955.

Lewis-Williams, David. *The Mind in the Cave: Consciousness and the Origins of Art.* London: Thames and Hudson, 2002.

Lindholm, Megan. *The Reindeer People*. New York: Ace, 1988.

———. *Wolf's Brother*. New York: Ace, 1988.

Lofficier, Jean-Marc, and Randy Lofficier. *French Science Fiction, Fantasy, Horror and Pulp Fiction: A Guide to Cinema, Television, Radio, Animation, Comic Books and Literature from the Middle Ages to the Present*. Jefferson, N.C.: McFarland, 2000.

London, Jack. *Before Adam*. New York: Macmillan, 1907.

———. *The Call of the Wild*. 1903. In London, *The Call of the Wild, White Fang, and Other Stories*, edited by Andrew Sinclair, 39–140. Harmondsworth, Middlesex, Eng.: Penguin, 1981.

———. *The Star Rover*. 1915. Reprint, Amherst, N.Y.: Prometheus, 1999.

———. "The Strength of the Strong." 1911. In London, *The Science Fiction of Jack London: An Anthology*, edited by Richard Gid Powers, 251–283. Boston: Gregg, 1975.

———. "When the World Was Young." 1910. In London, *The Science Fiction of Jack London: An Anthology*, edited by Richard Gid Powers, 219–250. Boston: Gregg, 1975.

Lovejoy, C. O. "The Origin of Man." *Science* 211 (1981): 341–350.

Lubbock, John. *Pre-Historic Times, as Illustrated by Ancient Remains, and the Manners and Customs of Modern Savages*. 1865. 4th ed. London: Frederic Norgate, 1878.

Lyell, Charles. *The Geological Evidences of the Antiquity of Man, with Remarks on Theories of the Origin of Species by Variation*. 1863. 2nd ed., revised. London: John Murray, 1863.

Lyon, John. "The Search for Fossil Man: Cinq Personnages à la Recherche du Temps Perdu." *Isis* 61 (Spring 1970): 68–84.

Lysøe, Eric. "*The War for Fire*: An Epic Vision of Evolution." Translated by Stephen Trussel. http://www.trussel.com/prehist/lysoe.htm.

Marcy, Mary E. *Stories of the Cave People*. Chicago: Charles H. Kerr, 1917.

Marshall, Edison. *Dian of the Lost Land*. New York: H. C. Kinsey, 1935.

———. *Ogden's Strange Story*. New York: H. C. Kinsey, 1934.

Mason, Otis Tufton. *Woman's Share in Primitive Culture*. London: Macmillan, 1895.

McCarthy, Susan. "Elizabeth Marshall Thomas." *Salon.com* (27 June 2000). http://archive.salon.com/people/bc/2000/06/27/thomas/index2.html.

McCord, P. B. *Wolf: The Memoirs of a Cave-Dweller*. New York: B. W. Dodge, 1908.

McLennan, John F. *Primitive Marriage: An Inquiry into the Origin of the Form of Capture in Marriage Ceremonies*. 1865. Edited by Peter Rivière. Chicago: University of Chicago Press, 1970.

McMorrow, Will. "Man o' Dreams." 1929. In Silverberg et al., eds., *Neanderthals*, 113–129.

Meunier, Mme. Stanislas. *Misère et grandeur de l'humanité primitive*. 1889. 5th ed. Paris: A. Picard et Kaan, 189?

Miller, P. Schuyler. "Old Man Mulligan." 1940. In *Isaac Asimov Presents the Great Science Fiction Stories*, vol. 2, *1940*, edited by Isaac Asimov and Martin H. Greenberg, 321–350. New York: DAW, 1979.

——. "The People of the Arrow." *Amazing Stories* 10 (July 1935): 63-70.

Missing Link. Directed by David and Carol Hughes. 92 minutes. 1988. MCA Home Video, videocassette.

Mitchell, J. Leslie. "The Diffusionist Heresy." *Twentieth Century* 2 (March 1931): 14–16.

——. *Three Go Back*. 1932. Edinburgh: Polygon, 2000.

——, [as Lewis Grassic Gibbon]. "The Woman of Leadenhall Street." In *Masterpiece of Thrills*, edited by John Gawsworth, 567–586. London: Daily Express, 1936.

Mitchison, Naomi. *Early in Orcadia*. Glasgow: Richard Drew, 1987.

Mivart, St. George. "Primitive Man: Tylor and Lubbock." *Quarterly Review* 137 (October 1874): 40–77.

Montagu, Ashley. *The Idea of Race*. Lincoln: University of Nebraska Press, 1965.

——. *The Nature of Human Aggression*. Oxford: Oxford University Press, 1976.

Morgan, Lewis Henry. *Ancient Society; or, Researches in the Lines of Human Progress from Savagery through Barbarism to Civilization*. 1877. Edited by Eleanor Burke Leacock. Cleveland, Ohio: Meridian, 1963.

Morris, Gouverneur. *The Pagan's Progress*. New York: A. S. Barnes, 1904.

Moser, Stephanie. *Ancestral Images: The Iconography of Human Origins*. Ithaca, N.Y.: Cornell University Press, 1998.

Munro, Ian S. *Leslie Mitchell: Lewis Grassic Gibbon*. Edinburgh: Oliver and Boyd, 1966.

Nida, William Lewis. *Ab the Cave Man: A Story of the Time of the Stone Age*. Chicago: A. Flanagan, 1911.

Nyst, Ray. *La Caverne: histoire pittoresque d'une famille humaine de vingt-neuf personnes, filles et garçons, petits et grands, à l'époque des luxuriantes forêts tertiaires et des saisons clémentes dans l'Europe centrale*. Brussels: the Author, 1909.

Olender, Maurice. *The Languages of Paradise: Race, Religion, and Philology in the Nineteenth Century*. Translated by Arthur Goldhammer. Cambridge, Mass.: Harvard University Press, 1992.

Oliver, Chad. *Mists of Dawn*. 1952. Reprint, Boston: Gregg, 1979.

One Million B.C. Directed by Hal Roach. 80 minutes. Hal Roach Studios, 1940.

One Million Years B.C. Directed by Don Chaffey. 91 minutes. Hammer / Twentieth–Century Fox, 1966. DVD.

Otis, Laura. *Organic Memory: History and the Body in the Late Nineteenth and Early Twentieth Centuries*. Lincoln: University of Nebraska Press, 1994.

Pelot, Pierre. *Avant la fin du ciel*. 2000. Paris: Denoël, 2003.

——. *Ceux qui parlent au bord de la pierre*. 2001. Paris: Denoël, 2003.

——. *Debout dans le ventre blanc du silence*. 1999. Paris: Denoël, 2003.

——. *Le Nom perdu du soleil*. 1998. Paris: Denoël, 1999.

——. *Sous le vent du monde. Qui regarde la montagne au loin*. 1996. Paris: Denoël, 1997.

——, and Yves Coppens. *Le Rêve de Lucy*. 1990. Paris: Seuil, 1997.

Pluciennik, Mark. "Archaeological Narratives and Other Ways of Telling." *Current Anthropology* 40 (December 1999): 653–678.

Pollak, Janet S. "Excavating Auel: The Gender Roles of Earth's Children." In *The Archaeology of Gender: Proceedings of the Twenty-Second Annual Conference of the Archaeological Association of the University of Calgary*, edited by Dale Walde and Noreen D. Willows, 297–300. Calgary: University of Calgary Archaeological Association, 1991.

Prestwich, Grace Ann. *Life and Letters of Sir Joseph Prestwich*. Edinburgh: Blackwood, 1899.

Pringle, David. Introduction to *Allan and the Ice-Gods*, by Haggard, v–xi.

Quest for Fire. Directed by Jean-Jacques Annaud. 100 minutes. International Cinema Corporation, 1981. DVD.

Reed, E. T. *Mr. Punch's "Prehistoric Peeps."* London: Bradbury, Agnew, c. 1896.

Ribeiro, Stella Carr. *Sambaqui: A Novel of Pre-History*. Translated by Claudia van der Heuvel. New York: Bard, 1987.

Richards, Robert J. "The Linguistic Creation of Man: Charles Darwin, August Schleicher, Ernst Haeckel, and the Missing Link in Nineteenth-Century Evolutionary Theory." In *Experimenting in Tongues: Studies in Science and Language*, edited by Matthias Doerres. Stanford, Calif.: Stanford University Press, 2002. http://home.uchicago.edu/~rjr6/articles/Schleicher—final.doc.

Roberts, Charles G. D. *In the Morning of Time*. 1912, 1919. New York: Dutton; London: Dent, 1924.

Robinson, C. H. *Longhead: The Story of the First Fire*. Boston: L. C. Page, 1913.

Rosny aîné, J.-H. *Les Conquérants du feu*. Paris: Portiques, 1929.

———. *Eyrimah*. 1896. In Baronian, 99–201.

———. "La Grande Enigme." 1920. In Baronian, 655–658.

———. *Helgvor of the Blue River*. Translated by George Surdez. *Argosy* (28 May 1932): 46–66; (4 June 1932): 57–78; (11 June 1932): 103–123; (18 June 1932): 111–125. http://www.trussel.com/prehist/helgvor1.htm.

———. "Les Hommes Sangliers." 1929. In Baronian, 659–684.

———. "Nomaï." 1897. In Baronian, 613–625.

———. *Les Origines*. Paris: L. Borel, 1895.

———. *Quest for Fire*. Translated by Harold Talbott. 1967. Harmondsworth, Middlesex, Eng.: Penguin, 1982.

———. *Quest of the Dawn Man*. Translated by the Hon. Lady Whitehead. 1924. New York: Ace, 1964.

———. *Vamireh: roman des temps primitif*. 1892. In Baronian, 17–97.

———. "Les Xipéhuz." 1887. In Baronian, 627–652.

Roudier, Emmanuel. *Vo'Hounâ*. Vol. 1, *La Saison d'Ao*. Paris: Soleil, 2002.

Rousseau, Jean-Jacques. "Essay on the Origin of Languages, in which Melody and Musical Imitation Are Treated." In Rousseau, *Essay on the Origin of Languages and Writings Related to Music*, translated and edited by John T. Scott, 289–332. Hanover, N.H.: University Press of New England, 1998.

Roveland, Blythe E. "Child the Creator: Children as Agents of Change in Juvenile Prehistoric Literature." *Visual Anthropology Review* 9 (Spring 1993): 147–153.

Ruddick, Nicholas. "Courtship with a Club: Wife-Capture in Prehistoric Fiction, 1865–1914." *Yearbook of English Studies* 37, no. 2 (2007): 45–63.

———. "Jules Verne and the Fossil Man Controversy: An Addendum to Allen A. Debus." *Science Fiction Studies* 34 (March 2007): 156–158.

———. "Sexual Paradise Regained? C. J. Cutcliffe Hyne's *New Eden* Project." *Foundation: The International Review of Science Fiction* 98 (Autumn 2006): 74–84.

Rudwick, Martin J. S. *Georges Cuvier, Fossil Bones, and Geological Catastrophes: New Translations and Interpretations of the Primary Texts*. Chicago: University of Chicago Press, 1997.

Russett, Cynthia Eagle. *Darwin in America: The Intellectual Response, 1865–1912*. San Francisco, Calif.: Freeman, 1976.

Rutherfurd, Edward. "James A. Michener." http://www.edwardrutherford.com/us/index/item.php?i=ngt4638ab657aa54.

———. *Sarum: The Novel of England*. 1987. New York: Ivy, 1988.

Sanders, Warren E. "The Memory Stream." *Amazing Stories* 8 (April 1933): 54–59.

Sawyer, Robert J. *Hominids*. 2002. New York: TOR, 2003.

Schwob, Marcel. "The Amber-Trader." In Schwob, *The King in the Golden Mask and Other Writings*, edited and translated by Iain White. Manchester: Carcanet, 1982. http://www.trussel.com/prehist/amber.htm.

———. "The Death of Odjigh." In Schwob, *The King in the Golden Mask and Other Writings*, edited and translated by Iain White, 80–83. Manchester: Carcanet, 1982.

Sheffield, Charles. "The Treasure of Odirex." 1978. In Silverberg et al., eds., *Neanderthals*, 130–195.

Shipman, Pat. *The Evolution of Racism: Human Differences and the Use and Abuse of Science*. New York: Simon and Schuster, 1994.

———. *The Man Who Found the Missing Link: Eugène Dubois and His Lifelong Quest to Prove Darwin Right*. New York: Simon and Schuster, 2001.

Shuler, Linda Lay. *She Who Remembers*. 1988. New York: Signet, 1989.

Sieveking, Ann. *The Cave Artists*. London: Thames and Hudson, 1979.

Silverberg, Robert. *Man before Adam: The Story of Man in Search of His Origins*. Philadelphia: Macrae Smith, 1964.

———, Martin H. Greenberg, and Charles G. Waugh, eds. *Neanderthals: Isaac Asimov's Wonderful Worlds of Science Fiction*, no. 6. New York: Signet, 1987.

Simak, Clifford D. "Grotto of the Dancing Deer." *Analog* 100 (April 1980): 144–159.

Slocum, Sally. "Woman the Gatherer: Male Bias in Anthropology." 1971. In *Toward an Anthropology of Women*, edited by Rayna R. Reiter, 36–50. New York: Monthly Review Press, 1975.

Solecki, Ralph S. *Shanidar: The First Flower People*. New York: Knopf, 1971.

Sollas, W. J. *Ancient Hunters and Their Modern Representatives*. London: Macmillan, 1911.

Sparks, Julie. "At the Intersection of Victorian Science and Fiction: Andrew Lang's 'Romance of the First Radical.'" *English Literature in Transition*, 42, no. 2 (1999): 124–142.

Sterling, George. "Babes in the Wood: The Saber-Tooth." *Popular Magazine* 31 (1 February 1914): 218–224. http://www.trussel.com/prehist/sterling.htm.

Stoczkowski, Wiktor. *Explaining Human Origins: Myth, Imagination and Conjecture.* Translated by Mary Turton. Cambridge: Cambridge University Press, 2002.

Stover, Leon E. Afterword to *Apeman, Spaceman*, edited by Leon E. Stover and Harry Harrison, 328–374. 1968. Harmondsworth, Middlesex, Eng.: Penguin, 1972.

Stringer, Christopher, and Robin McKie. *African Exodus: The Origins of Modern Humanity.* New York: Holt, 1996.

Sullivan, Alan. *In the Beginning.* New York: Dutton, 1927.

Taine, John. *Before the Dawn.* Baltimore: Williams and Wilkins, 1934.

Tattersall, Ian. *The Last Neanderthal: The Rise, Success, and Mysterious Extinction of Our Closest Human Relatives.* 1995. Rev. ed. New York: Westview, 1999.

Thomas, Elizabeth Marshall. *The Animal Wife.* 1990. New York: Pocket Star, 1991.

———. *Reindeer Moon.* Boston: Houghton Mifflin, 1987.

Thomas, Ted. "The Doctor." 1967. In Greenberg, et al., eds., 90–99.

Three Ages, The. Directed by Buster Keaton. 63 minutes. Buster Keaton Productions, 1923. DVD.

Tiptree, James, Jr. "The Color of Neanderthal Eyes." 1988. In Tiptree, *Meet Me at Infinity*, 112–182. New York: Orb, 2001.

Tooker, Richard. *The Day of the Brown Horde.* New York: Payson and Clarke, 1929.

Treece, Henry. *The Golden Strangers.* 1956. London: Hodder and Stoughton, 1967.

Trinkaus, Erik, and Pat Shipman. *The Neandertals: Changing the Image of Mankind.* New York: Knopf, 1993.

Trussel, Steve. "Prehistoric Fiction." http://www.trussel.com/f_prehis.htm.

2001: A Space Odyssey. Directed by Stanley Kubrick. 148 minutes. Warner Brothers, 1968. DVD.

Tylor, Edward Burnett. *The Origins of Culture* [vol. 1 of *Primitive Culture*]. 1871. New York: Harper and Row, 1958.

Ucko, Peter J., and Andrée Rosenfeld. *Palaeolithic Cave Art.* London: Weidenfeld and Nicolson, 1967.

Van Riper, A. Bowdoin. *Men among the Mammoths: Victorian Science and the Discovery of Human Prehistory.* Chicago: University of Chicago Press, 1993.

"Vardis (Alvero) Fisher, 1895–1968." *Contemporary Authors Online.* Gale, 2003.

Vercors. *Borderline.* Translated by Rita Barisse. 1953. London: NEL, 1976.

Verne, Jules. *Journey to the Centre of the Earth.* Translated by Robert Baldick. Harmondsworth, Middlesex, Eng.: Penguin, 1965.

———. *The Village in the Treetops.* Translated by I. O. Evans. New York: Ace, 1964.

———. *Voyage au centre de la Terre.* Paris: J. Hetzel, 1864.

Vernier, J.-P. "The SF of J.H. Rosny the Elder." *Science Fiction Studies* 2 (July 1975): 156–163.

Versins, Pierre. *Encyclopédie de l'utopie, des voyages extraordinaires, et de la science fiction.* 1972. 2nd ed. Lausanne: L'Age d'homme, 1984.

Vogt, Carl. *Lectures on Man: His Place in Creation, and in the History of the Earth.* Translated and edited by James Hunt. London: Longman, Green, Longman, and Roberts, 1864.

Walker, Alan, and Pat Shipman. *The Wisdom of the Bones: In Search of Human Origins.* 1996. New York: Vintage, 1997.

Walker, Martin. *The Caves of Périgord.* New York: Simon and Schuster, 2002.

Washburn, Sherwood L., and C. S. Lancaster. "The Evolution of Hunting." In *Man the Hunter,* edited by Richard B. Lee and Irven DeVore, 293–303. Chicago: Aldine, 1968.

Waterloo, Stanley. "Christmas 200,000 B.C." In Waterloo, *The Wolf's Long Howl,* 231–239. Chicago: Herbert S. Stone, 1899.

———. *A Son of the Ages: The Reincarnations and Adventures of Scar, the Link. A Story of Man from the Beginning.* Garden City, N.Y.: Doubleday, Page, 1914.

———. *The Story of Ab: A Tale of the Time of the Cave Man.* Chicago: Way and Williams, 1897.

Wells, H.G. "The Grisly Folk." 1921. In Wells, *The Complete Short Stories of H. G. Wells,* 607–621. 1927. London: A. & C. Black, 1987.

———. *Mr. Belloc Objects to "The Outline of History."* London: Watts, 1926.

———. *The Outline of History: Being a Plain History of Life and Mankind.* 1920. Rev. ed. 2 vols. Garden City, N.Y.: Garden City Books, 1949.

———. Preface to *Seven Famous Novels,* by Wells, vii–x. New York: Knopf, 1934.

———. "A Story of the Days to Come." 1897. In Wells, *The Complete Short Stories of H. G. Wells,* 715–806. 1927. London: A. & C. Black, 1987.

———. "A Story of the Stone Age." 1897. In Wells, *The Complete Short Stories of H. G. Wells,* 656–714. 1927. London: A. & C. Black, 1987.

———. "Stories of the Stone Age. 1. Ugh-Lomi and Uya." *Idler* 11 (May 1897): 418–429.

———. *The Time Machine: An Invention.* 1895. Edited by Nicholas Ruddick. Peterborough, Ontario: Broadview, 2001.

———. "Zoological Retrogression." 1891. In Wells, *Early Writings in Science and Science Fiction,* edited by Robert M. Philmus and David Y. Hughes, 158–168. Berkeley and Los Angeles: University of California Press, 1975.

Wendt, Herbert. *In Search of Adam: The Story of Man's Quest for the Truth about His Earliest Ancestors.* Translated by James Cleugh. New York: Collier, 1963.

Wilcox, Clyde. "The Not-So-Failed Feminism of Jean Auel." *Journal of Popular Culture* 28 (Winter 1994): 63–70.

Williams, Raymond. *People of the Black Mountains.* Vol. 1, *The Beginning. . . .* London: Chatto and Windus, 1989.

Wilson, Edward O. *On Human Nature.* 1978. Cambridge, Mass.: Harvard University Press, 2004.

Wright, S. Fowler. *Dream; or, The Simian Maid.* London: Harrap, 1931.

————, [as Anthony Wingrave]. *The Vengeance of Gwa*. London: Thornton Butterworth, 1935.

Young, Matthew. "The London Skull." *Biometrika* 29 (February 1938): 277–321.

Zihlman, Adrienne. "The Paleolithic Glass Ceiling: Women in Human Evolution." In *Women in Human Evolution*, edited by Lori D. Hager, 91–113. London: Routledge, 1997.

Illustration Credits

Every attempt has been made by the author to obtain permission to reprint copyrighted material. The author apologizes if any material has been used without consent.

Figure 1.1. Illustration after drawing by Pierre Boitard from his *Paris avant les hommes* (1861).

Figure 1.2. Illustration by Yan' Dargent from S.-H. Berthoud's *L'Homme depuis cinq mille ans* (1865).

Figure 1.3. Illustration by Edouard Riou from Jules Verne's *Voyage au centre de la Terre* (1867).

Figure 1.4. Illustration by Emile Bayard after drawing by Adrien Arcelin from Louis Figuier's *L'Homme primitif* (1870).

Figure 1.5. Thomas Henry Huxley's sketch of "Homo Hercules Columarum," or the Man of the Pillars of Hercules, 19 July 1864. Huxley Archives, Imperial College of Science, Technology and Medicine, London.

Figure 1.6. Illustration by Cosmo Rowe from H. G. Wells's "Stories of the Stone Age" as serialized in *Idler* (May 1897).

Figure 1.7. Illustration by Frederick Gardner from Charles G. D. Roberts's "In the Morning of Time" as serialized in *London Magazine* (20 June 1912).

Figure 1.8. Illustration by H. R. Heaton from Austin Bierbower's *From Monkey to Man* (1894).

Figure 1.9. Illustration by Charles Livingston Bull from Jack London's *Before Adam* (1907).

Figure 2.1. Fernand Cormon's painting *Caïn* (1880). Musée d'Orsay, Paris.

Figure 2.2. Illustration by Françoise Boudignon from J.-H. Rosny's *La Guerre du feu* (Livre de Poche Jeunesse edition, 1980). J.-H. Rosny, *La Guerre du feu*, © Le Livre de Poche Jeunesse, 1980.

Figure 2.3 and 2.4. Illustrations by J. F. Horrabin from H. G. Wells's *The Outline of History* (1920).

Figure 2.5. Cover art by Calder from Max Bégouën's *Bison of Clay* (1926).

Figure 3.1. Illustration by MacGregor from Carleton S. Coon's *The Races of Europe* (1939).

Figure 3.2. Illustration by Ralph Ray from Jim Kjelgaard's *Fire-Hunter* (1951).

Credit: Reprinted from *Fire-Hunter* by Jim Kjelgaard by permission of Holiday House.

Figure 3.3. Illustration by William Hewison from Roy Lewis's *What We Did to Father* (1960).

Figure 3.4. Cover art by Geoff Taylor from Elizabeth Marshall Thomas's *The Animal Wife* (1990). "Animal Wife" illustration by © Geoff Taylor.

Figure 3.5. Cover art by Emmanuel Roudier from his graphic novel *Vo'Hounâ I: La Saison d'Ao* (2002). © MC Productions / Roudier.

Figure 4.1. Illustration by Simon Harmon Vedder from Stanley Waterloo's *A Tale of the Time of the Cave Men* (a 1904 British reissue of *The Story of Ab*).

Figure 4.2. Back cover art by R. Marcello from comic book adaptation by Raymonde Borel-Rosny (1982) of J.-H. Rosny's *La Guerre du feu*.

Figure 5.1. Liverpool-Manchester Railway Centenary pageant, 1930 (photograph). National Railway Museum / Science & Society Picture Library.

Figure 5.2. Dijon version of the 1887 sculpture by Emmanuel Frémiet known as *Gorille enlevant une négresse*. Emmanuel Frémiet, "Gorille enlevant une négresse," photograph © Musée des Beaux-Arts de Dijon.

Figure 5.3. Illustration by P. B. McCord from his *Wolf: The Memoirs of a Cave-Dweller* (1908).

Figure 5.4. Illustration by Norman Lindsay from Dulcie Deamer's *As It Was in the Beginning* (1929).

Figure 7.1. Illustration by Pierre Bonnard from Claude Anet's *The End of a World* (1927).

Index

▼